CREATED BY

ROBERT SCOTT M. CHRIS
KIRKMAN GIMPLE BURNHAM

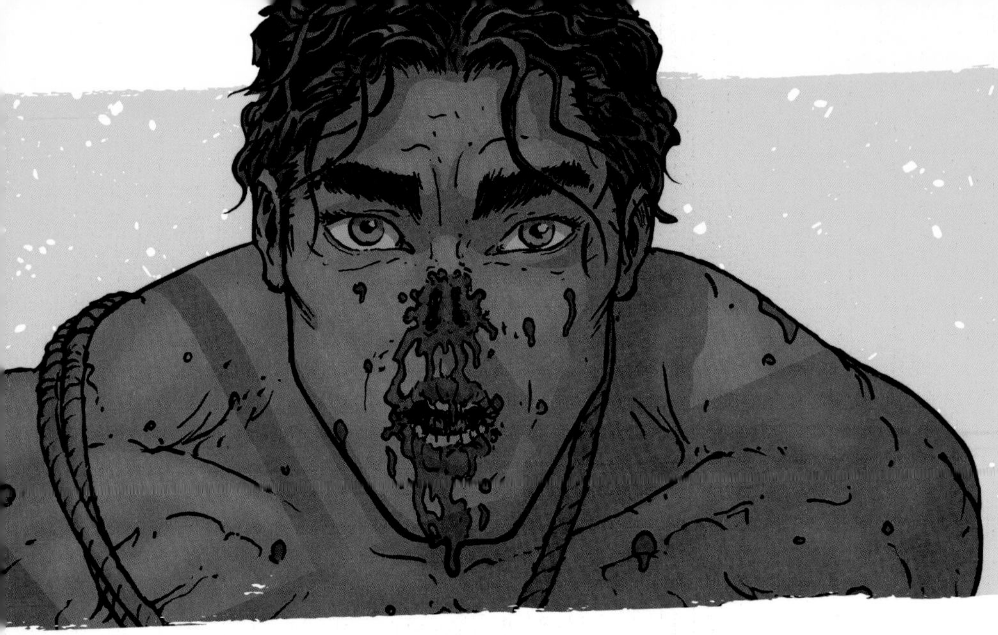

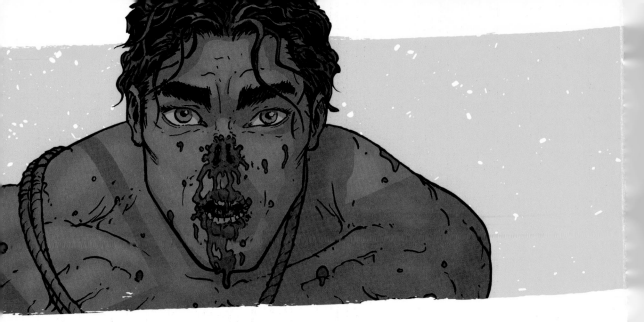

NATHAN FAIRBAIRN
COLORIST

RUS WOOTON
LETTERER

ARIELLE BASICH
ASSOCIATE EDITOR

SEAN MACKIEWICZ
EDITOR

ANDRES JUAREZ
LOGO & PRODUCTION DESIGN

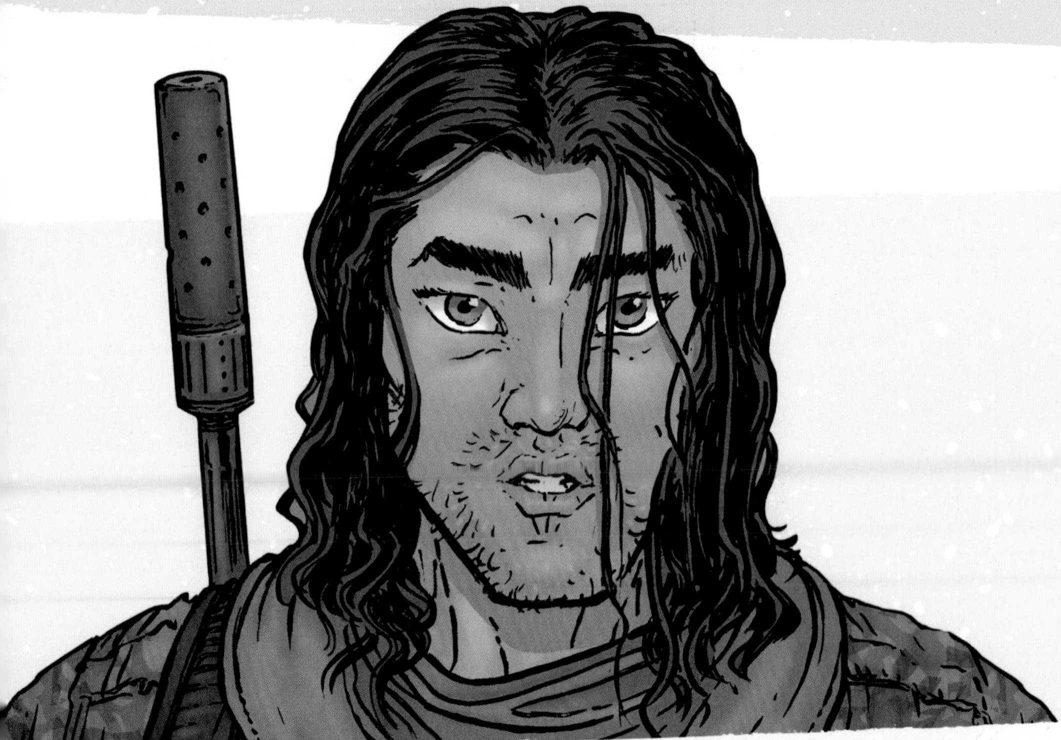

ROBERT KIRKMAN
WRITER, CREATOR

SCOTT M. GIMPLE
CO-PLOT, CREATOR

CHRIS BURNHAM
ARTIST, CREATOR

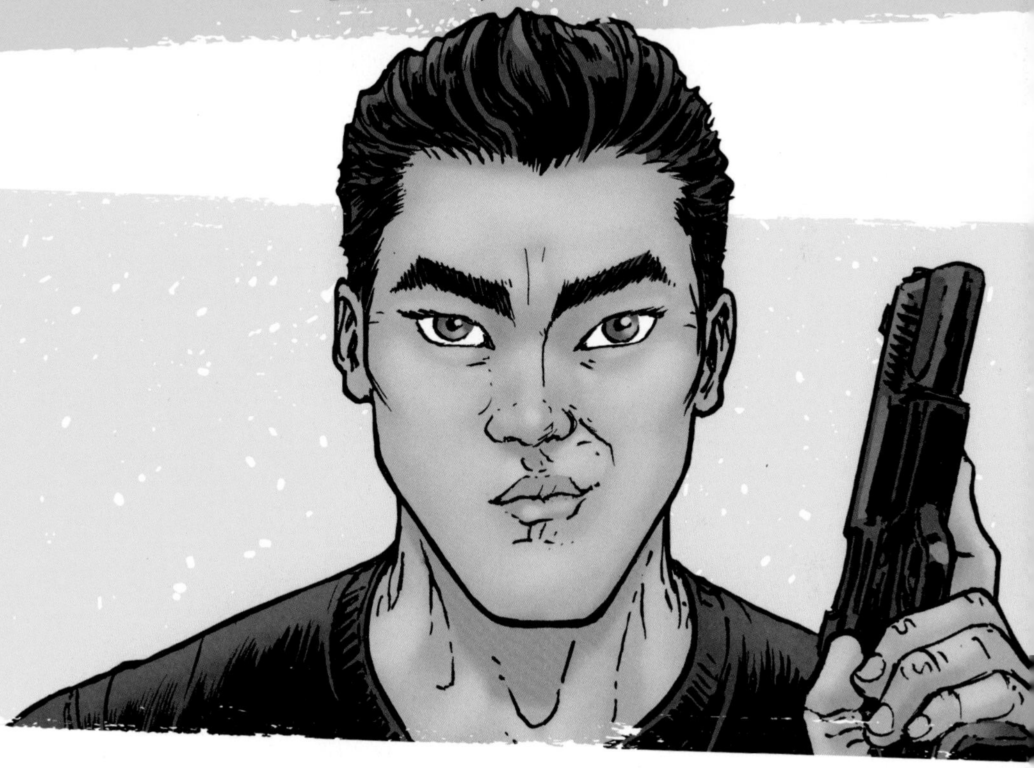

SKYBOUND LLC.

ROBERT KIRKMAN Chairman
DAVID ALPERT CEO
SEAN MACKIEWICZ SVP, Editor-in-Chief
SHAWN KIRKHAM SVP, Business Development
BRIAN HUNTINGTON VP, Online Content
SHAUNA WYNNE Publicity Director
ANDRES JUAREZ Art Director
JON MOISAN Editor
ARIELLE BASICH Associate Editor
KATE CAUDILL Assistant Editor
CARINA TAYLOR Production Artist
PAUL SHIN Business Development Manager
JOHNNY O'DELL Social Media Manager
DAN PETERSEN Sr. Director of Operations & Events

FOREIGN RIGHTS INQUIRIES: ag@sequentialrights.com
OTHER LICENSING INQUIRIES: contact@skybound.com

WWW.SKYBOUND.COM

IMAGE COMICS, INC.

ROBERT KIRKMAN Chief Operating Officer
ERIK LARSEN Chief Financial Officer
TODD MCFARLANE President
MARC SILVESTRI Chief Executive Officer
JIM VALENTINO Vice President
ERIC STEPHENSON Publisher / Chief Creative Officer
JEFF BOISON Director of Publishing Planning & Book Trade Sales
CHRIS ROSS Director of Digital Sales
JEFF STANG Director of Specialty Sales
KAT SALAZAR Director of PR & Marketing
DREW GILL Art Director
HEATHER DOORNINK Production Director
NICOLE LAPALME Controller

WWW.IMAGECOMICS.COM

DIE!DIE!DIE! Volume One. First Printing. Published by Image Comics, Inc. Office of publication: 2701 NW Vaughn St., Ste. 780, Portland, OR 97210.

ISBN: 978-1-5343-1214-2

VOLUME
ONE

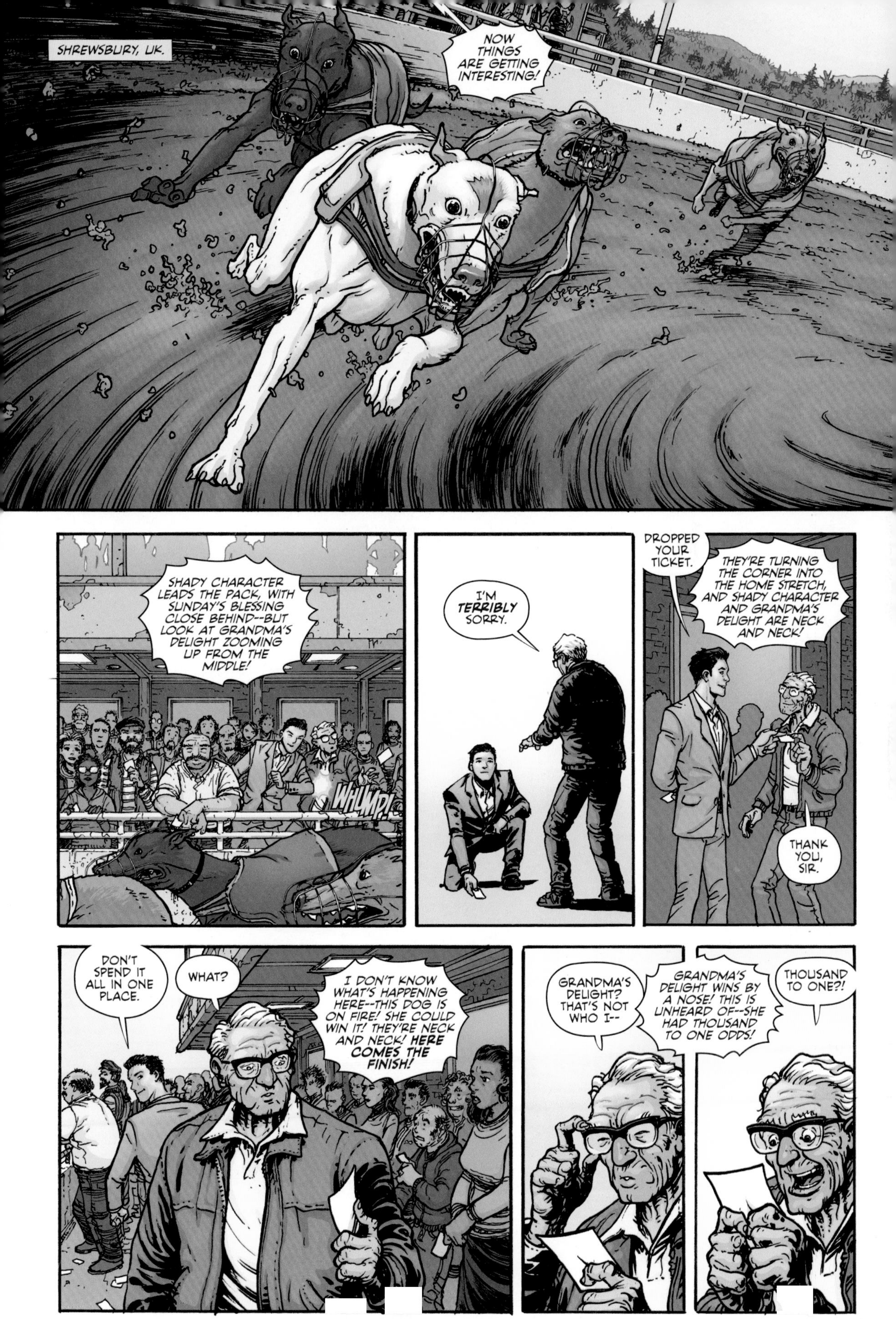
SHREWSBURY, UK.
NOW THINGS ARE GETTING INTERESTING!
SHADY CHARACTER LEADS THE PACK, WITH SUNDAY'S BLESSING CLOSE BEHIND--BUT LOOK AT GRANDMA'S DELIGHT ZOOMING UP FROM THE MIDDLE!
WHUMP!
I'M **TERRIBLY** SORRY.
DROPPED YOUR TICKET.
THEY'RE TURNING THE CORNER INTO THE HOME STRETCH, AND SHADY CHARACTER AND GRANDMA'S DELIGHT ARE NECK AND NECK!
THANK YOU, SIR.
DON'T SPEND IT ALL IN ONE PLACE.
WHAT?
I DON'T KNOW WHAT'S HAPPENING HERE--THIS DOG IS ON FIRE! SHE COULD WIN IT! THEY'RE NECK AND NECK! **HERE COMES THE FINISH!**
GRANDMA'S DELIGHT? THAT'S NOT WHO I--
GRANDMA'S DELIGHT WINS BY A NOSE! THIS IS UNHEARD OF--SHE HAD THOUSAND TO ONE ODDS!
THOUSAND TO ONE?!

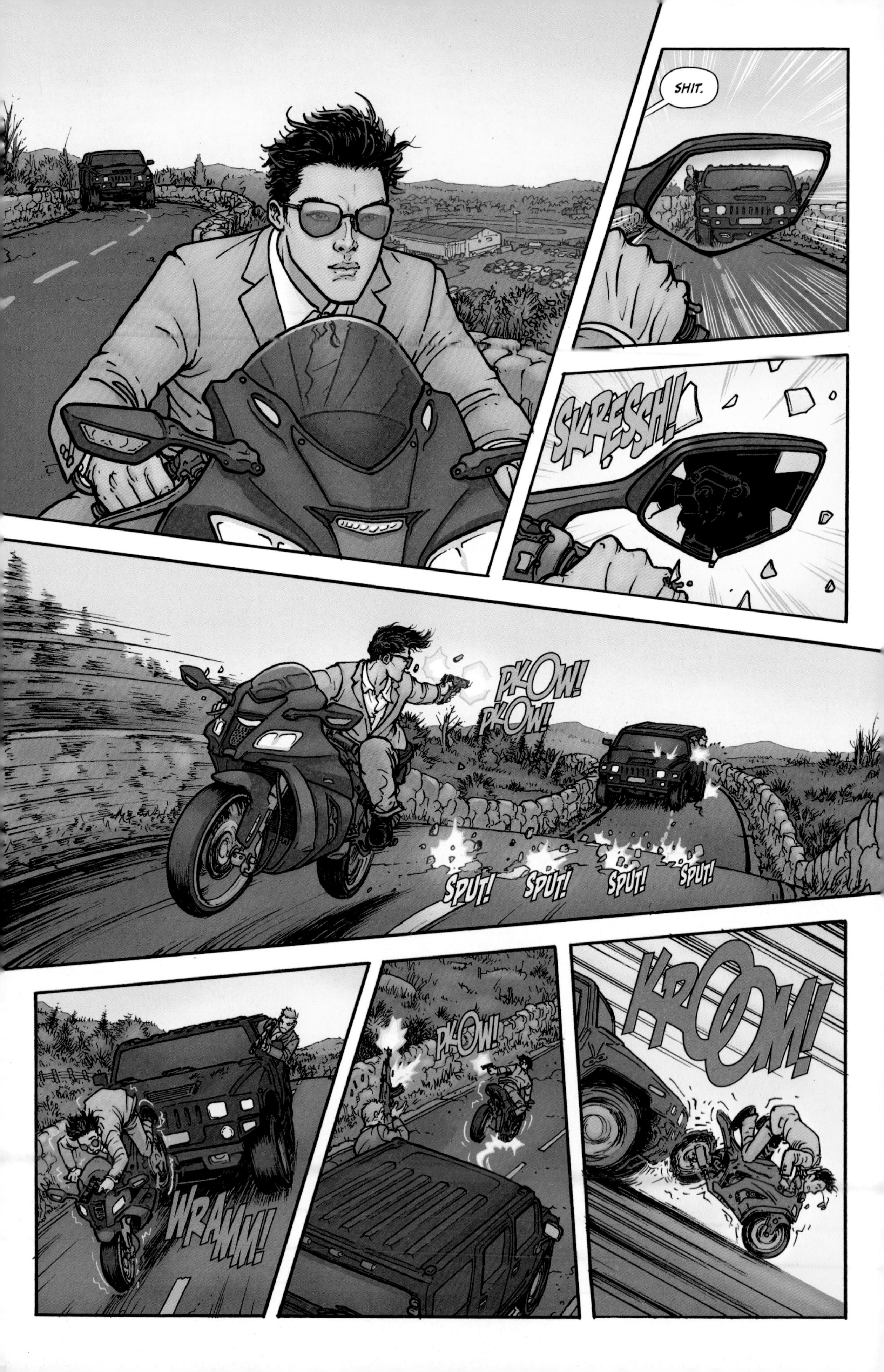
SHIT.
SKRESSH!
PKOW!
PKOW!
SPUT!
SPUT!
SPUT!
SPUT!
WRAMM!
PKOW!
KROOM!

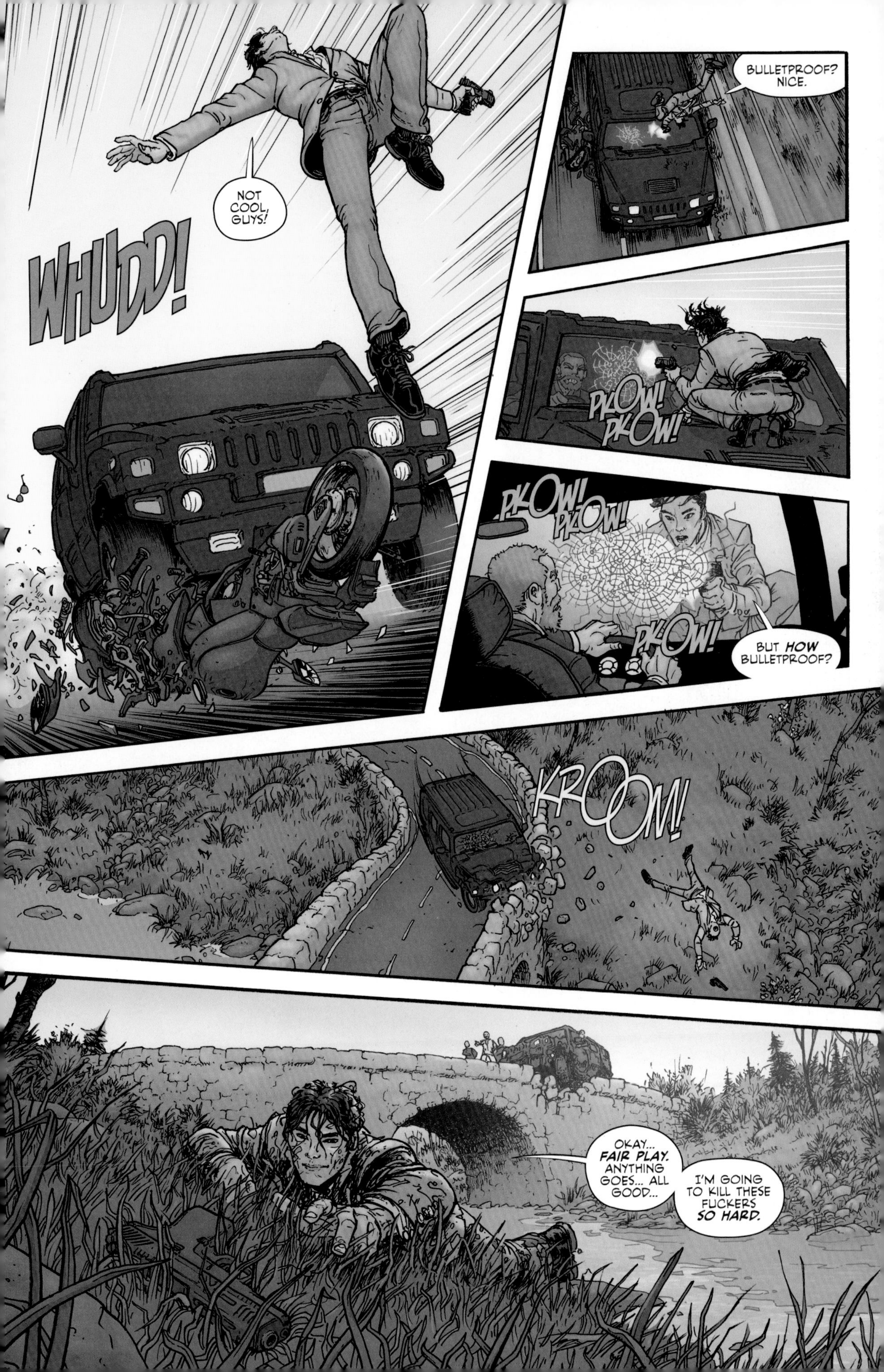
NOT COOL, GUYS!
WHUDD!
BULLETPROOF? NICE.
PKOW! PKOW!
PKOW! PKOW!
PKOW!
BUT HOW BULLETPROOF?
KROOM!
OKAY... FAIR PLAY. ANYTHING GOES... ALL GOOD...
I'M GOING TO KILL THESE FUCKERS SO HARD.

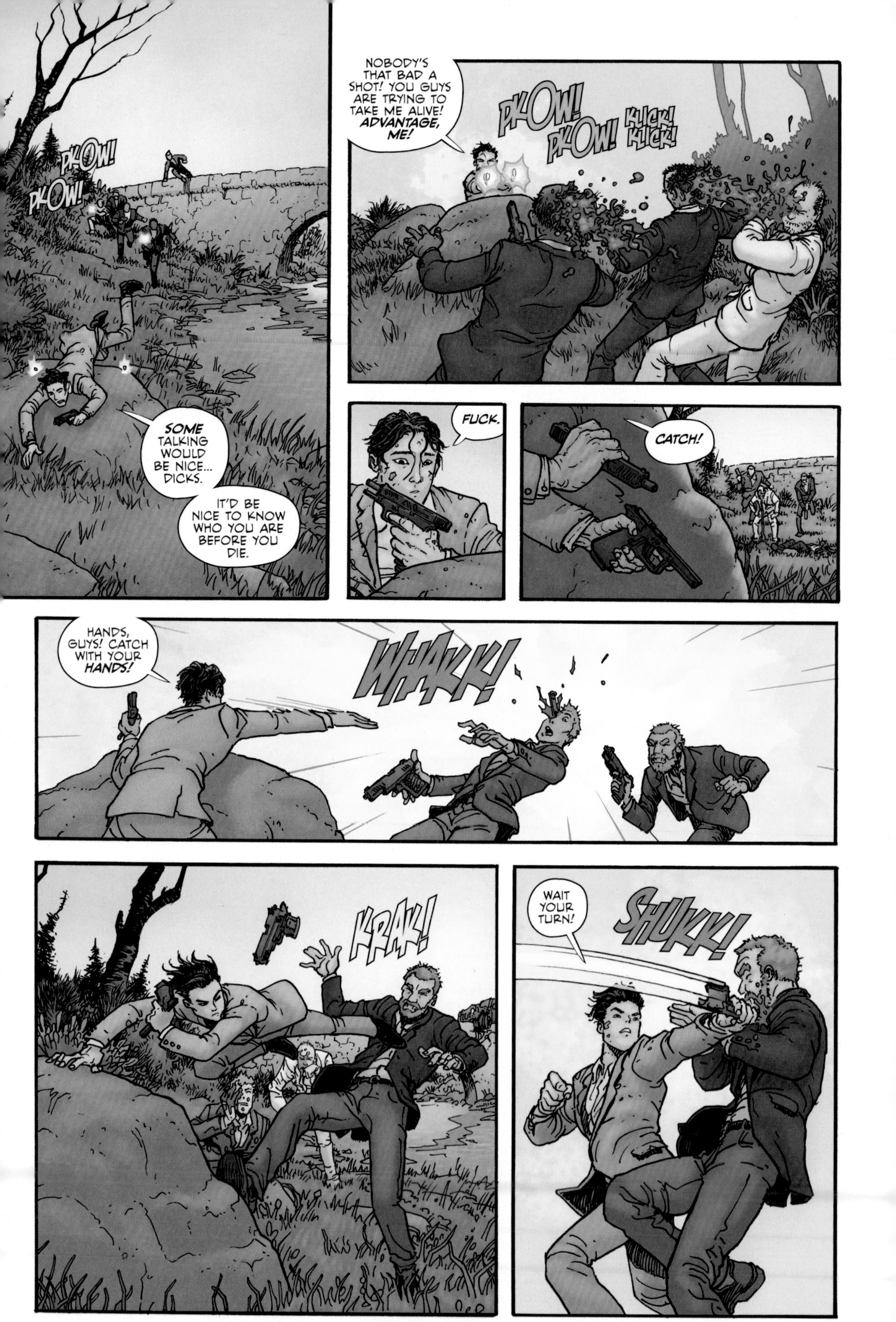
PKOW!
PKOW!
SOME TALKING WOULD BE NICE... DICKS.
IT'D BE NICE TO KNOW WHO YOU ARE BEFORE YOU DIE.
NOBODY'S THAT BAD A SHOT! YOU GUYS ARE TRYING TO TAKE ME ALIVE! ADVANTAGE, ME!
PKOW! PKOW!
KLICK! KLICK!
FUCK.
CATCH!
HANDS, GUYS! CATCH WITH YOUR HANDS!
WHAKK!
KRAK!
WAIT YOUR TURN!
SHUKK!

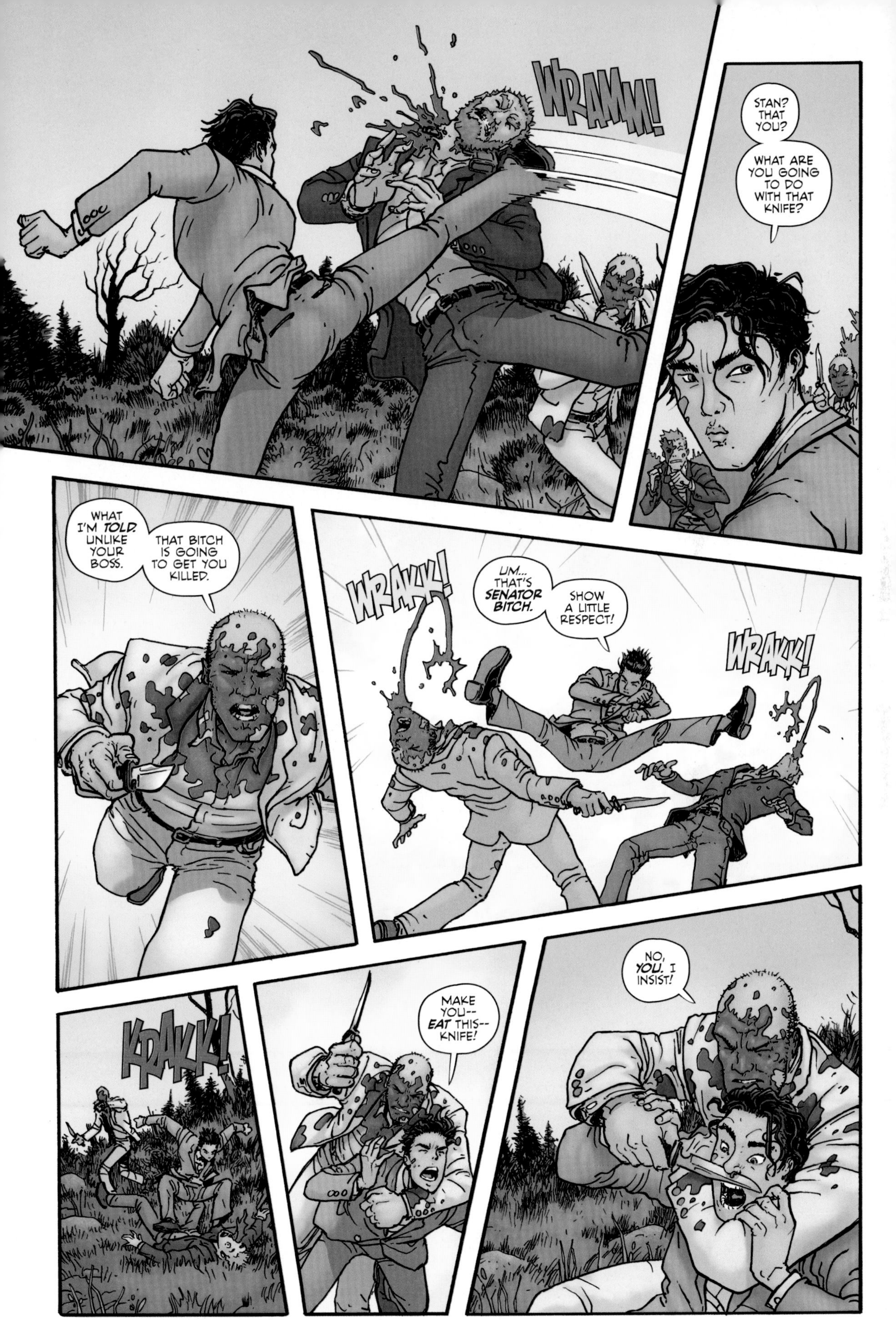
WRAMM!
STAN? THAT YOU?
WHAT ARE YOU GOING TO DO WITH THAT KNIFE?
WHAT I'M TOLD. UNLIKE YOUR BOSS.
THAT BITCH IS GOING TO GET YOU KILLED.
WRAKK!
UM... THAT'S SENATOR BITCH.
SHOW A LITTLE RESPECT!
WRAKK!
KRAKK!
MAKE YOU-- EAT THIS-- KNIFE!
NO, YOU. I INSIST!

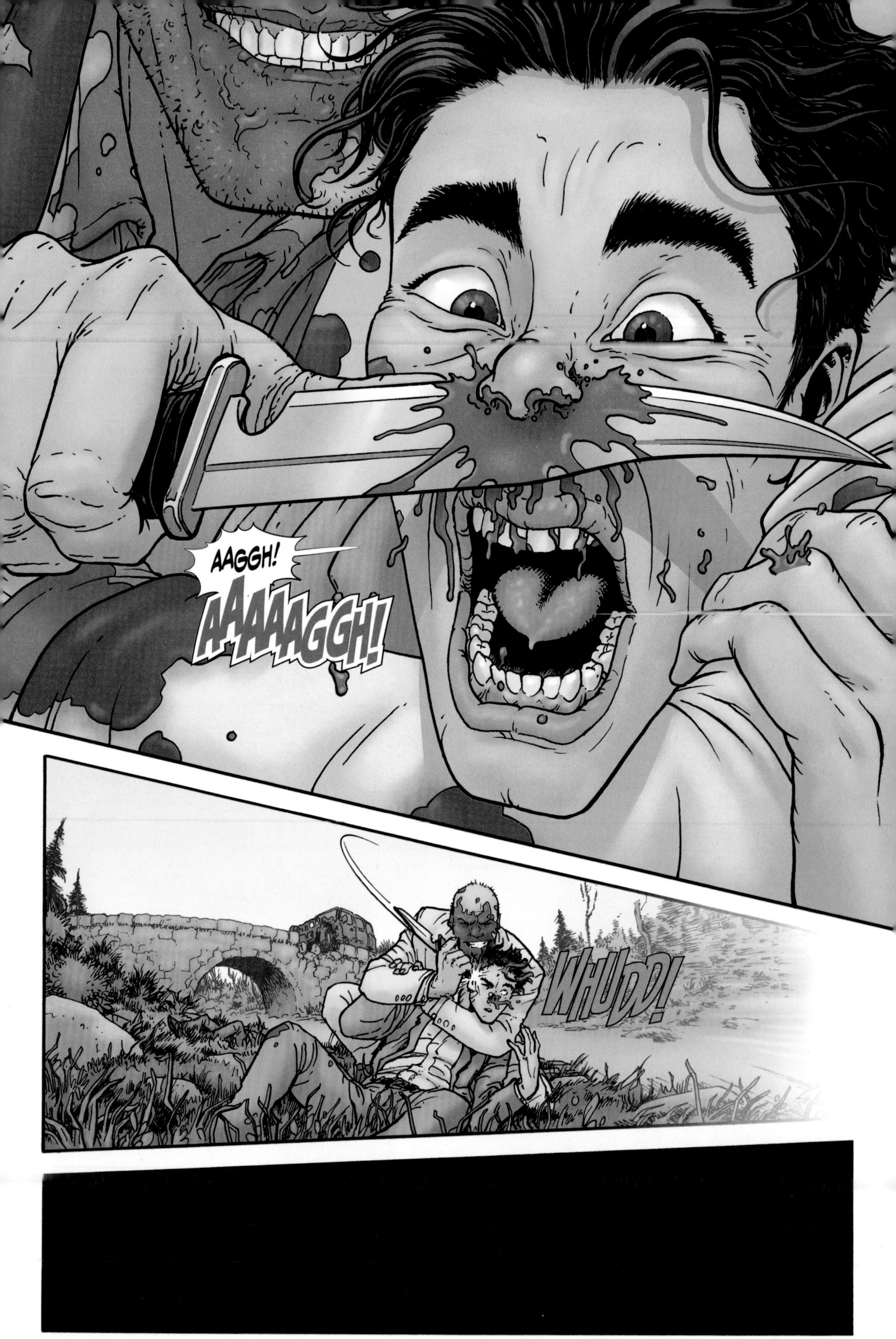
AAGGH!
AAAAAGGH!
WHUDD!

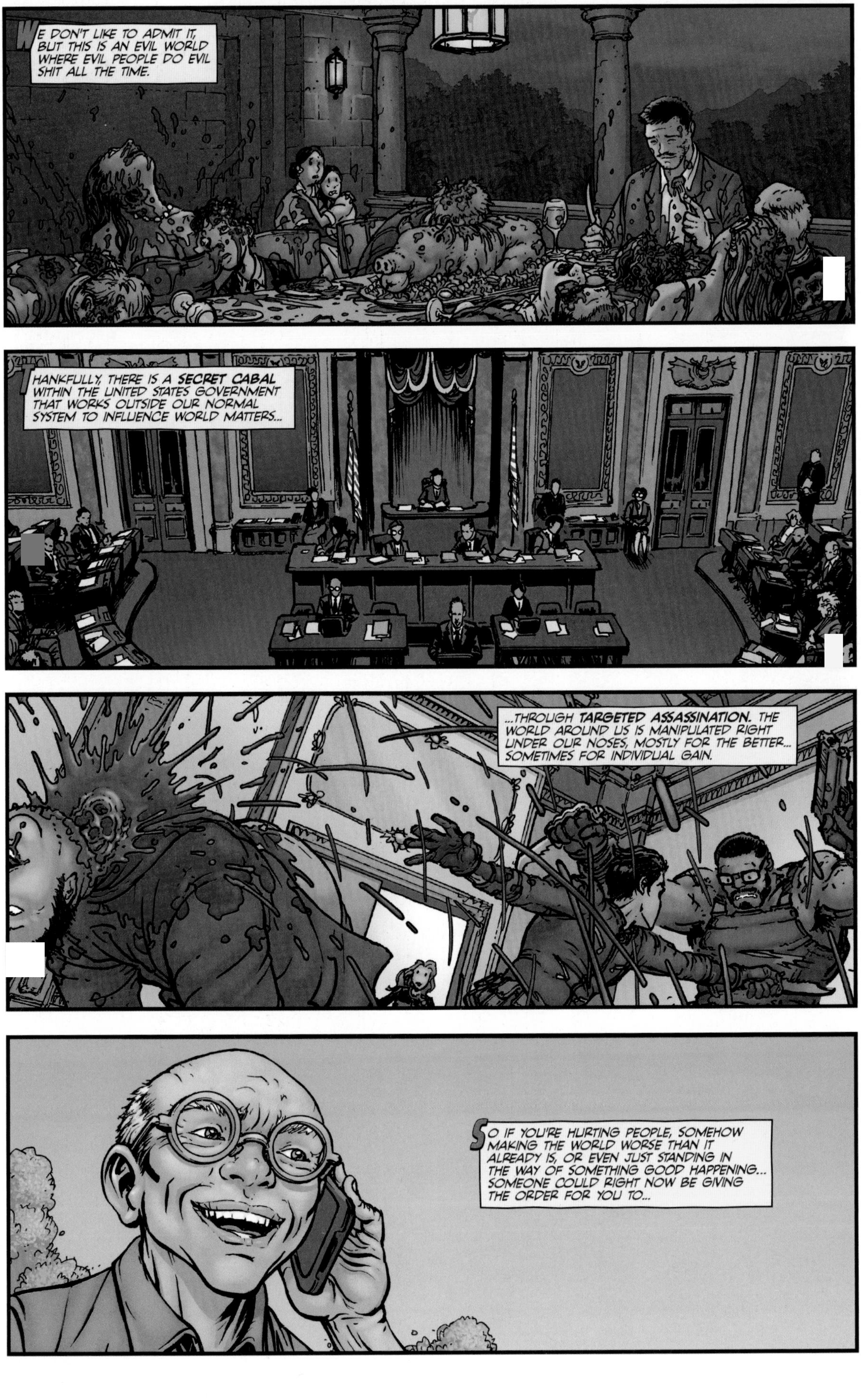
WE DON'T LIKE TO ADMIT IT, BUT THIS IS AN EVIL WORLD WHERE EVIL PEOPLE DO EVIL SHIT ALL THE TIME.
THANKFULLY, THERE IS A SECRET CABAL WITHIN THE UNITED STATES GOVERNMENT THAT WORKS OUTSIDE OUR NORMAL SYSTEM TO INFLUENCE WORLD MATTERS...
...THROUGH TARGETED ASSASSINATION. THE WORLD AROUND US IS MANIPULATED RIGHT UNDER OUR NOSES, MOSTLY FOR THE BETTER... SOMETIMES FOR INDIVIDUAL GAIN.
SO IF YOU'RE HURTING PEOPLE, SOMEHOW MAKING THE WORLD WORSE THAN IT ALREADY IS, OR EVEN JUST STANDING IN THE WAY OF SOMETHING GOOD HAPPENING... SOMEONE COULD RIGHT NOW BE GIVING THE ORDER FOR YOU TO...

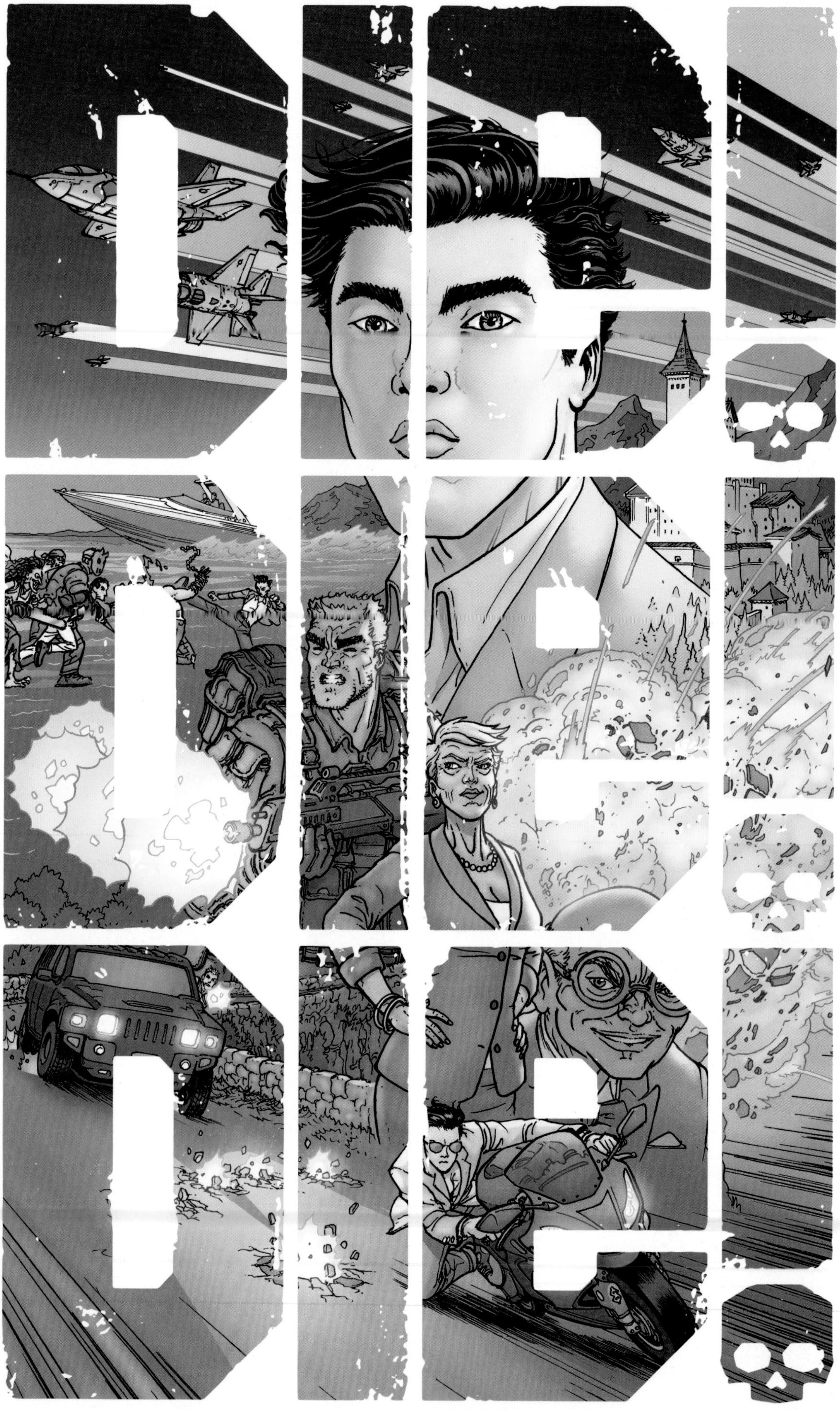
DIE!
DIE!
DIE!

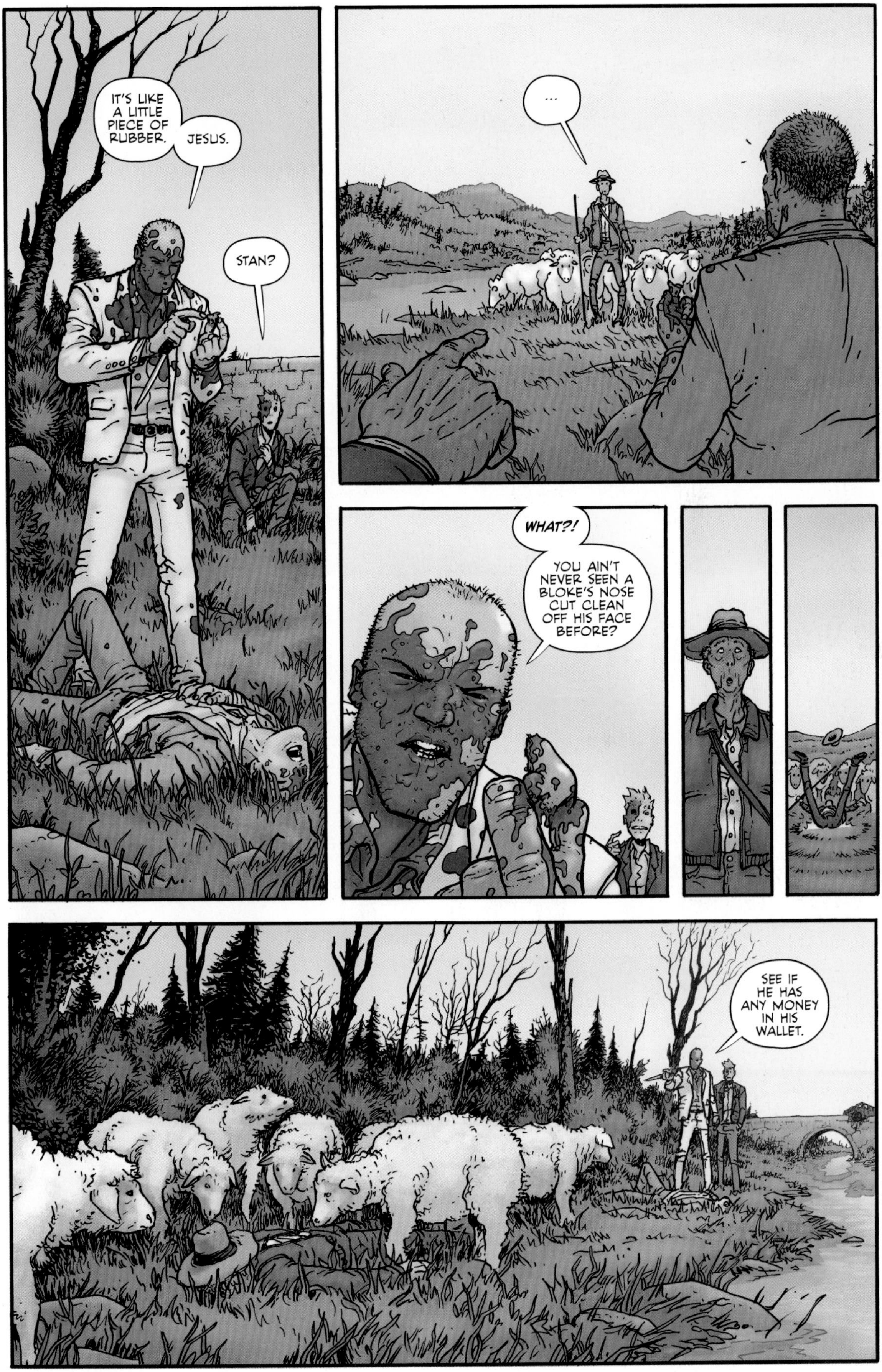

IT'S LIKE A LITTLE PIECE OF RUBBER.
JESUS.
STAN?
...
WHAT?!
YOU AIN'T NEVER SEEN A BLOKE'S NOSE CUT CLEAN OFF HIS FACE BEFORE?
SEE IF HE HAS ANY MONEY IN HIS WALLET.

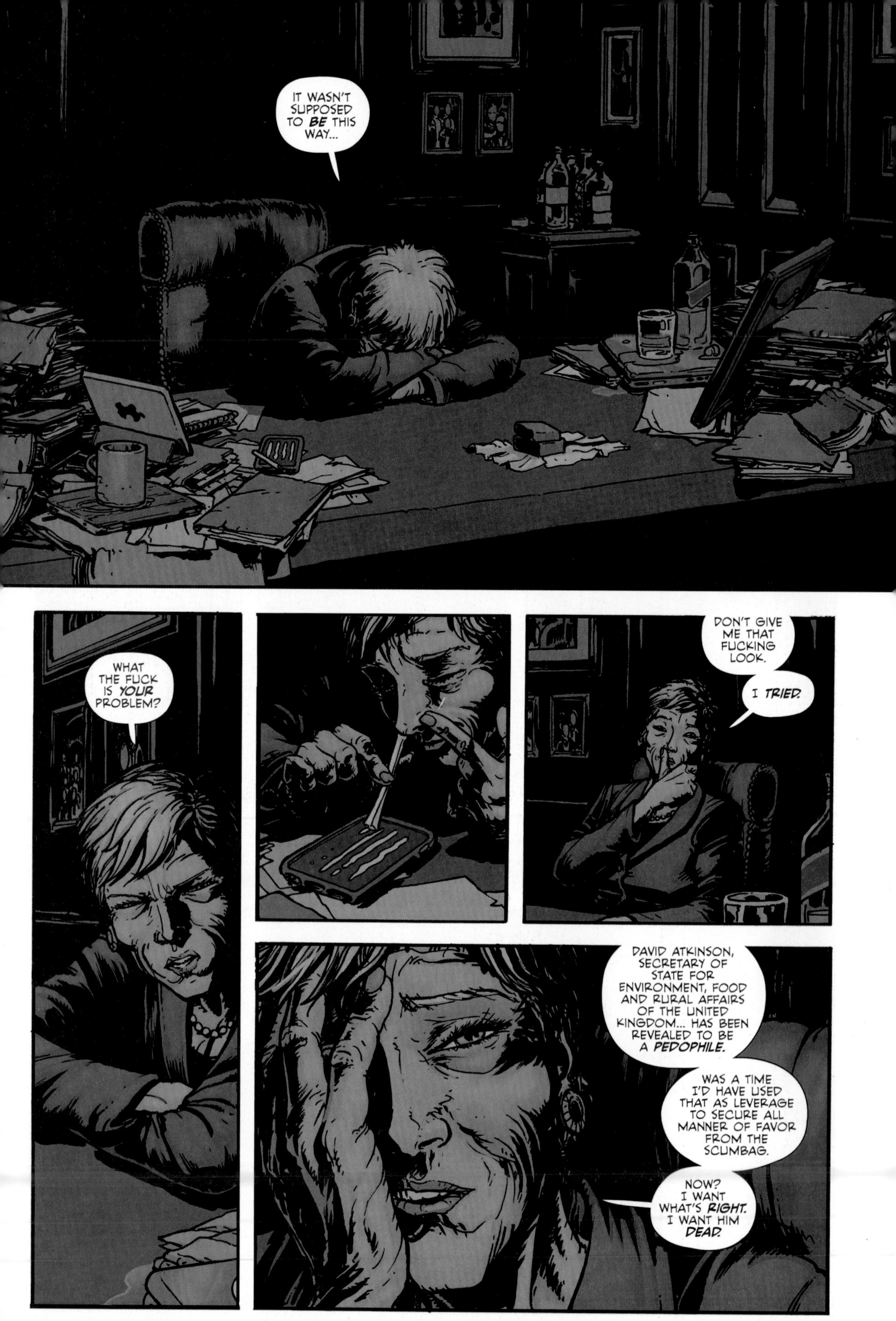
IT WASN'T SUPPOSED TO *BE* THIS WAY...
WHAT THE FUCK IS *YOUR* PROBLEM?
DON'T GIVE ME THAT FUCKING LOOK.
I *TRIED.*
DAVID ATKINSON, SECRETARY OF STATE FOR ENVIRONMENT, FOOD AND RURAL AFFAIRS OF THE UNITED KINGDOM... HAS BEEN REVEALED TO BE A *PEDOPHILE.*
WAS A TIME I'D HAVE USED THAT AS LEVERAGE TO SECURE ALL MANNER OF FAVOR FROM THE SCUMBAG.
NOW? I WANT WHAT'S *RIGHT.* I WANT HIM *DEAD.*

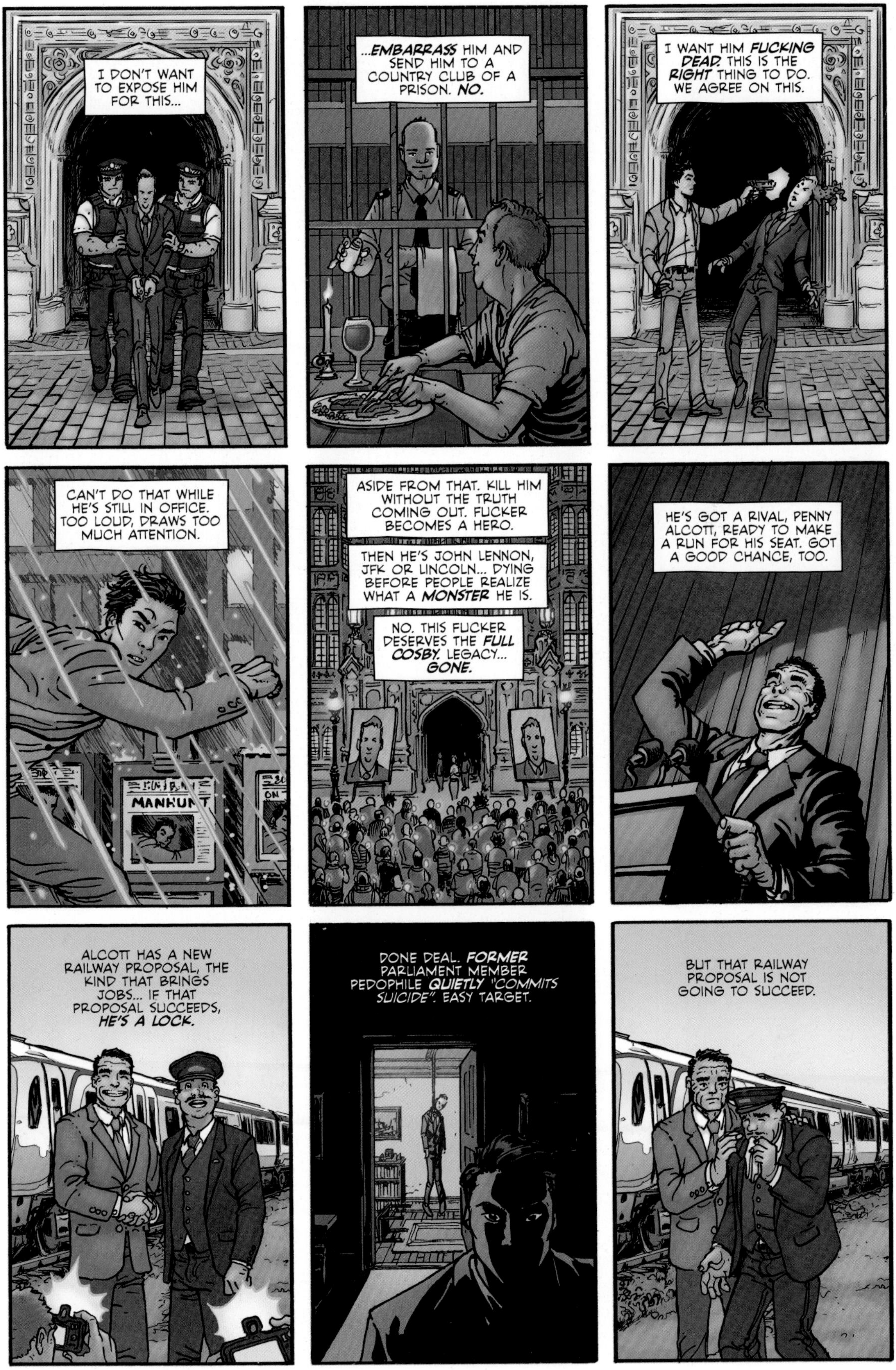
I DON'T WANT TO EXPOSE HIM FOR THIS...
...EMBARRASS HIM AND SEND HIM TO A COUNTRY CLUB OF A PRISON. NO.
I WANT HIM FUCKING DEAD. THIS IS THE RIGHT THING TO DO. WE AGREE ON THIS.
CAN'T DO THAT WHILE HE'S STILL IN OFFICE. TOO LOUD, DRAWS TOO MUCH ATTENTION.
MANHUNT
ASIDE FROM THAT. KILL HIM WITHOUT THE TRUTH COMING OUT. FUCKER BECOMES A HERO.
THEN HE'S JOHN LENNON, JFK OR LINCOLN... DYING BEFORE PEOPLE REALIZE WHAT A MONSTER HE IS.
NO. THIS FUCKER DESERVES THE FULL COSBY. LEGACY... GONE.
HE'S GOT A RIVAL, PENNY ALCOTT, READY TO MAKE A RUN FOR HIS SEAT. GOT A GOOD CHANCE, TOO.
ALCOTT HAS A NEW RAILWAY PROPOSAL, THE KIND THAT BRINGS JOBS... IF THAT PROPOSAL SUCCEEDS, HE'S A LOCK.
DONE DEAL. FORMER PARLIAMENT MEMBER PEDOPHILE QUIETLY "COMMITS SUICIDE". EASY TARGET.
BUT THAT RAILWAY PROPOSAL IS NOT GOING TO SUCCEED.

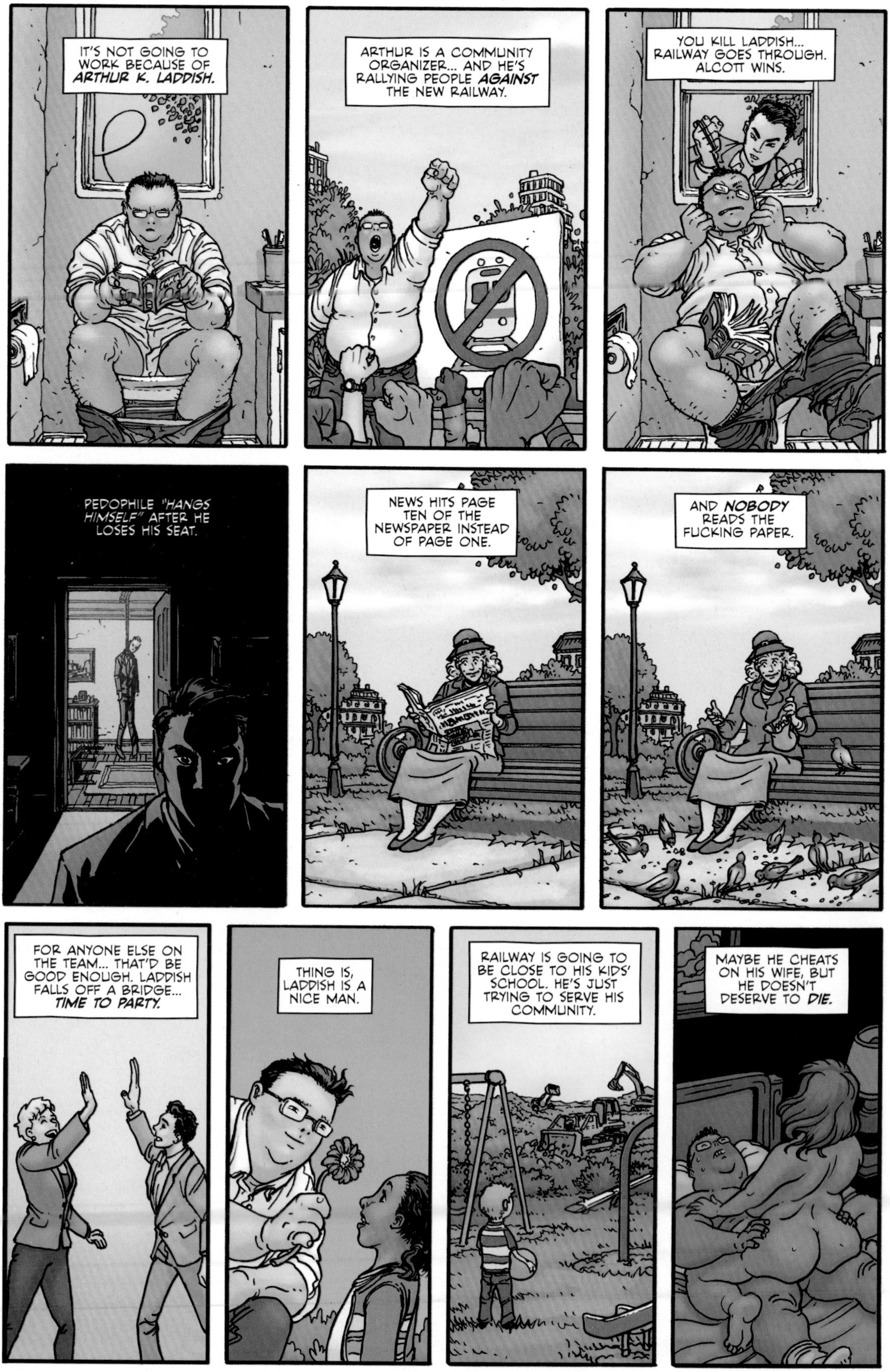
IT'S NOT GOING TO WORK BECAUSE OF *ARTHUR K. LADDISH.*
ARTHUR IS A COMMUNITY ORGANIZER... AND HE'S RALLYING PEOPLE *AGAINST* THE NEW RAILWAY.
YOU KILL LADDISH... RAILWAY GOES THROUGH. ALCOTT WINS.
PEDOPHILE *"HANGS HIMSELF"* AFTER HE LOSES HIS SEAT.
NEWS HITS PAGE TEN OF THE NEWSPAPER INSTEAD OF PAGE ONE.
AND *NOBODY* READS THE FUCKING PAPER.
FOR ANYONE ELSE ON THE TEAM... THAT'D BE GOOD ENOUGH. LADDISH FALLS OFF A BRIDGE... *TIME TO PARTY.*
THING IS, LADDISH IS A NICE MAN.
RAILWAY IS GOING TO BE CLOSE TO HIS KIDS' SCHOOL. HE'S JUST TRYING TO SERVE HIS COMMUNITY.
MAYBE HE CHEATS ON HIS WIFE, BUT HE DOESN'T DESERVE TO *DIE.*

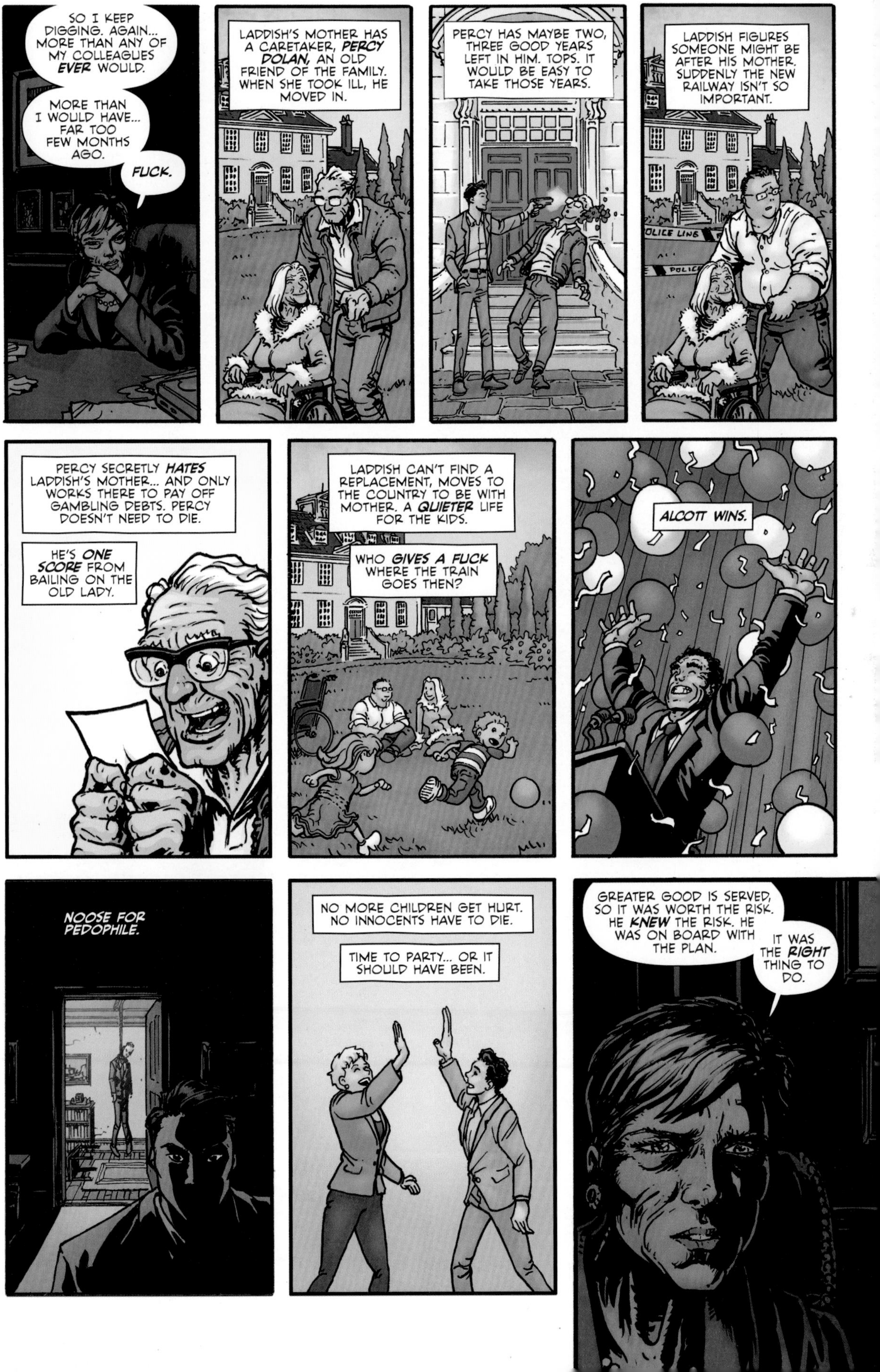
SO I KEEP DIGGING. AGAIN... MORE THAN ANY OF MY COLLEAGUES EVER WOULD.
MORE THAN I WOULD HAVE... FAR TOO FEW MONTHS AGO.
FUCK.
LADDISH'S MOTHER HAS A CARETAKER, PERCY DOLAN, AN OLD FRIEND OF THE FAMILY. WHEN SHE TOOK ILL, HE MOVED IN.
PERCY HAS MAYBE TWO, THREE GOOD YEARS LEFT IN HIM. TOPS. IT WOULD BE EASY TO TAKE THOSE YEARS.
LADDISH FIGURES SOMEONE MIGHT BE AFTER HIS MOTHER. SUDDENLY THE NEW RAILWAY ISN'T SO IMPORTANT.
PERCY SECRETLY HATES LADDISH'S MOTHER... AND ONLY WORKS THERE TO PAY OFF GAMBLING DEBTS. PERCY DOESN'T NEED TO DIE.
HE'S ONE SCORE FROM BAILING ON THE OLD LADY.
LADDISH CAN'T FIND A REPLACEMENT, MOVES TO THE COUNTRY TO BE WITH MOTHER. A QUIETER LIFE FOR THE KIDS.
WHO GIVES A FUCK WHERE THE TRAIN GOES THEN?
ALCOTT WINS.
NOOSE FOR PEDOPHILE.
NO MORE CHILDREN GET HURT. NO INNOCENTS HAVE TO DIE.
TIME TO PARTY... OR IT SHOULD HAVE BEEN.
GREATER GOOD IS SERVED, SO IT WAS WORTH THE RISK. HE KNEW THE RISK. HE WAS ON BOARD WITH THE PLAN.
IT WAS THE RIGHT THING TO DO.

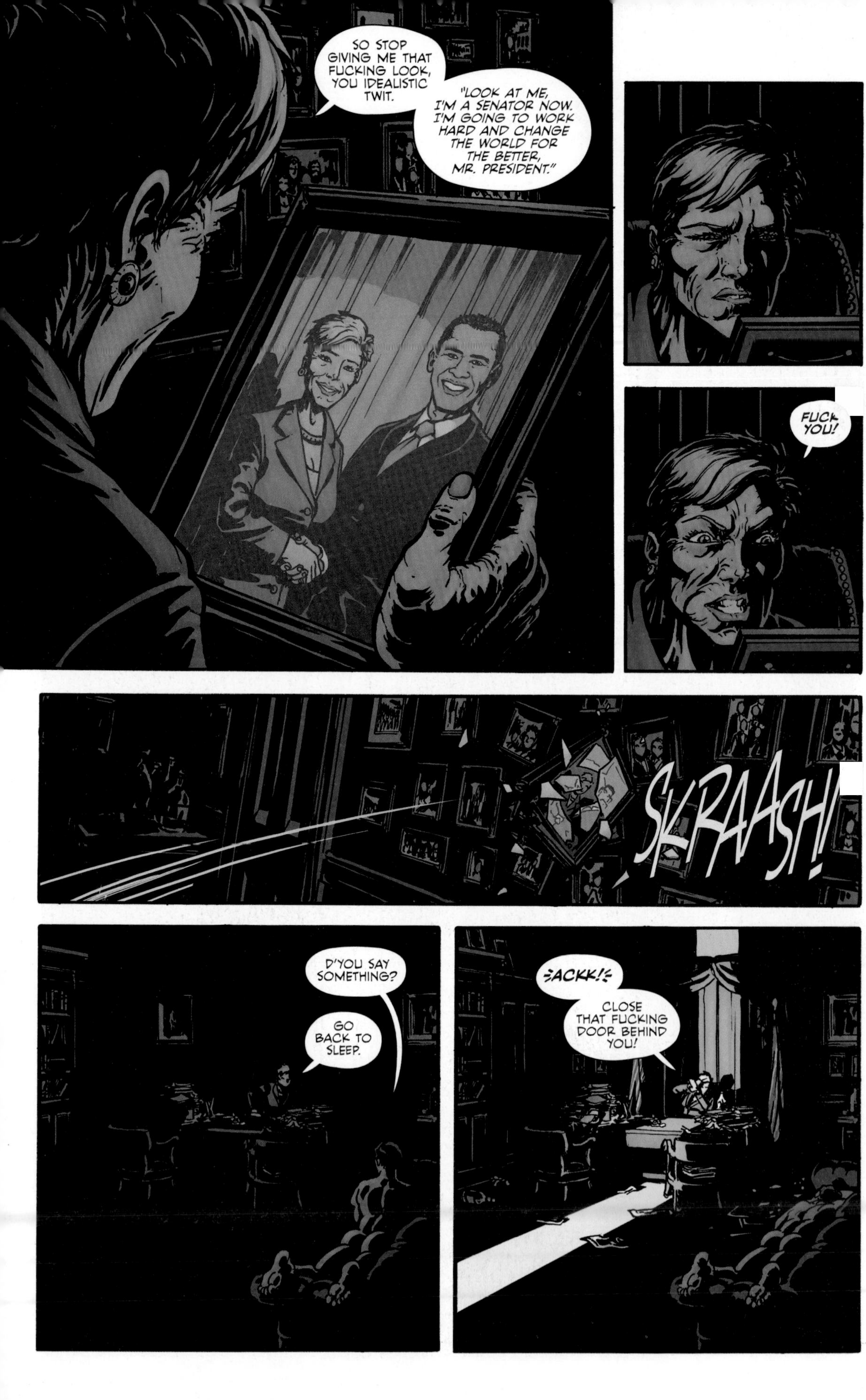
SO STOP GIVING ME THAT FUCKING LOOK, YOU IDEALISTIC TWIT.
"LOOK AT ME, I'M A SENATOR NOW. I'M GOING TO WORK HARD AND CHANGE THE WORLD FOR THE BETTER, MR. PRESIDENT."
FUCK YOU!
SKRAASH!
D'YOU SAY SOMETHING?
GO BACK TO SLEEP.
ACKK!
CLOSE THAT FUCKING DOOR BEHIND YOU!

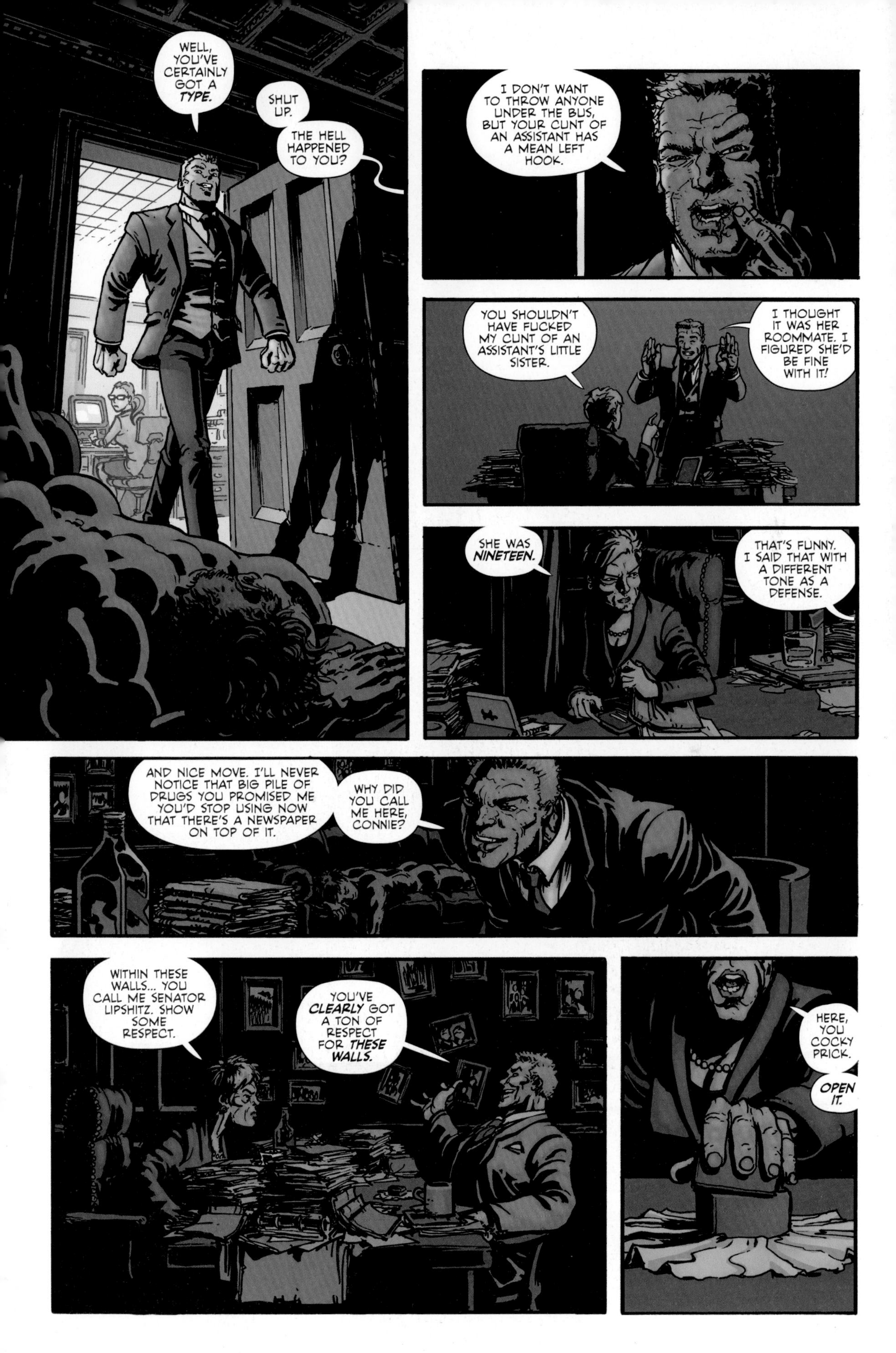
WELL, YOU'VE CERTAINLY GOT A *TYPE.*
SHUT UP.
THE HELL HAPPENED TO YOU?
I DON'T WANT TO THROW ANYONE UNDER THE BUS, BUT YOUR CUNT OF AN ASSISTANT HAS A MEAN LEFT HOOK.
YOU SHOULDN'T HAVE FUCKED MY CUNT OF AN ASSISTANT'S LITTLE SISTER.
I THOUGHT IT WAS HER ROOMMATE. I FIGURED SHE'D BE FINE WITH IT!
SHE WAS *NINETEEN.*
THAT'S FUNNY. I SAID THAT WITH A DIFFERENT TONE AS A DEFENSE.
AND NICE MOVE. I'LL NEVER NOTICE THAT BIG PILE OF DRUGS YOU PROMISED ME YOU'D STOP USING NOW THAT THERE'S A NEWSPAPER ON TOP OF IT.
WHY DID YOU CALL ME HERE, CONNIE?
WITHIN THESE WALLS... YOU CALL ME SENATOR LIPSHITZ. SHOW SOME RESPECT.
YOU'VE *CLEARLY* GOT A TON OF RESPECT FOR *THESE WALLS.*
HERE, YOU COCKY PRICK.
OPEN IT.

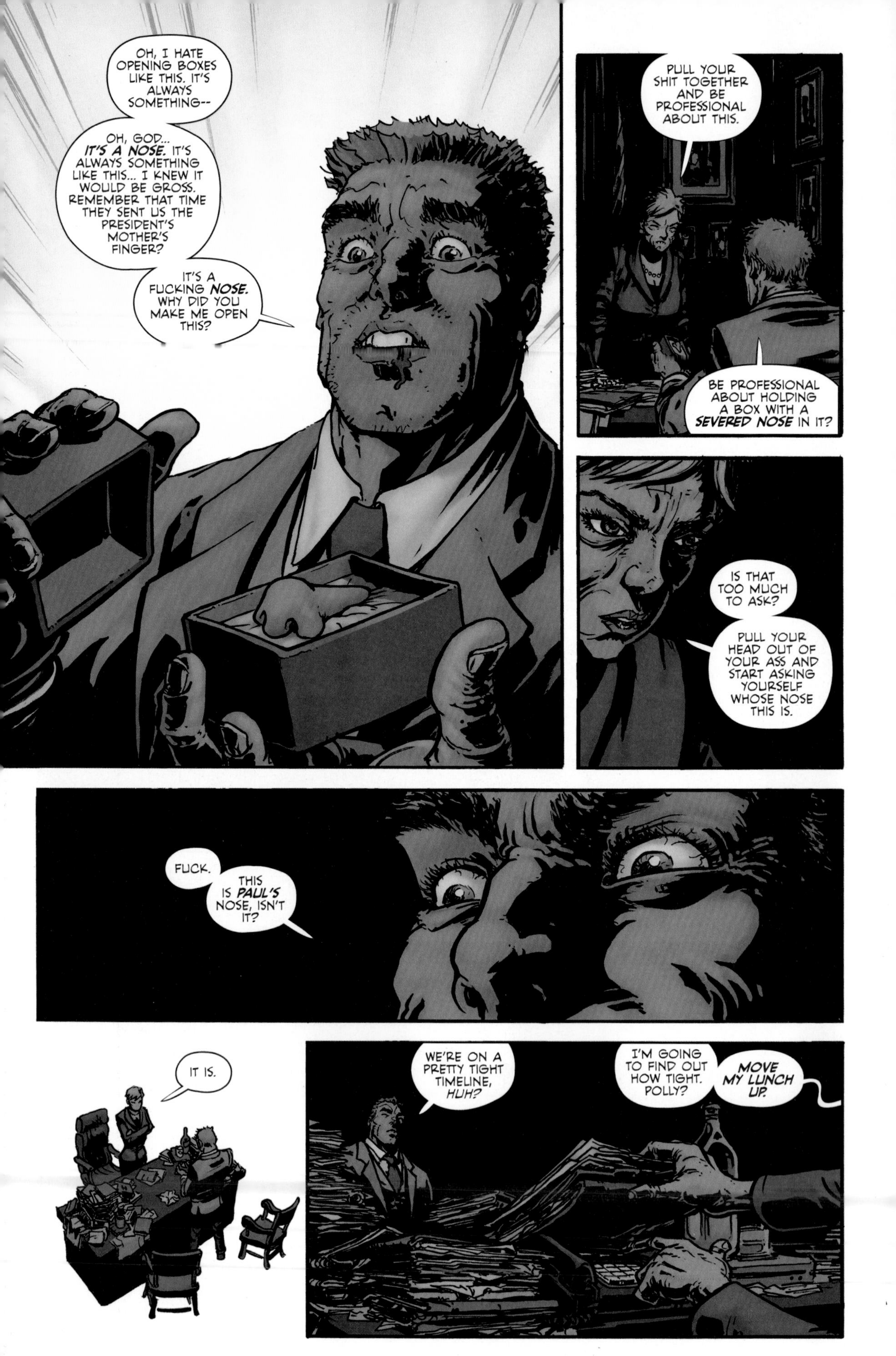
OH, I HATE OPENING BOXES LIKE THIS. IT'S ALWAYS SOMETHING--
OH, GOD... IT'S A NOSE. IT'S ALWAYS SOMETHING LIKE THIS... I KNEW IT WOULD BE GROSS. REMEMBER THAT TIME THEY SENT US THE PRESIDENT'S MOTHER'S FINGER?
IT'S A FUCKING NOSE. WHY DID YOU MAKE ME OPEN THIS?
PULL YOUR SHIT TOGETHER AND BE PROFESSIONAL ABOUT THIS.
BE PROFESSIONAL ABOUT HOLDING A BOX WITH A SEVERED NOSE IN IT?
IS THAT TOO MUCH TO ASK?
PULL YOUR HEAD OUT OF YOUR ASS AND START ASKING YOURSELF WHOSE NOSE THIS IS.
FUCK.
THIS IS PAUL'S NOSE, ISN'T IT?
IT IS.
WE'RE ON A PRETTY TIGHT TIMELINE, HUH?
I'M GOING TO FIND OUT HOW TIGHT. POLLY?
MOVE MY LUNCH UP.

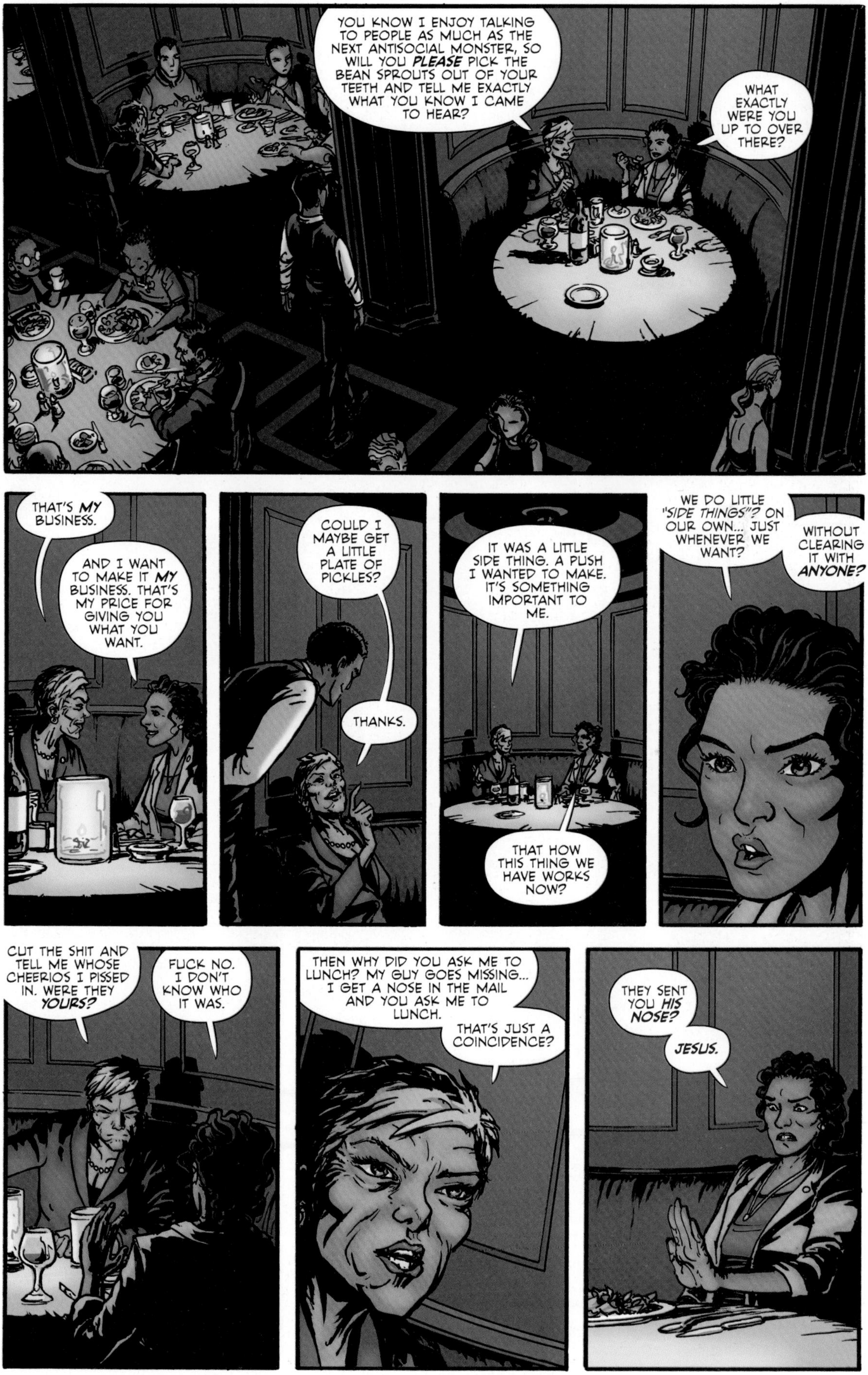
YOU KNOW I ENJOY TALKING TO PEOPLE AS MUCH AS THE NEXT ANTISOCIAL MONSTER, SO WILL YOU *PLEASE* PICK THE BEAN SPROUTS OUT OF YOUR TEETH AND TELL ME EXACTLY WHAT YOU KNOW I CAME TO HEAR?
WHAT EXACTLY WERE YOU UP TO OVER THERE?
THAT'S *MY* BUSINESS.
AND I WANT TO MAKE IT *MY* BUSINESS. THAT'S MY PRICE FOR GIVING YOU WHAT YOU WANT.
COULD I MAYBE GET A LITTLE PLATE OF PICKLES?
THANKS.
IT WAS A LITTLE SIDE THING. A PUSH I WANTED TO MAKE. IT'S SOMETHING IMPORTANT TO ME.
THAT HOW THIS THING WE HAVE WORKS NOW?
WE DO LITTLE *"SIDE THINGS"?* ON OUR OWN... JUST WHENEVER WE WANT?
WITHOUT CLEARING IT WITH *ANYONE?*
CUT THE SHIT AND TELL ME WHOSE CHEERIOS I PISSED IN. WERE THEY *YOURS?*
FUCK NO. I DON'T KNOW WHO IT WAS.
THEN WHY DID YOU ASK ME TO LUNCH? MY GUY GOES MISSING... I GET A NOSE IN THE MAIL AND YOU ASK ME TO LUNCH.
THAT'S JUST A COINCIDENCE?
THEY SENT YOU *HIS NOSE?*
JESUS.

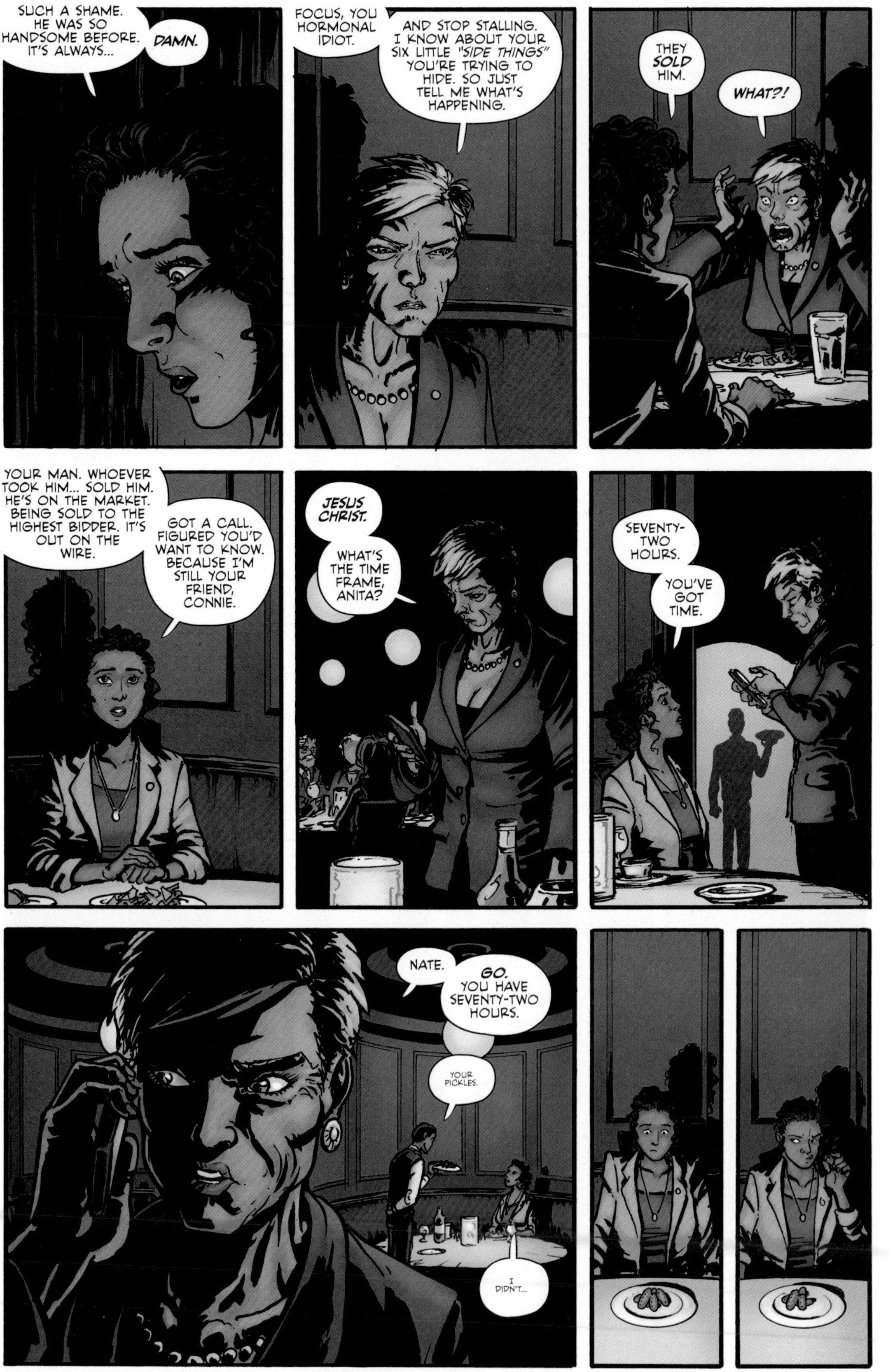
SUCH A SHAME. HE WAS SO HANDSOME BEFORE. IT'S ALWAYS...
DAMN.
FOCUS, YOU HORMONAL IDIOT.
AND STOP STALLING. I KNOW ABOUT YOUR SIX LITTLE "SIDE THINGS" YOU'RE TRYING TO HIDE. SO JUST TELL ME WHAT'S HAPPENING.
THEY SOLD HIM.
WHAT?!
YOUR MAN. WHOEVER TOOK HIM... SOLD HIM. HE'S ON THE MARKET. BEING SOLD TO THE HIGHEST BIDDER. IT'S OUT ON THE WIRE.
GOT A CALL. FIGURED YOU'D WANT TO KNOW. BECAUSE I'M STILL YOUR FRIEND, CONNIE.
JESUS CHRIST.
WHAT'S THE TIME FRAME, ANITA?
SEVENTY-TWO HOURS.
YOU'VE GOT TIME.
NATE.
GO. YOU HAVE SEVENTY-TWO HOURS.
YOUR PICKLES.
I DIDN'T...

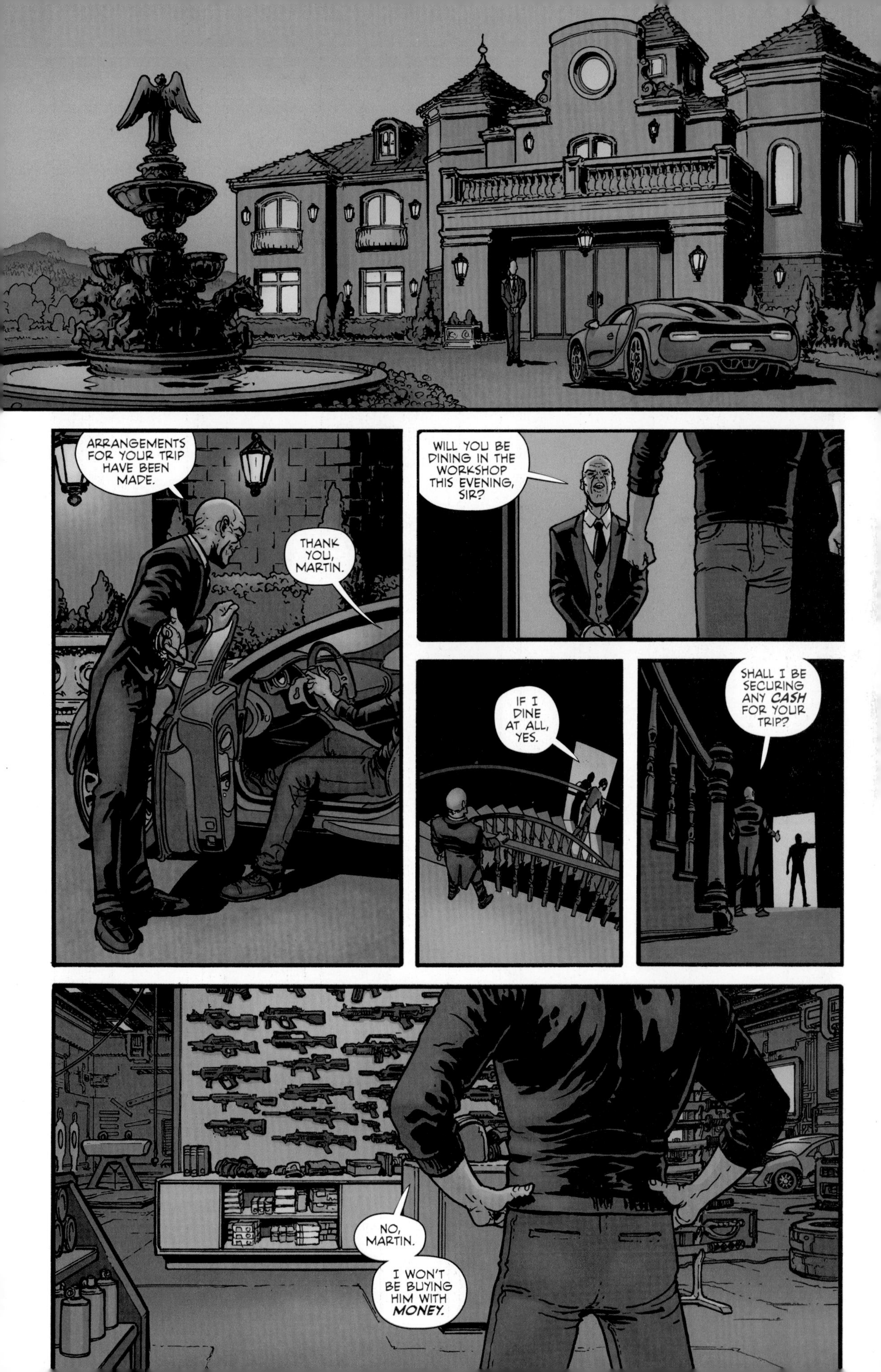
ARRANGEMENTS FOR YOUR TRIP HAVE BEEN MADE.
THANK YOU, MARTIN.
WILL YOU BE DINING IN THE WORKSHOP THIS EVENING, SIR?
IF I DINE AT ALL, YES.
SHALL I BE SECURING ANY *CASH* FOR YOUR TRIP?
NO, MARTIN.
I WON'T BE BUYING HIM WITH ***MONEY.***

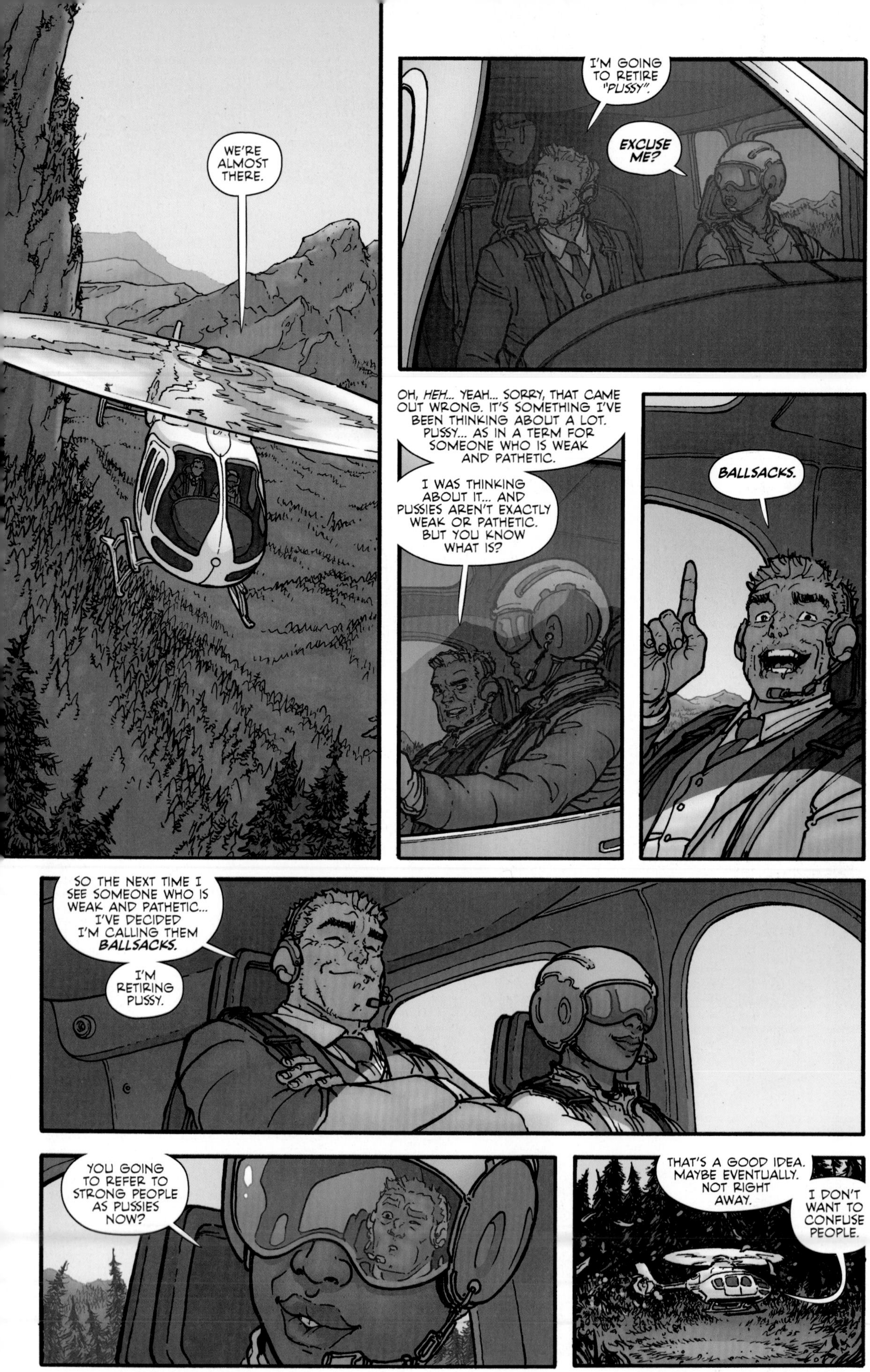
WE'RE ALMOST THERE.
I'M GOING TO RETIRE "PUSSY".
EXCUSE ME?
OH, HEH... YEAH... SORRY, THAT CAME OUT WRONG. IT'S SOMETHING I'VE BEEN THINKING ABOUT A LOT. PUSSY... AS IN A TERM FOR SOMEONE WHO IS WEAK AND PATHETIC.
I WAS THINKING ABOUT IT... AND PUSSIES AREN'T EXACTLY WEAK OR PATHETIC. BUT YOU KNOW WHAT IS?
BALLSACKS.
SO THE NEXT TIME I SEE SOMEONE WHO IS WEAK AND PATHETIC... I'VE DECIDED I'M CALLING THEM BALLSACKS.
I'M RETIRING PUSSY.
YOU GOING TO REFER TO STRONG PEOPLE AS PUSSIES NOW?
THAT'S A GOOD IDEA. MAYBE EVENTUALLY. NOT RIGHT AWAY.
I DON'T WANT TO CONFUSE PEOPLE.

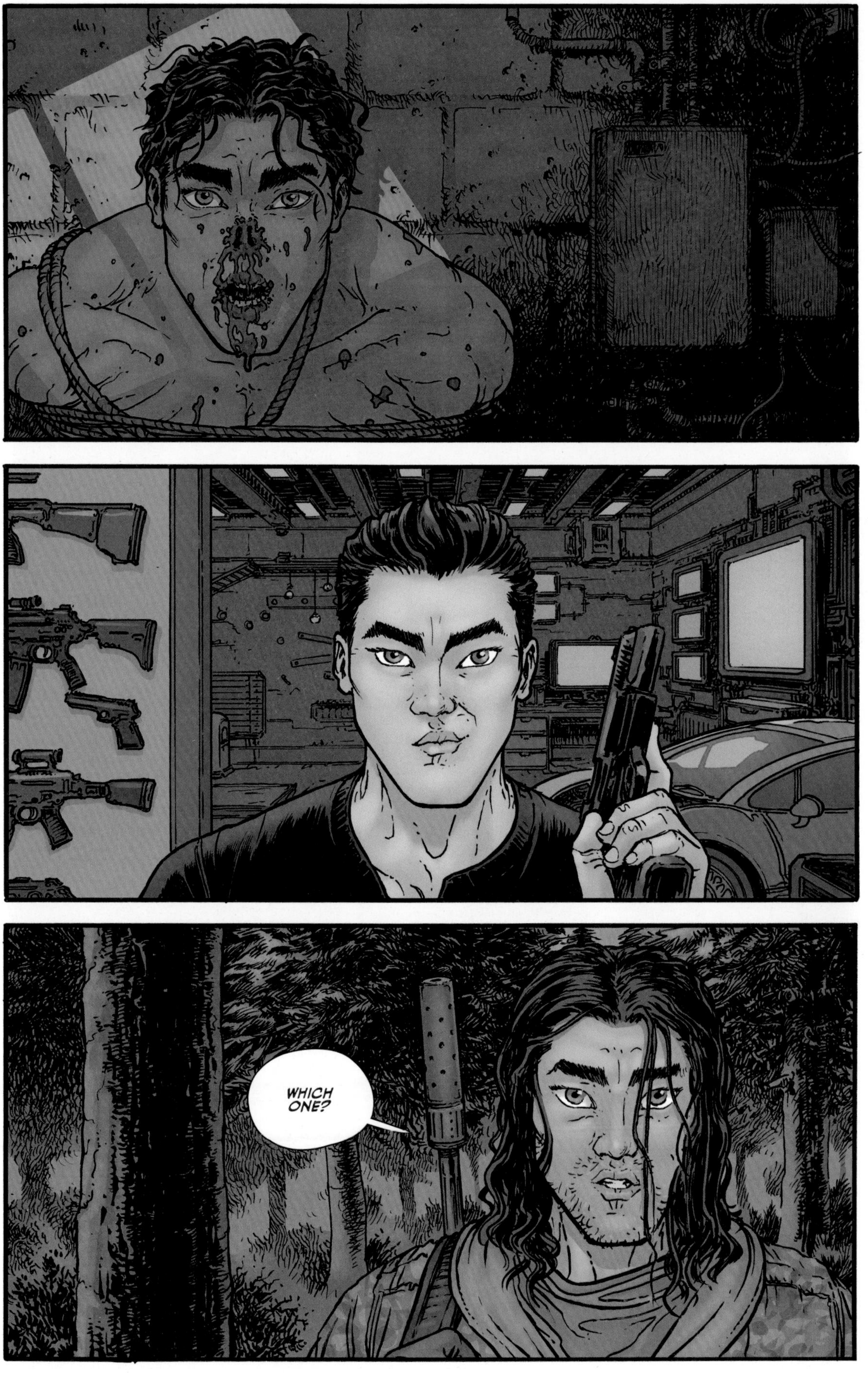
WHICH ONE?

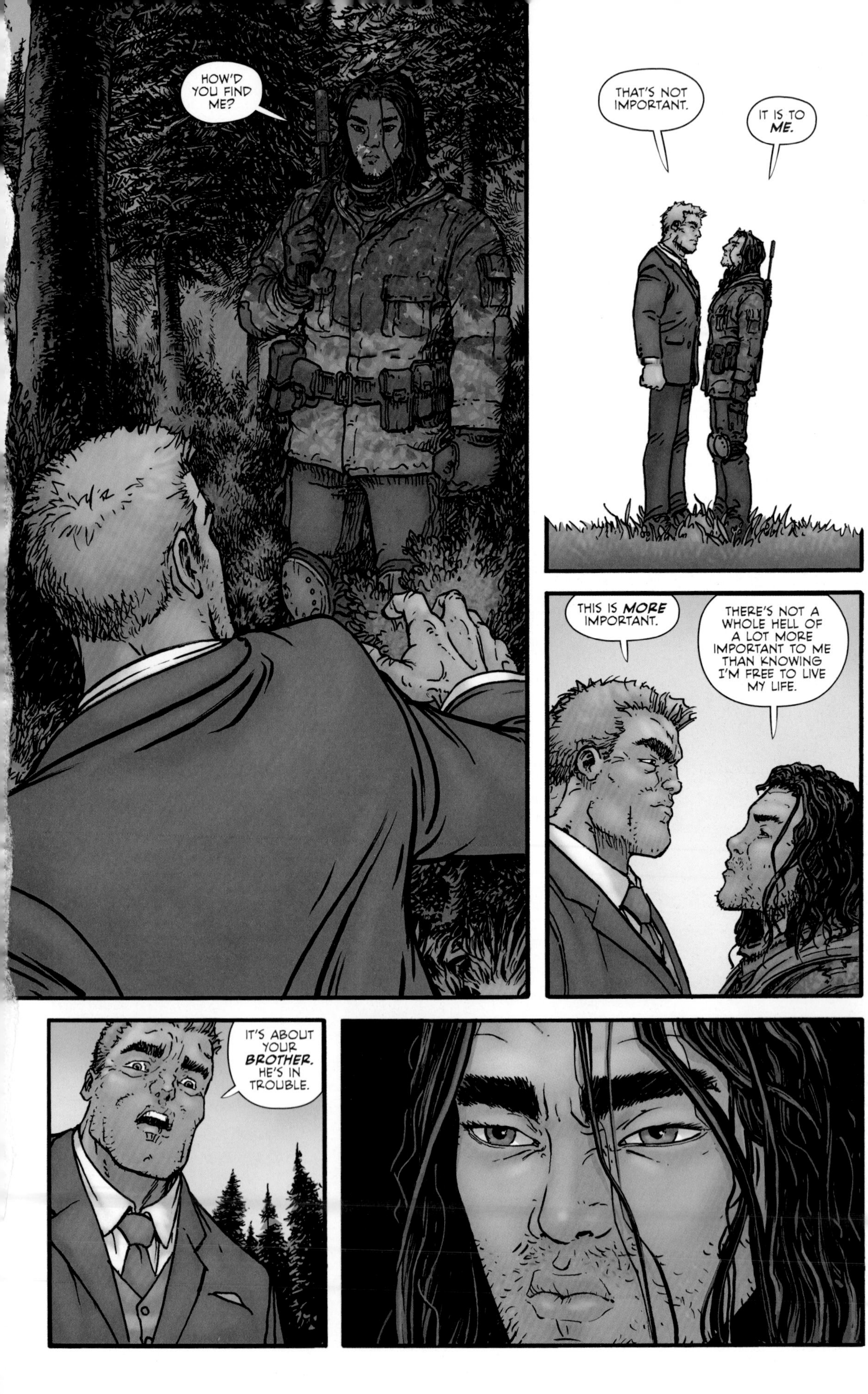
HOW'D YOU FIND ME?
THAT'S NOT IMPORTANT.
IT IS TO *ME.*
THIS IS *MORE* IMPORTANT.
THERE'S NOT A WHOLE HELL OF A LOT MORE IMPORTANT TO ME THAN KNOWING I'M FREE TO LIVE MY LIFE.
IT'S ABOUT YOUR *BROTHER.* HE'S IN TROUBLE.

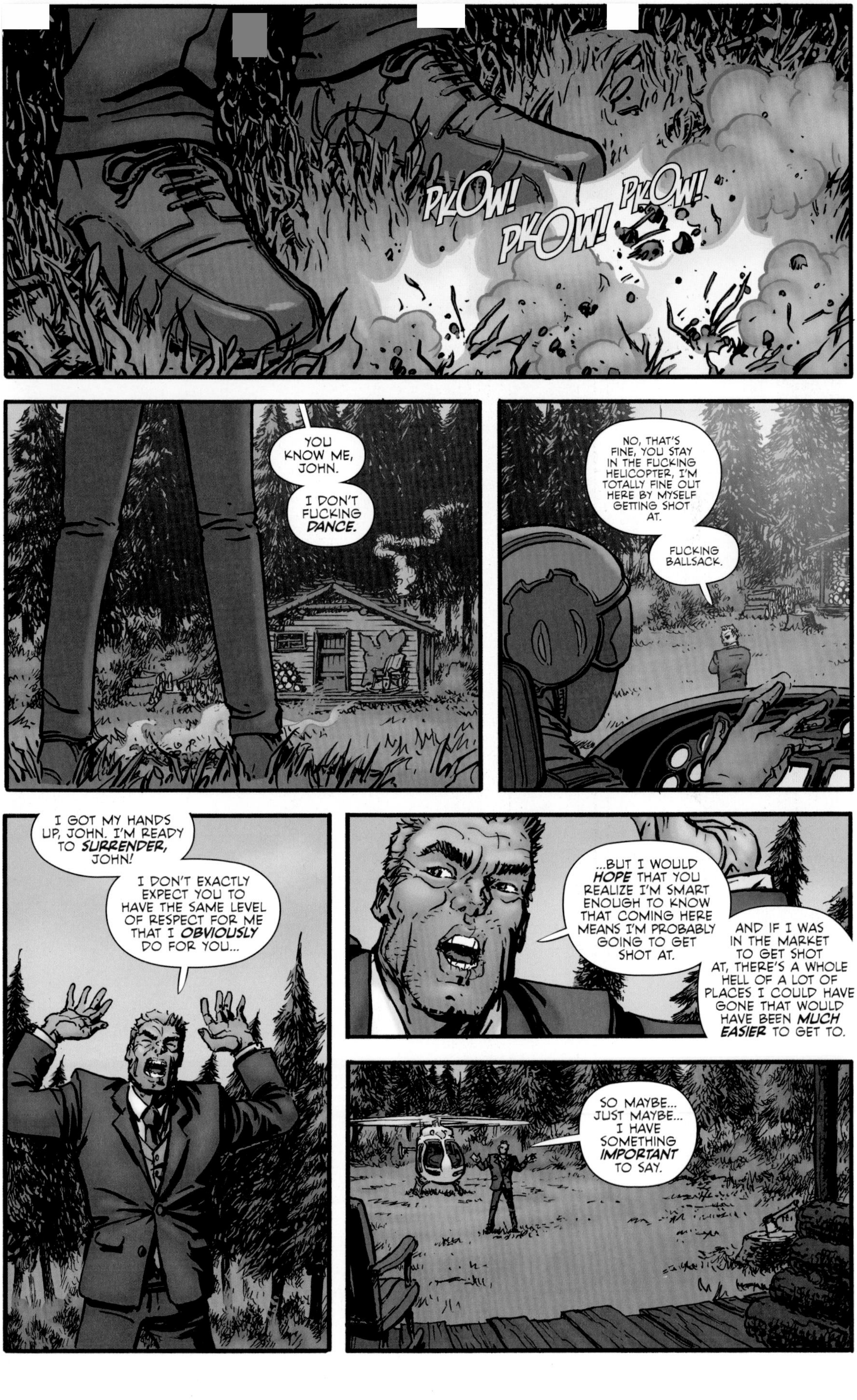
PKOW!
PKOW!
PKOW!
YOU KNOW ME, JOHN.
I DON'T FUCKING DANCE.
NO, THAT'S FINE, YOU STAY IN THE FUCKING HELICOPTER, I'M TOTALLY FINE OUT HERE BY MYSELF GETTING SHOT AT.
FUCKING BALLSACK.
I GOT MY HANDS UP, JOHN. I'M READY TO SURRENDER, JOHN!
I DON'T EXACTLY EXPECT YOU TO HAVE THE SAME LEVEL OF RESPECT FOR ME THAT I OBVIOUSLY DO FOR YOU...
...BUT I WOULD HOPE THAT YOU REALIZE I'M SMART ENOUGH TO KNOW THAT COMING HERE MEANS I'M PROBABLY GOING TO GET SHOT AT.
AND IF I WAS IN THE MARKET TO GET SHOT AT, THERE'S A WHOLE HELL OF A LOT OF PLACES I COULD HAVE GONE THAT WOULD HAVE BEEN MUCH EASIER TO GET TO.
SO MAYBE... JUST MAYBE... I HAVE SOMETHING IMPORTANT TO SAY.

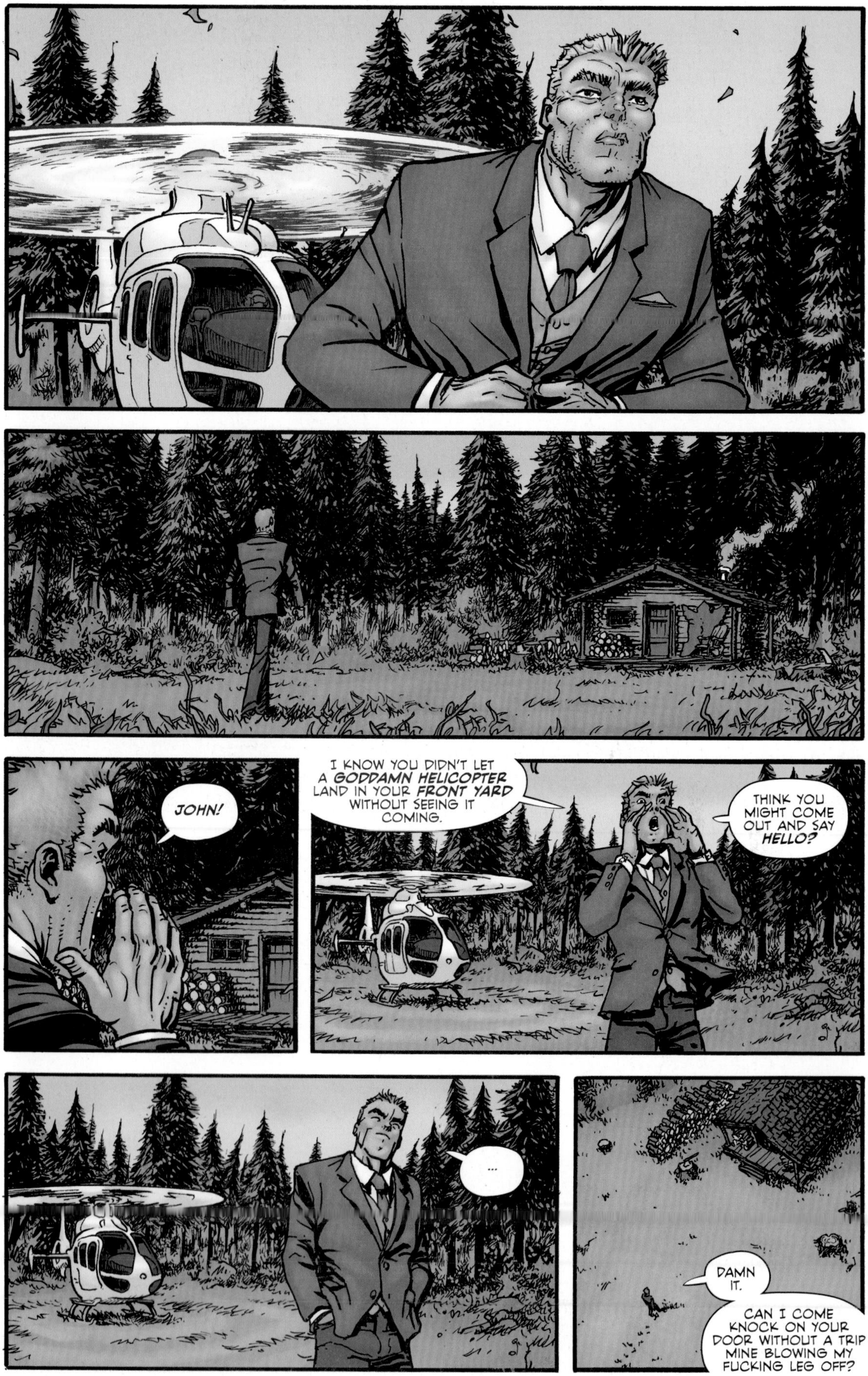
JOHN!
I KNOW YOU DIDN'T LET A GODDAMN HELICOPTER LAND IN YOUR FRONT YARD WITHOUT SEEING IT COMING.
THINK YOU MIGHT COME OUT AND SAY HELLO?
...
DAMN IT.
CAN I COME KNOCK ON YOUR DOOR WITHOUT A TRIP MINE BLOWING MY FUCKING LEG OFF?

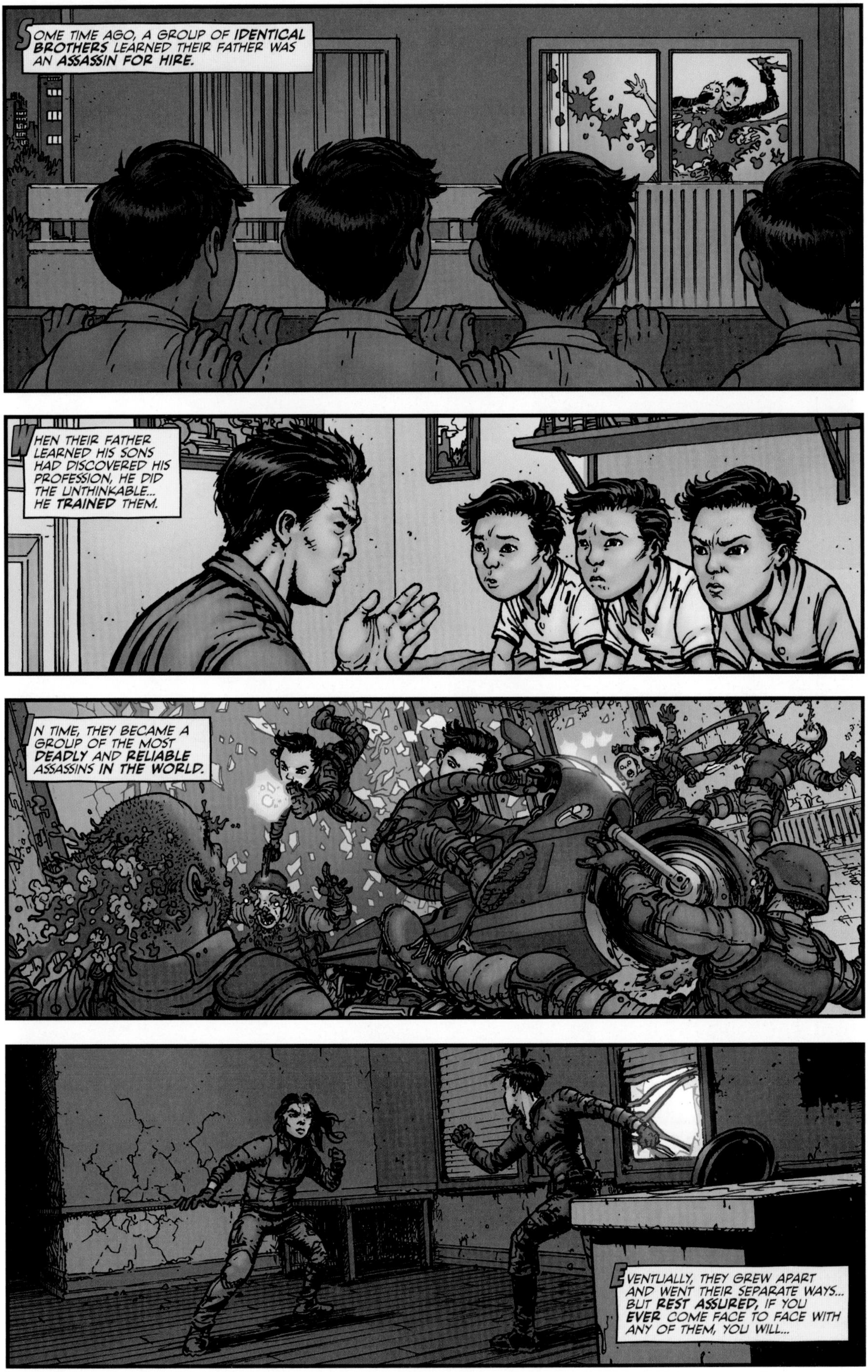
SOME TIME AGO, A GROUP OF IDENTICAL BROTHERS LEARNED THEIR FATHER WAS AN ASSASSIN FOR HIRE.
WHEN THEIR FATHER LEARNED HIS SONS HAD DISCOVERED HIS PROFESSION, HE DID THE UNTHINKABLE... HE TRAINED THEM.
IN TIME, THEY BECAME A GROUP OF THE MOST DEADLY AND RELIABLE ASSASSINS IN THE WORLD.
EVENTUALLY, THEY GREW APART AND WENT THEIR SEPARATE WAYS... BUT REST ASSURED, IF YOU EVER COME FACE TO FACE WITH ANY OF THEM, YOU WILL...

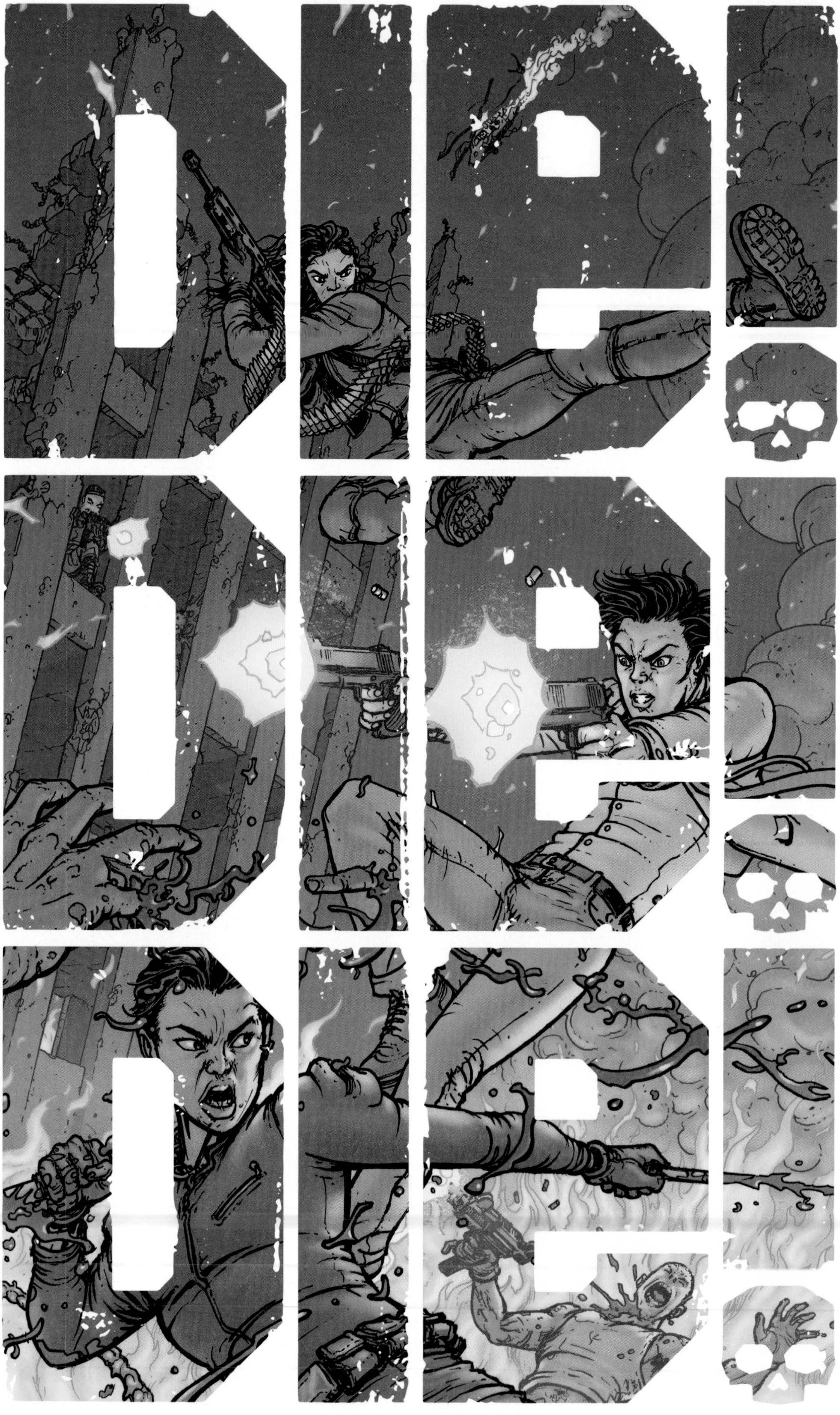
DIE!
DIE!
DIE!

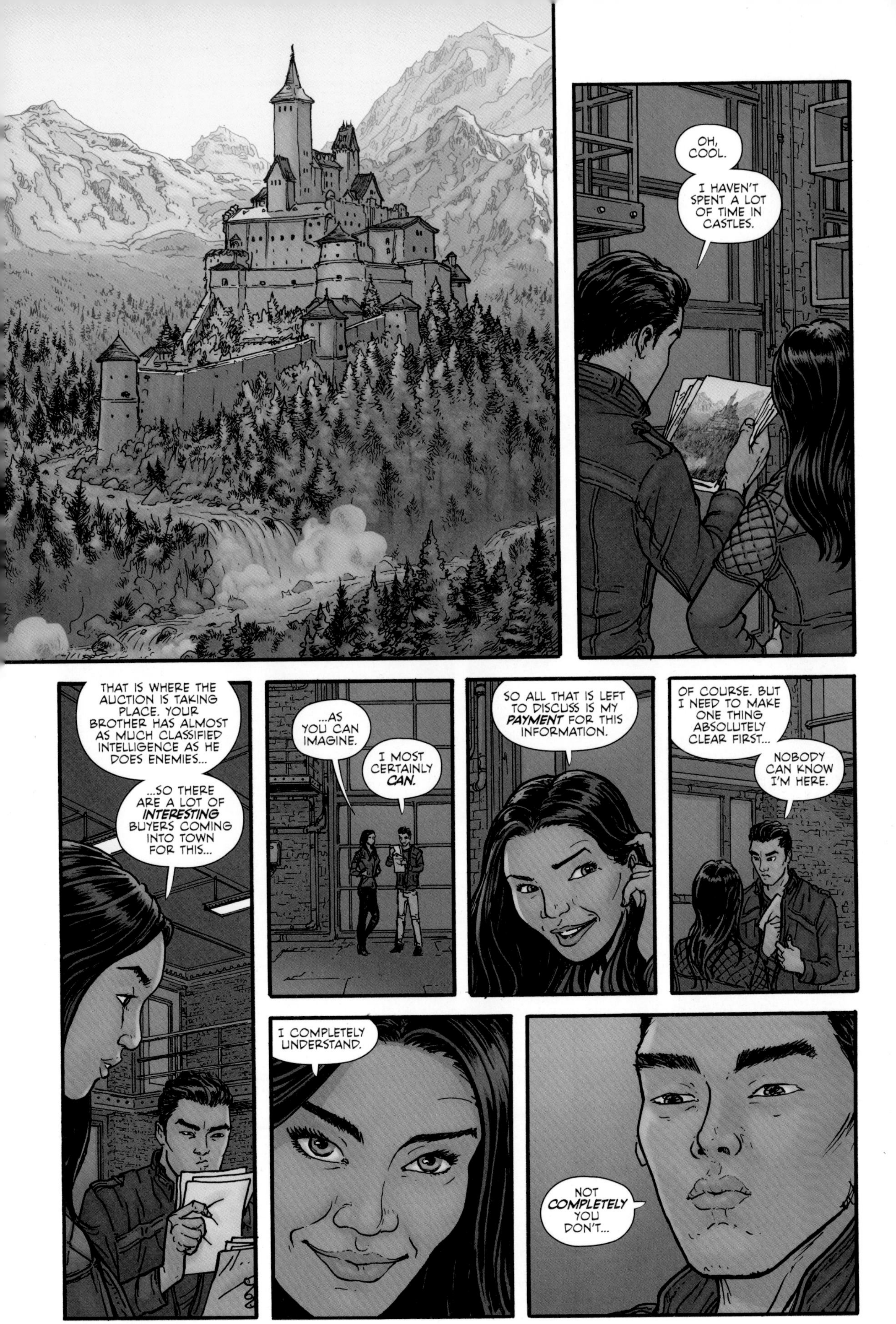

OH, COOL.
I HAVEN'T SPENT A LOT OF TIME IN CASTLES.
THAT IS WHERE THE AUCTION IS TAKING PLACE. YOUR BROTHER HAS ALMOST AS MUCH CLASSIFIED INTELLIGENCE AS HE DOES ENEMIES...
...SO THERE ARE A LOT OF INTERESTING BUYERS COMING INTO TOWN FOR THIS...
...AS YOU CAN IMAGINE.
I MOST CERTAINLY CAN.
SO ALL THAT IS LEFT TO DISCUSS IS MY PAYMENT FOR THIS INFORMATION.
OF COURSE. BUT I NEED TO MAKE ONE THING ABSOLUTELY CLEAR FIRST...
NOBODY CAN KNOW I'M HERE.
I COMPLETELY UNDERSTAND.
NOT COMPLETELY YOU DON'T...

BZZT.

BZZT.

YES. THE TEXT CAME THROUGH. I SEE IT NOW.

NOW I'M *HERE* TALKING TO *YOUR GUY* ABOUT WHEN HE'S COMING OVER TO MEET HER. THEY'LL NAB HIM AS SOON AS THE BODY IS FOUND.

I'LL HAVE THE GUN TO YOU WITHIN THE HOUR. YOU CAN PLANT IT AND *YOUR* PHONE IN HIS APARTMENT TONIGHT.

ABSOLUTELY NOT. THIS ONE IS A FREEBIE. I NEEDED THE INFORMATION AND NOW I DON'T HAVE TO PAY FOR IT. FRAMING YOUR GUY SAVES *ME* MONEY.

I'M NICE LIKE THAT...

...AND I--

YOU'VE DONE YOUR HOMEWORK. IMPRESSIVE. SHE DOES HAVE A HIT ON HER FROM THE STAZULLI FAMILY. WHY DO ONE JOB WHEN YOU CAN DO *THREE* AT ONCE, I ALWAYS SAY.

NO, I WILL *NOT* BE SPLITTING THAT MONEY WITH YOU. I AM DELIVERING A *GUN* TO YOU... WOULD YOU LIKE AN ADDITIONAL *BULLET* TO COME WITH IT?

SMART MAN. SEE YOU SOON.

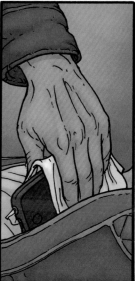

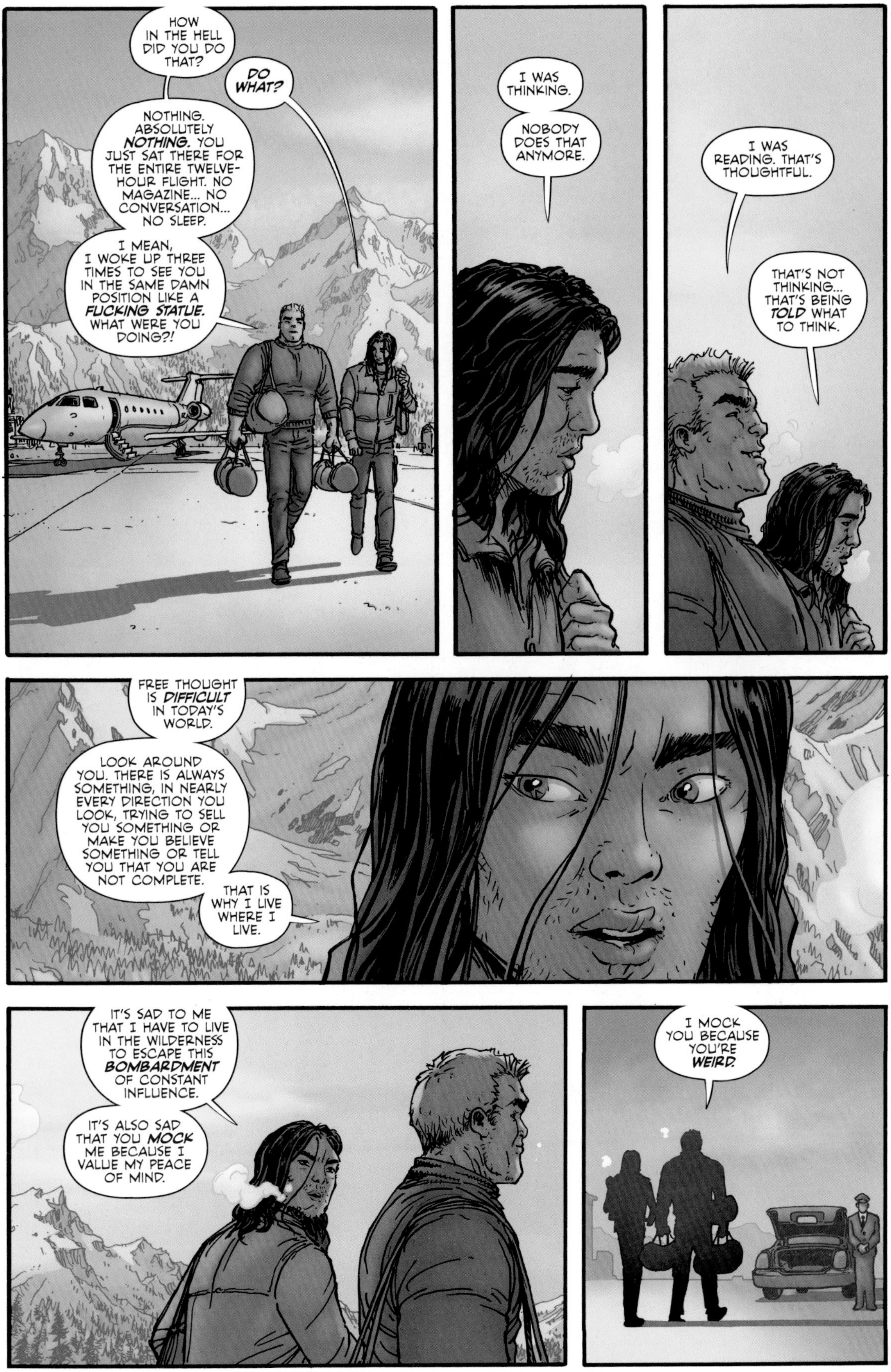
HOW IN THE HELL DID YOU DO THAT?
DO WHAT?
NOTHING. ABSOLUTELY NOTHING. YOU JUST SAT THERE FOR THE ENTIRE TWELVE-HOUR FLIGHT. NO MAGAZINE... NO CONVERSATION... NO SLEEP.
I MEAN, I WOKE UP THREE TIMES TO SEE YOU IN THE SAME DAMN POSITION LIKE A FUCKING STATUE. WHAT WERE YOU DOING?!
I WAS THINKING.
NOBODY DOES THAT ANYMORE.
I WAS READING. THAT'S THOUGHTFUL.
THAT'S NOT THINKING... THAT'S BEING TOLD WHAT TO THINK.
FREE THOUGHT IS DIFFICULT IN TODAY'S WORLD.
LOOK AROUND YOU. THERE IS ALWAYS SOMETHING, IN NEARLY EVERY DIRECTION YOU LOOK, TRYING TO SELL YOU SOMETHING OR MAKE YOU BELIEVE SOMETHING OR TELL YOU THAT YOU ARE NOT COMPLETE.
THAT IS WHY I LIVE WHERE I LIVE.
IT'S SAD TO ME THAT I HAVE TO LIVE IN THE WILDERNESS TO ESCAPE THIS BOMBARDMENT OF CONSTANT INFLUENCE.
IT'S ALSO SAD THAT YOU MOCK ME BECAUSE I VALUE MY PEACE OF MIND.
I MOCK YOU BECAUSE YOU'RE WEIRD.

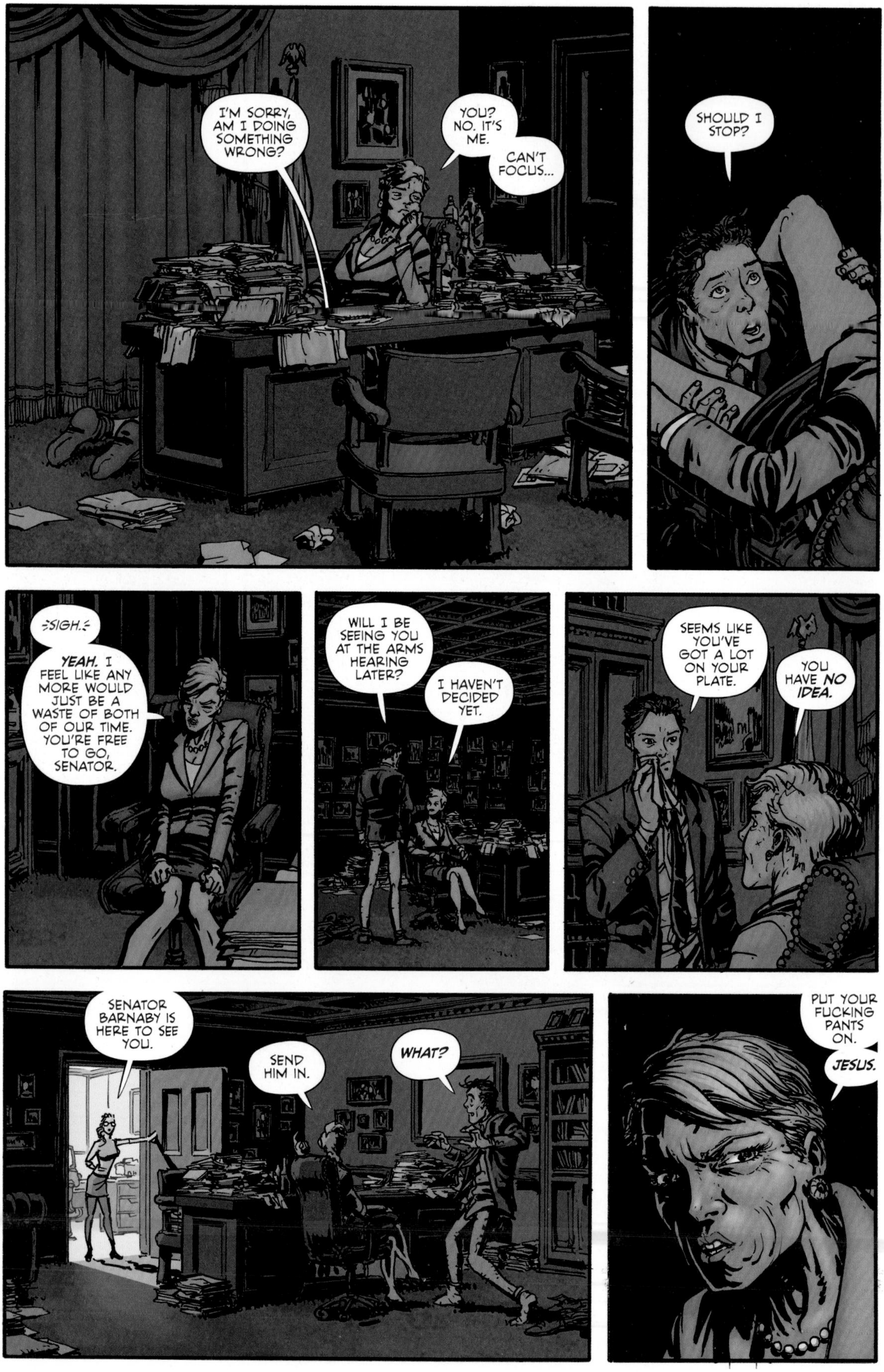
I'M SORRY, AM I DOING SOMETHING WRONG?
YOU? NO. IT'S ME.
CAN'T FOCUS...
SHOULD I STOP?
SIGH.
YEAH. I FEEL LIKE ANY MORE WOULD JUST BE A WASTE OF BOTH OF OUR TIME. YOU'RE FREE TO GO, SENATOR.
WILL I BE SEEING YOU AT THE ARMS HEARING LATER?
I HAVEN'T DECIDED YET.
SEEMS LIKE YOU'VE GOT A LOT ON YOUR PLATE.
YOU HAVE NO IDEA.
SENATOR BARNABY IS HERE TO SEE YOU.
SEND HIM IN.
WHAT?
PUT YOUR FUCKING PANTS ON.
JESUS.

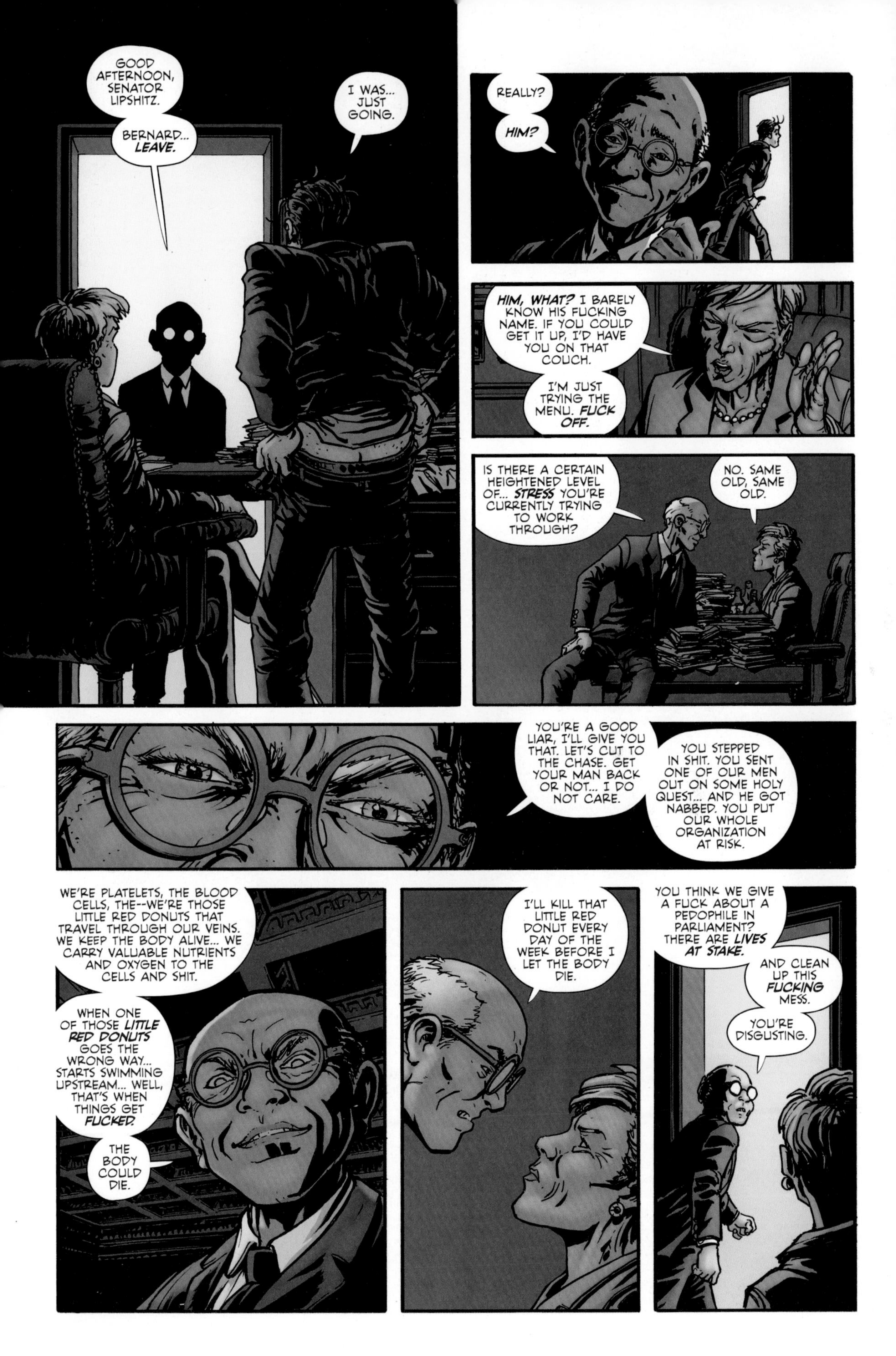
GOOD AFTERNOON, SENATOR LIPSHITZ.
BERNARD... LEAVE.
I WAS... JUST GOING.
REALLY?
HIM?
HIM, WHAT? I BARELY KNOW HIS FUCKING NAME. IF YOU COULD GET IT UP, I'D HAVE YOU ON THAT COUCH.
I'M JUST TRYING THE MENU. FUCK OFF.
IS THERE A CERTAIN HEIGHTENED LEVEL OF... STRESS YOU'RE CURRENTLY TRYING TO WORK THROUGH?
NO. SAME OLD, SAME OLD.
YOU'RE A GOOD LIAR, I'LL GIVE YOU THAT. LET'S CUT TO THE CHASE. GET YOUR MAN BACK OR NOT... I DO NOT CARE.
YOU STEPPED IN SHIT. YOU SENT ONE OF OUR MEN OUT ON SOME HOLY QUEST... AND HE GOT NABBED. YOU PUT OUR WHOLE ORGANIZATION AT RISK.
WE'RE PLATELETS, THE BLOOD CELLS, THE--WE'RE THOSE LITTLE RED DONUTS THAT TRAVEL THROUGH OUR VEINS. WE KEEP THE BODY ALIVE... WE CARRY VALUABLE NUTRIENTS AND OXYGEN TO THE CELLS AND SHIT.
WHEN ONE OF THOSE LITTLE RED DONUTS GOES THE WRONG WAY... STARTS SWIMMING UPSTREAM... WELL, THAT'S WHEN THINGS GET FUCKED.
THE BODY COULD DIE.
I'LL KILL THAT LITTLE RED DONUT EVERY DAY OF THE WEEK BEFORE I LET THE BODY DIE.
YOU THINK WE GIVE A FUCK ABOUT A PEDOPHILE IN PARLIAMENT? THERE ARE LIVES AT STAKE.
AND CLEAN UP THIS FUCKING MESS.
YOU'RE DISGUSTING.

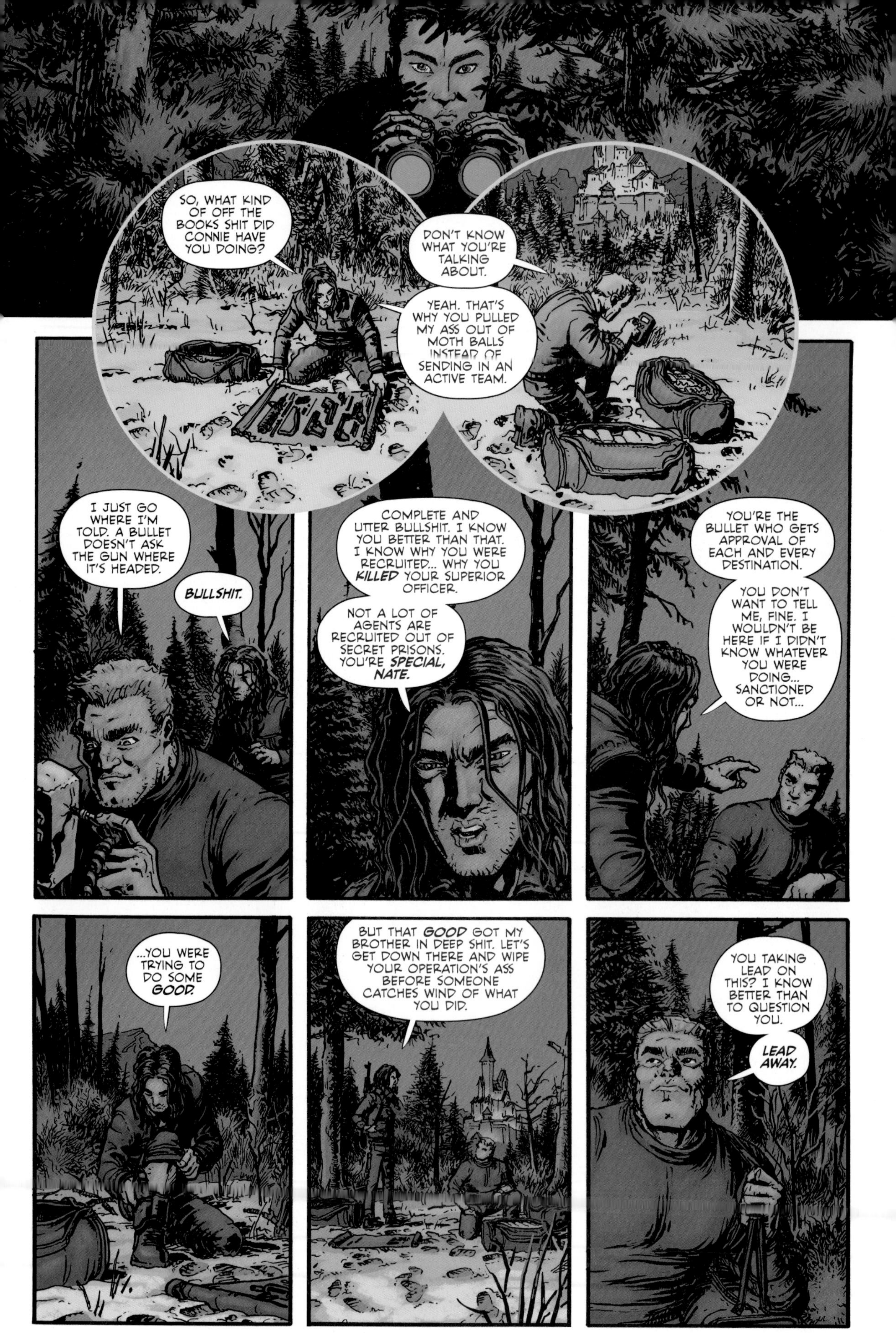
SO, WHAT KIND OF OFF THE BOOKS SHIT DID CONNIE HAVE YOU DOING?
DON'T KNOW WHAT YOU'RE TALKING ABOUT.
YEAH. THAT'S WHY YOU PULLED MY ASS OUT OF MOTH BALLS INSTEAD OF SENDING IN AN ACTIVE TEAM.
I JUST GO WHERE I'M TOLD. A BULLET DOESN'T ASK THE GUN WHERE IT'S HEADED.
BULLSHIT.
COMPLETE AND UTTER BULLSHIT. I KNOW YOU BETTER THAN THAT. I KNOW WHY YOU WERE RECRUITED... WHY YOU KILLED YOUR SUPERIOR OFFICER.
NOT A LOT OF AGENTS ARE RECRUITED OUT OF SECRET PRISONS. YOU'RE SPECIAL, NATE.
YOU'RE THE BULLET WHO GETS APPROVAL OF EACH AND EVERY DESTINATION.
YOU DON'T WANT TO TELL ME, FINE. I WOULDN'T BE HERE IF I DIDN'T KNOW WHATEVER YOU WERE DOING... SANCTIONED OR NOT...
...YOU WERE TRYING TO DO SOME GOOD.
BUT THAT GOOD GOT MY BROTHER IN DEEP SHIT. LET'S GET DOWN THERE AND WIPE YOUR OPERATION'S ASS BEFORE SOMEONE CATCHES WIND OF WHAT YOU DID.
YOU TAKING LEAD ON THIS? I KNOW BETTER THAN TO QUESTION YOU.
LEAD AWAY.

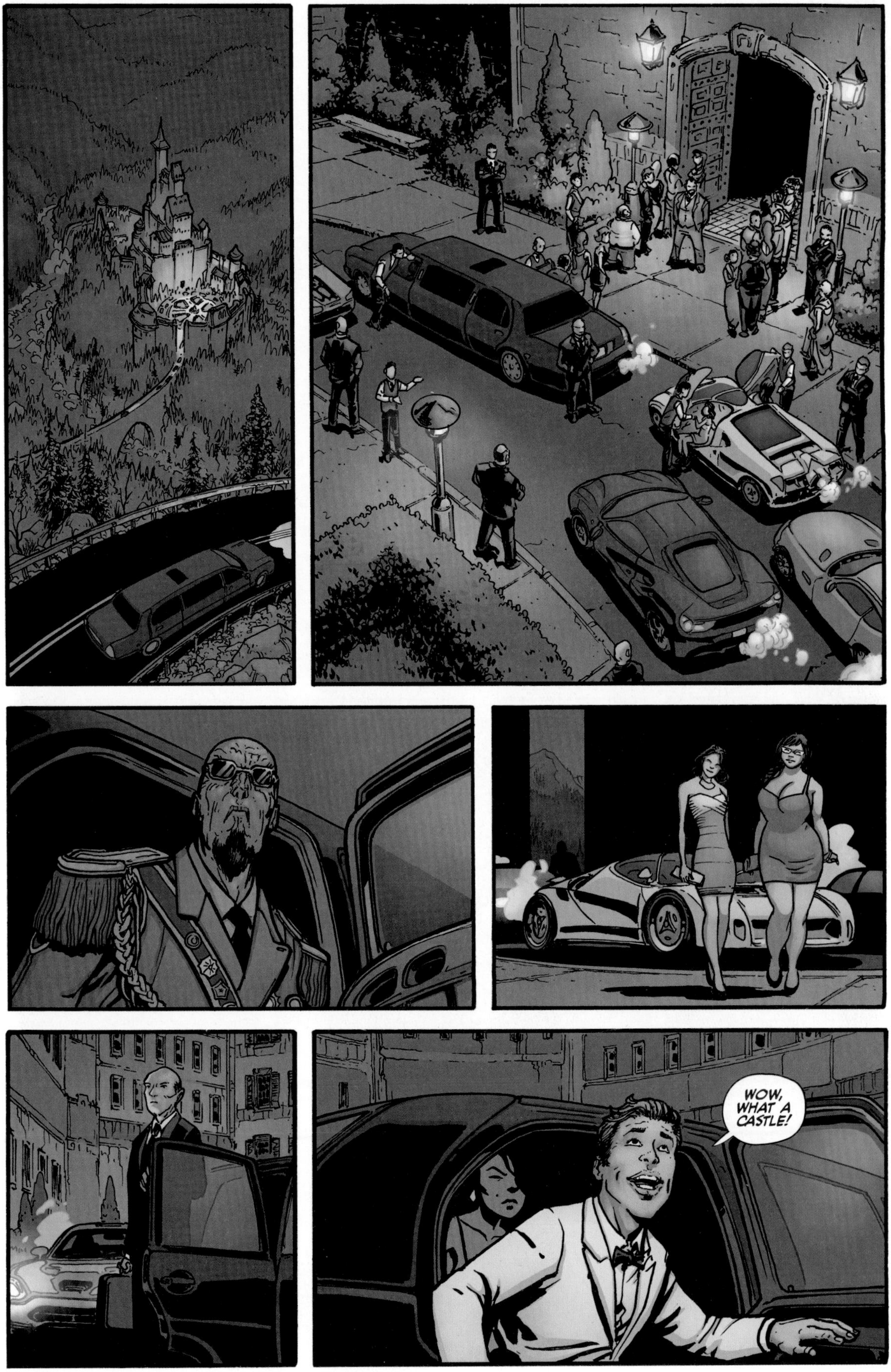
WOW, WHAT A CASTLE!

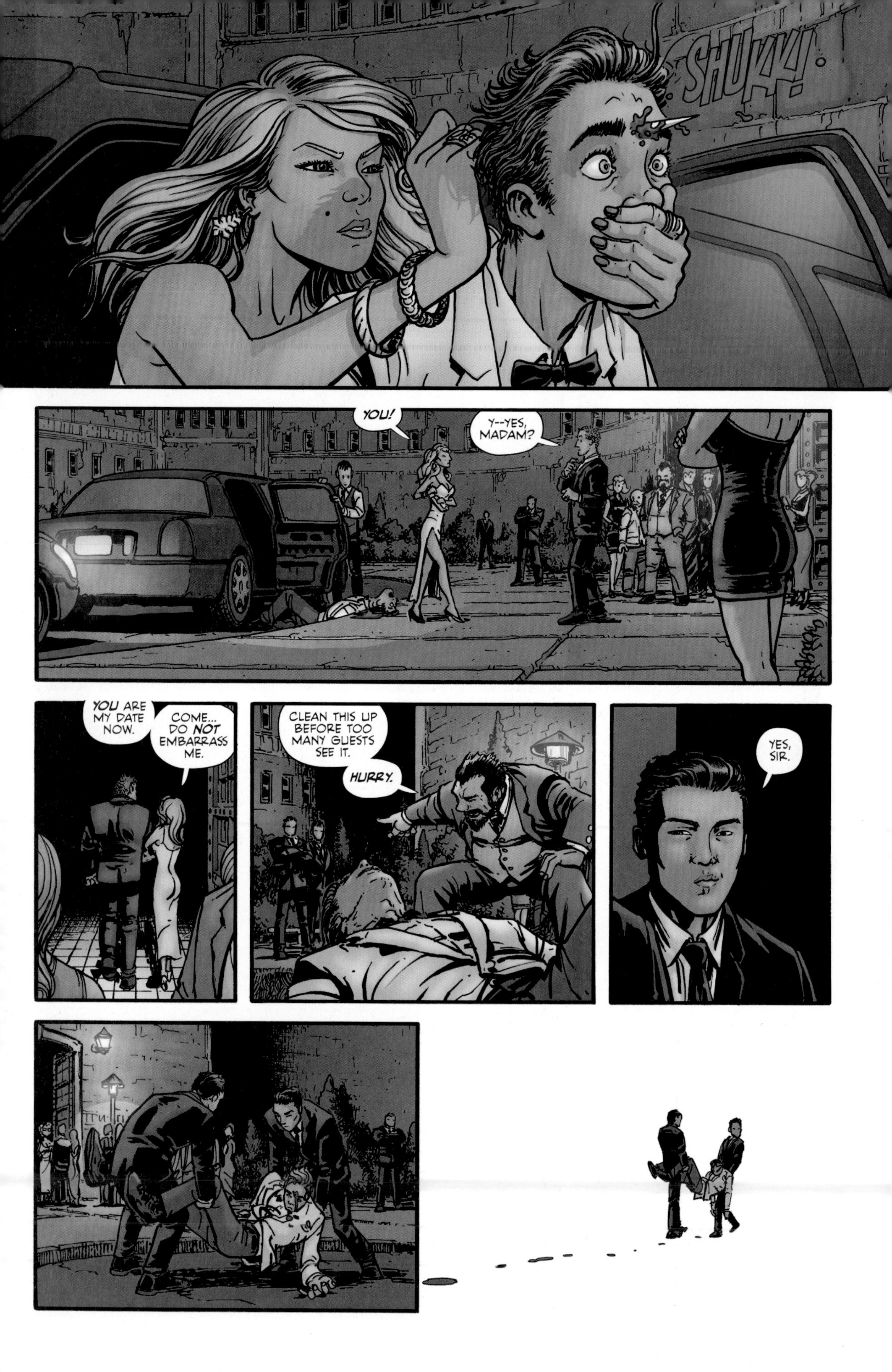
SHUKK!
YOU!
Y--YES, MADAM?
YOU ARE MY DATE NOW.
COME... DO NOT EMBARRASS ME.
CLEAN THIS UP BEFORE TOO MANY GUESTS SEE IT.
HURRY.
YES, SIR.

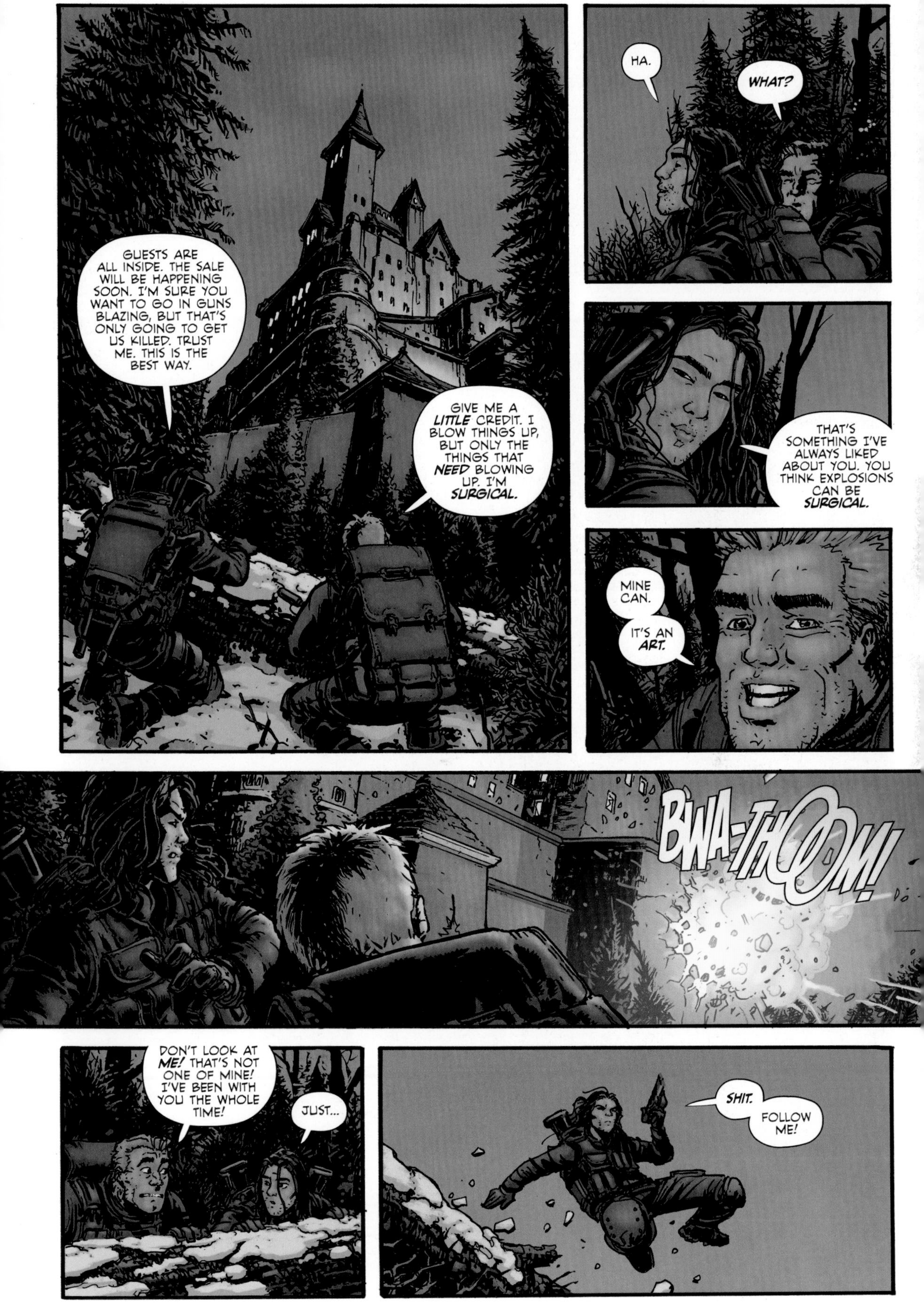

GUESTS ARE ALL INSIDE. THE SALE WILL BE HAPPENING SOON. I'M SURE YOU WANT TO GO IN GUNS BLAZING, BUT THAT'S ONLY GOING TO GET US KILLED. TRUST ME. THIS IS THE BEST WAY.
GIVE ME A LITTLE CREDIT. I BLOW THINGS UP, BUT ONLY THE THINGS THAT NEED BLOWING UP. I'M SURGICAL.
HA.
WHAT?
THAT'S SOMETHING I'VE ALWAYS LIKED ABOUT YOU. YOU THINK EXPLOSIONS CAN BE SURGICAL.
MINE CAN.
IT'S AN ART.
BWA-THOOM!
DON'T LOOK AT ME! THAT'S NOT ONE OF MINE! I'VE BEEN WITH YOU THE WHOLE TIME!
JUST...
SHIT.
FOLLOW ME!

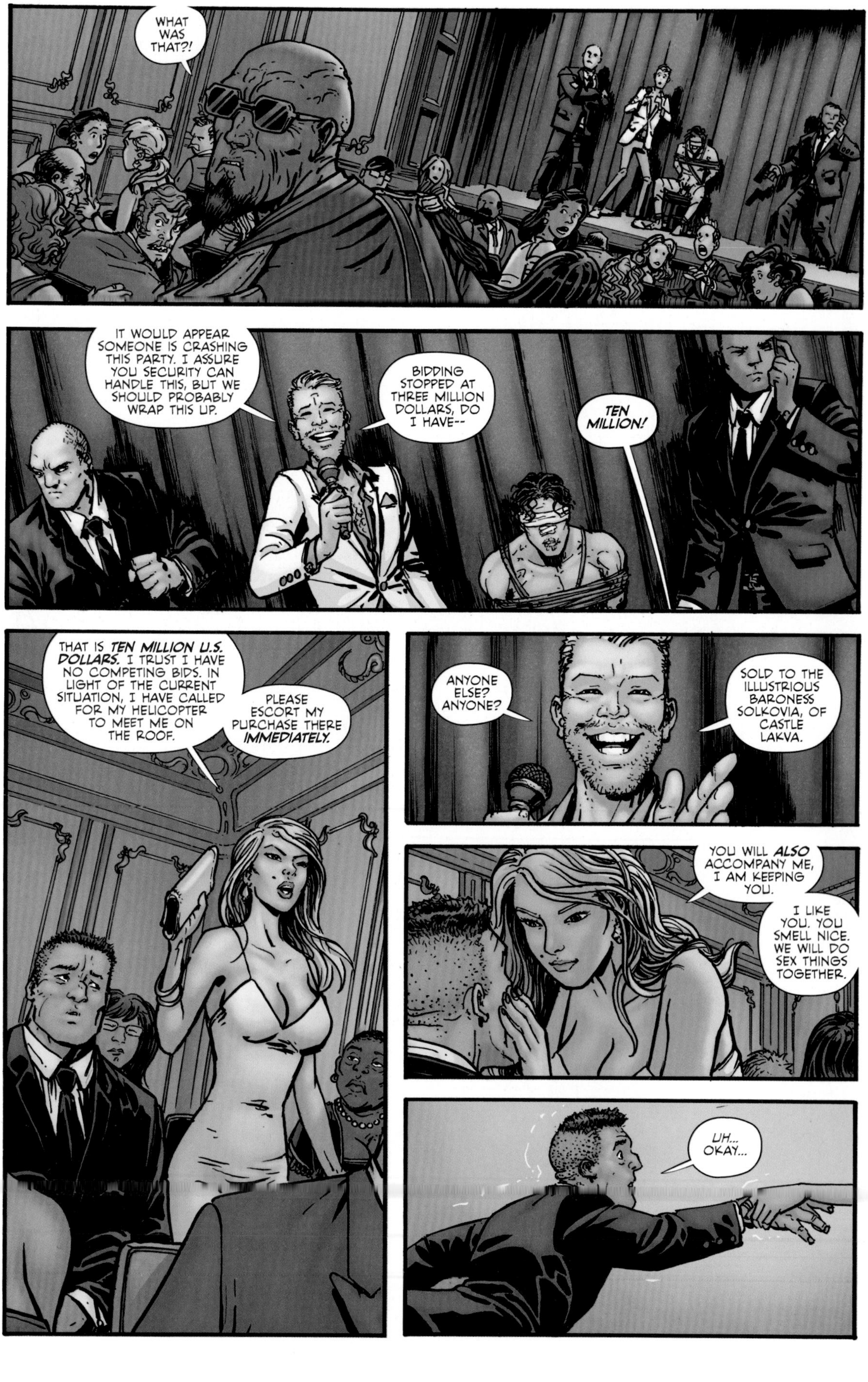
WHAT WAS THAT?!
IT WOULD APPEAR SOMEONE IS CRASHING THIS PARTY. I ASSURE YOU SECURITY CAN HANDLE THIS, BUT WE SHOULD PROBABLY WRAP THIS UP.
BIDDING STOPPED AT THREE MILLION DOLLARS, DO I HAVE--
TEN MILLION!
THAT IS TEN MILLION U.S. DOLLARS. I TRUST I HAVE NO COMPETING BIDS. IN LIGHT OF THE CURRENT SITUATION, I HAVE CALLED FOR MY HELICOPTER TO MEET ME ON THE ROOF.
PLEASE ESCORT MY PURCHASE THERE IMMEDIATELY.
ANYONE ELSE? ANYONE?
SOLD TO THE ILLUSTRIOUS BARONESS SOLKOVIA, OF CASTLE LAKVA.
YOU WILL ALSO ACCOMPANY ME, I AM KEEPING YOU.
I LIKE YOU. YOU SMELL NICE. WE WILL DO SEX THINGS TOGETHER.
UH... OKAY...

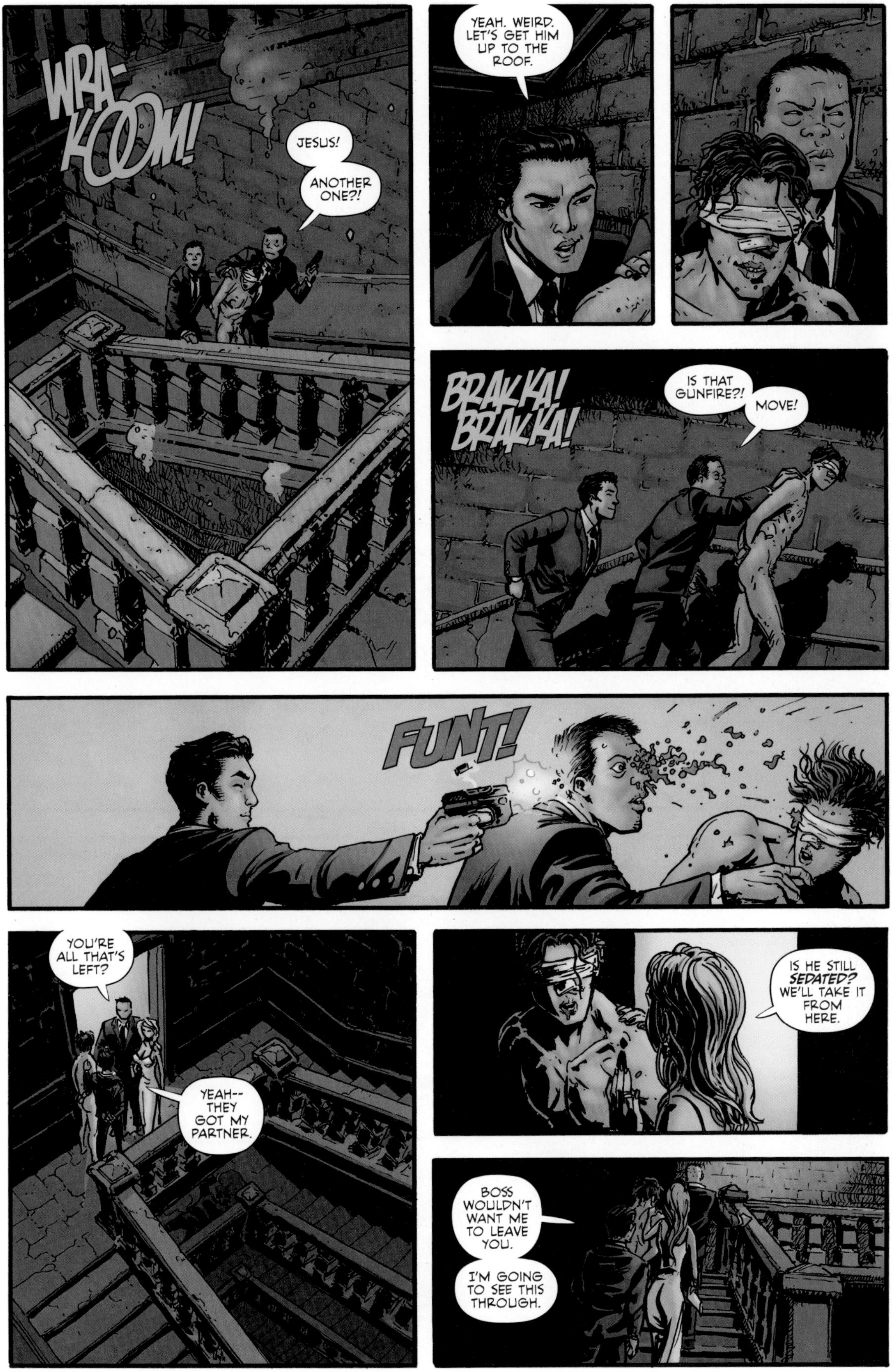
WRA-KOOM!
JESUS!
ANOTHER ONE?!
YEAH. WEIRD. LET'S GET HIM UP TO THE ROOF.
BRAKKA! BRAKKA!
IS THAT GUNFIRE?!
MOVE!
FUNT!
YOU'RE ALL THAT'S LEFT?
YEAH-- THEY GOT MY PARTNER.
IS HE STILL SEDATED? WE'LL TAKE IT FROM HERE.
BOSS WOULDN'T WANT ME TO LEAVE YOU.
I'M GOING TO SEE THIS THROUGH.

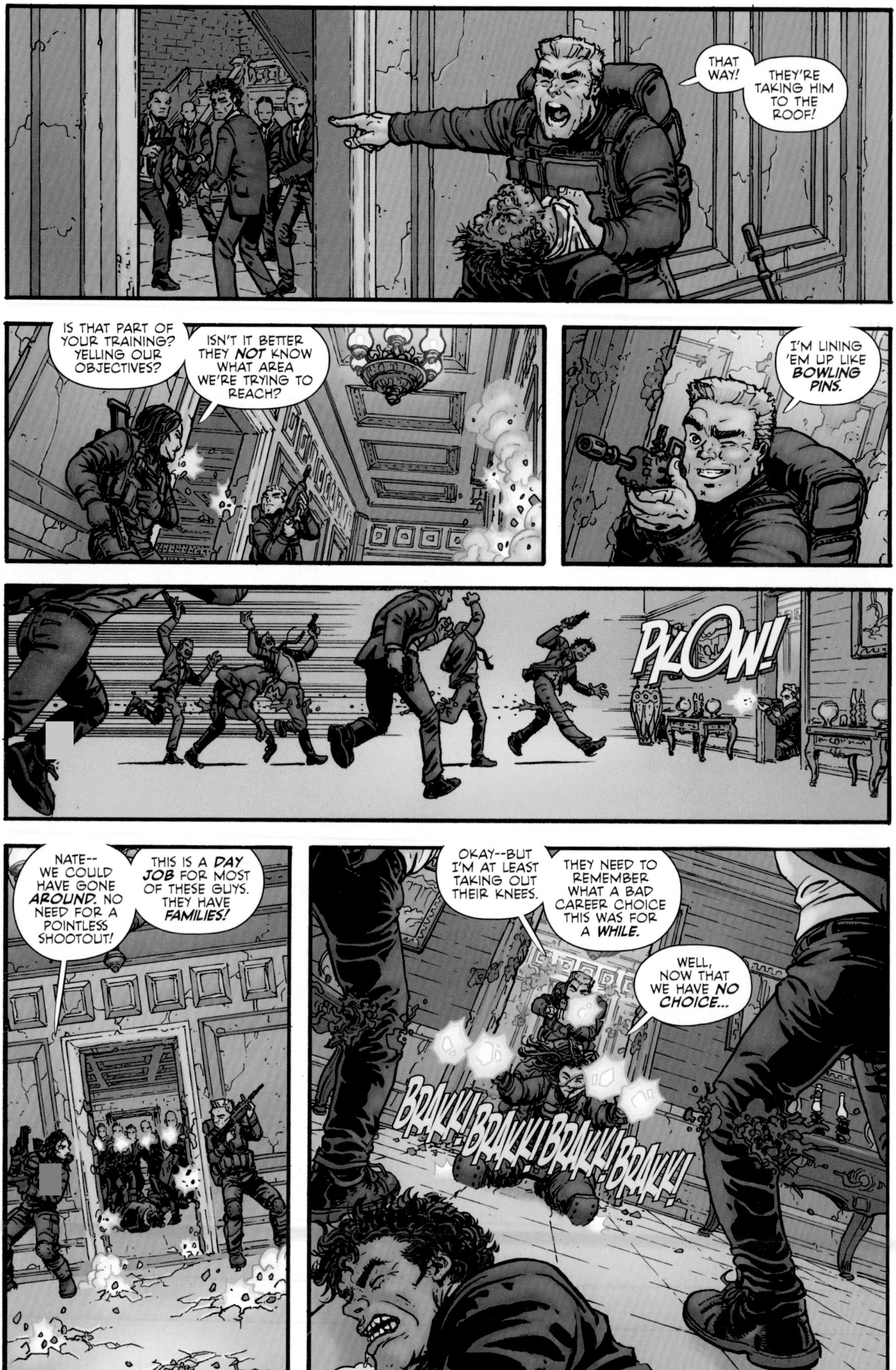
THAT WAY!
THEY'RE TAKING HIM TO THE ROOF!
IS THAT PART OF YOUR TRAINING? YELLING OUR OBJECTIVES?
ISN'T IT BETTER THEY NOT KNOW WHAT AREA WE'RE TRYING TO REACH?
I'M LINING 'EM UP LIKE BOWLING PINS.
PKOW!
NATE-- WE COULD HAVE GONE AROUND. NO NEED FOR A POINTLESS SHOOTOUT!
THIS IS A DAY JOB FOR MOST OF THESE GUYS. THEY HAVE FAMILIES!
OKAY--BUT I'M AT LEAST TAKING OUT THEIR KNEES.
THEY NEED TO REMEMBER WHAT A BAD CAREER CHOICE THIS WAS FOR A WHILE.
WELL, NOW THAT WE HAVE NO CHOICE...
BRAKK! BRAKK! BRAKK! BRAKK!

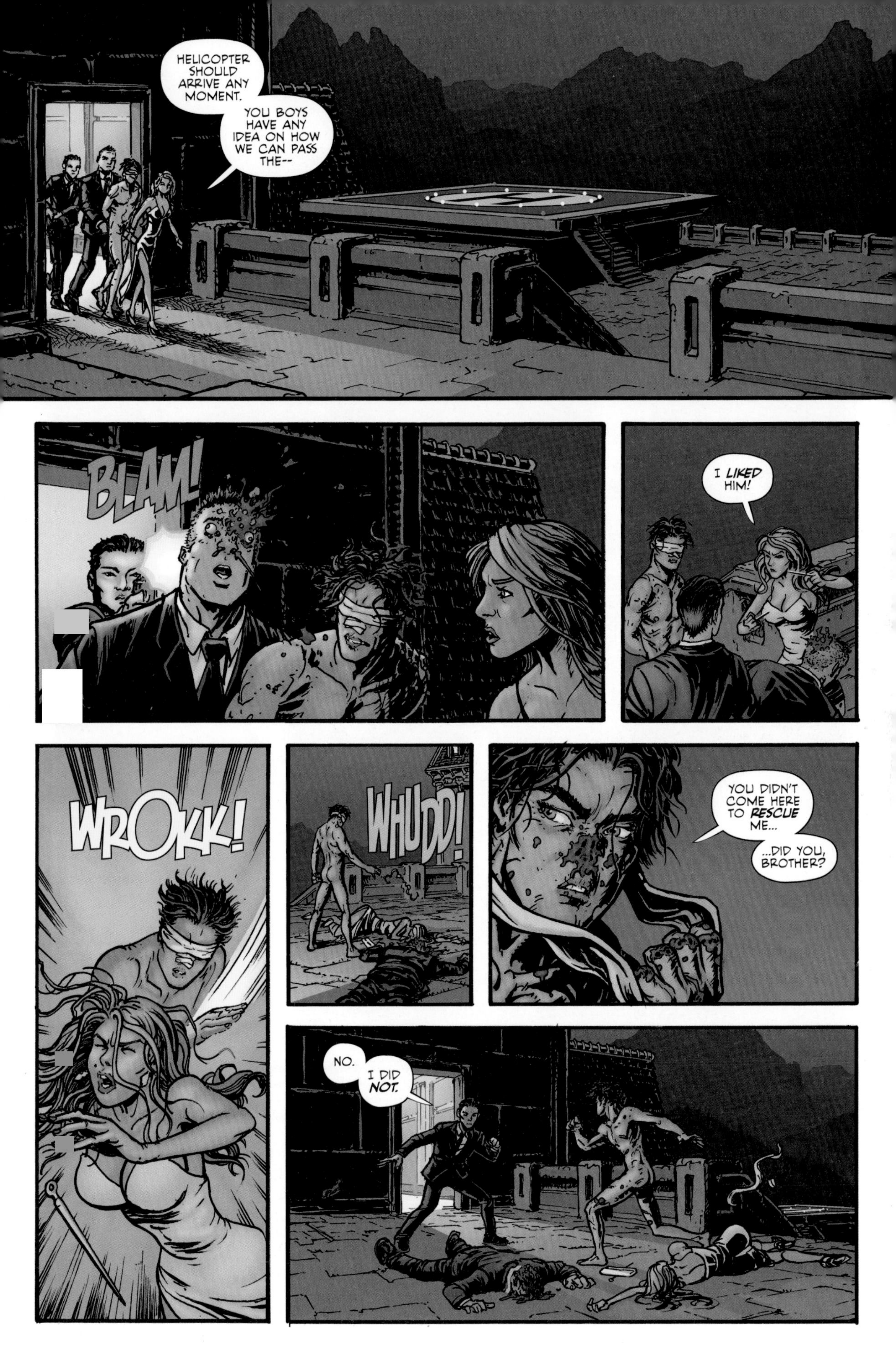

HELICOPTER SHOULD ARRIVE ANY MOMENT.
YOU BOYS HAVE ANY IDEA ON HOW WE CAN PASS THE--
BLAM!
I LIKED HIM!
WROKK!
WHUDD!
YOU DIDN'T COME HERE TO RESCUE ME...
...DID YOU, BROTHER?
NO.
I DID NOT.

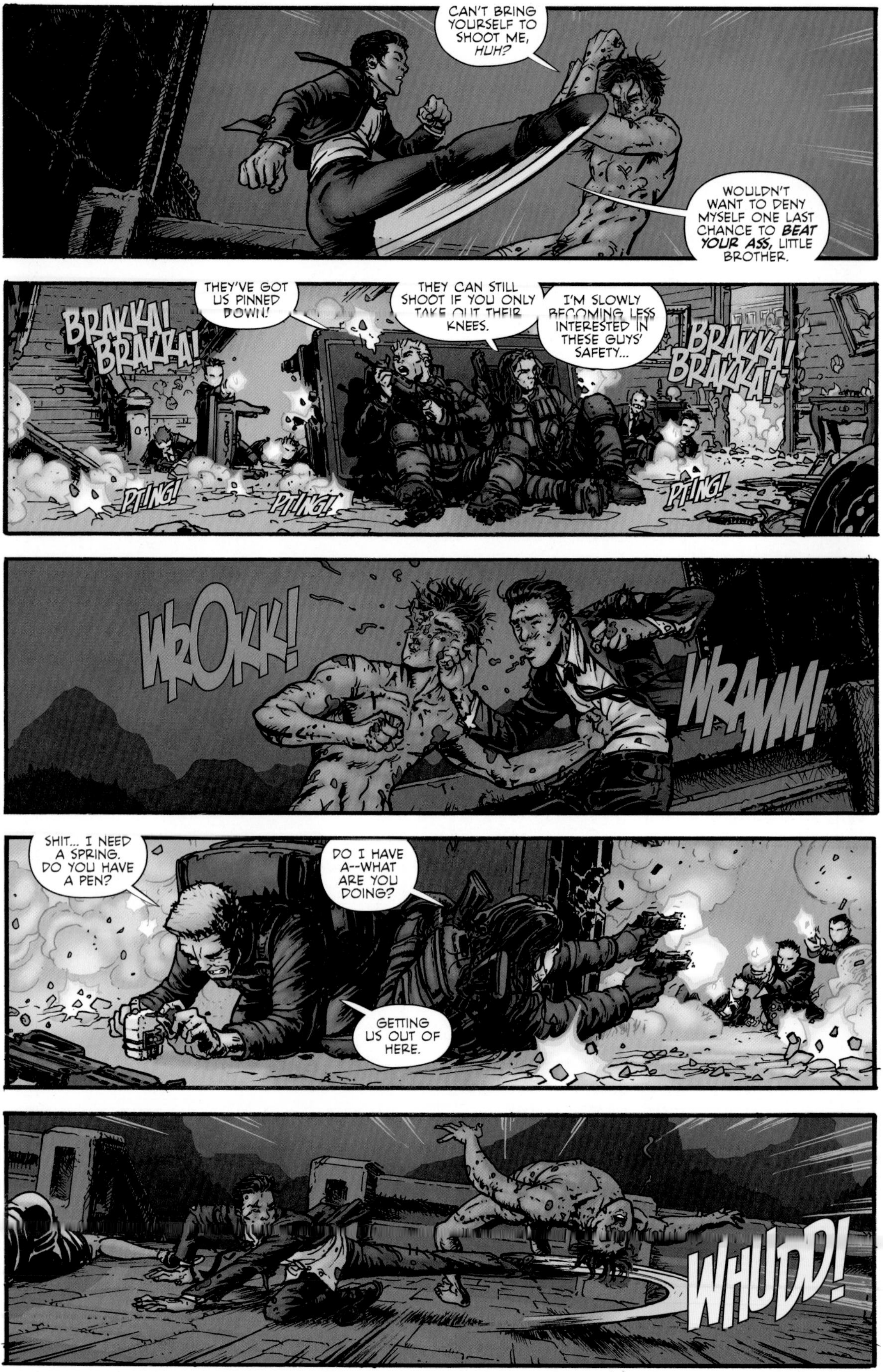
CAN'T BRING YOURSELF TO SHOOT ME, HUH?
WOULDN'T WANT TO DENY MYSELF ONE LAST CHANCE TO BEAT YOUR ASS, LITTLE BROTHER.
BRAKKA! BRAKKA!
THEY'VE GOT US PINNED DOWN!
THEY CAN STILL SHOOT IF YOU ONLY TAKE OUT THEIR KNEES.
I'M SLOWLY BECOMING LESS INTERESTED IN THESE GUYS' SAFETY...
BRAKKA! BRAKKA!
PTING!
PTING!
PTING!
WROKK!
WRAMM!
SHIT... I NEED A SPRING. DO YOU HAVE A PEN?
DO I HAVE A--WHAT ARE YOU DOING?
GETTING US OUT OF HERE.
WHUDD!

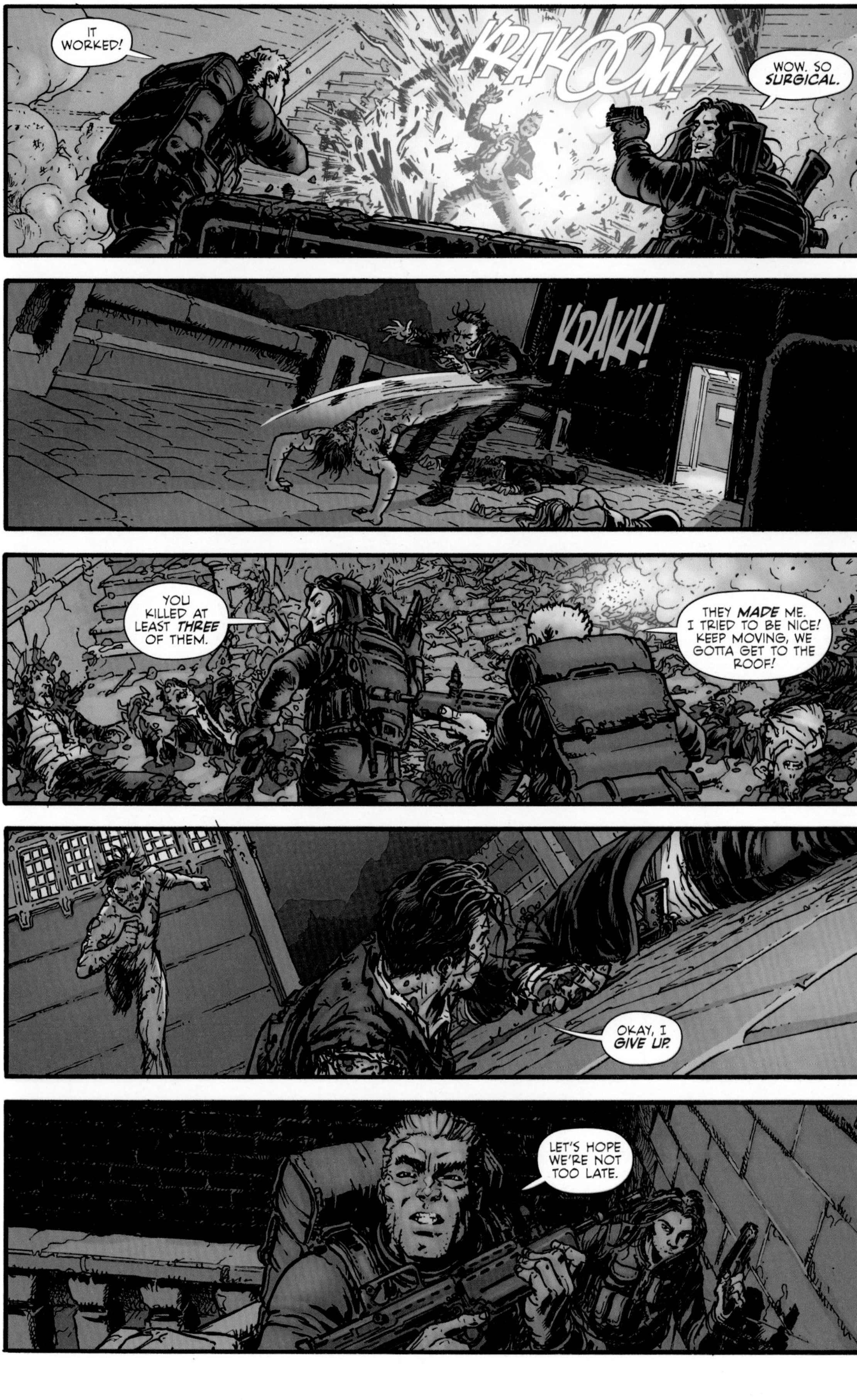
IT WORKED!
KRAKOOM!
WOW. SO SURGICAL.
KRAKK!
YOU KILLED AT LEAST THREE OF THEM.
THEY MADE ME. I TRIED TO BE NICE! KEEP MOVING, WE GOTTA GET TO THE ROOF!
OKAY, I GIVE UP.
LET'S HOPE WE'RE NOT TOO LATE.

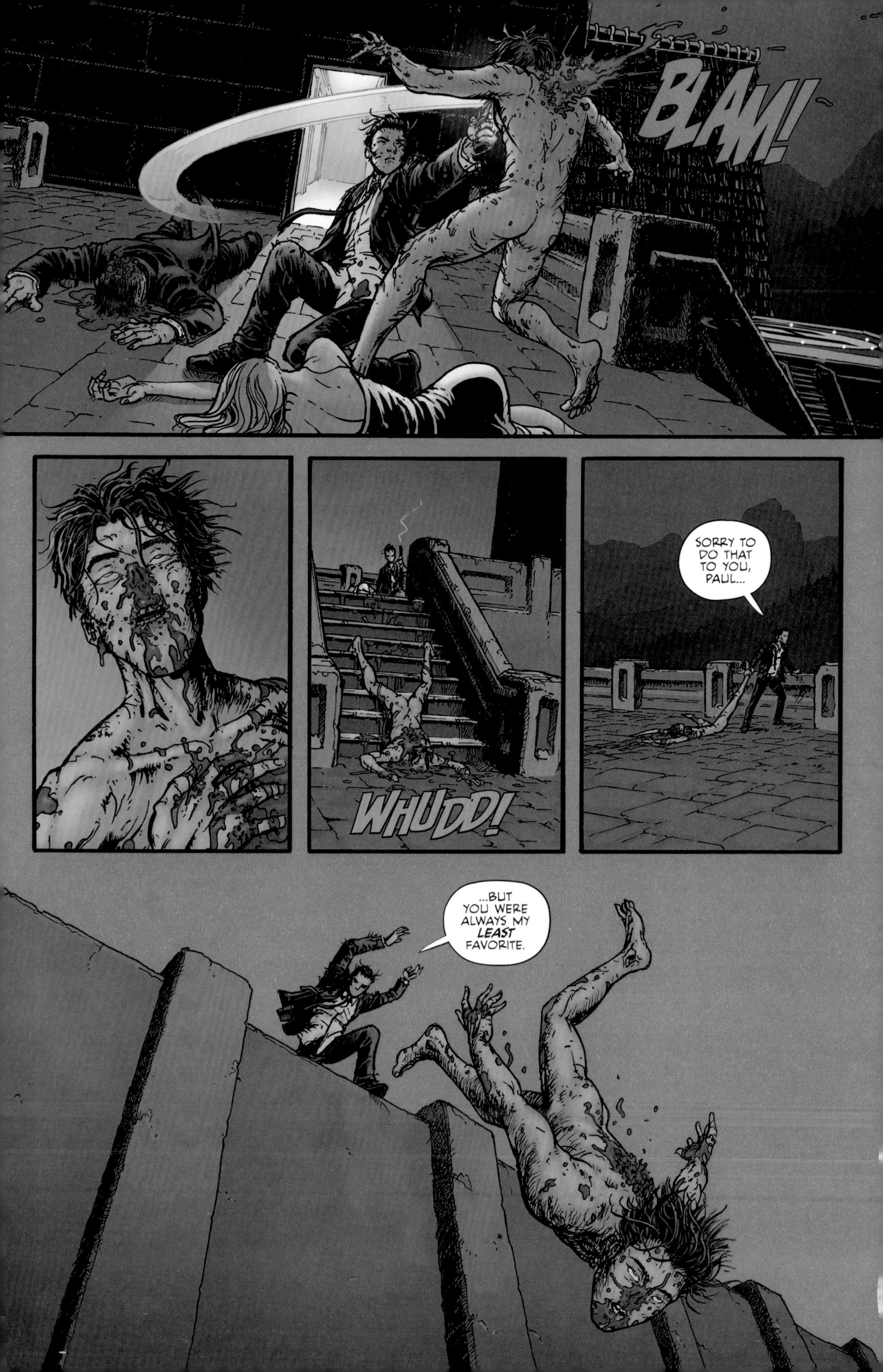
BLAM!
WHUDD!
SORRY TO DO THAT TO YOU, PAUL...
...BUT YOU WERE ALWAYS MY *LEAST* FAVORITE.

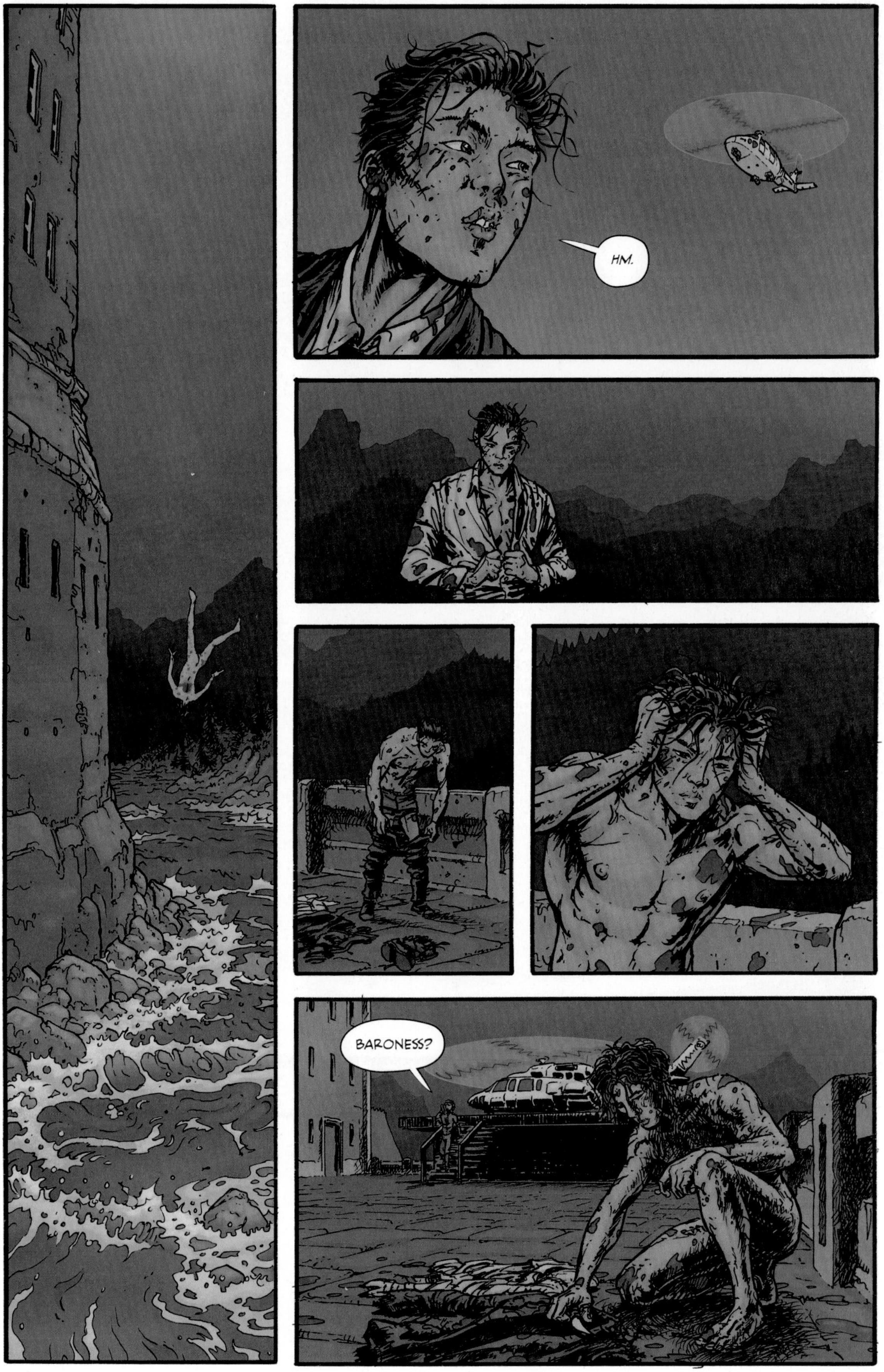
HM.
BARONESS?

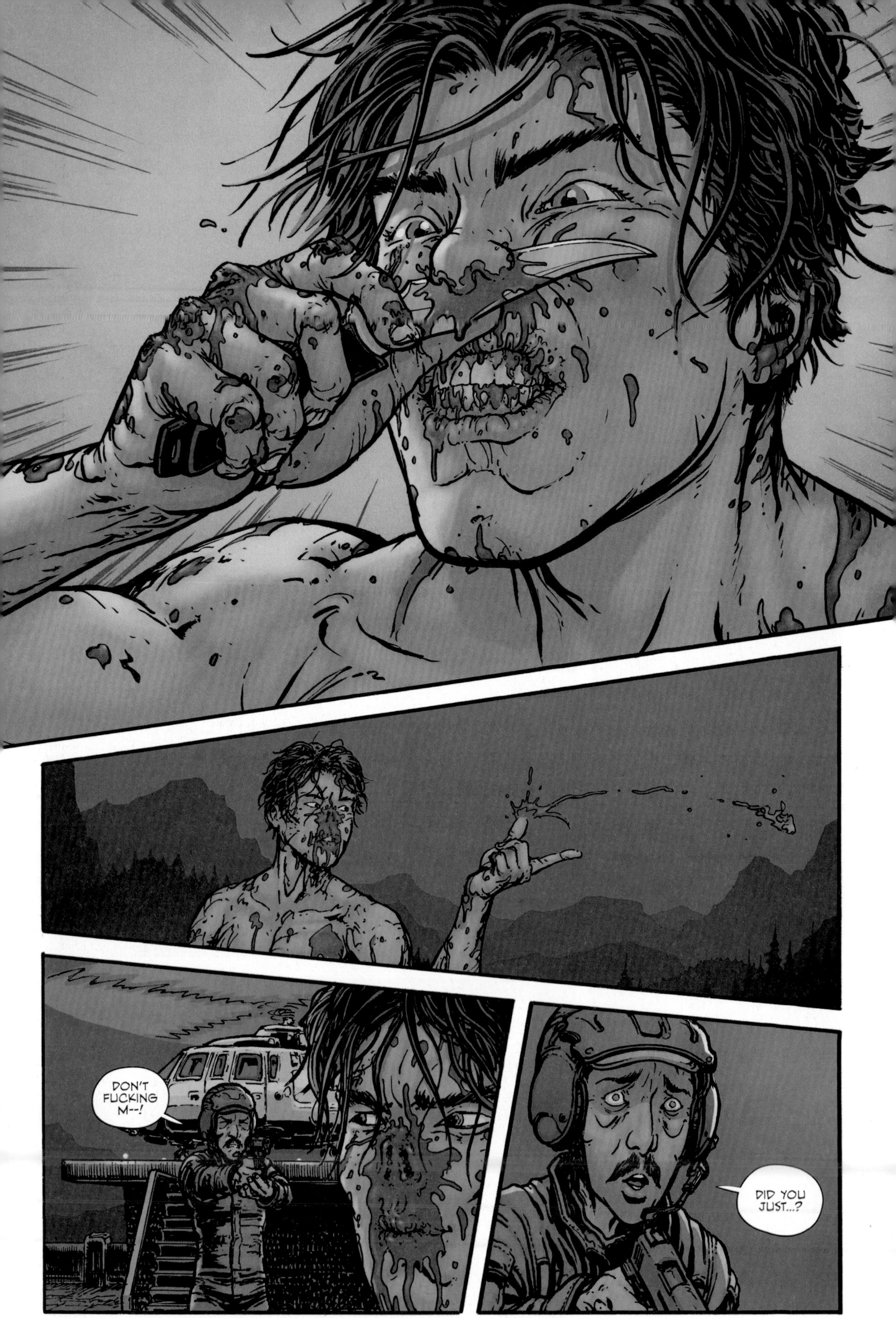
DON'T FUCKING M--!
DID YOU JUST...?

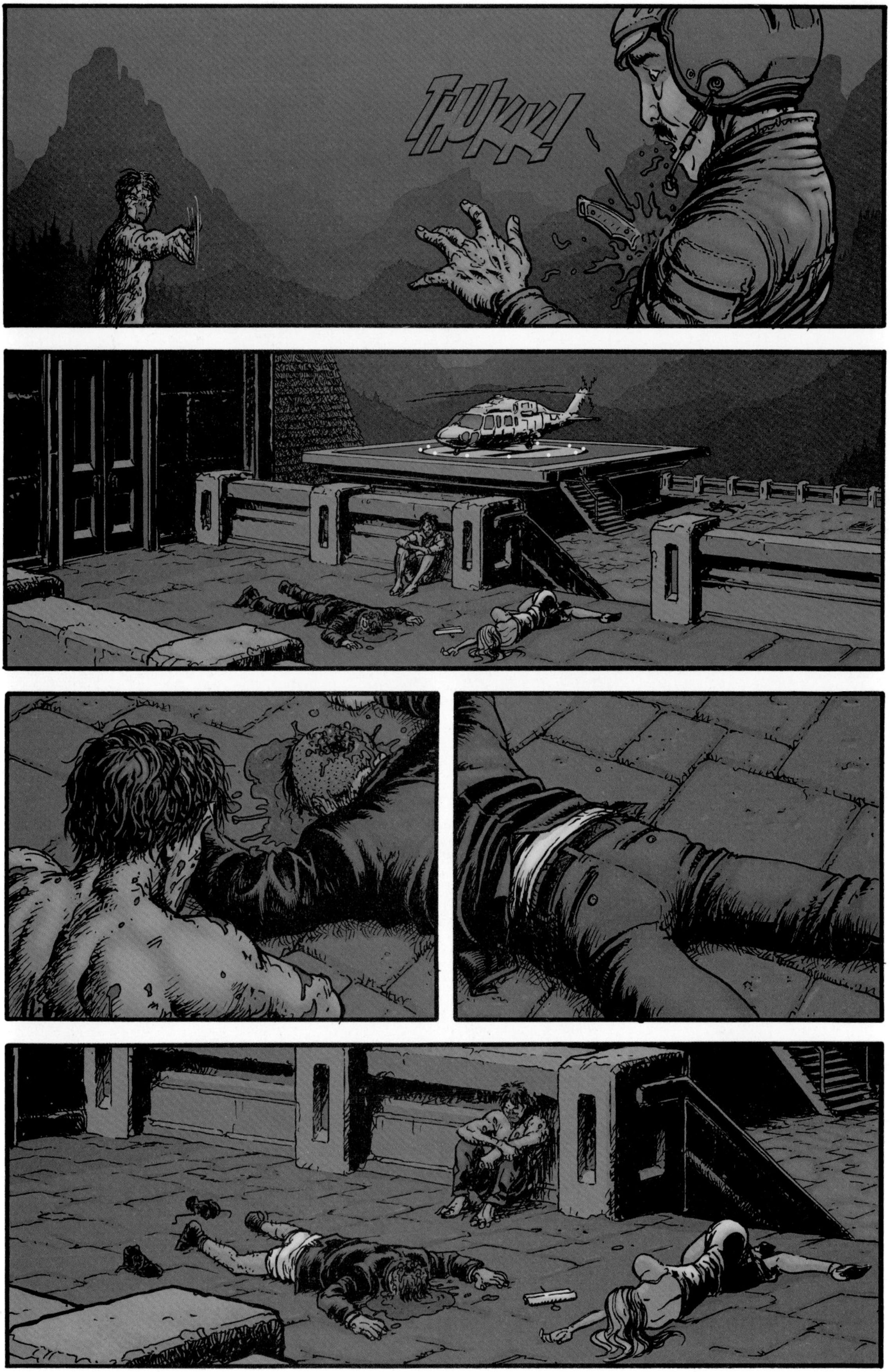
THUKK!

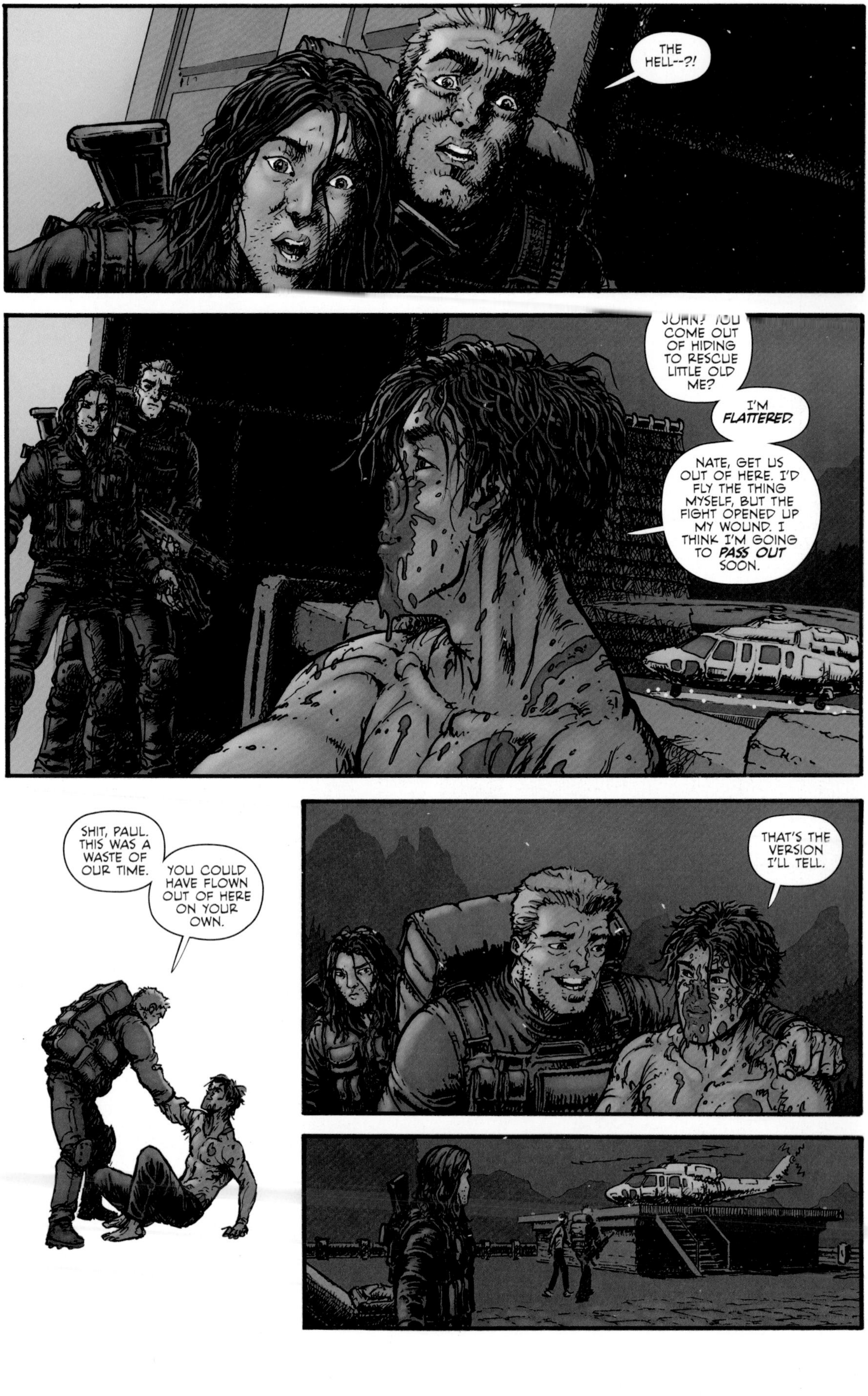
THE HELL--?!
JOHN? YOU COME OUT OF HIDING TO RESCUE LITTLE OLD ME?
I'M FLATTERED.
NATE, GET US OUT OF HERE. I'D FLY THE THING MYSELF, BUT THE FIGHT OPENED UP MY WOUND. I THINK I'M GOING TO PASS OUT SOON.
SHIT, PAUL. THIS WAS A WASTE OF OUR TIME.
YOU COULD HAVE FLOWN OUT OF HERE ON YOUR OWN.
THAT'S THE VERSION I'LL TELL.

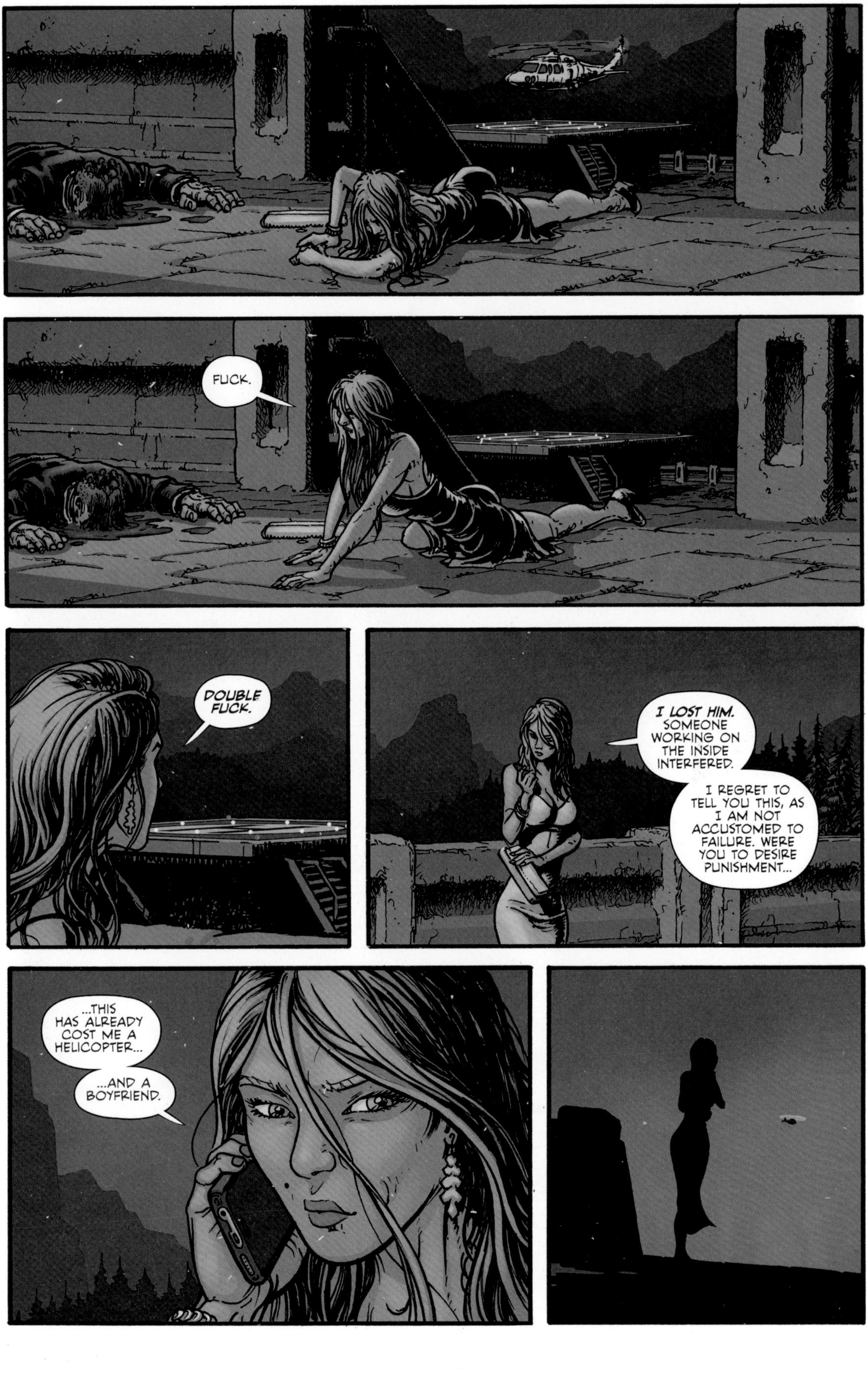
FUCK.
DOUBLE FUCK.
I LOST HIM. SOMEONE WORKING ON THE INSIDE INTERFERED.
I REGRET TO TELL YOU THIS, AS I AM NOT ACCUSTOMED TO FAILURE. WERE YOU TO DESIRE PUNISHMENT...
...THIS HAS ALREADY COST ME A HELICOPTER...
...AND A BOYFRIEND.

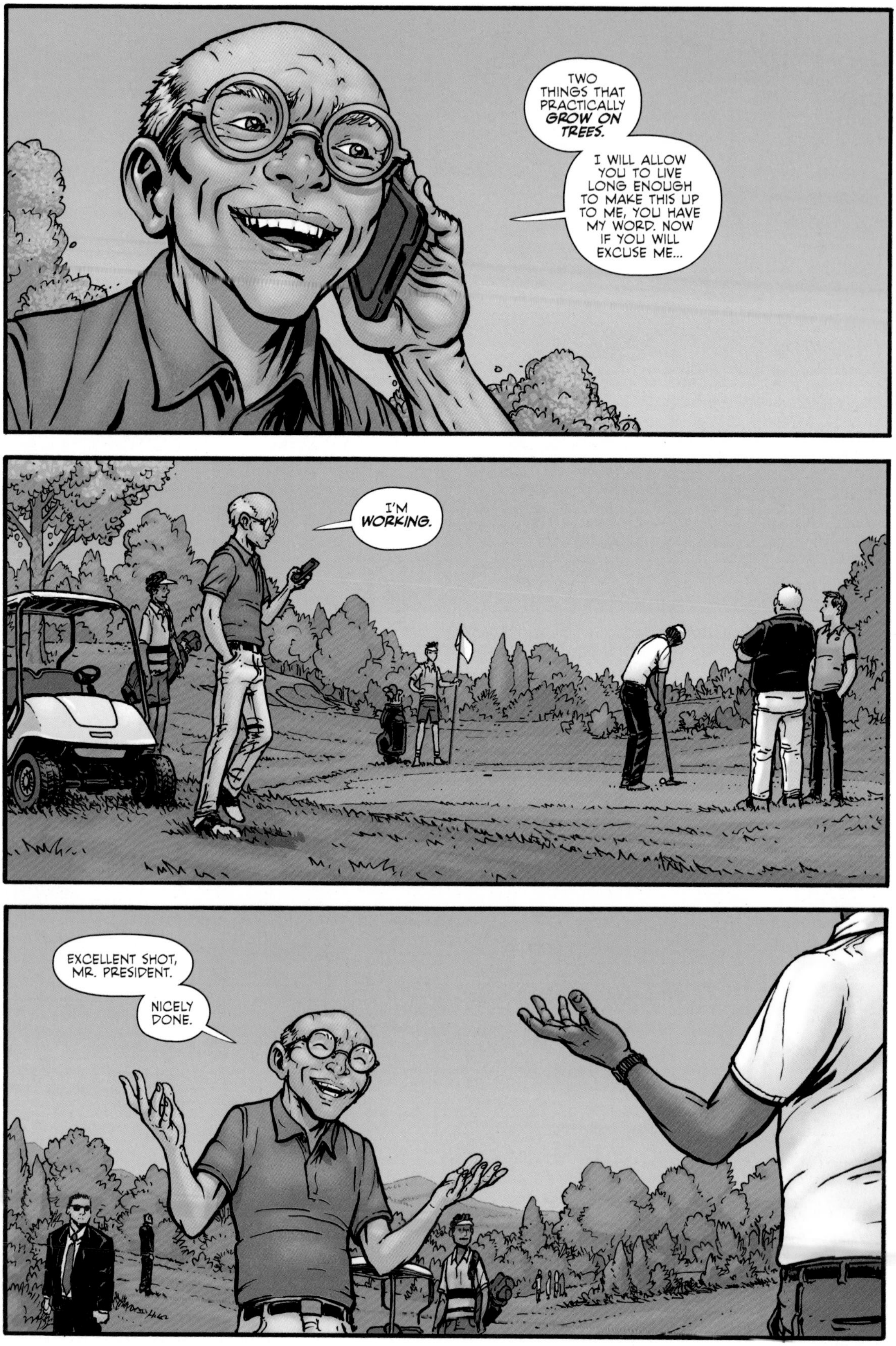
TWO THINGS THAT PRACTICALLY *GROW ON TREES.*
I WILL ALLOW YOU TO LIVE LONG ENOUGH TO MAKE THIS UP TO ME, YOU HAVE MY WORD. NOW IF YOU WILL EXCUSE ME...
I'M *WORKING.*
EXCELLENT SHOT, MR. PRESIDENT.
NICELY DONE.

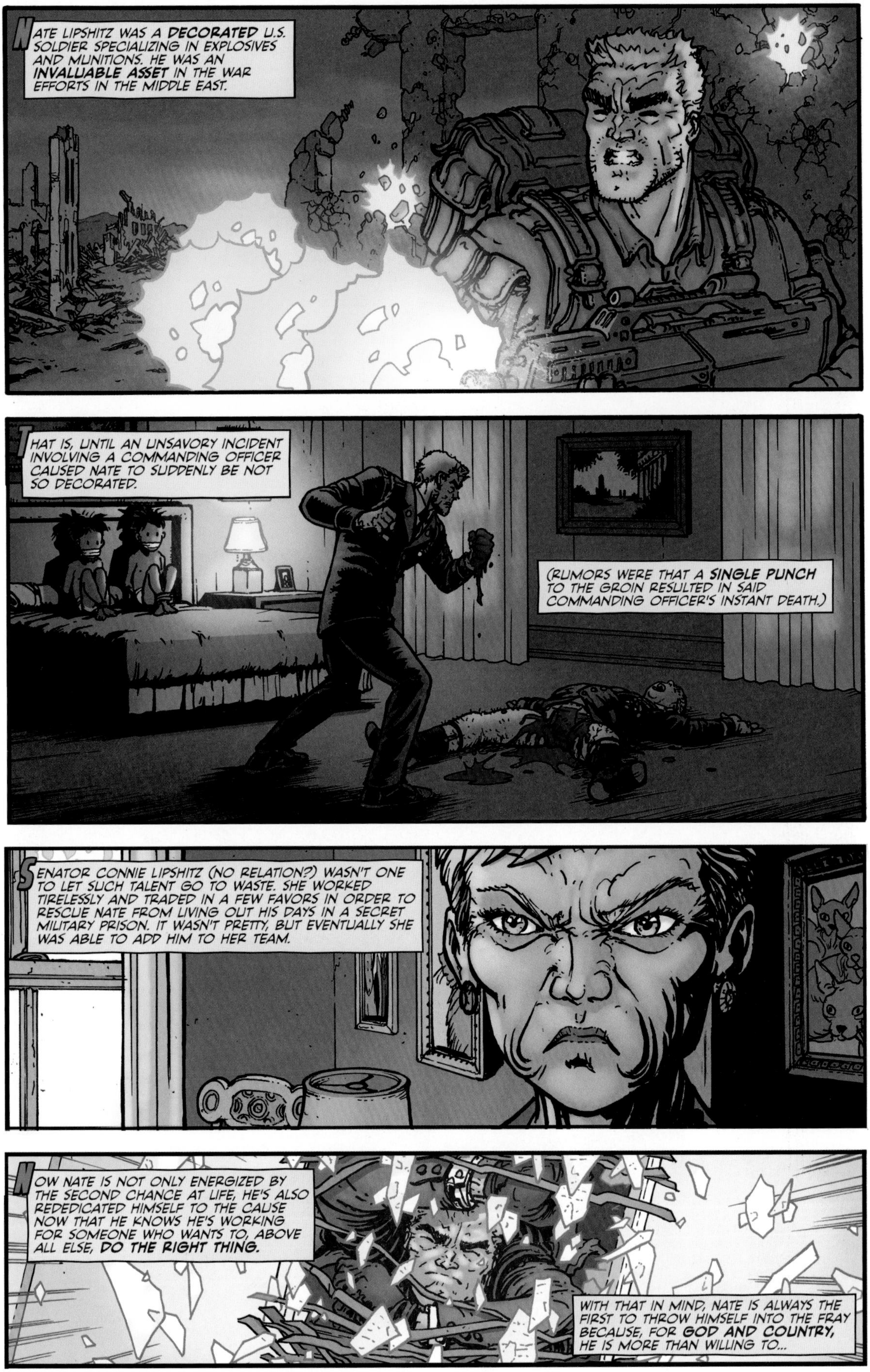
NATE LIPSHITZ WAS A DECORATED U.S. SOLDIER SPECIALIZING IN EXPLOSIVES AND MUNITIONS. HE WAS AN INVALUABLE ASSET IN THE WAR EFFORTS IN THE MIDDLE EAST.
THAT IS, UNTIL AN UNSAVORY INCIDENT INVOLVING A COMMANDING OFFICER CAUSED NATE TO SUDDENLY BE NOT SO DECORATED.
(RUMORS WERE THAT A SINGLE PUNCH TO THE GROIN RESULTED IN SAID COMMANDING OFFICER'S INSTANT DEATH.)
SENATOR CONNIE LIPSHITZ (NO RELATION?) WASN'T ONE TO LET SUCH TALENT GO TO WASTE. SHE WORKED TIRELESSLY AND TRADED IN A FEW FAVORS IN ORDER TO RESCUE NATE FROM LIVING OUT HIS DAYS IN A SECRET MILITARY PRISON. IT WASN'T PRETTY, BUT EVENTUALLY SHE WAS ABLE TO ADD HIM TO HER TEAM.
NOW NATE IS NOT ONLY ENERGIZED BY THE SECOND CHANCE AT LIFE, HE'S ALSO REDEDICATED HIMSELF TO THE CAUSE NOW THAT HE KNOWS HE'S WORKING FOR SOMEONE WHO WANTS TO, ABOVE ALL ELSE, DO THE RIGHT THING.
WITH THAT IN MIND, NATE IS ALWAYS THE FIRST TO THROW HIMSELF INTO THE FRAY BECAUSE, FOR GOD AND COUNTRY, HE IS MORE THAN WILLING TO...

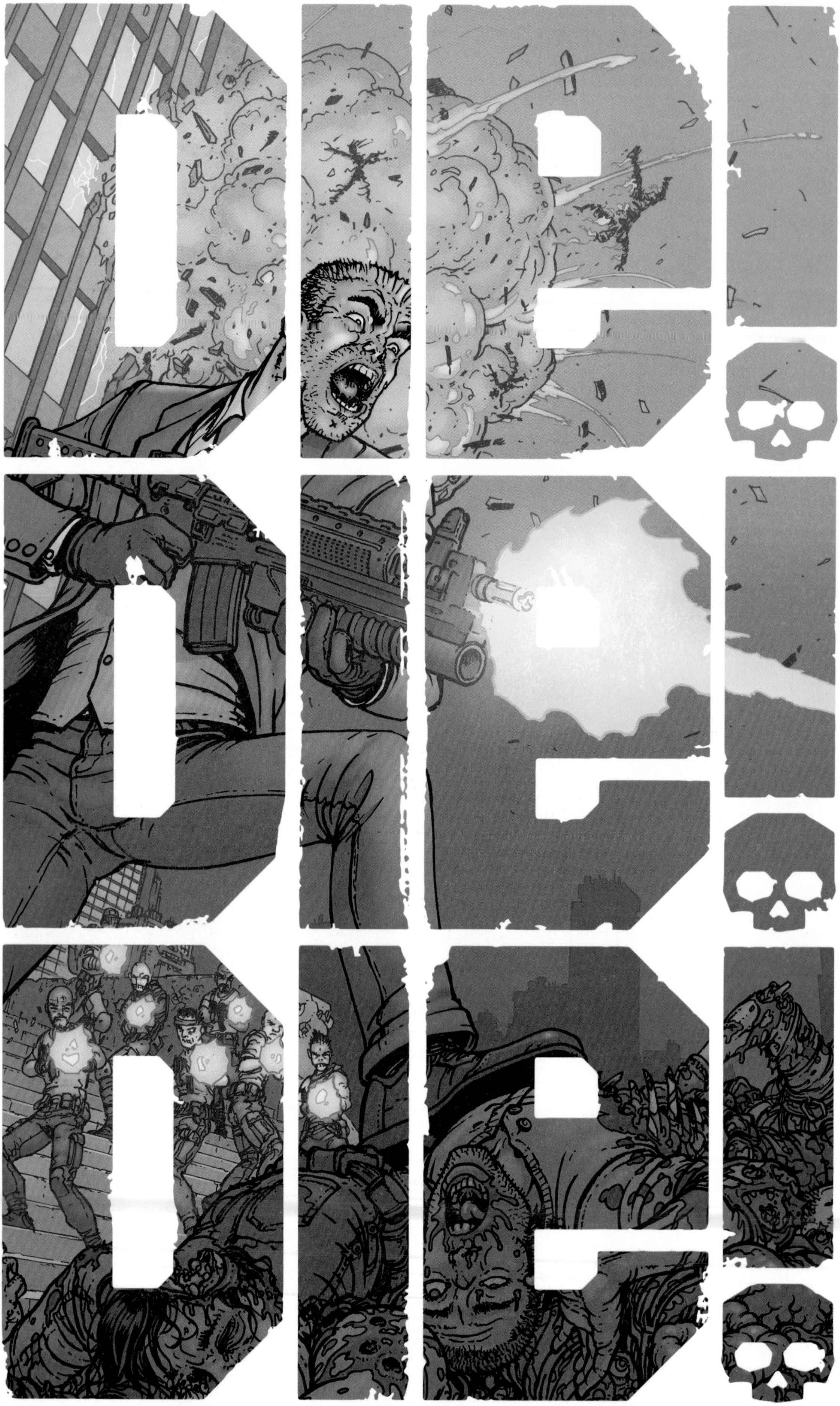
DIE!
DIE!
DIE!

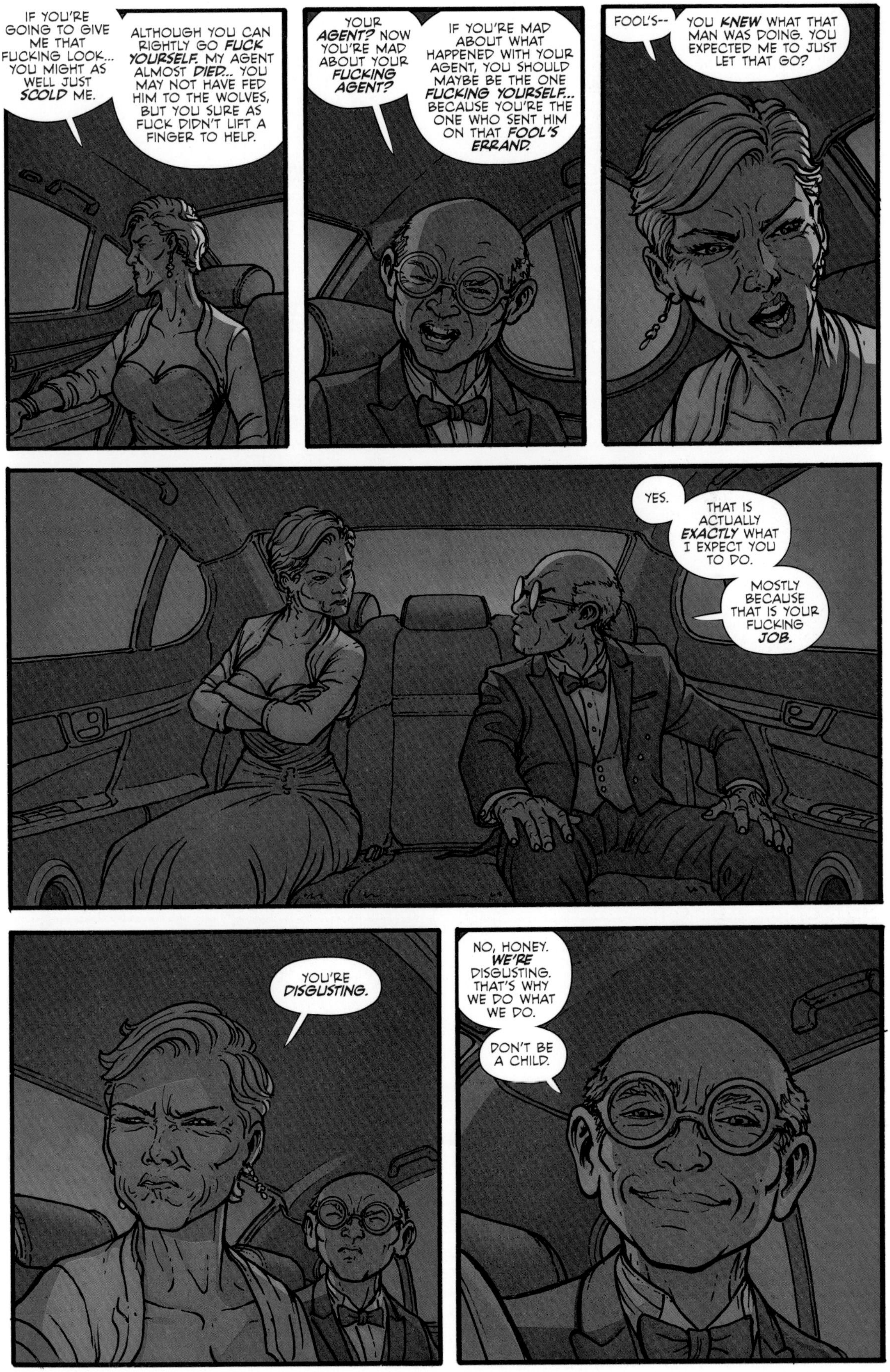
IF YOU'RE GOING TO GIVE ME THAT FUCKING LOOK... YOU MIGHT AS WELL JUST SCOLD ME.
ALTHOUGH YOU CAN RIGHTLY GO FUCK YOURSELF. MY AGENT ALMOST DIED... YOU MAY NOT HAVE FED HIM TO THE WOLVES, BUT YOU SURE AS FUCK DIDN'T LIFT A FINGER TO HELP.
YOUR AGENT? NOW YOU'RE MAD ABOUT YOUR FUCKING AGENT?
IF YOU'RE MAD ABOUT WHAT HAPPENED WITH YOUR AGENT, YOU SHOULD MAYBE BE THE ONE FUCKING YOURSELF... BECAUSE YOU'RE THE ONE WHO SENT HIM ON THAT FOOL'S ERRAND.
FOOL'S--
YOU KNEW WHAT THAT MAN WAS DOING. YOU EXPECTED ME TO JUST LET THAT GO?
YES.
THAT IS ACTUALLY EXACTLY WHAT I EXPECT YOU TO DO.
MOSTLY BECAUSE THAT IS YOUR FUCKING JOB.
YOU'RE DISGUSTING.
NO, HONEY. WE'RE DISGUSTING. THAT'S WHY WE DO WHAT WE DO.
DON'T BE A CHILD.

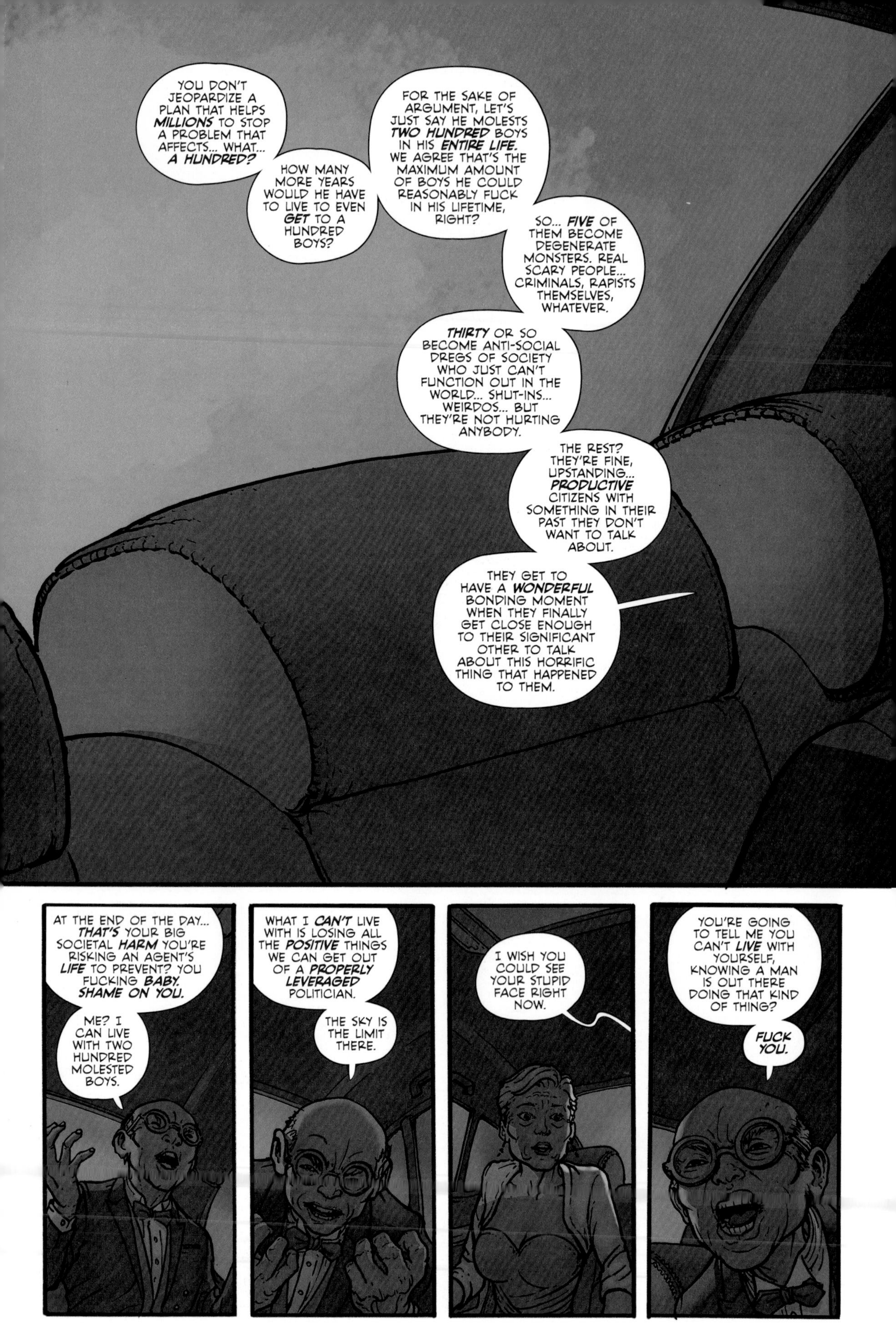
YOU DON'T JEOPARDIZE A PLAN THAT HELPS MILLIONS TO STOP A PROBLEM THAT AFFECTS... WHAT... A HUNDRED?
HOW MANY MORE YEARS WOULD HE HAVE TO LIVE TO EVEN GET TO A HUNDRED BOYS?
FOR THE SAKE OF ARGUMENT, LET'S JUST SAY HE MOLESTS TWO HUNDRED BOYS IN HIS ENTIRE LIFE. WE AGREE THAT'S THE MAXIMUM AMOUNT OF BOYS HE COULD REASONABLY FUCK IN HIS LIFETIME, RIGHT?
SO... FIVE OF THEM BECOME DEGENERATE MONSTERS. REAL SCARY PEOPLE... CRIMINALS, RAPISTS THEMSELVES, WHATEVER.
THIRTY OR SO BECOME ANTI-SOCIAL DREGS OF SOCIETY WHO JUST CAN'T FUNCTION OUT IN THE WORLD... SHUT-INS... WEIRDOS... BUT THEY'RE NOT HURTING ANYBODY.
THE REST? THEY'RE FINE, UPSTANDING... PRODUCTIVE CITIZENS WITH SOMETHING IN THEIR PAST THEY DON'T WANT TO TALK ABOUT.
THEY GET TO HAVE A WONDERFUL BONDING MOMENT WHEN THEY FINALLY GET CLOSE ENOUGH TO THEIR SIGNIFICANT OTHER TO TALK ABOUT THIS HORRIFIC THING THAT HAPPENED TO THEM.
AT THE END OF THE DAY... THAT'S YOUR BIG SOCIETAL HARM YOU'RE RISKING AN AGENT'S LIFE TO PREVENT? YOU FUCKING BABY. SHAME ON YOU.
ME? I CAN LIVE WITH TWO HUNDRED MOLESTED BOYS.
WHAT I CAN'T LIVE WITH IS LOSING ALL THE POSITIVE THINGS WE CAN GET OUT OF A PROPERLY LEVERAGED POLITICIAN.
THE SKY IS THE LIMIT THERE.
I WISH YOU COULD SEE YOUR STUPID FACE RIGHT NOW.
YOU'RE GOING TO TELL ME YOU CAN'T LIVE WITH YOURSELF, KNOWING A MAN IS OUT THERE DOING THAT KIND OF THING?
FUCK YOU.

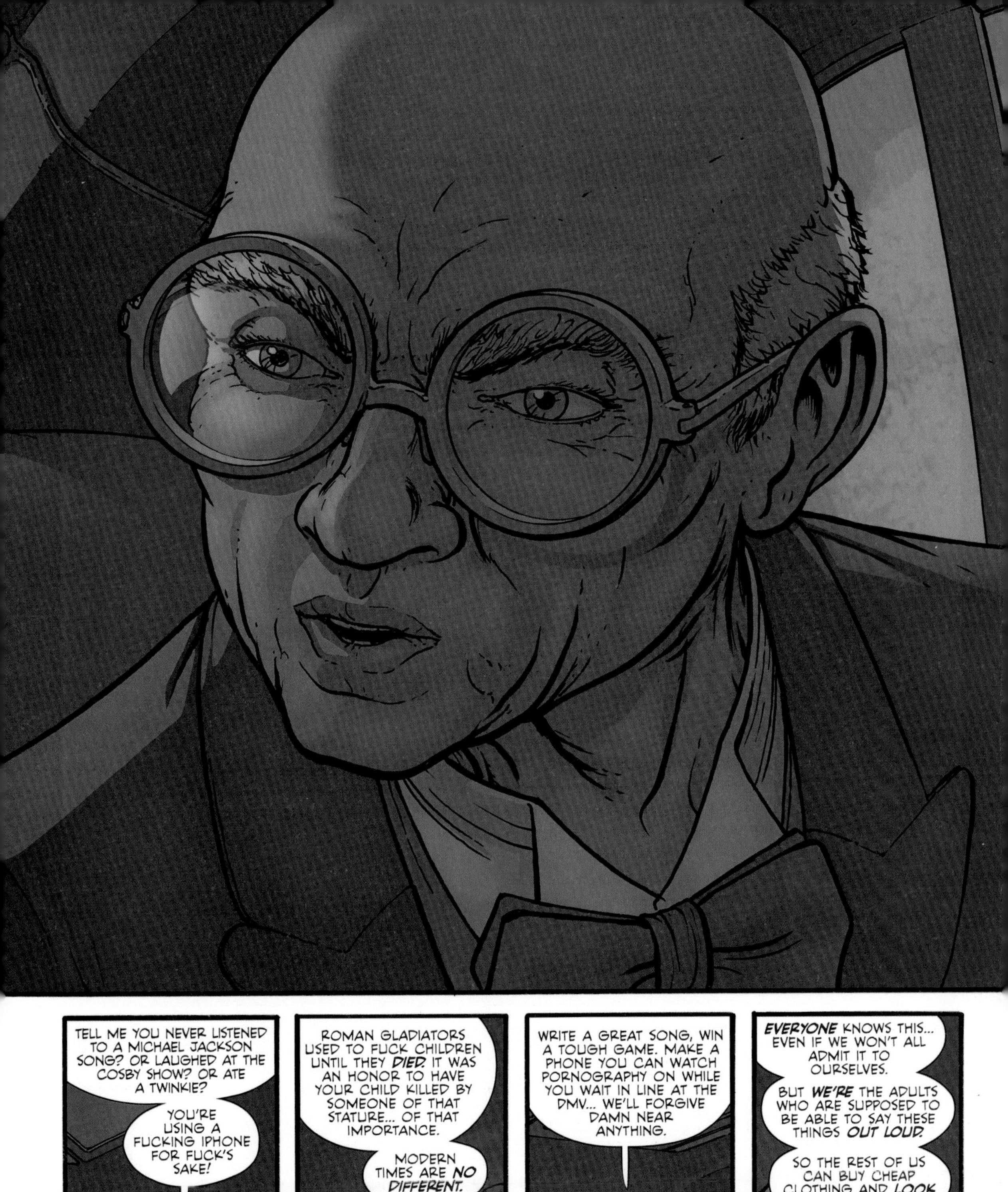

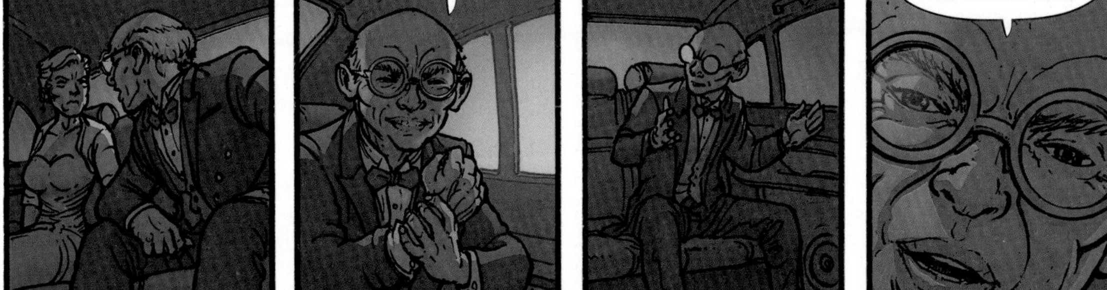
TELL ME YOU NEVER LISTENED TO A MICHAEL JACKSON SONG? OR LAUGHED AT THE COSBY SHOW? OR ATE A TWINKIE?
YOU'RE USING A FUCKING IPHONE FOR FUCK'S SAKE!
ROMAN GLADIATORS USED TO FUCK CHILDREN UNTIL THEY *DIED.* IT WAS AN HONOR TO HAVE YOUR CHILD KILLED BY SOMEONE OF THAT STATURE... OF THAT IMPORTANCE.
MODERN TIMES ARE *NO DIFFERENT.*
WRITE A GREAT SONG, WIN A TOUGH GAME. MAKE A PHONE YOU CAN WATCH PORNOGRAPHY ON WHILE YOU WAIT IN LINE AT THE DMV... WE'LL FORGIVE DAMN NEAR ANYTHING.
EVERYONE KNOWS THIS... EVEN IF WE WON'T ALL ADMIT IT TO OURSELVES.
BUT *WE'RE* THE ADULTS WHO ARE SUPPOSED TO BE ABLE TO SAY THESE THINGS *OUT LOUD.*
SO THE REST OF US CAN BUY CHEAP CLOTHING AND *LOOK THE OTHER WAY.*

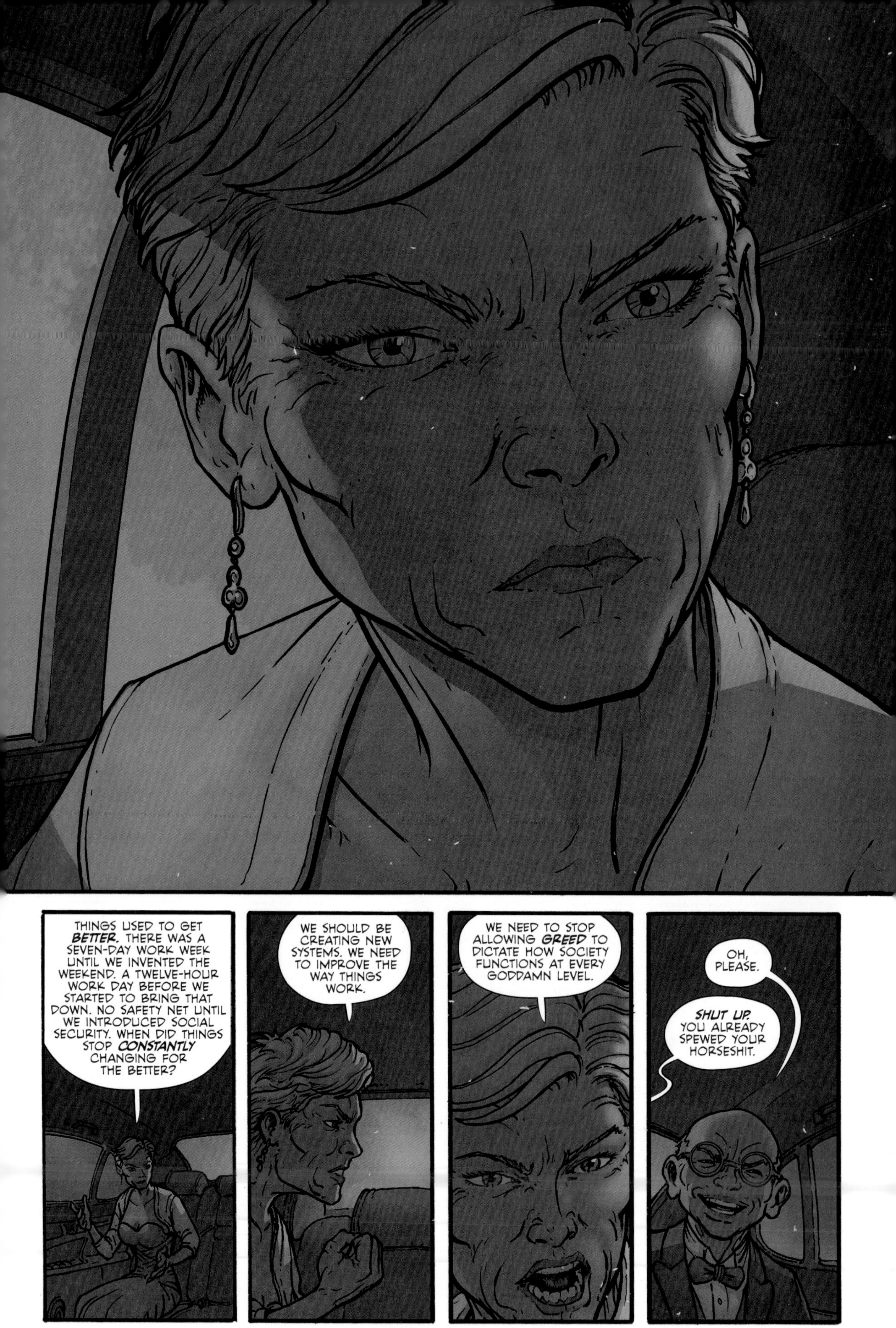

THINGS USED TO GET BETTER. THERE WAS A SEVEN-DAY WORK WEEK UNTIL WE INVENTED THE WEEKEND. A TWELVE-HOUR WORK DAY BEFORE WE STARTED TO BRING THAT DOWN. NO SAFETY NET UNTIL WE INTRODUCED SOCIAL SECURITY. WHEN DID THINGS STOP CONSTANTLY CHANGING FOR THE BETTER?
WE SHOULD BE CREATING NEW SYSTEMS. WE NEED TO IMPROVE THE WAY THINGS WORK.
WE NEED TO STOP ALLOWING GREED TO DICTATE HOW SOCIETY FUNCTIONS AT EVERY GODDAMN LEVEL.
OH, PLEASE.
SHUT UP. YOU ALREADY SPEWED YOUR HORSESHIT.

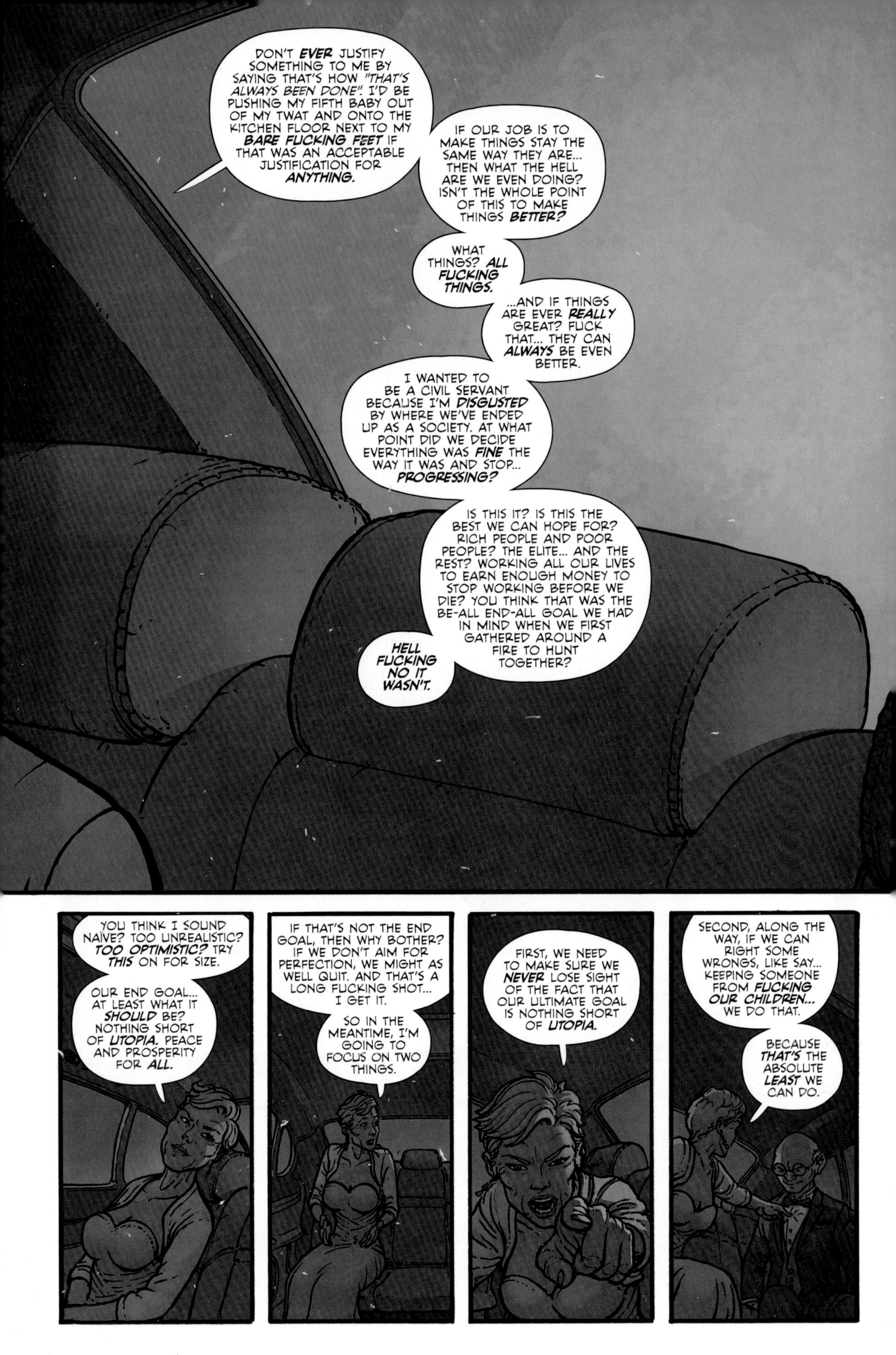
DON'T EVER JUSTIFY SOMETHING TO ME BY SAYING THAT'S HOW "THAT'S ALWAYS BEEN DONE". I'D BE PUSHING MY FIFTH BABY OUT OF MY TWAT AND ONTO THE KITCHEN FLOOR NEXT TO MY BARE FUCKING FEET IF THAT WAS AN ACCEPTABLE JUSTIFICATION FOR ANYTHING.
IF OUR JOB IS TO MAKE THINGS STAY THE SAME WAY THEY ARE... THEN WHAT THE HELL ARE WE EVEN DOING? ISN'T THE WHOLE POINT OF THIS TO MAKE THINGS BETTER?
WHAT THINGS? ALL FUCKING THINGS.
...AND IF THINGS ARE EVER REALLY GREAT? FUCK THAT... THEY CAN ALWAYS BE EVEN BETTER.
I WANTED TO BE A CIVIL SERVANT BECAUSE I'M DISGUSTED BY WHERE WE'VE ENDED UP AS A SOCIETY. AT WHAT POINT DID WE DECIDE EVERYTHING WAS FINE THE WAY IT WAS AND STOP... PROGRESSING?
IS THIS IT? IS THIS THE BEST WE CAN HOPE FOR? RICH PEOPLE AND POOR PEOPLE? THE ELITE... AND THE REST? WORKING ALL OUR LIVES TO EARN ENOUGH MONEY TO STOP WORKING BEFORE WE DIE? YOU THINK THAT WAS THE BE-ALL END-ALL GOAL WE HAD IN MIND WHEN WE FIRST GATHERED AROUND A FIRE TO HUNT TOGETHER?
HELL FUCKING NO IT WASN'T.
YOU THINK I SOUND NAÏVE? TOO UNREALISTIC? TOO OPTIMISTIC? TRY THIS ON FOR SIZE.
OUR END GOAL... AT LEAST WHAT IT SHOULD BE? NOTHING SHORT OF UTOPIA. PEACE AND PROSPERITY FOR ALL.
IF THAT'S NOT THE END GOAL, THEN WHY BOTHER? IF WE DON'T AIM FOR PERFECTION, WE MIGHT AS WELL QUIT. AND THAT'S A LONG FUCKING SHOT... I GET IT.
SO IN THE MEANTIME, I'M GOING TO FOCUS ON TWO THINGS.
FIRST, WE NEED TO MAKE SURE WE NEVER LOSE SIGHT OF THE FACT THAT OUR ULTIMATE GOAL IS NOTHING SHORT OF UTOPIA.
SECOND, ALONG THE WAY, IF WE CAN RIGHT SOME WRONGS, LIKE SAY... KEEPING SOMEONE FROM FUCKING OUR CHILDREN... WE DO THAT.
BECAUSE THAT'S THE ABSOLUTE LEAST WE CAN DO.

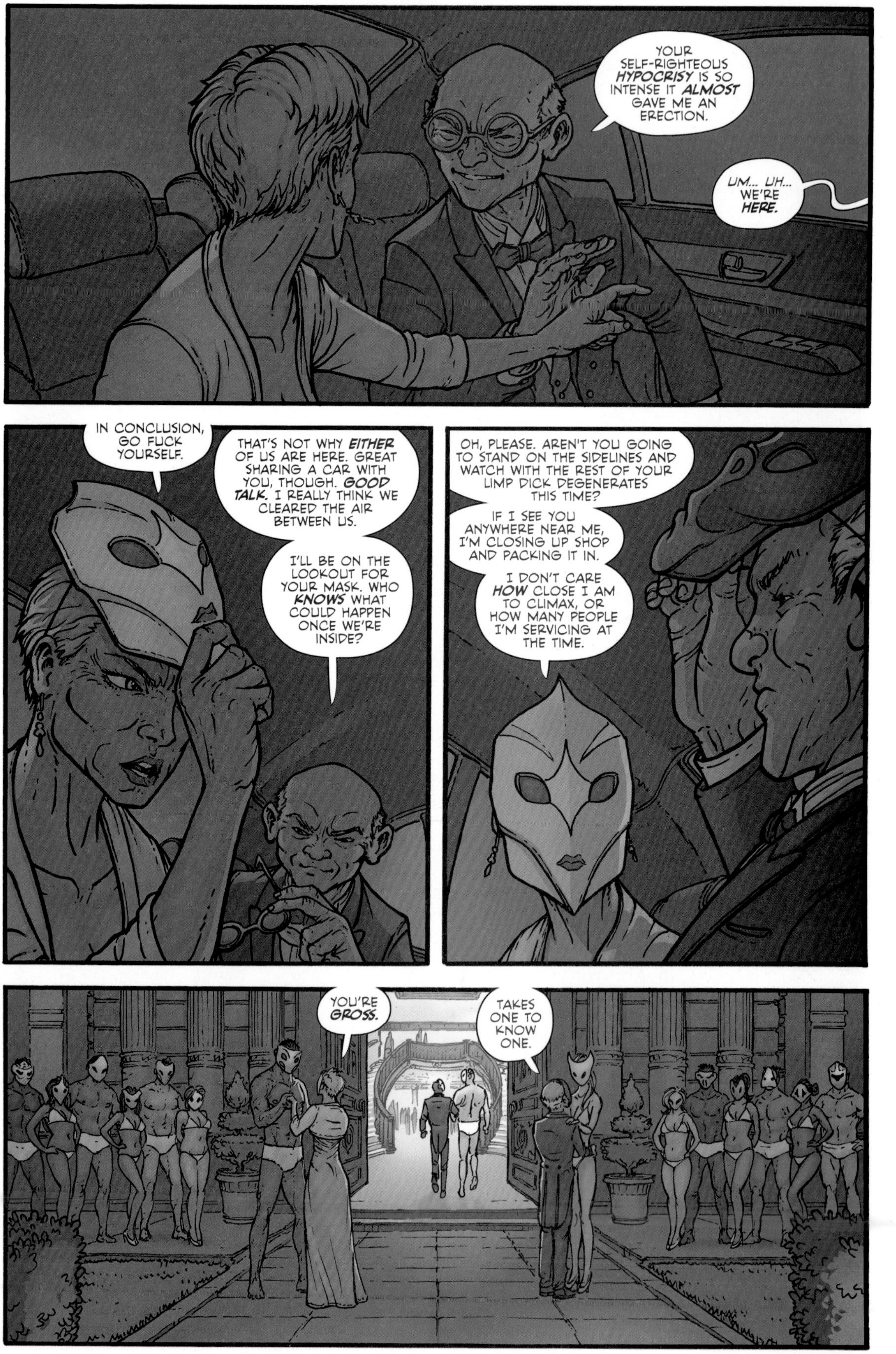
YOUR SELF-RIGHTEOUS HYPOCRISY IS SO INTENSE IT ALMOST GAVE ME AN ERECTION.
UM... UH... WE'RE HERE.
IN CONCLUSION, GO FUCK YOURSELF.
THAT'S NOT WHY EITHER OF US ARE HERE. GREAT SHARING A CAR WITH YOU, THOUGH. GOOD TALK. I REALLY THINK WE CLEARED THE AIR BETWEEN US.
I'LL BE ON THE LOOKOUT FOR YOUR MASK. WHO KNOWS WHAT COULD HAPPEN ONCE WE'RE INSIDE?
OH, PLEASE. AREN'T YOU GOING TO STAND ON THE SIDELINES AND WATCH WITH THE REST OF YOUR LIMP DICK DEGENERATES THIS TIME?
IF I SEE YOU ANYWHERE NEAR ME, I'M CLOSING UP SHOP AND PACKING IT IN.
I DON'T CARE HOW CLOSE I AM TO CLIMAX, OR HOW MANY PEOPLE I'M SERVICING AT THE TIME.
YOU'RE GROSS.
TAKES ONE TO KNOW ONE.

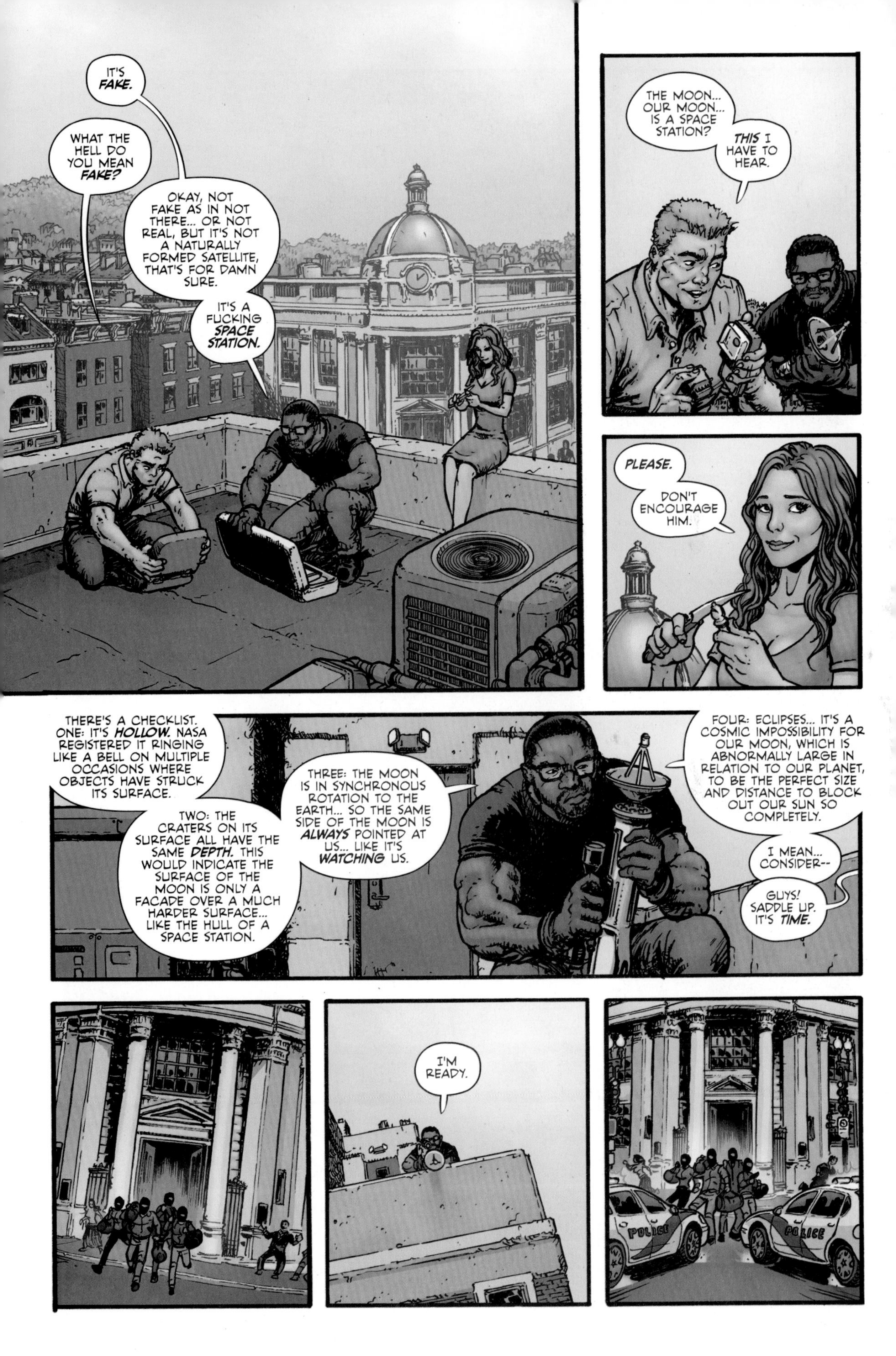
IT'S FAKE.
WHAT THE HELL DO YOU MEAN FAKE?
OKAY, NOT FAKE AS IN NOT THERE... OR NOT REAL, BUT IT'S NOT A NATURALLY FORMED SATELLITE, THAT'S FOR DAMN SURE.
IT'S A FUCKING SPACE STATION.
THE MOON... OUR MOON... IS A SPACE STATION?
THIS I HAVE TO HEAR.
PLEASE.
DON'T ENCOURAGE HIM.
THERE'S A CHECKLIST. ONE: IT'S HOLLOW. NASA REGISTERED IT RINGING LIKE A BELL ON MULTIPLE OCCASIONS WHERE OBJECTS HAVE STRUCK ITS SURFACE.
TWO: THE CRATERS ON ITS SURFACE ALL HAVE THE SAME DEPTH. THIS WOULD INDICATE THE SURFACE OF THE MOON IS ONLY A FACADE OVER A MUCH HARDER SURFACE... LIKE THE HULL OF A SPACE STATION.
THREE: THE MOON IS IN SYNCHRONOUS ROTATION TO THE EARTH... SO THE SAME SIDE OF THE MOON IS ALWAYS POINTED AT US... LIKE IT'S WATCHING US.
FOUR: ECLIPSES... IT'S A COSMIC IMPOSSIBILITY FOR OUR MOON, WHICH IS ABNORMALLY LARGE IN RELATION TO OUR PLANET, TO BE THE PERFECT SIZE AND DISTANCE TO BLOCK OUT OUR SUN SO COMPLETELY.
I MEAN... CONSIDER--
GUYS! SADDLE UP. IT'S TIME.
I'M READY.
POLICE
POLICE

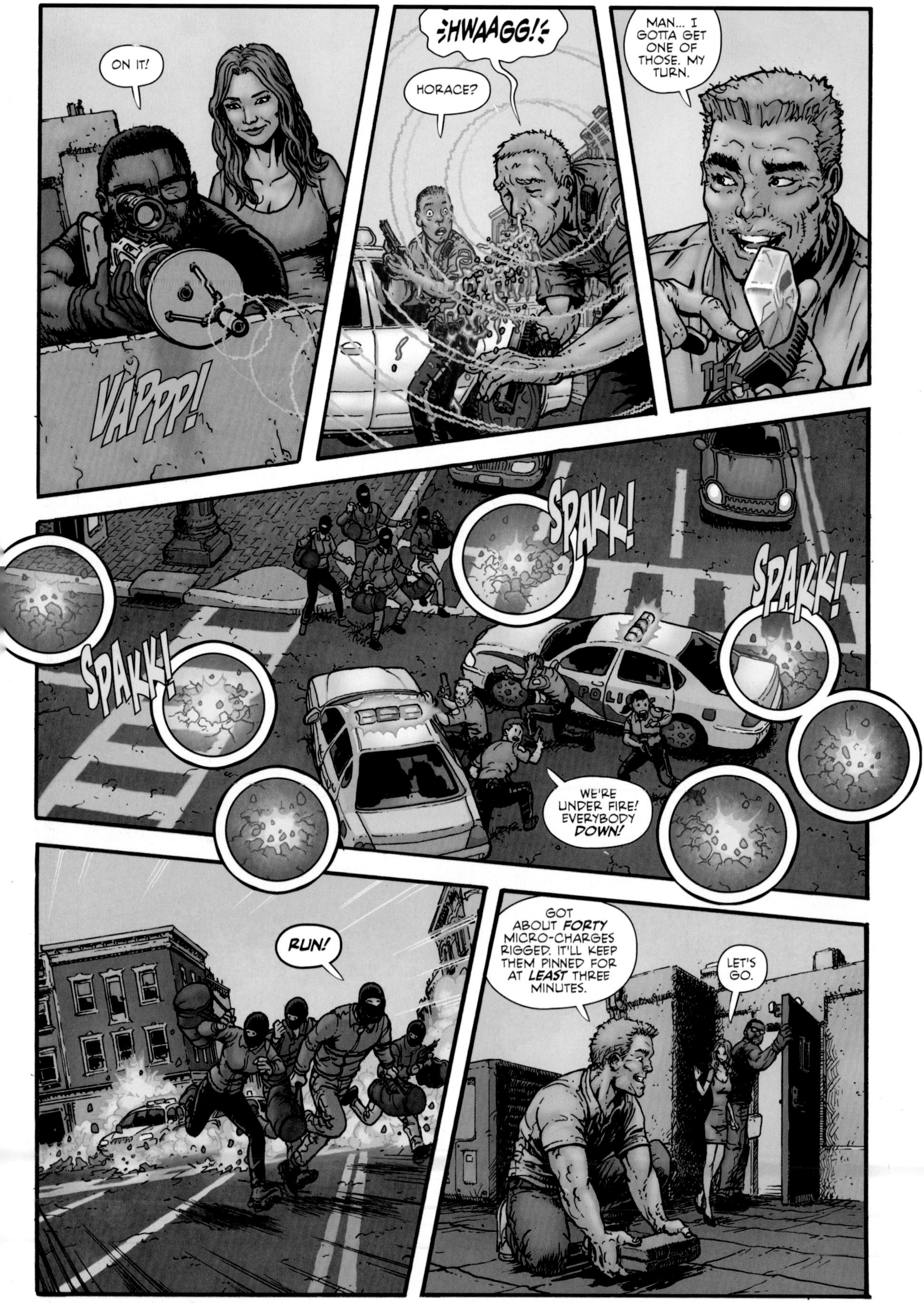
ON IT!
VAPPP!
HWAAGG!
HORACE?
MAN... I GOTTA GET ONE OF THOSE. MY TURN.
SPAKK!
SPAKK!
SPAKK!
WE'RE UNDER FIRE! EVERYBODY DOWN!
RUN!
GOT ABOUT FORTY MICRO-CHARGES RIGGED. IT'LL KEEP THEM PINNED FOR AT LEAST THREE MINUTES.
LET'S GO.

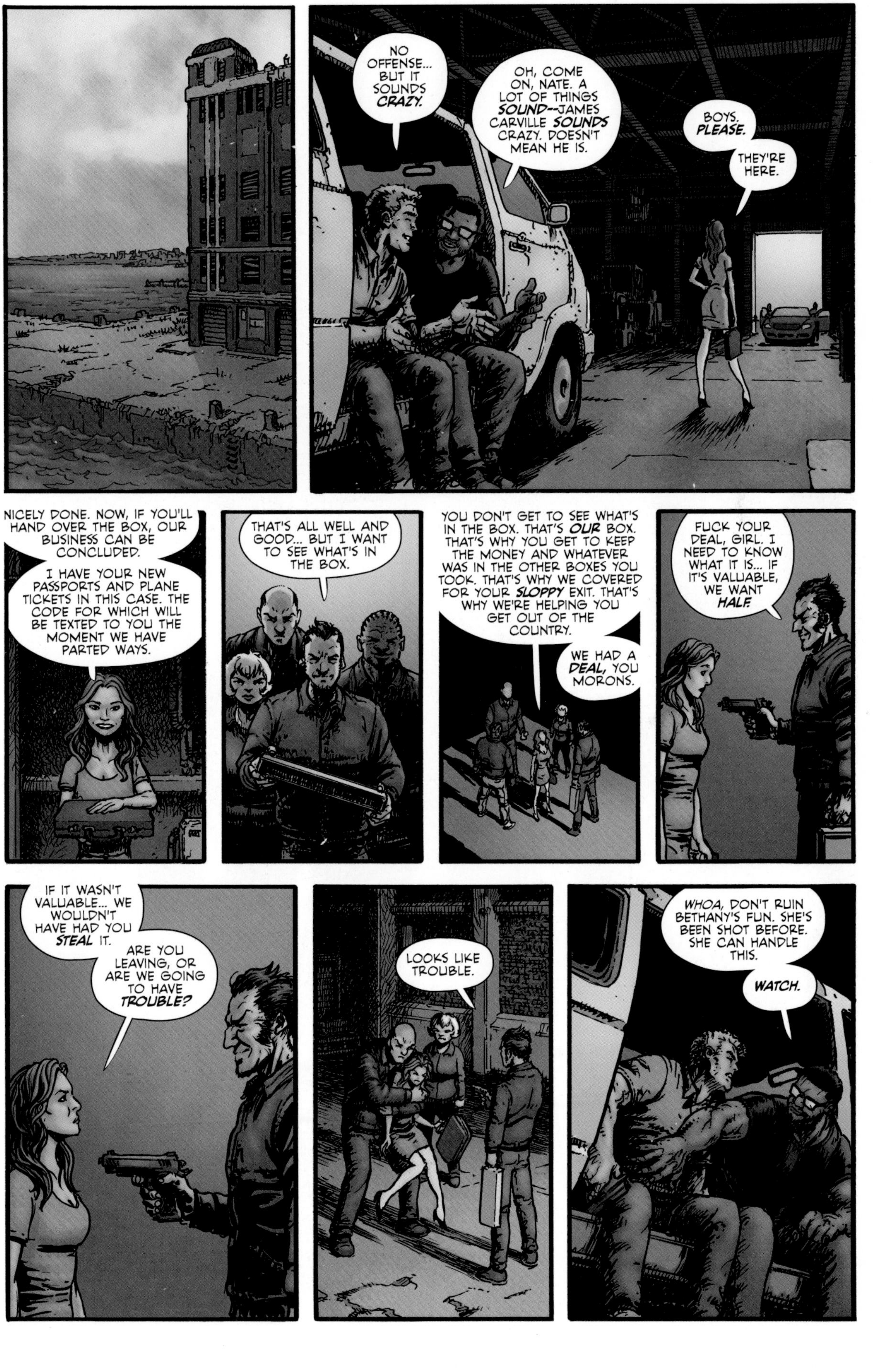
NO OFFENSE... BUT IT SOUNDS CRAZY.
OH, COME ON, NATE. A LOT OF THINGS SOUND--JAMES CARVILLE SOUNDS CRAZY. DOESN'T MEAN HE IS.
BOYS. PLEASE.
THEY'RE HERE.
NICELY DONE. NOW, IF YOU'LL HAND OVER THE BOX, OUR BUSINESS CAN BE CONCLUDED.
I HAVE YOUR NEW PASSPORTS AND PLANE TICKETS IN THIS CASE. THE CODE FOR WHICH WILL BE TEXTED TO YOU THE MOMENT WE HAVE PARTED WAYS.
THAT'S ALL WELL AND GOOD... BUT I WANT TO SEE WHAT'S IN THE BOX.
YOU DON'T GET TO SEE WHAT'S IN THE BOX. THAT'S OUR BOX. THAT'S WHY YOU GET TO KEEP THE MONEY AND WHATEVER WAS IN THE OTHER BOXES YOU TOOK. THAT'S WHY WE COVERED FOR YOUR SLOPPY EXIT. THAT'S WHY WE'RE HELPING YOU GET OUT OF THE COUNTRY.
WE HAD A DEAL, YOU MORONS.
FUCK YOUR DEAL, GIRL. I NEED TO KNOW WHAT IT IS... IF IT'S VALUABLE, WE WANT HALF.
IF IT WASN'T VALUABLE... WE WOULDN'T HAVE HAD YOU STEAL IT.
ARE YOU LEAVING, OR ARE WE GOING TO HAVE TROUBLE?
LOOKS LIKE TROUBLE.
WHOA, DON'T RUIN BETHANY'S FUN. SHE'S BEEN SHOT BEFORE. SHE CAN HANDLE THIS.
WATCH.

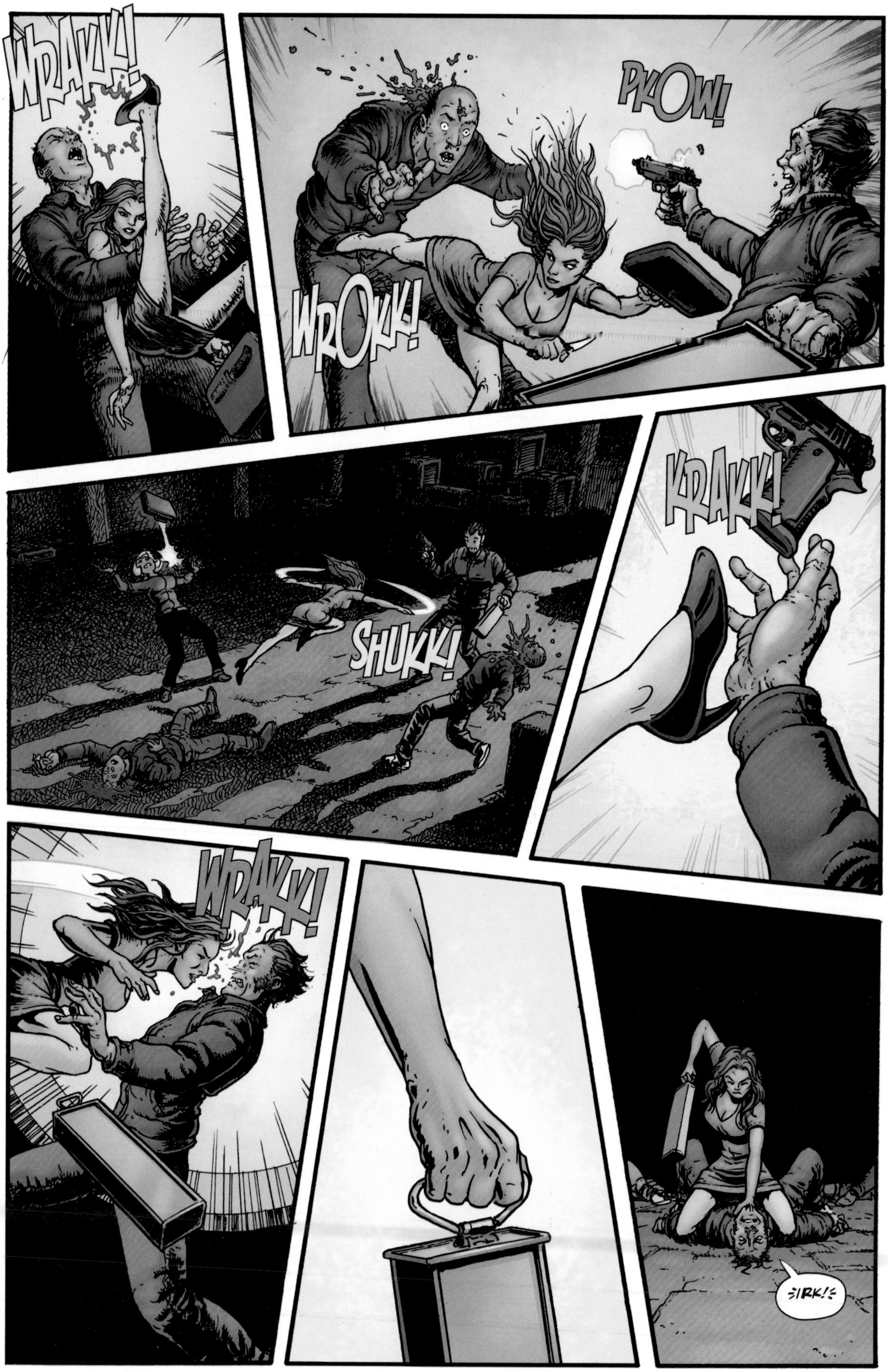
WRAKK!
PKOW!
WROKK!
SHUKK!
KRAKK!
WRAKK!
IRK!

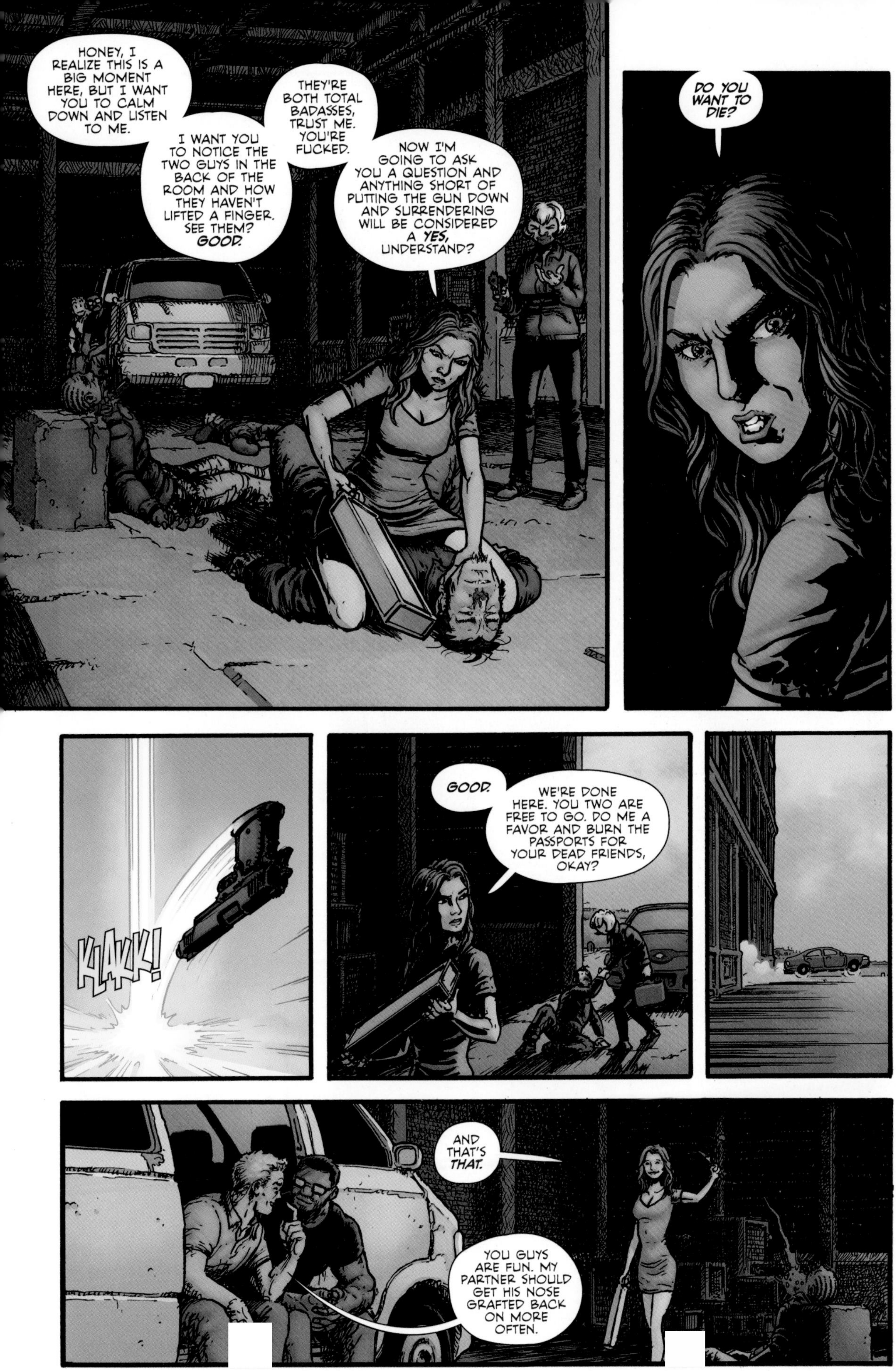
HONEY, I REALIZE THIS IS A BIG MOMENT HERE, BUT I WANT YOU TO CALM DOWN AND LISTEN TO ME.
I WANT YOU TO NOTICE THE TWO GUYS IN THE BACK OF THE ROOM AND HOW THEY HAVEN'T LIFTED A FINGER. SEE THEM? GOOD.
THEY'RE BOTH TOTAL BADASSES, TRUST ME. YOU'RE FUCKED.
NOW I'M GOING TO ASK YOU A QUESTION AND ANYTHING SHORT OF PUTTING THE GUN DOWN AND SURRENDERING WILL BE CONSIDERED A YES, UNDERSTAND?
DO YOU WANT TO DIE?
KLAKK!
GOOD.
WE'RE DONE HERE. YOU TWO ARE FREE TO GO. DO ME A FAVOR AND BURN THE PASSPORTS FOR YOUR DEAD FRIENDS, OKAY?
AND THAT'S THAT.
YOU GUYS ARE FUN. MY PARTNER SHOULD GET HIS NOSE GRAFTED BACK ON MORE OFTEN.

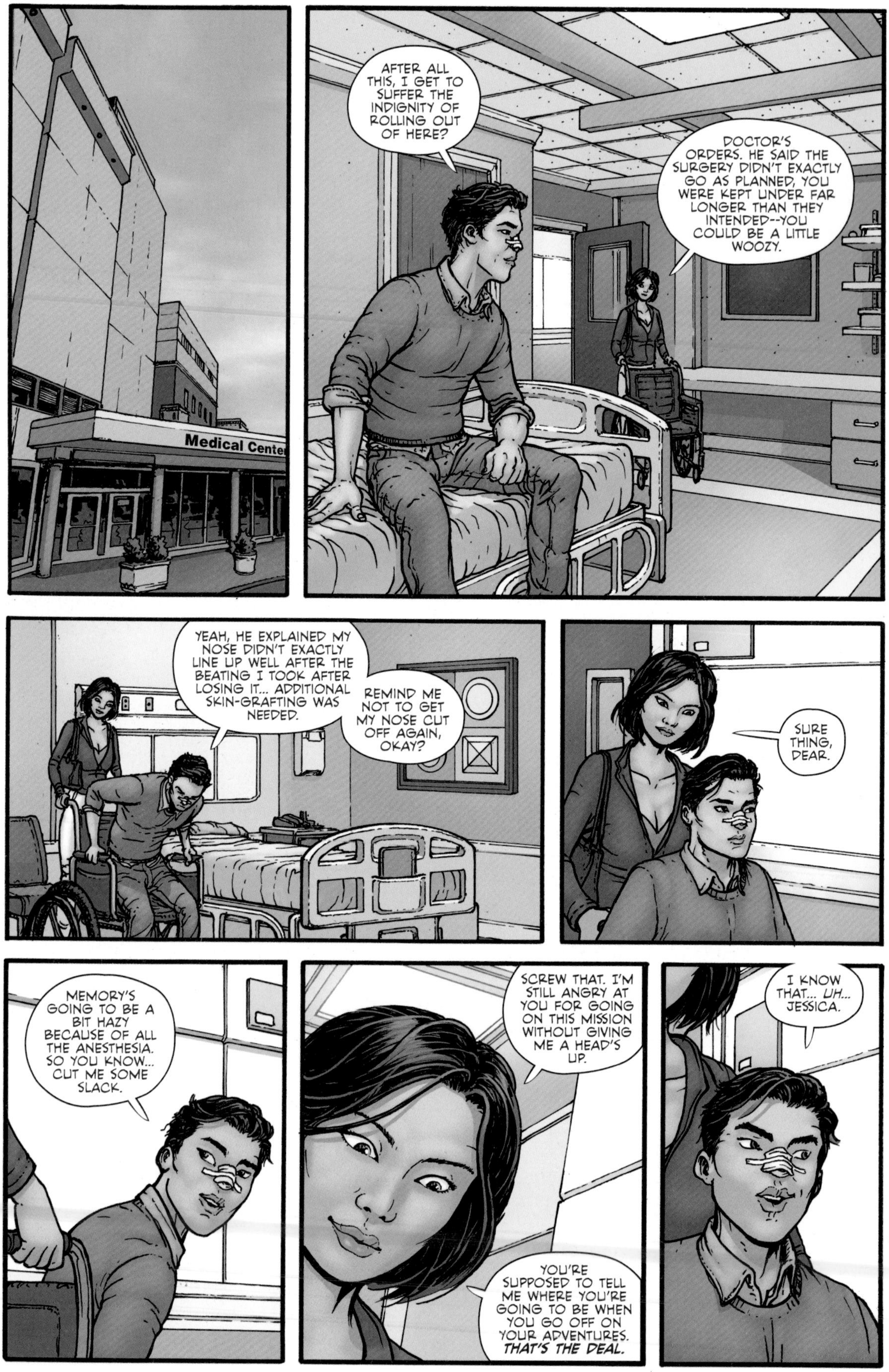
Medical Center
AFTER ALL THIS, I GET TO SUFFER THE INDIGNITY OF ROLLING OUT OF HERE?
DOCTOR'S ORDERS. HE SAID THE SURGERY DIDN'T EXACTLY GO AS PLANNED, YOU WERE KEPT UNDER FAR LONGER THAN THEY INTENDED--YOU COULD BE A LITTLE WOOZY.
YEAH, HE EXPLAINED MY NOSE DIDN'T EXACTLY LINE UP WELL AFTER THE BEATING I TOOK AFTER LOSING IT... ADDITIONAL SKIN-GRAFTING WAS NEEDED.
REMIND ME NOT TO GET MY NOSE CUT OFF AGAIN, OKAY?
SURE THING, DEAR.
MEMORY'S GOING TO BE A BIT HAZY BECAUSE OF ALL THE ANESTHESIA. SO YOU KNOW... CUT ME SOME SLACK.
SCREW THAT. I'M STILL ANGRY AT YOU FOR GOING ON THIS MISSION WITHOUT GIVING ME A HEAD'S UP.
YOU'RE SUPPOSED TO TELL ME WHERE YOU'RE GOING TO BE WHEN YOU GO OFF ON YOUR ADVENTURES. THAT'S THE DEAL.
I KNOW THAT... UH... JESSICA.

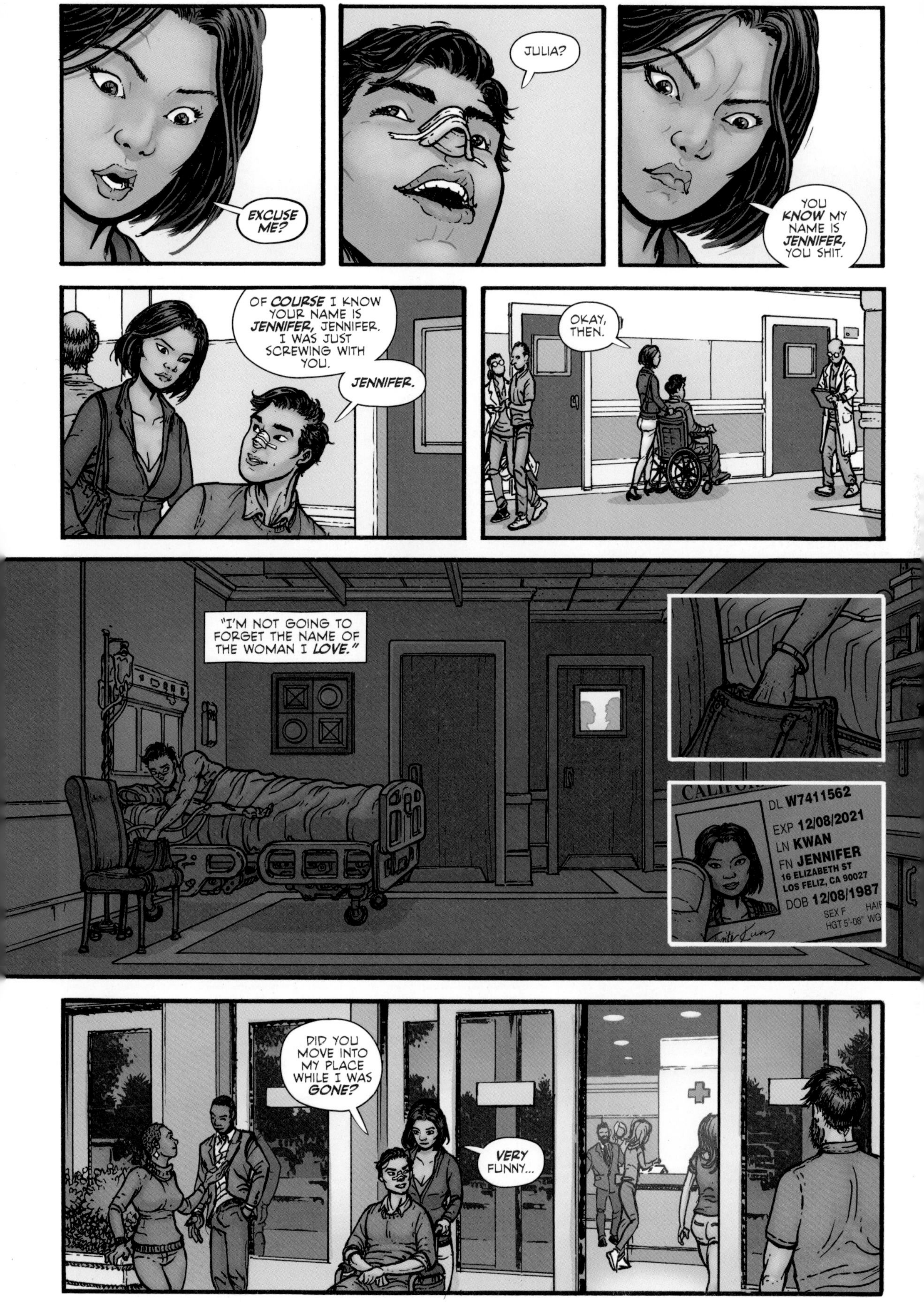
EXCUSE ME?
JULIA?
YOU KNOW MY NAME IS JENNIFER, YOU SHIT.
OF COURSE I KNOW YOUR NAME IS JENNIFER, JENNIFER. I WAS JUST SCREWING WITH YOU.
JENNIFER.
OKAY, THEN.
"I'M NOT GOING TO FORGET THE NAME OF THE WOMAN I LOVE."
CALIFO
DL W7411562
EXP 12/08/2021
LN KWAN
FN JENNIFER
16 ELIZABETH ST
LOS FELIZ, CA 90027
DOB 12/08/1987
SEX F
HGT 5'-08"
DID YOU MOVE INTO MY PLACE WHILE I WAS GONE?
VERY FUNNY...

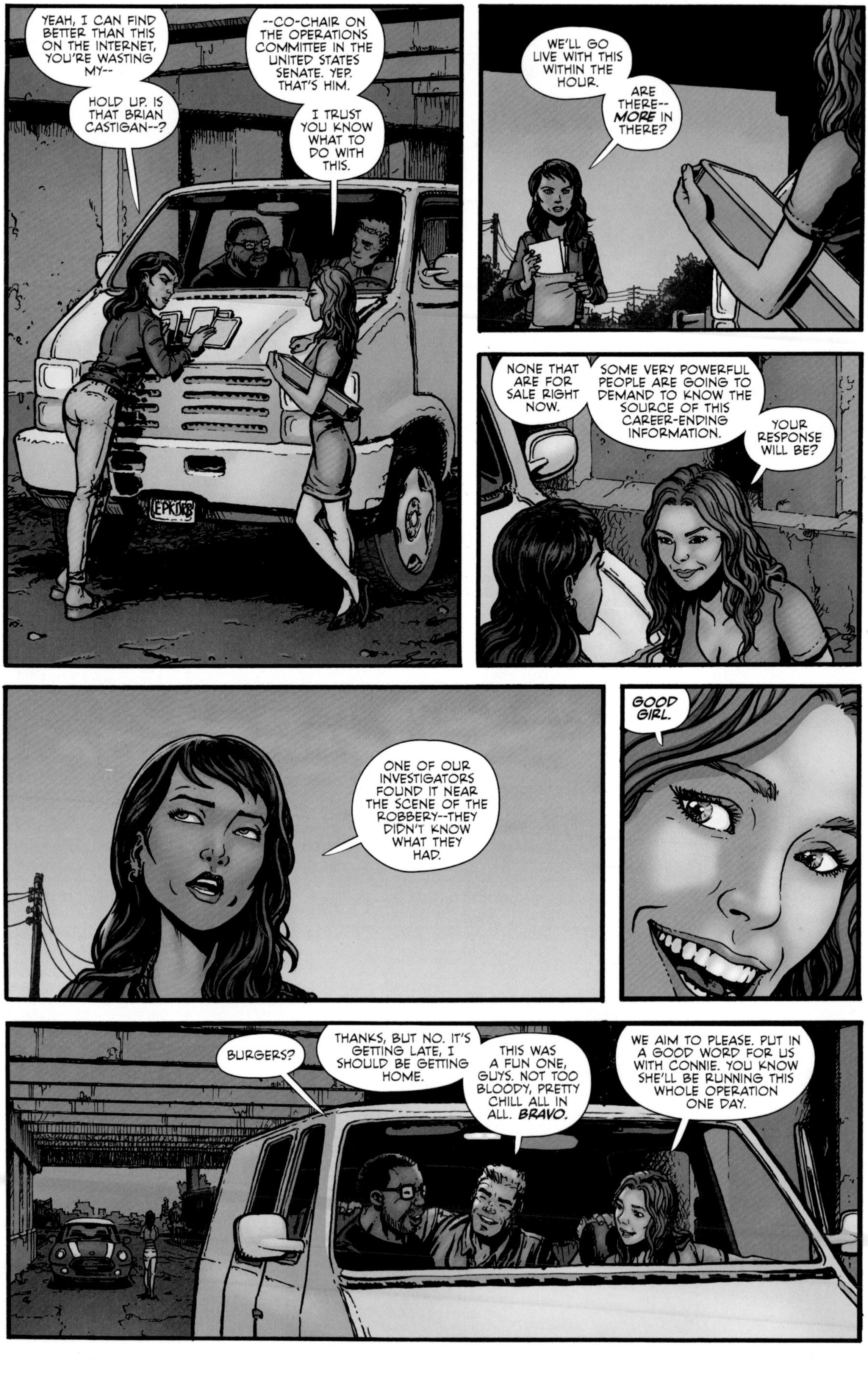
YEAH, I CAN FIND BETTER THAN THIS ON THE INTERNET, YOU'RE WASTING MY--
HOLD UP. IS THAT BRIAN CASTIGAN--?
--CO-CHAIR ON THE OPERATIONS COMMITTEE IN THE UNITED STATES SENATE. YEP. THAT'S HIM.
I TRUST YOU KNOW WHAT TO DO WITH THIS.
WE'LL GO LIVE WITH THIS WITHIN THE HOUR.
ARE THERE-- MORE IN THERE?
NONE THAT ARE FOR SALE RIGHT NOW.
SOME VERY POWERFUL PEOPLE ARE GOING TO DEMAND TO KNOW THE SOURCE OF THIS CAREER-ENDING INFORMATION.
YOUR RESPONSE WILL BE?
ONE OF OUR INVESTIGATORS FOUND IT NEAR THE SCENE OF THE ROBBERY--THEY DIDN'T KNOW WHAT THEY HAD.
GOOD GIRL.
BURGERS?
THANKS, BUT NO. IT'S GETTING LATE, I SHOULD BE GETTING HOME.
THIS WAS A FUN ONE, GUYS. NOT TOO BLOODY, PRETTY CHILL ALL IN ALL. BRAVO.
WE AIM TO PLEASE. PUT IN A GOOD WORD FOR US WITH CONNIE. YOU KNOW SHE'LL BE RUNNING THIS WHOLE OPERATION ONE DAY.

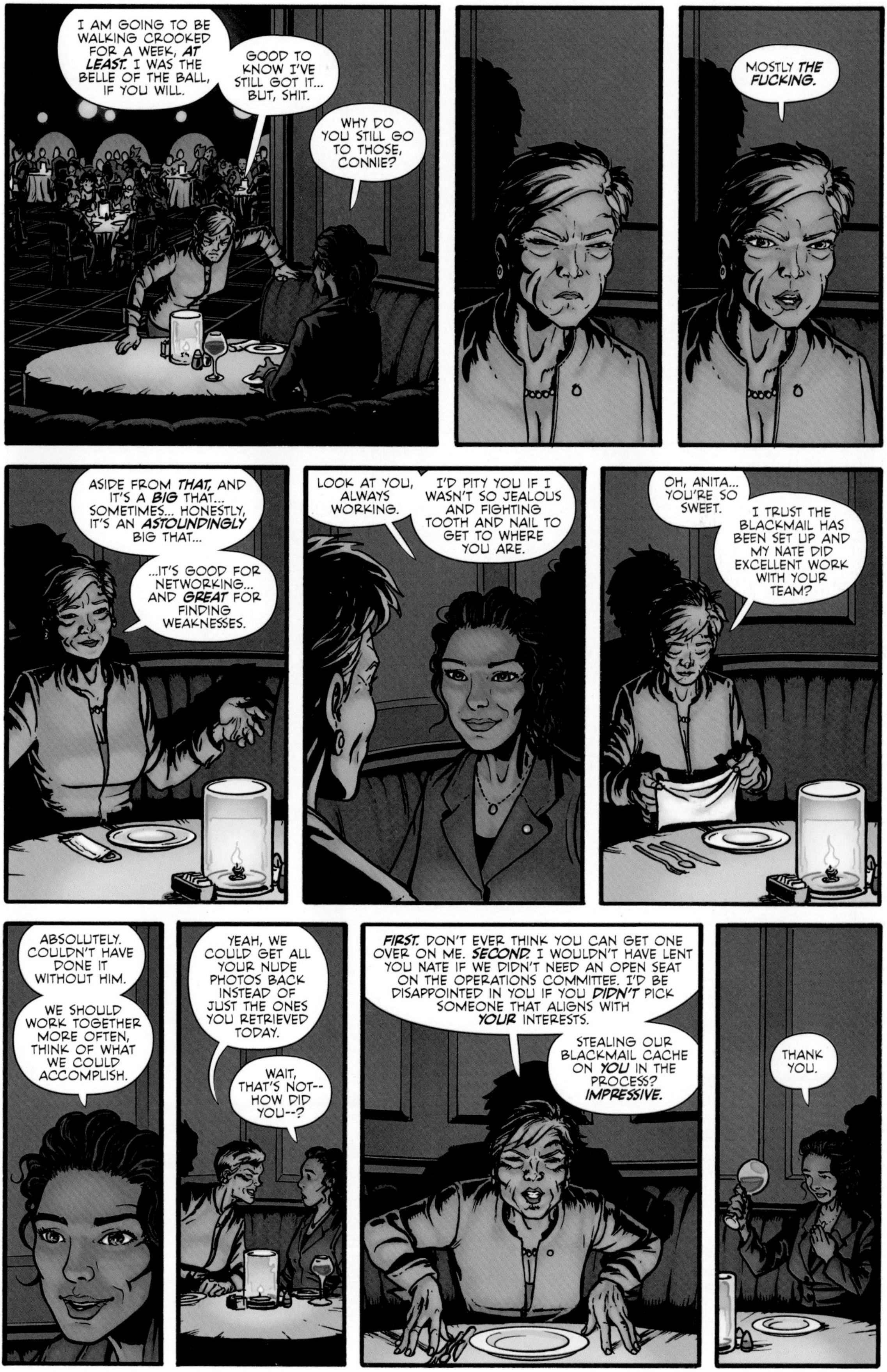
I AM GOING TO BE WALKING CROOKED FOR A WEEK, AT LEAST. I WAS THE BELLE OF THE BALL, IF YOU WILL.
GOOD TO KNOW I'VE STILL GOT IT... BUT, SHIT.
WHY DO YOU STILL GO TO THOSE, CONNIE?
MOSTLY THE FUCKING.
ASIDE FROM THAT, AND IT'S A BIG THAT... SOMETIMES... HONESTLY, IT'S AN ASTOUNDINGLY BIG THAT...
...IT'S GOOD FOR NETWORKING... AND GREAT FOR FINDING WEAKNESSES.
LOOK AT YOU, ALWAYS WORKING.
I'D PITY YOU IF I WASN'T SO JEALOUS AND FIGHTING TOOTH AND NAIL TO GET TO WHERE YOU ARE.
OH, ANITA... YOU'RE SO SWEET.
I TRUST THE BLACKMAIL HAS BEEN SET UP AND MY NATE DID EXCELLENT WORK WITH YOUR TEAM?
ABSOLUTELY. COULDN'T HAVE DONE IT WITHOUT HIM.
WE SHOULD WORK TOGETHER MORE OFTEN, THINK OF WHAT WE COULD ACCOMPLISH.
YEAH, WE COULD GET ALL YOUR NUDE PHOTOS BACK INSTEAD OF JUST THE ONES YOU RETRIEVED TODAY.
WAIT, THAT'S NOT-- HOW DID YOU--?
FIRST. DON'T EVER THINK YOU CAN GET ONE OVER ON ME. SECOND. I WOULDN'T HAVE LENT YOU NATE IF WE DIDN'T NEED AN OPEN SEAT ON THE OPERATIONS COMMITTEE. I'D BE DISAPPOINTED IN YOU IF YOU DIDN'T PICK SOMEONE THAT ALIGNS WITH YOUR INTERESTS.
STEALING OUR BLACKMAIL CACHE ON YOU IN THE PROCESS? IMPRESSIVE.
THANK YOU.

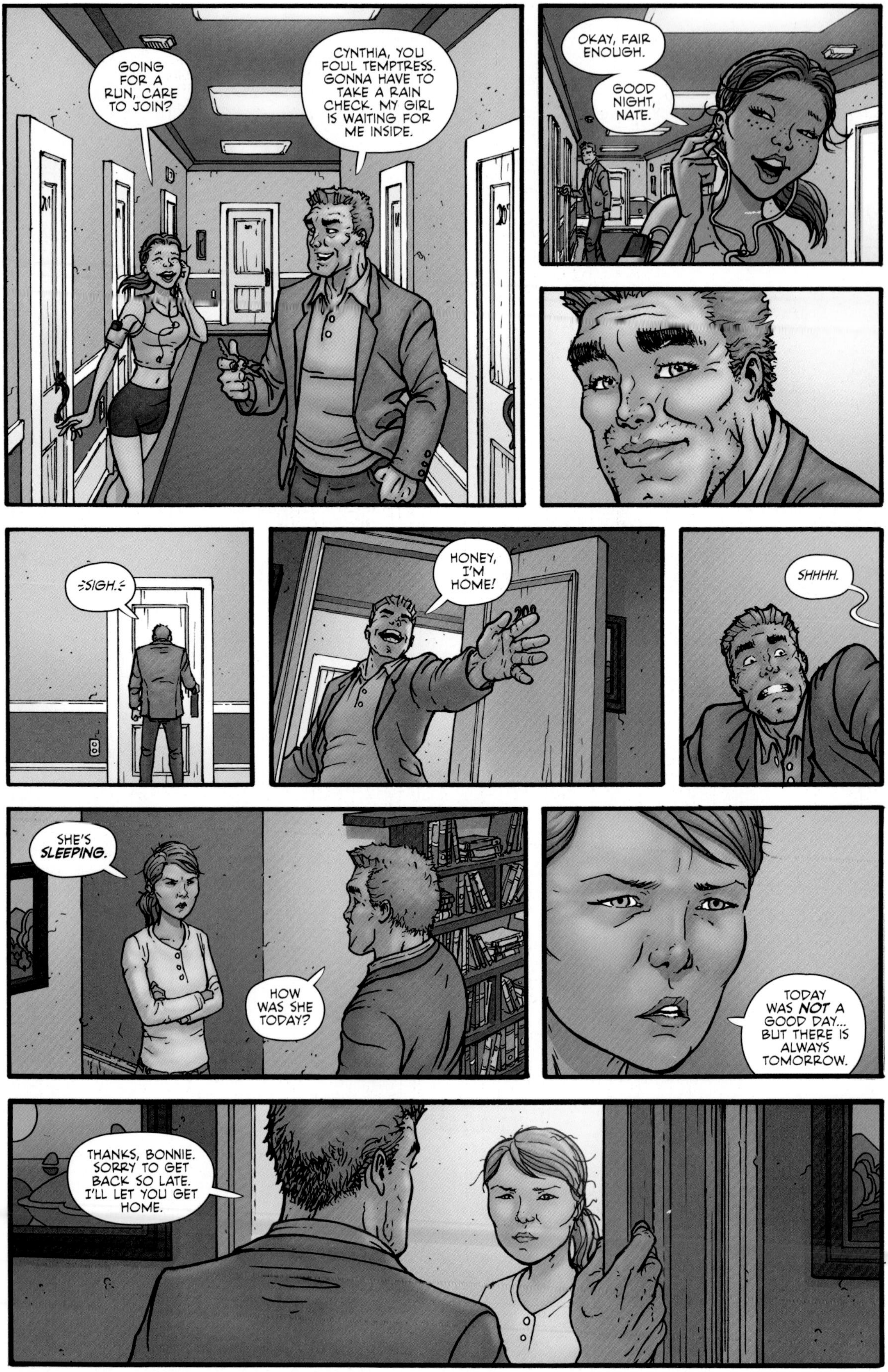
GOING FOR A RUN, CARE TO JOIN?
CYNTHIA, YOU FOUL TEMPTRESS. GONNA HAVE TO TAKE A RAIN CHECK. MY GIRL IS WAITING FOR ME INSIDE.
OKAY, FAIR ENOUGH.
GOOD NIGHT, NATE.
SIGH.
HONEY, I'M HOME!
SHHHH.
SHE'S *SLEEPING.*
HOW WAS SHE TODAY?
TODAY WAS *NOT* A GOOD DAY... BUT THERE IS ALWAYS TOMORROW.
THANKS, BONNIE. SORRY TO GET BACK SO LATE. I'LL LET YOU GET HOME.

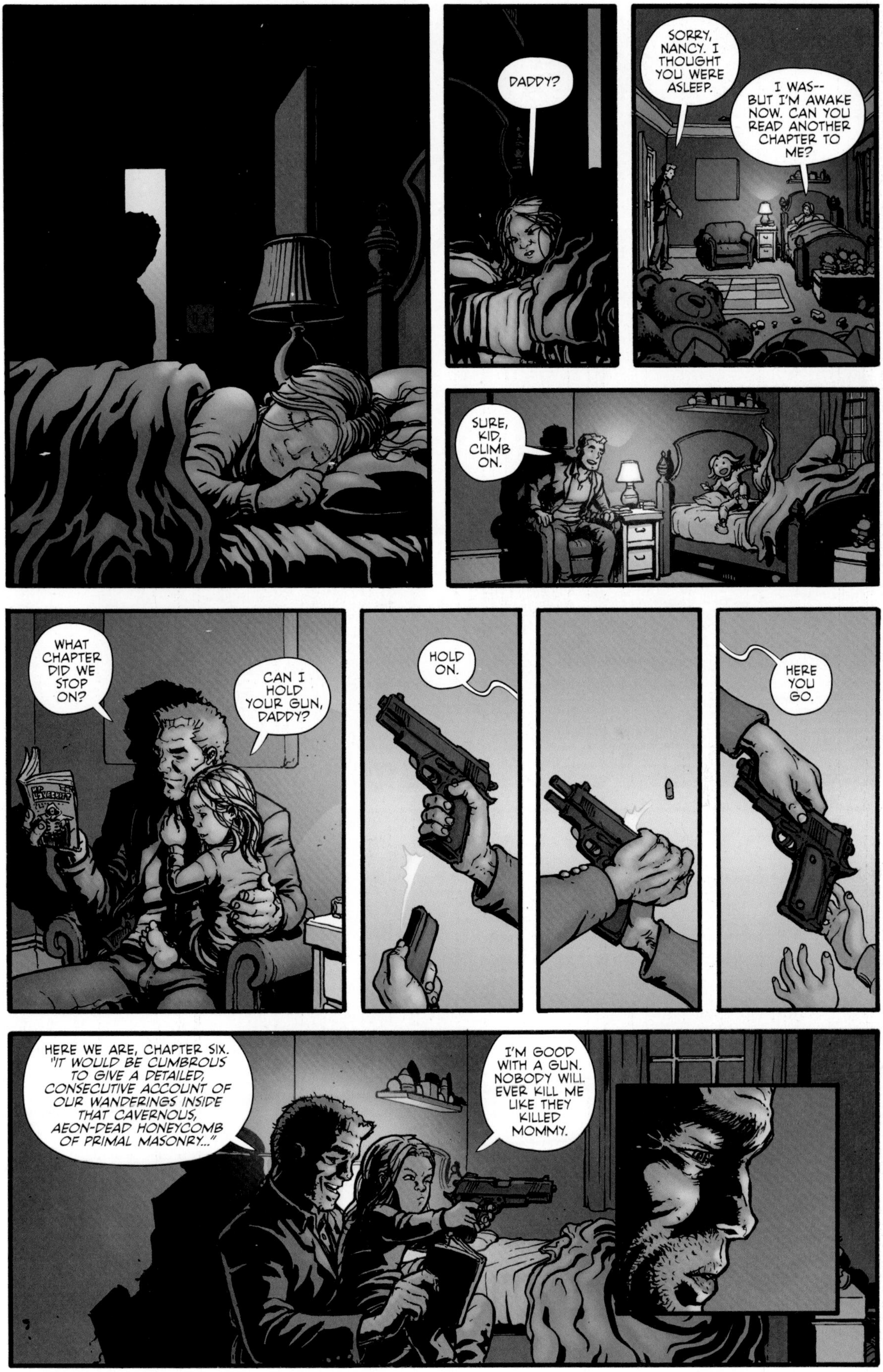
DADDY?
SORRY, NANCY. I THOUGHT YOU WERE ASLEEP.
I WAS-- BUT I'M AWAKE NOW. CAN YOU READ ANOTHER CHAPTER TO ME?
SURE, KID, CLIMB ON.
WHAT CHAPTER DID WE STOP ON?
CAN I HOLD YOUR GUN, DADDY?
HOLD ON.
HERE YOU GO.
HERE WE ARE, CHAPTER SIX. "IT WOULD BE CUMBROUS TO GIVE A DETAILED, CONSECUTIVE ACCOUNT OF OUR WANDERINGS INSIDE THAT CAVERNOUS, AEON-DEAD HONEYCOMB OF PRIMAL MASONRY..."
I'M GOOD WITH A GUN. NOBODY WILL EVER KILL ME LIKE THEY KILLED MOMMY.

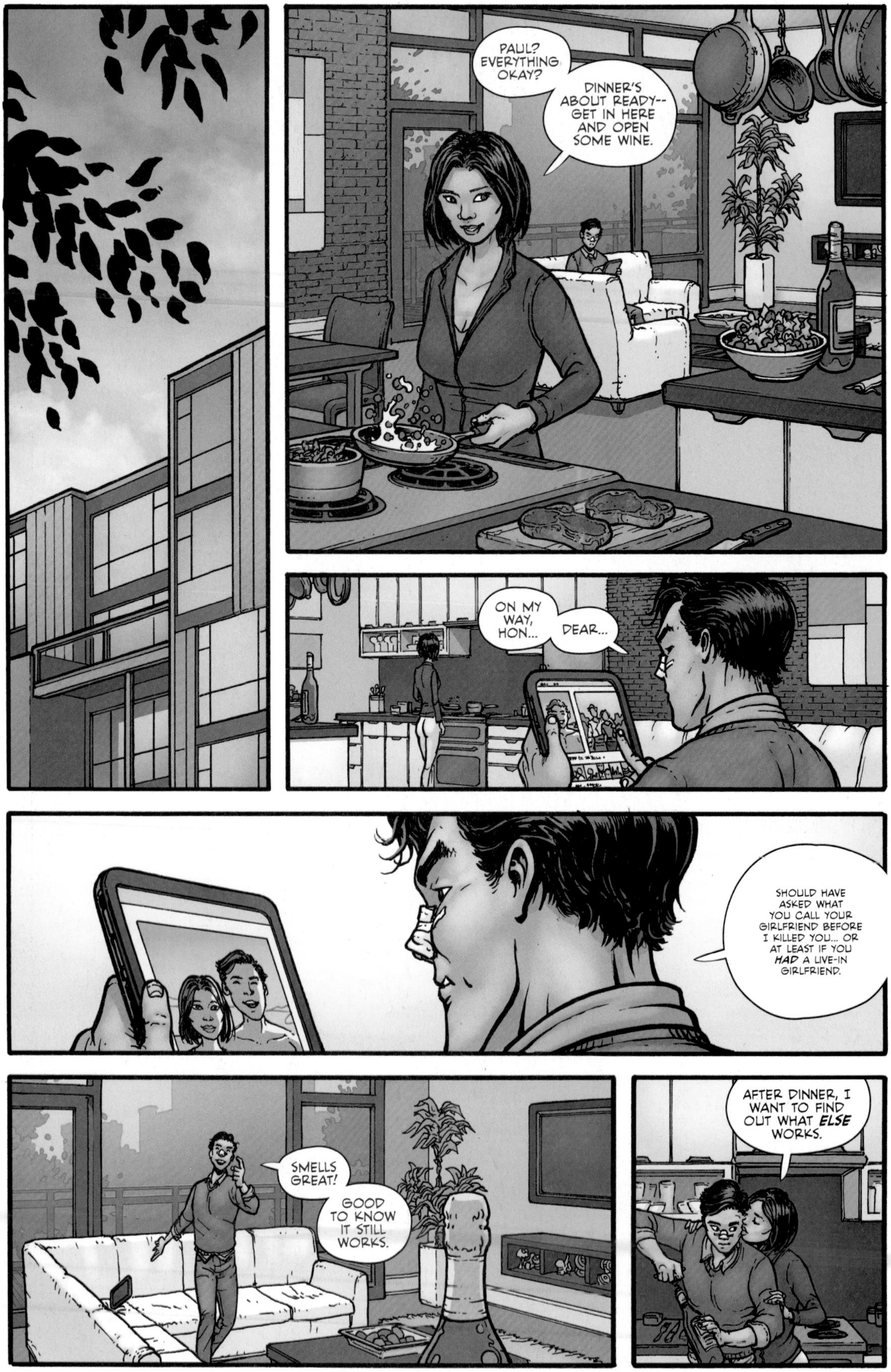
PAUL? EVERYTHING OKAY?
DINNER'S ABOUT READY-- GET IN HERE AND OPEN SOME WINE.
ON MY WAY, HON...
DEAR...
SHOULD HAVE ASKED WHAT YOU CALL YOUR GIRLFRIEND BEFORE I KILLED YOU... OR AT LEAST IF YOU *HAD* A LIVE-IN GIRLFRIEND.
SMELLS GREAT!
GOOD TO KNOW IT STILL WORKS.
AFTER DINNER, I WANT TO FIND OUT WHAT *ELSE* WORKS.

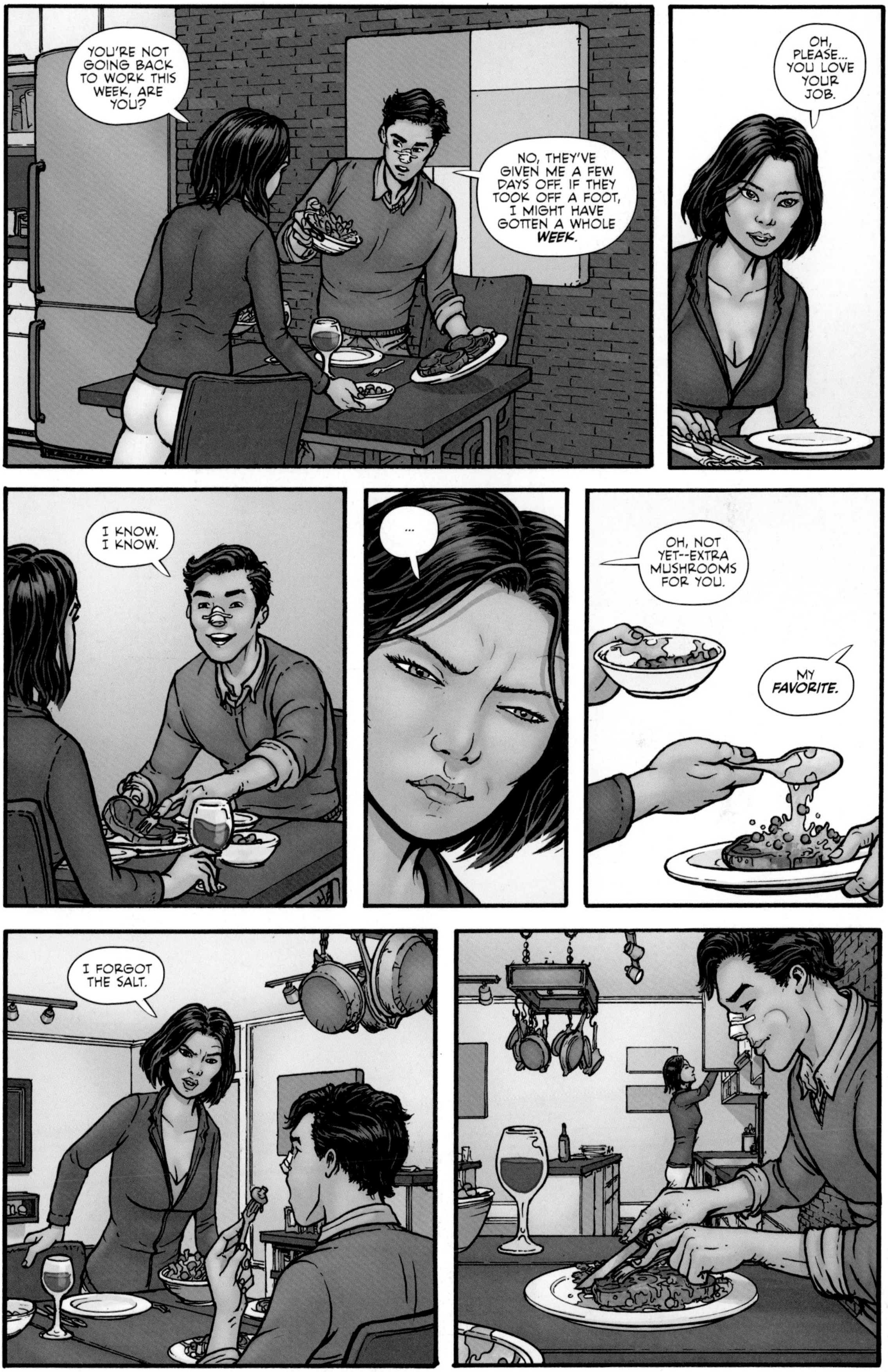
YOU'RE NOT GOING BACK TO WORK THIS WEEK, ARE YOU?
NO, THEY'VE GIVEN ME A FEW DAYS OFF. IF THEY TOOK OFF A FOOT, I MIGHT HAVE GOTTEN A WHOLE WEEK.
OH, PLEASE... YOU LOVE YOUR JOB.
I KNOW. I KNOW.
...
OH, NOT YET--EXTRA MUSHROOMS FOR YOU.
MY FAVORITE.
I FORGOT THE SALT.

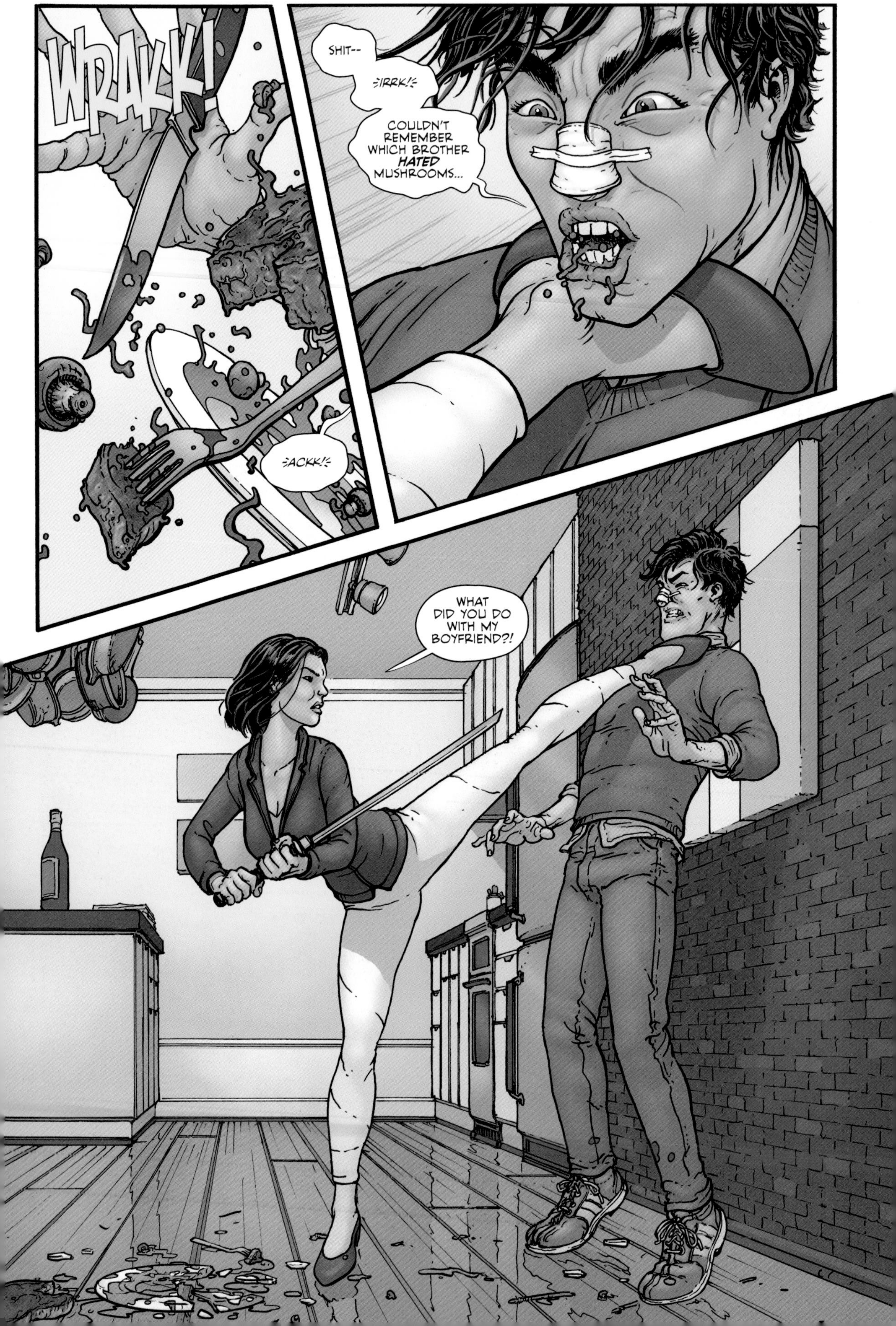
WRAKK!
SHIT--
IRRK!
COULDN'T REMEMBER WHICH BROTHER HATED MUSHROOMS...
ACKK!
WHAT DID YOU DO WITH MY BOYFRIEND?!

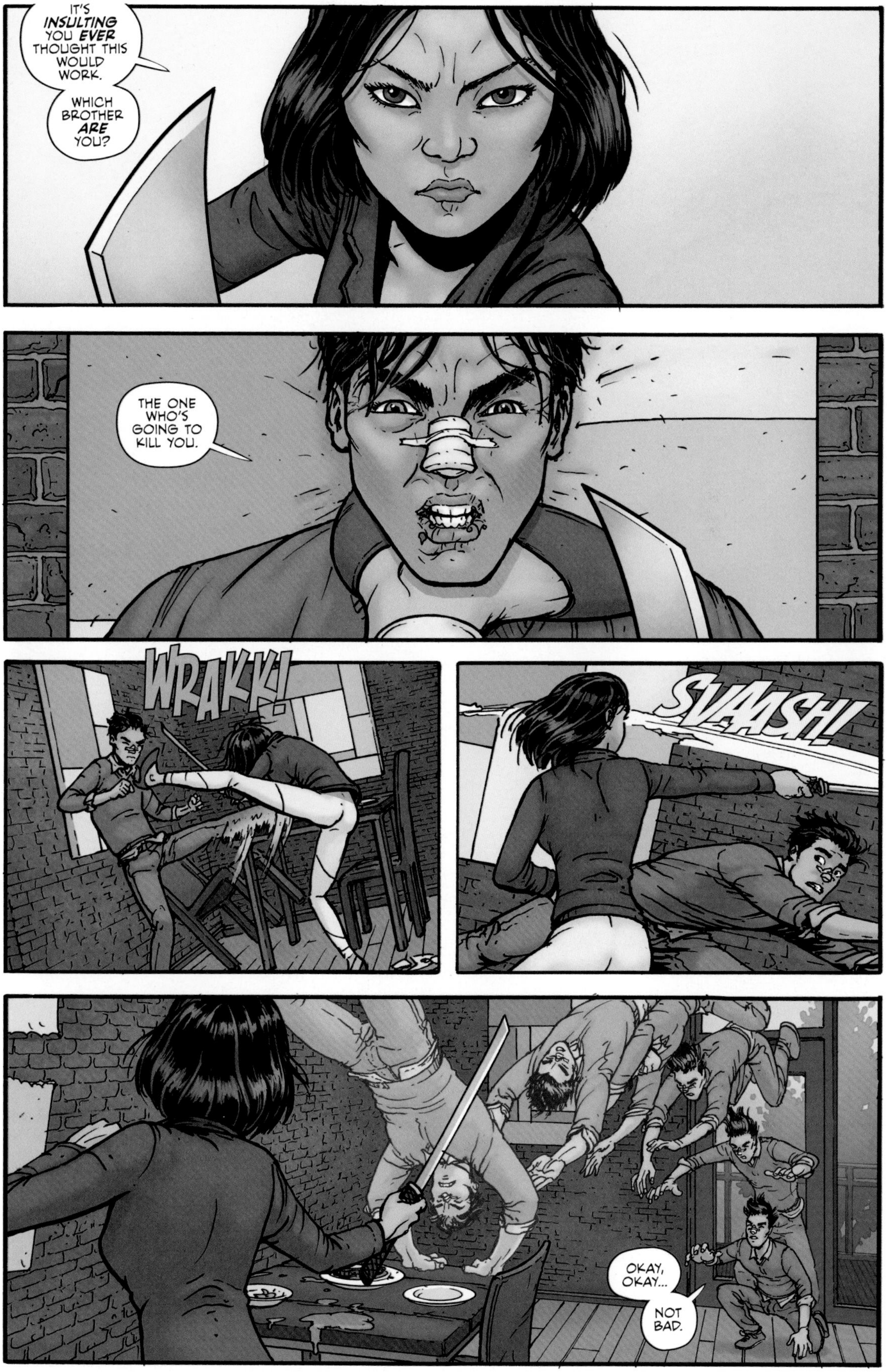
IT'S INSULTING YOU EVER THOUGHT THIS WOULD WORK.
WHICH BROTHER ARE YOU?
THE ONE WHO'S GOING TO KILL YOU.
WRAKK!
SVAASH!
OKAY, OKAY...
NOT BAD.

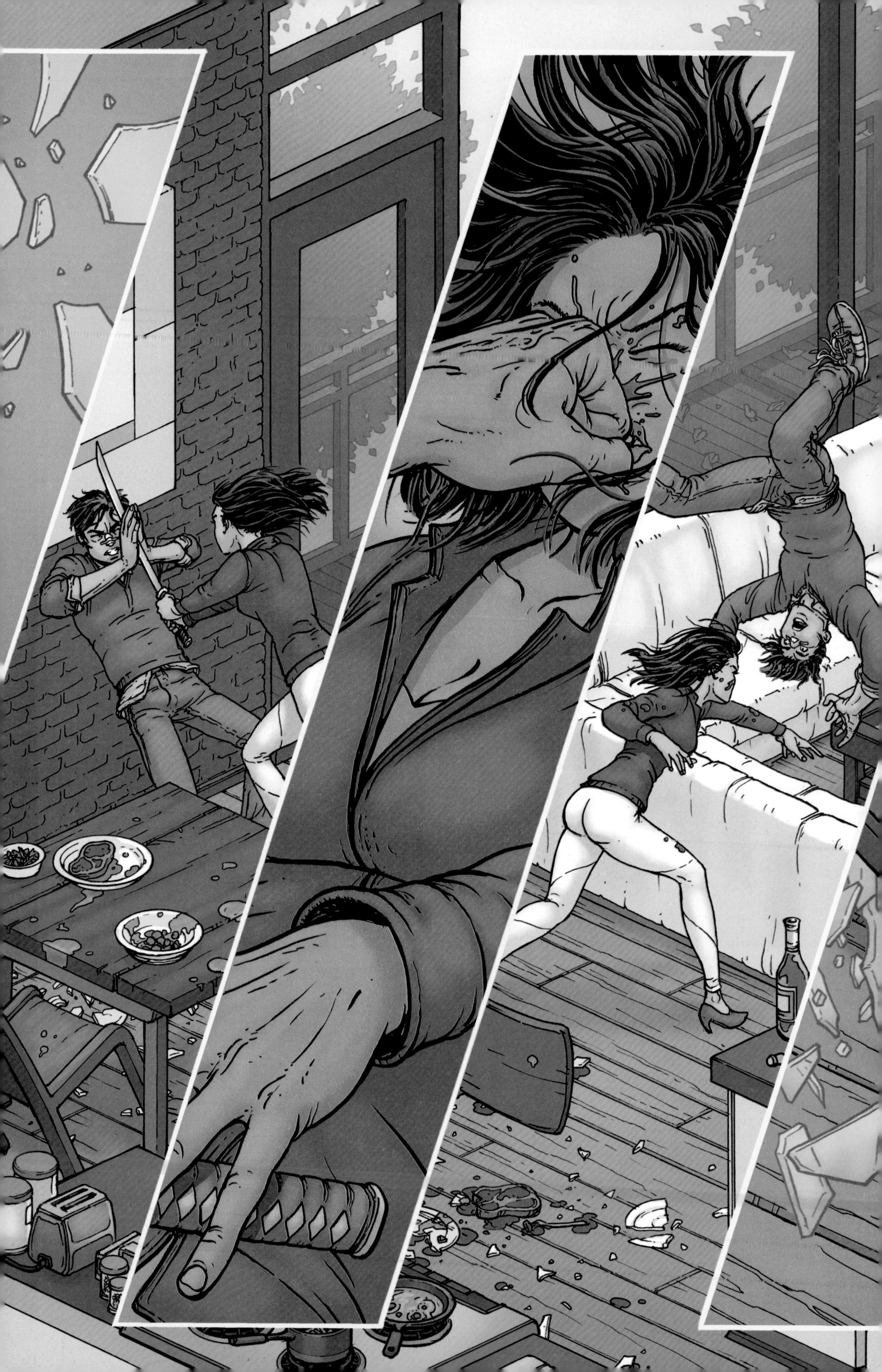

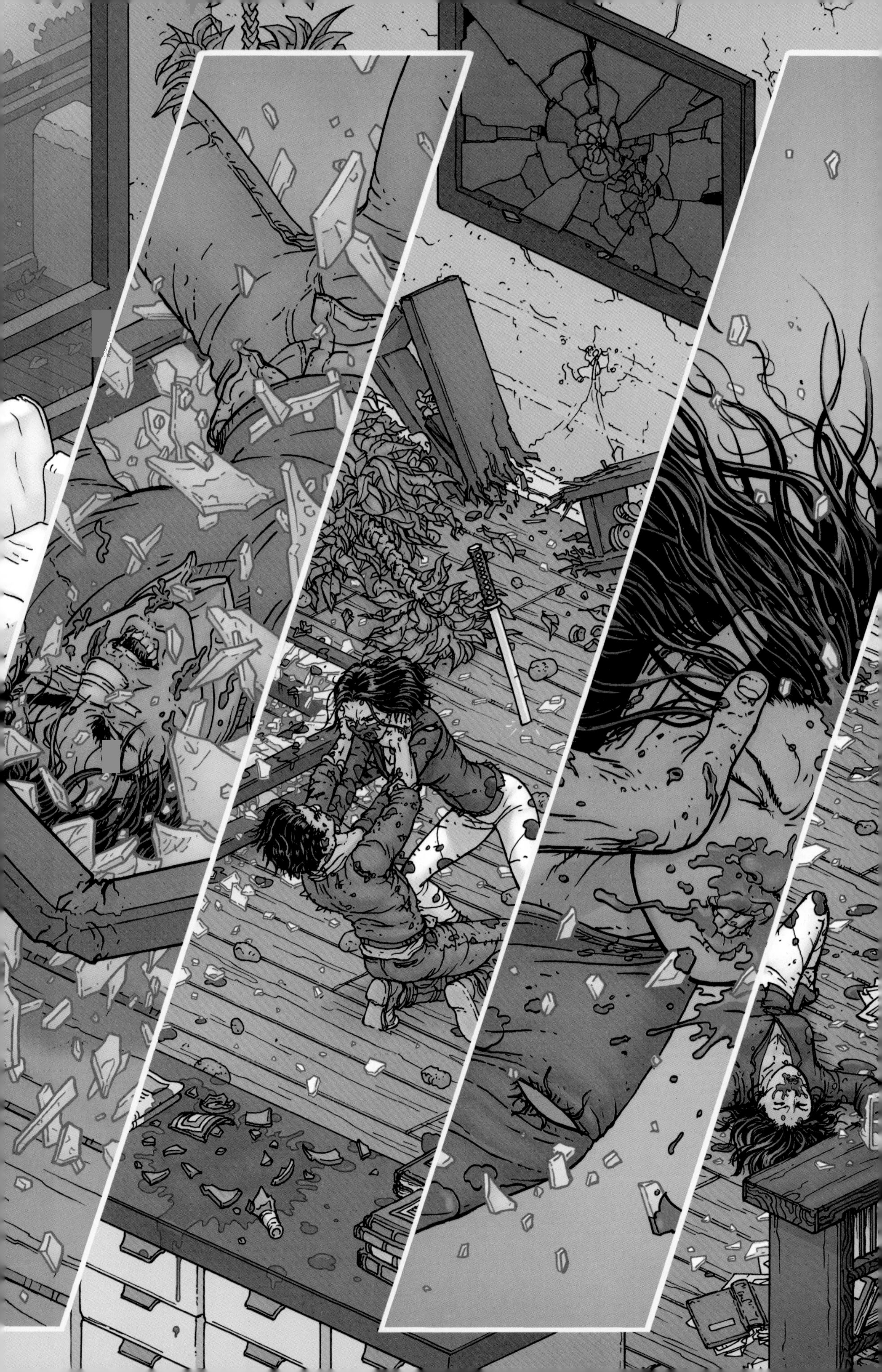

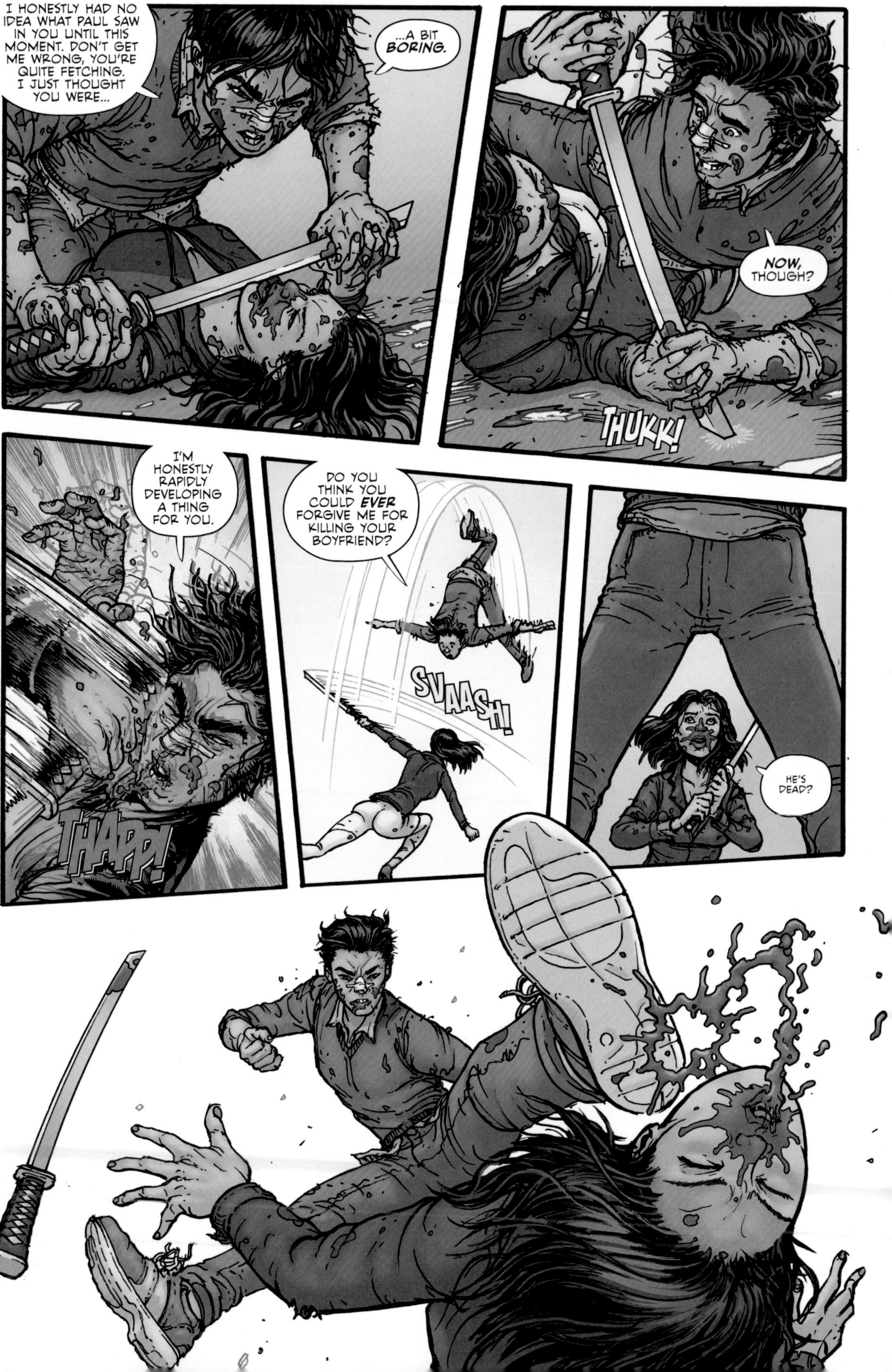

I HONESTLY HAD NO IDEA WHAT PAUL SAW IN YOU UNTIL THIS MOMENT. DON'T GET ME WRONG, YOU'RE QUITE FETCHING. I JUST THOUGHT YOU WERE...
...A BIT BORING.
NOW, THOUGH?
THUKK!
I'M HONESTLY RAPIDLY DEVELOPING A THING FOR YOU.
THAPP!
DO YOU THINK YOU COULD EVER FORGIVE ME FOR KILLING YOUR BOYFRIEND?
SVAASH!
HE'S DEAD?

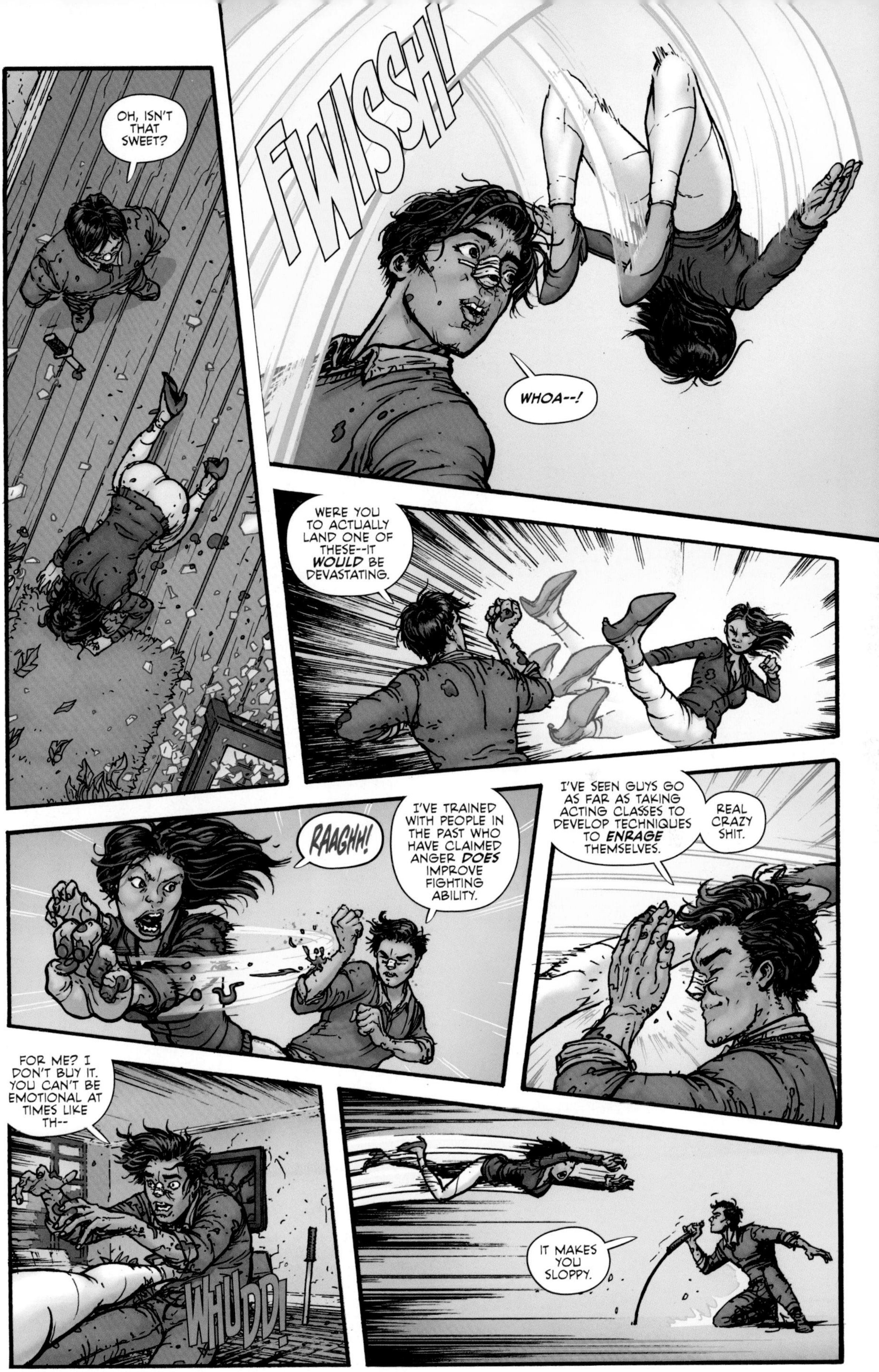
OH, ISN'T THAT SWEET?
FWISSH!
WHOA--!
WERE YOU TO ACTUALLY LAND ONE OF THESE--IT WOULD BE DEVASTATING.
RAAGHH!
I'VE TRAINED WITH PEOPLE IN THE PAST WHO HAVE CLAIMED ANGER DOES IMPROVE FIGHTING ABILITY.
I'VE SEEN GUYS GO AS FAR AS TAKING ACTING CLASSES TO DEVELOP TECHNIQUES TO ENRAGE THEMSELVES.
REAL CRAZY SHIT.
FOR ME? I DON'T BUY IT. YOU CAN'T BE EMOTIONAL AT TIMES LIKE TH--
WHUDD!
IT MAKES YOU SLOPPY.

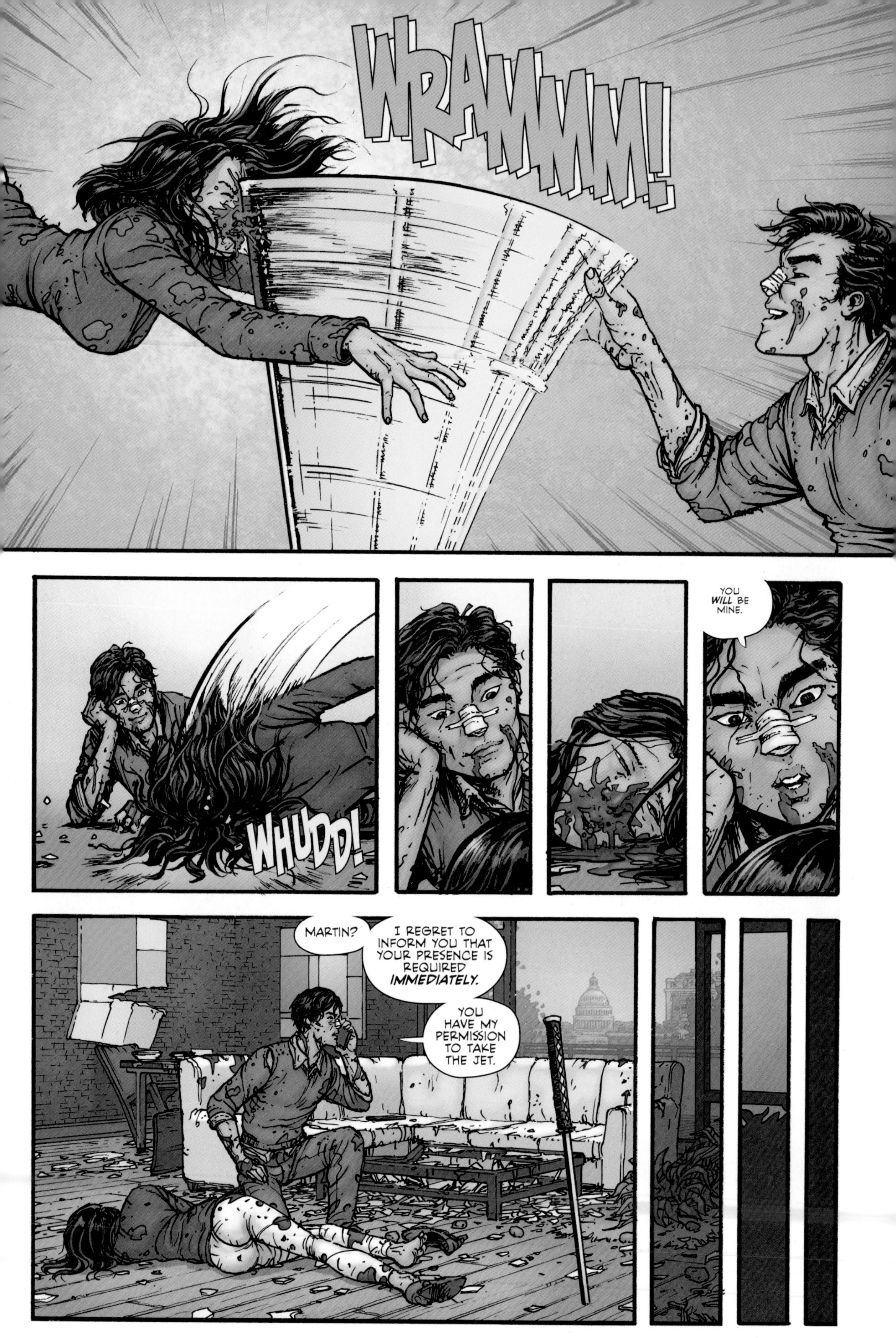
WRAMMM!
WHUDD!
YOU WILL BE MINE.
MARTIN?
I REGRET TO INFORM YOU THAT YOUR PRESENCE IS REQUIRED IMMEDIATELY.
YOU HAVE MY PERMISSION TO TAKE THE JET.

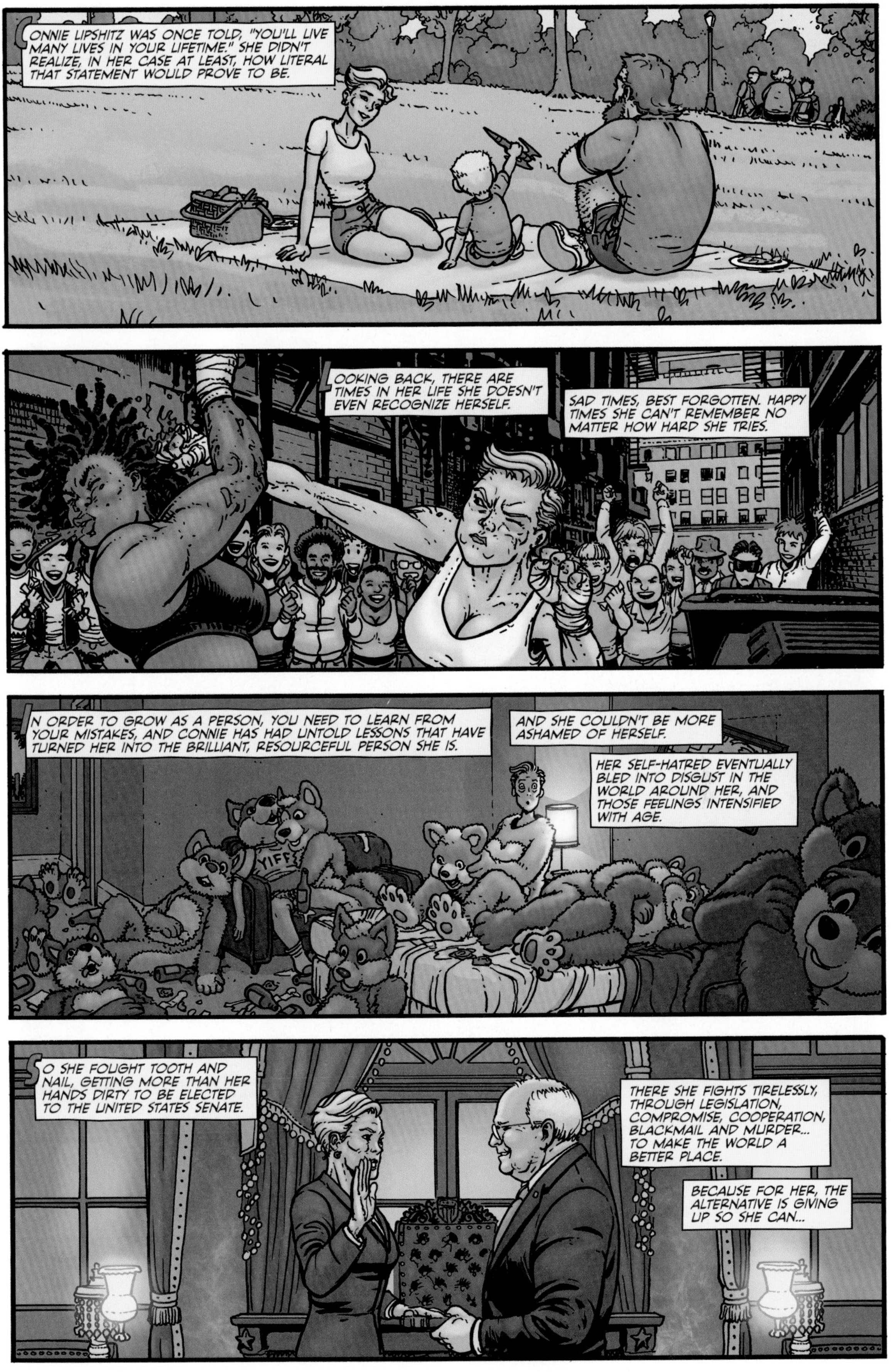
CONNIE LIPSHITZ WAS ONCE TOLD, "YOU'LL LIVE MANY LIVES IN YOUR LIFETIME." SHE DIDN'T REALIZE, IN HER CASE AT LEAST, HOW LITERAL THAT STATEMENT WOULD PROVE TO BE.
LOOKING BACK, THERE ARE TIMES IN HER LIFE SHE DOESN'T EVEN RECOGNIZE HERSELF.
SAD TIMES, BEST FORGOTTEN. HAPPY TIMES SHE CAN'T REMEMBER NO MATTER HOW HARD SHE TRIES.
IN ORDER TO GROW AS A PERSON, YOU NEED TO LEARN FROM YOUR MISTAKES, AND CONNIE HAS HAD UNTOLD LESSONS THAT HAVE TURNED HER INTO THE BRILLIANT, RESOURCEFUL PERSON SHE IS.
AND SHE COULDN'T BE MORE ASHAMED OF HERSELF.
HER SELF-HATRED EVENTUALLY BLED INTO DISGUST IN THE WORLD AROUND HER, AND THOSE FEELINGS INTENSIFIED WITH AGE.
YIFF
SO SHE FOUGHT TOOTH AND NAIL, GETTING MORE THAN HER HANDS DIRTY TO BE ELECTED TO THE UNITED STATES SENATE.
THERE SHE FIGHTS TIRELESSLY, THROUGH LEGISLATION, COMPROMISE, COOPERATION, BLACKMAIL AND MURDER... TO MAKE THE WORLD A BETTER PLACE.
BECAUSE FOR HER, THE ALTERNATIVE IS GIVING UP SO SHE CAN...

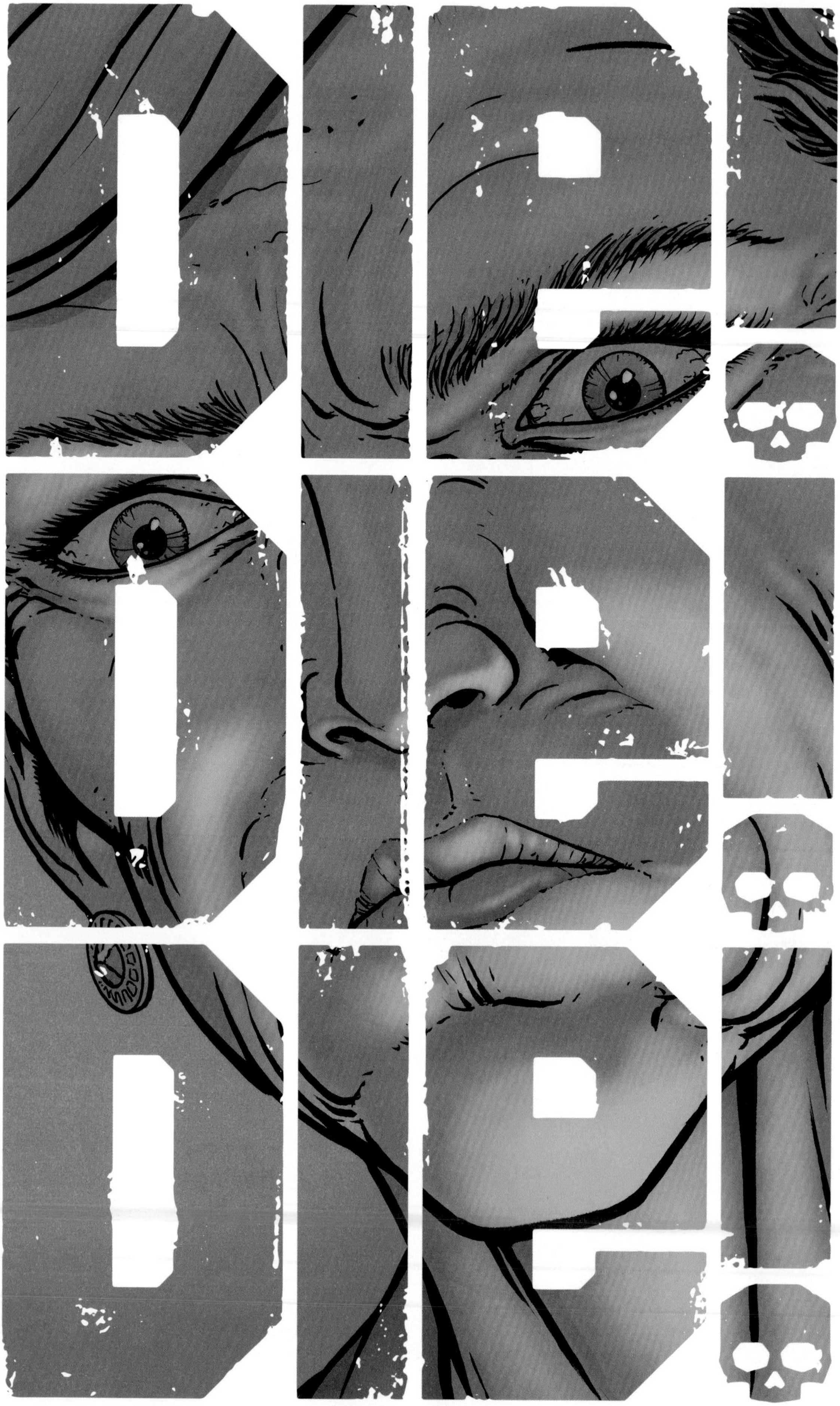
DIE!
DIE!
DIE!

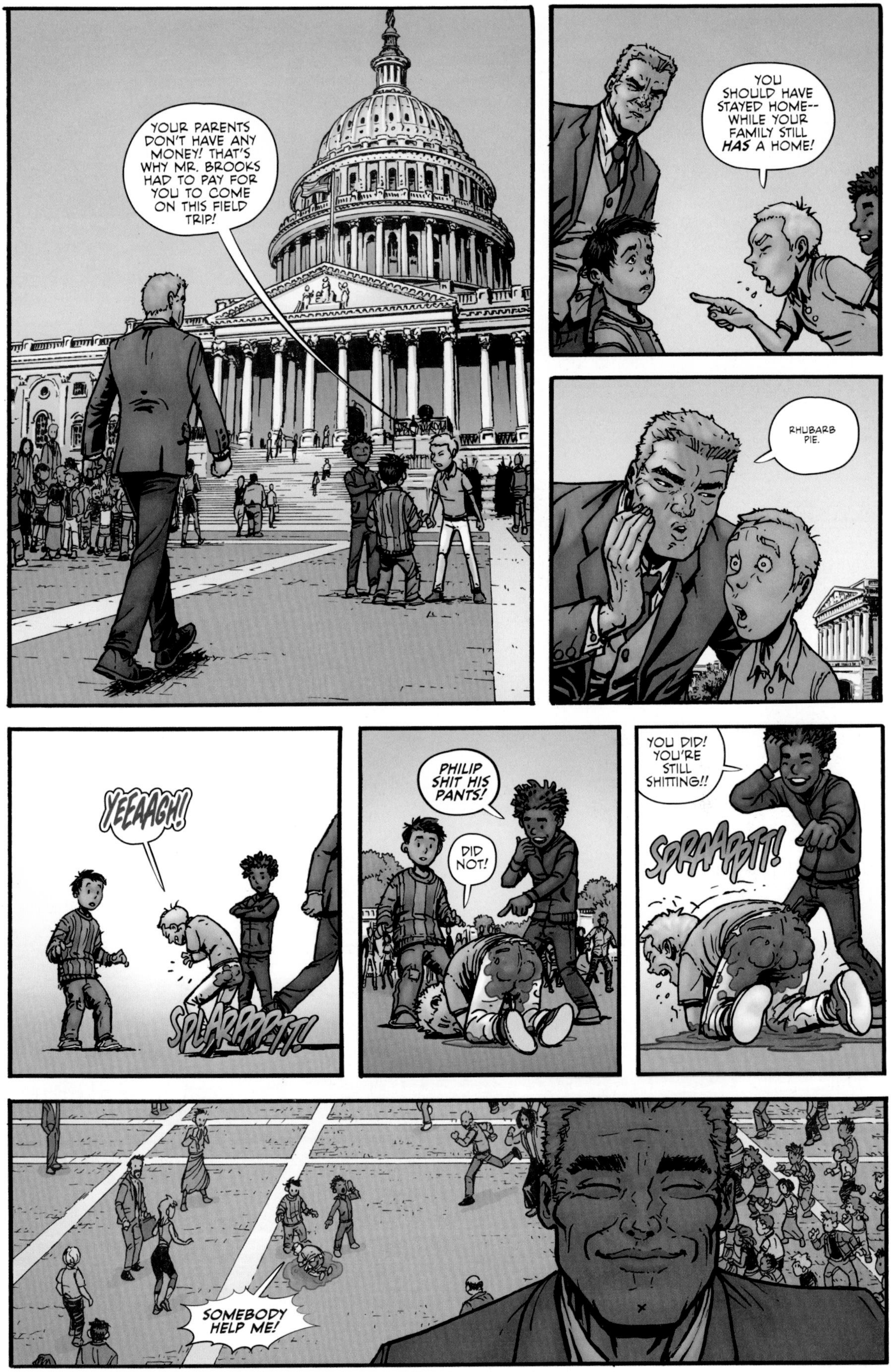
YOUR PARENTS DON'T HAVE ANY MONEY! THAT'S WHY MR. BROOKS HAD TO PAY FOR YOU TO COME ON THIS FIELD TRIP!
YOU SHOULD HAVE STAYED HOME-- WHILE YOUR FAMILY STILL HAS A HOME!
RHUBARB PIE.
YEEAAGH!
SPLARRPPTT!
PHILIP SHIT HIS PANTS!
DID NOT!
YOU DID! YOU'RE STILL SHITTING!!
SPRAAPTT!
SOMEBODY HELP ME!

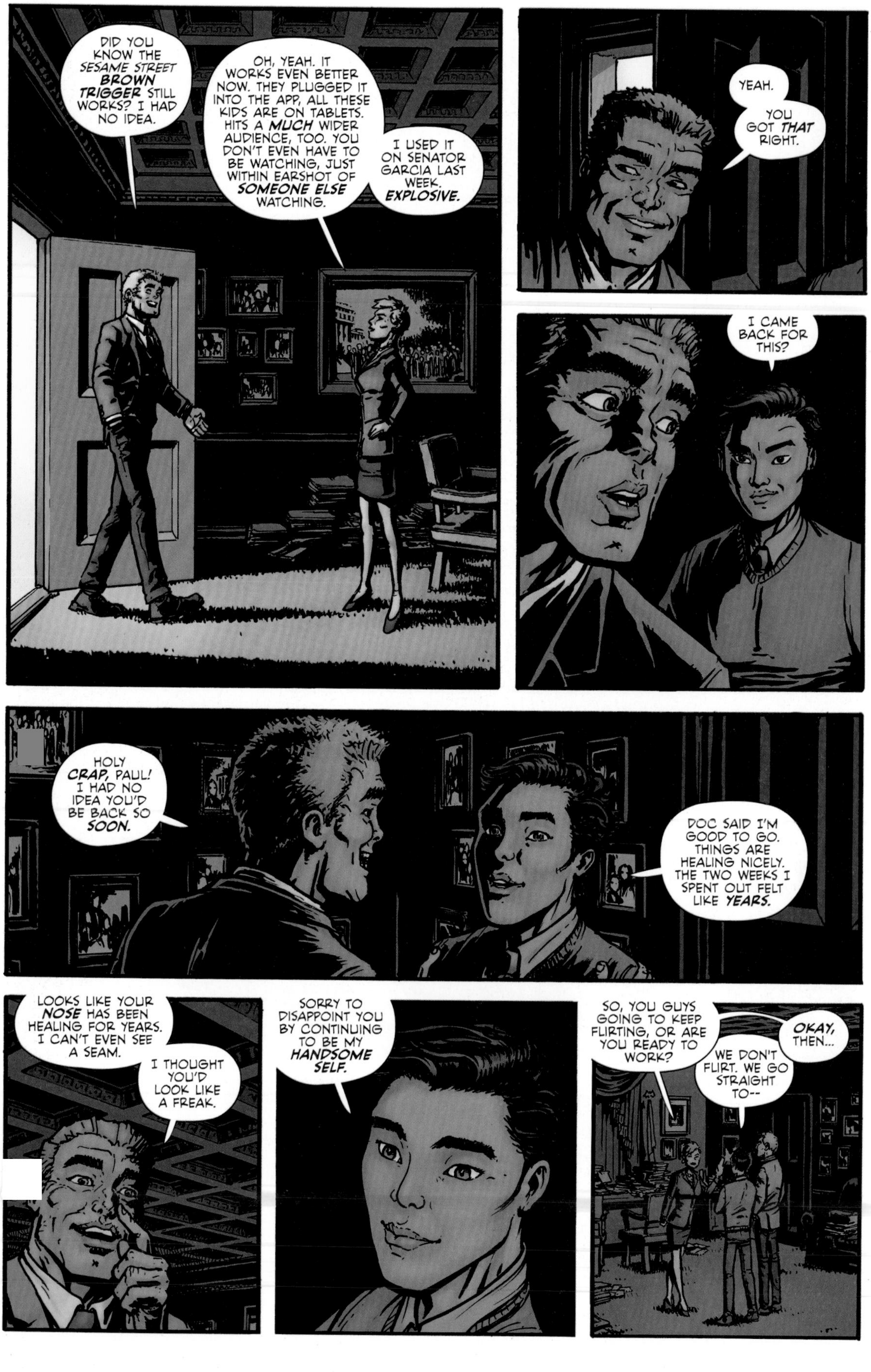

DID YOU KNOW THE SESAME STREET BROWN TRIGGER STILL WORKS? I HAD NO IDEA.
OH, YEAH. IT WORKS EVEN BETTER NOW. THEY PLUGGED IT INTO THE APP, ALL THESE KIDS ARE ON TABLETS. HITS A MUCH WIDER AUDIENCE, TOO. YOU DON'T EVEN HAVE TO BE WATCHING, JUST WITHIN EARSHOT OF SOMEONE ELSE WATCHING.
I USED IT ON SENATOR GARCIA LAST WEEK. EXPLOSIVE.
YEAH.
YOU GOT THAT RIGHT.
I CAME BACK FOR THIS?
HOLY CRAP, PAUL! I HAD NO IDEA YOU'D BE BACK SO SOON.
DOC SAID I'M GOOD TO GO. THINGS ARE HEALING NICELY. THE TWO WEEKS I SPENT OUT FELT LIKE YEARS.
LOOKS LIKE YOUR NOSE HAS BEEN HEALING FOR YEARS. I CAN'T EVEN SEE A SEAM.
I THOUGHT YOU'D LOOK LIKE A FREAK.
SORRY TO DISAPPOINT YOU BY CONTINUING TO BE MY HANDSOME SELF.
SO, YOU GUYS GOING TO KEEP FLIRTING, OR ARE YOU READY TO WORK?
WE DON'T FLIRT. WE GO STRAIGHT TO--
OKAY, THEN...

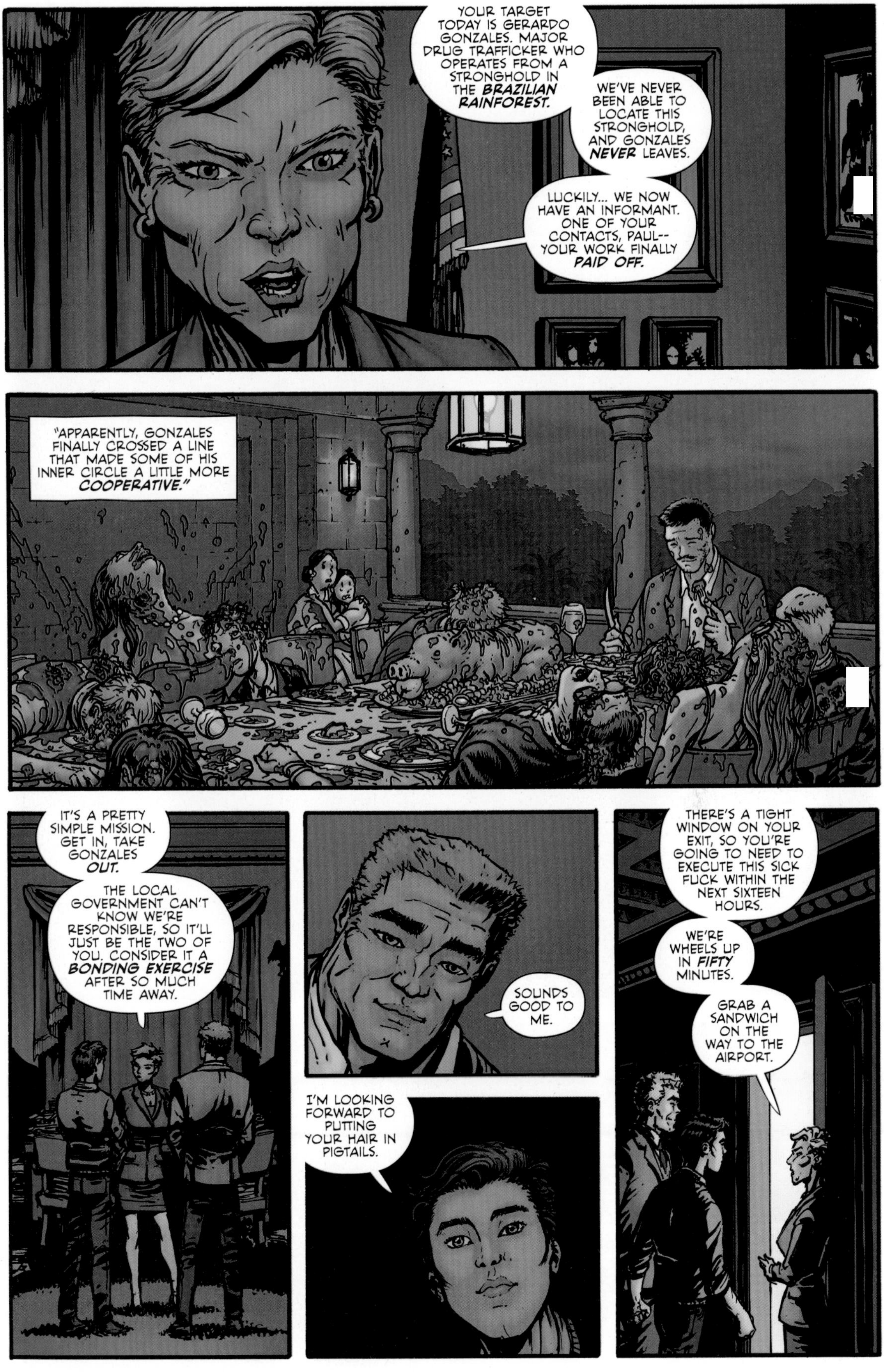
YOUR TARGET TODAY IS GERARDO GONZALES. MAJOR DRUG TRAFFICKER WHO OPERATES FROM A STRONGHOLD IN THE BRAZILIAN RAINFOREST.
WE'VE NEVER BEEN ABLE TO LOCATE THIS STRONGHOLD, AND GONZALES NEVER LEAVES.
LUCKILY... WE NOW HAVE AN INFORMANT. ONE OF YOUR CONTACTS, PAUL-- YOUR WORK FINALLY PAID OFF.
"APPARENTLY, GONZALES FINALLY CROSSED A LINE THAT MADE SOME OF HIS INNER CIRCLE A LITTLE MORE COOPERATIVE."
IT'S A PRETTY SIMPLE MISSION. GET IN, TAKE GONZALES OUT.
THE LOCAL GOVERNMENT CAN'T KNOW WE'RE RESPONSIBLE, SO IT'LL JUST BE THE TWO OF YOU. CONSIDER IT A BONDING EXERCISE AFTER SO MUCH TIME AWAY.
SOUNDS GOOD TO ME.
I'M LOOKING FORWARD TO PUTTING YOUR HAIR IN PIGTAILS.
THERE'S A TIGHT WINDOW ON YOUR EXIT, SO YOU'RE GOING TO NEED TO EXECUTE THIS SICK FUCK WITHIN THE NEXT SIXTEEN HOURS.
WE'RE WHEELS UP IN FIFTY MINUTES.
GRAB A SANDWICH ON THE WAY TO THE AIRPORT.

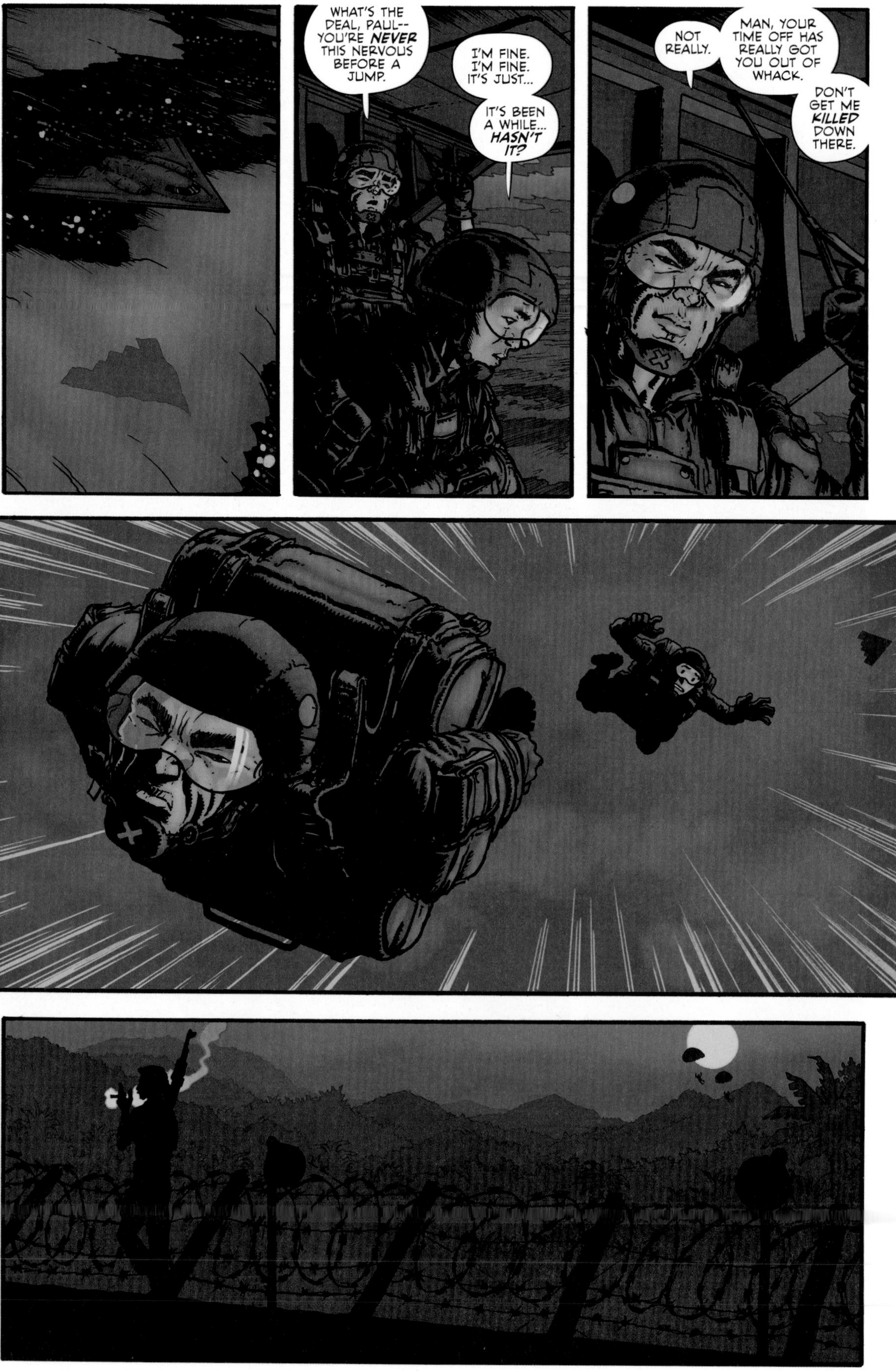

WHAT'S THE DEAL, PAUL-- YOU'RE NEVER THIS NERVOUS BEFORE A JUMP.
I'M FINE. I'M FINE. IT'S JUST...
IT'S BEEN A WHILE... HASN'T IT?
NOT REALLY.
MAN, YOUR TIME OFF HAS REALLY GOT YOU OUT OF WHACK.
DON'T GET ME KILLED DOWN THERE.

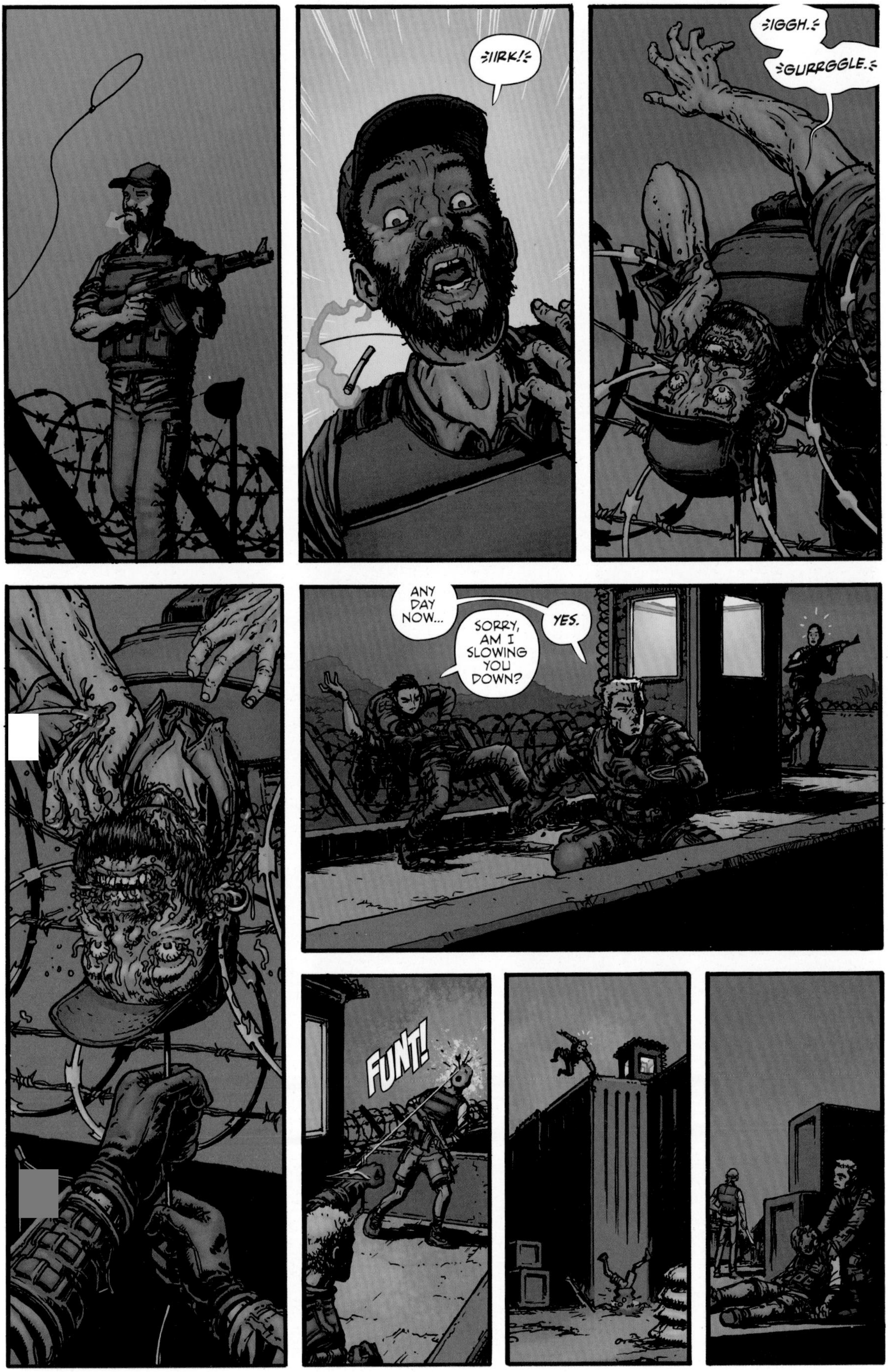
IIRK!
IGGH.
GURRGGLE.
ANY DAY NOW...
SORRY, AM I SLOWING YOU DOWN?
YES.
FUNT!

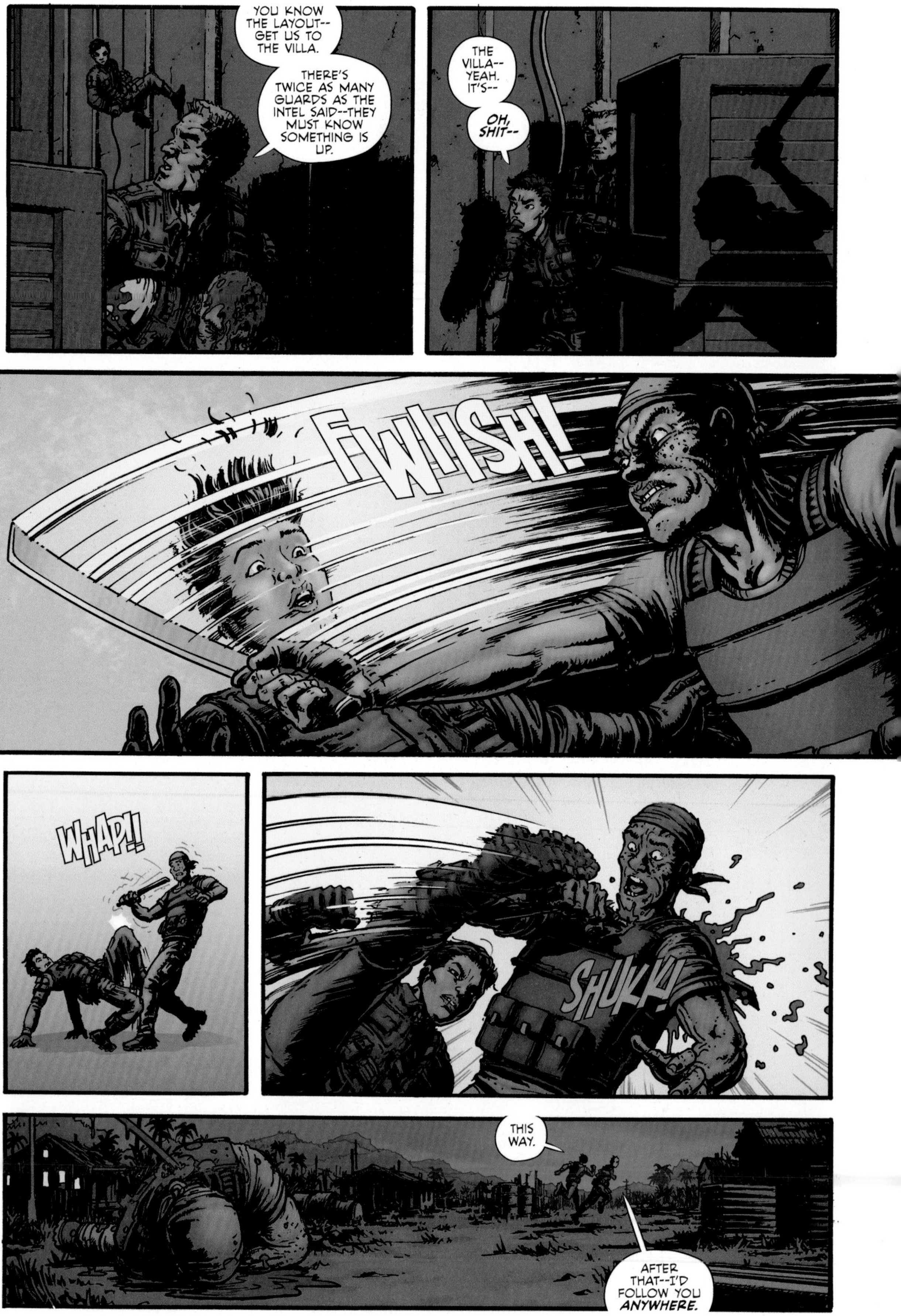

YOU KNOW THE LAYOUT--GET US TO THE VILLA.
THERE'S TWICE AS MANY GUARDS AS THE INTEL SAID--THEY MUST KNOW SOMETHING IS UP.
THE VILLA--YEAH. IT'S--
OH, SHIT--
FWISH!
WHAP!!
SHUKK!
THIS WAY.
AFTER THAT--I'D FOLLOW YOU ANYWHERE.

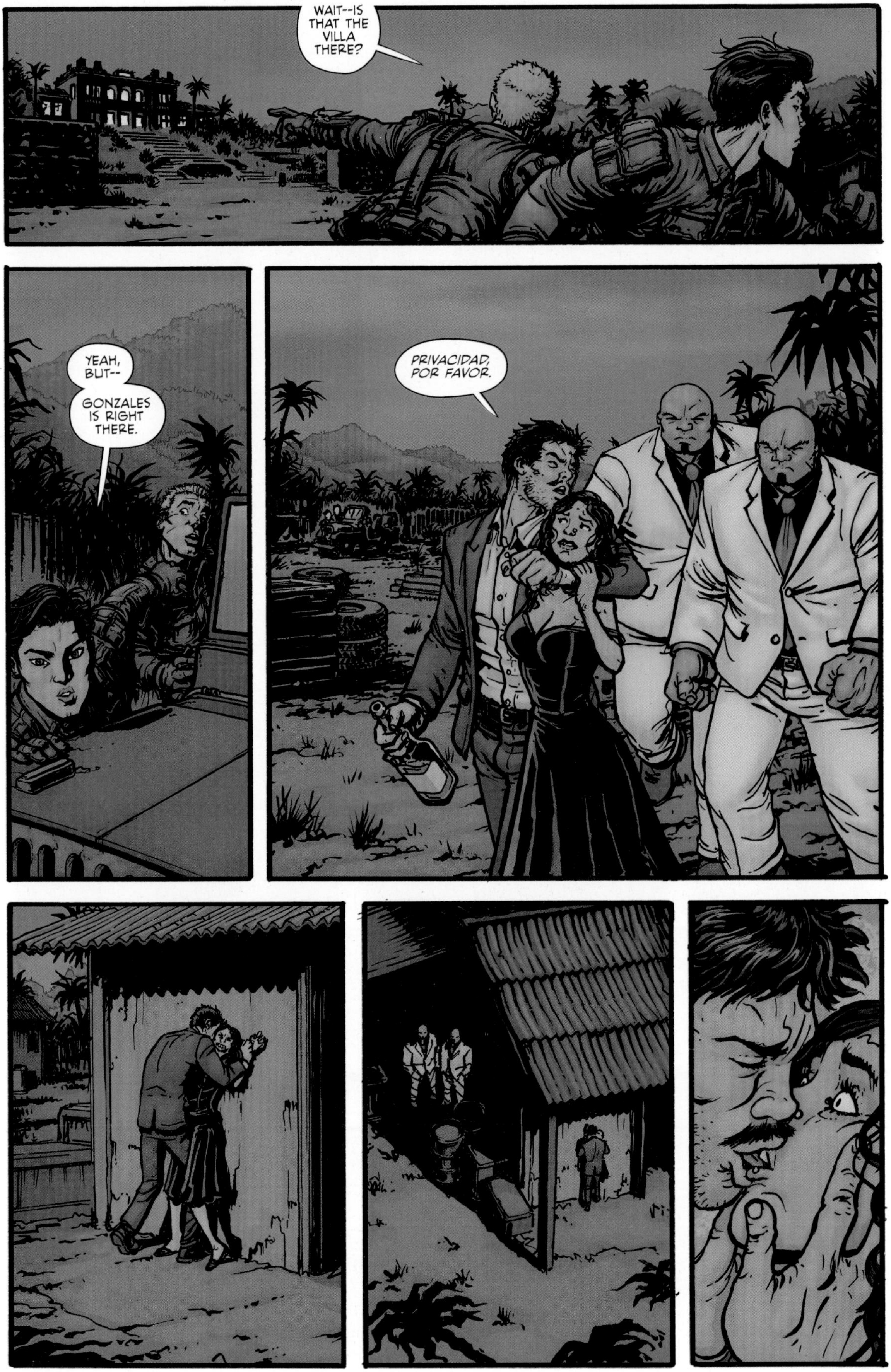
WAIT--IS THAT THE VILLA THERE?
YEAH, BUT--
GONZALES IS RIGHT THERE.
PRIVACIDAD, POR FAVOR.

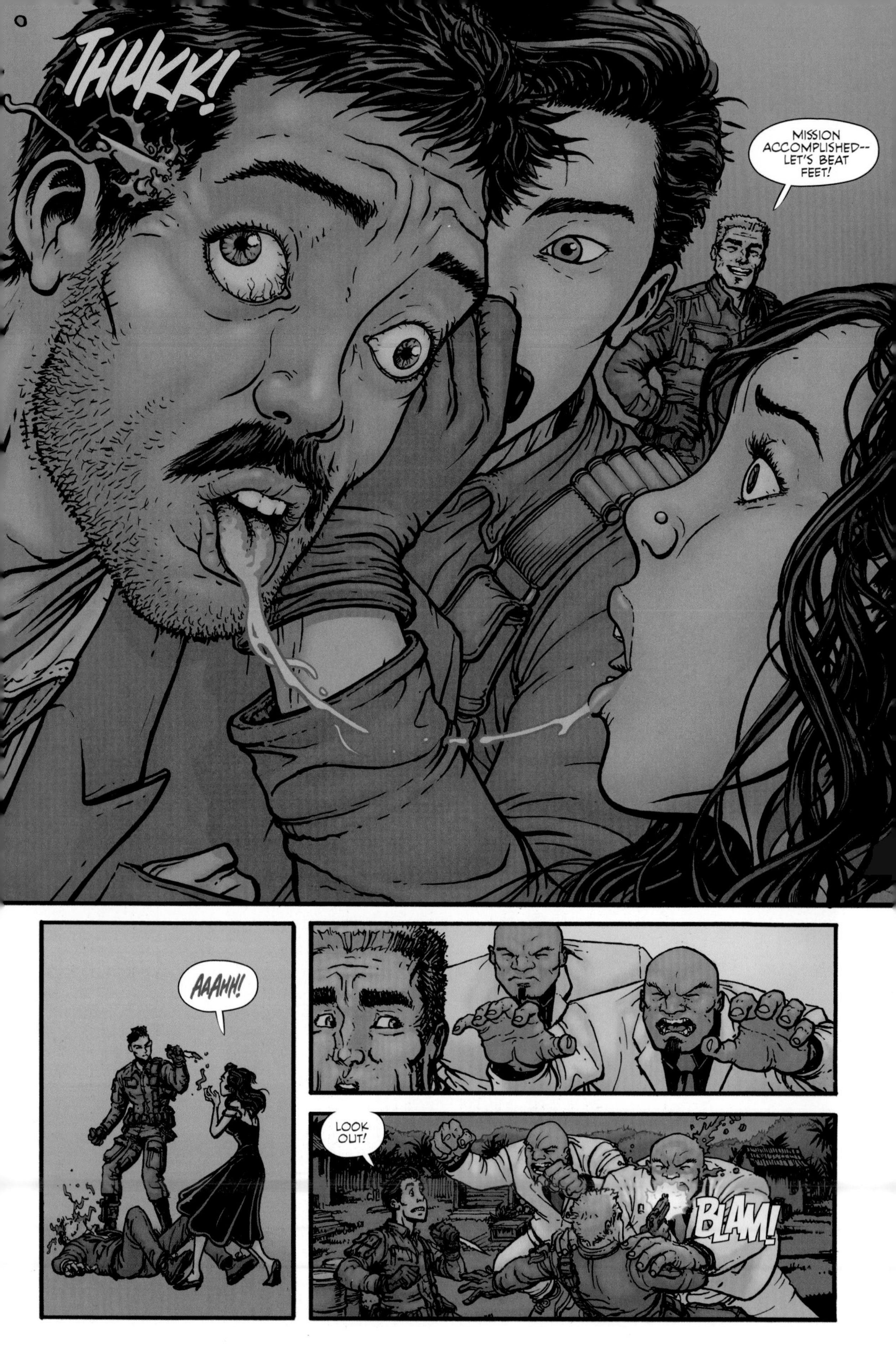
THUKK!
MISSION ACCOMPLISHED-- LET'S BEAT FEET!
AAAHH!
LOOK OUT!
BLAM!

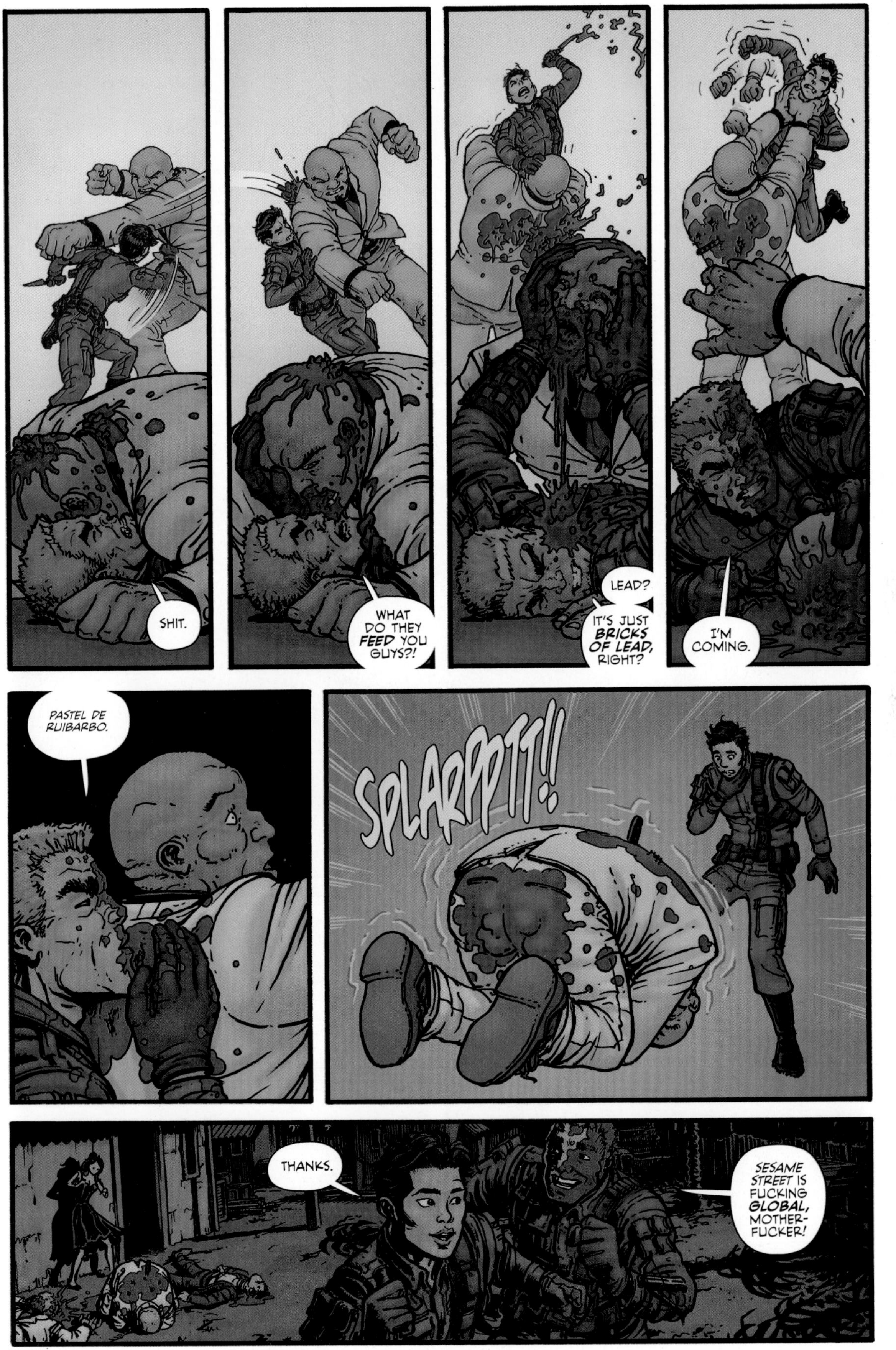
SHIT.
WHAT DO THEY FEED YOU GUYS?!
LEAD?
IT'S JUST BRICKS OF LEAD, RIGHT?
I'M COMING.
PASTEL DE RUIBARBO.
SPLARPPTT!!
THANKS.
SESAME STREET IS FUCKING GLOBAL, MOTHER-FUCKER!

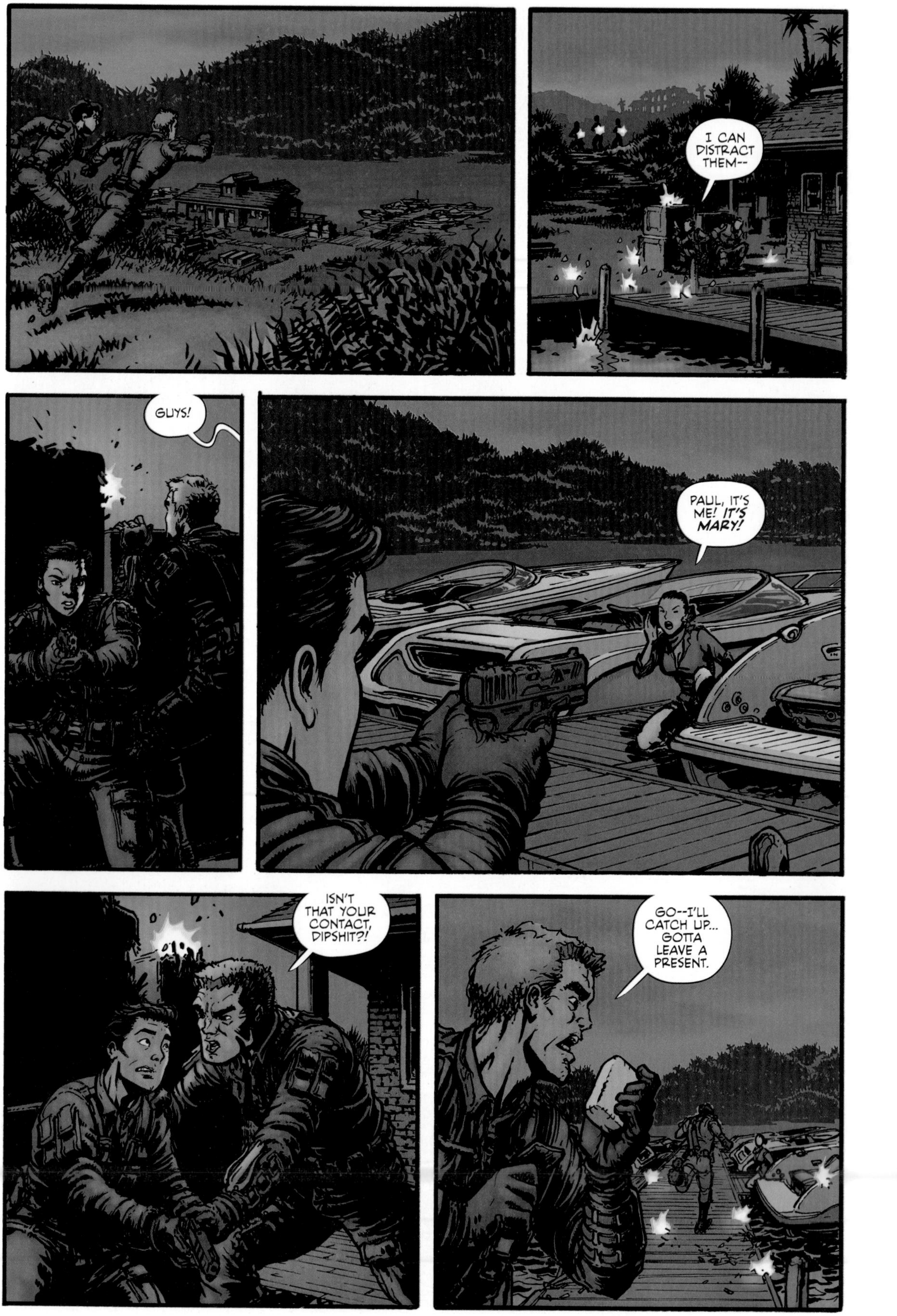
I CAN DISTRACT THEM--
GUYS!
PAUL, IT'S ME! *IT'S MARY!*
ISN'T THAT YOUR CONTACT, DIPSHIT?!
GO--I'LL CATCH UP... GOTTA LEAVE A PRESENT.

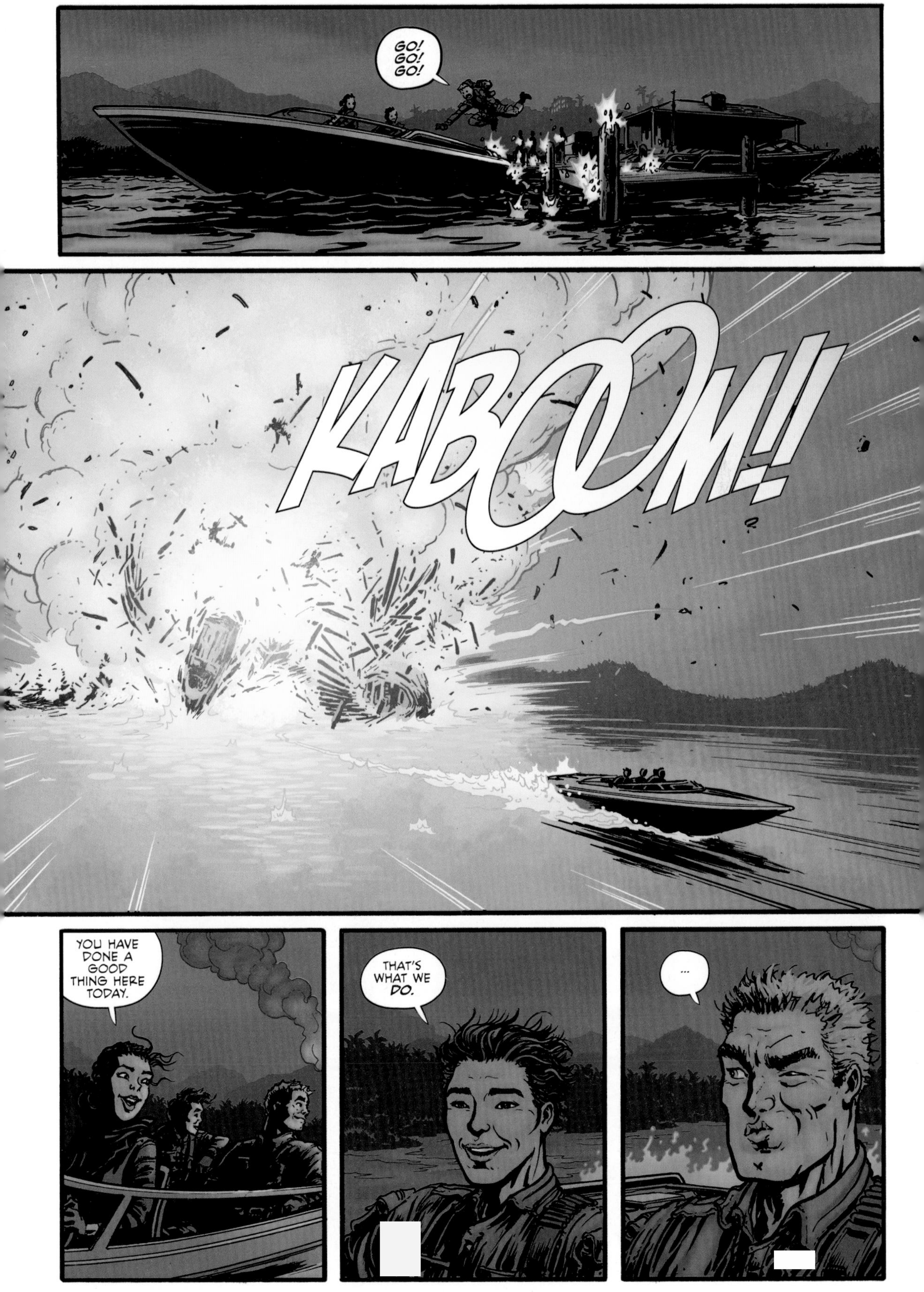
GO! GO! GO!
KABOOM!!
YOU HAVE DONE A GOOD THING HERE TODAY.
THAT'S WHAT WE DO.
...

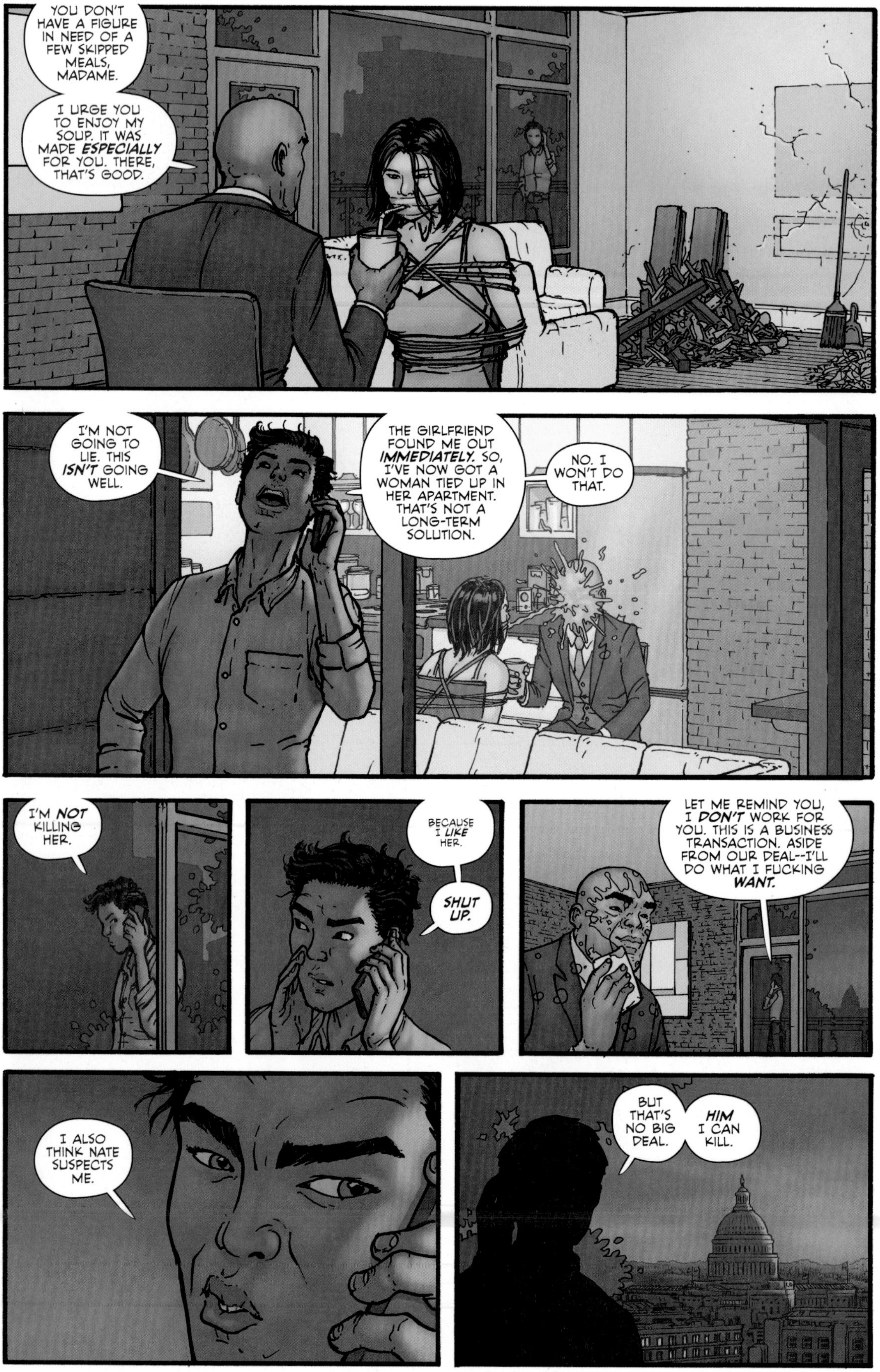
YOU DON'T HAVE A FIGURE IN NEED OF A FEW SKIPPED MEALS, MADAME.
I URGE YOU TO ENJOY MY SOUP. IT WAS MADE ESPECIALLY FOR YOU. THERE, THAT'S GOOD.
I'M NOT GOING TO LIE. THIS ISN'T GOING WELL.
THE GIRLFRIEND FOUND ME OUT IMMEDIATELY. SO, I'VE NOW GOT A WOMAN TIED UP IN HER APARTMENT. THAT'S NOT A LONG-TERM SOLUTION.
NO. I WON'T DO THAT.
I'M NOT KILLING HER.
BECAUSE I LIKE HER.
SHUT UP.
LET ME REMIND YOU, I DON'T WORK FOR YOU. THIS IS A BUSINESS TRANSACTION. ASIDE FROM OUR DEAL--I'LL DO WHAT I FUCKING WANT.
I ALSO THINK NATE SUSPECTS ME.
BUT THAT'S NO BIG DEAL.
HIM I CAN KILL.

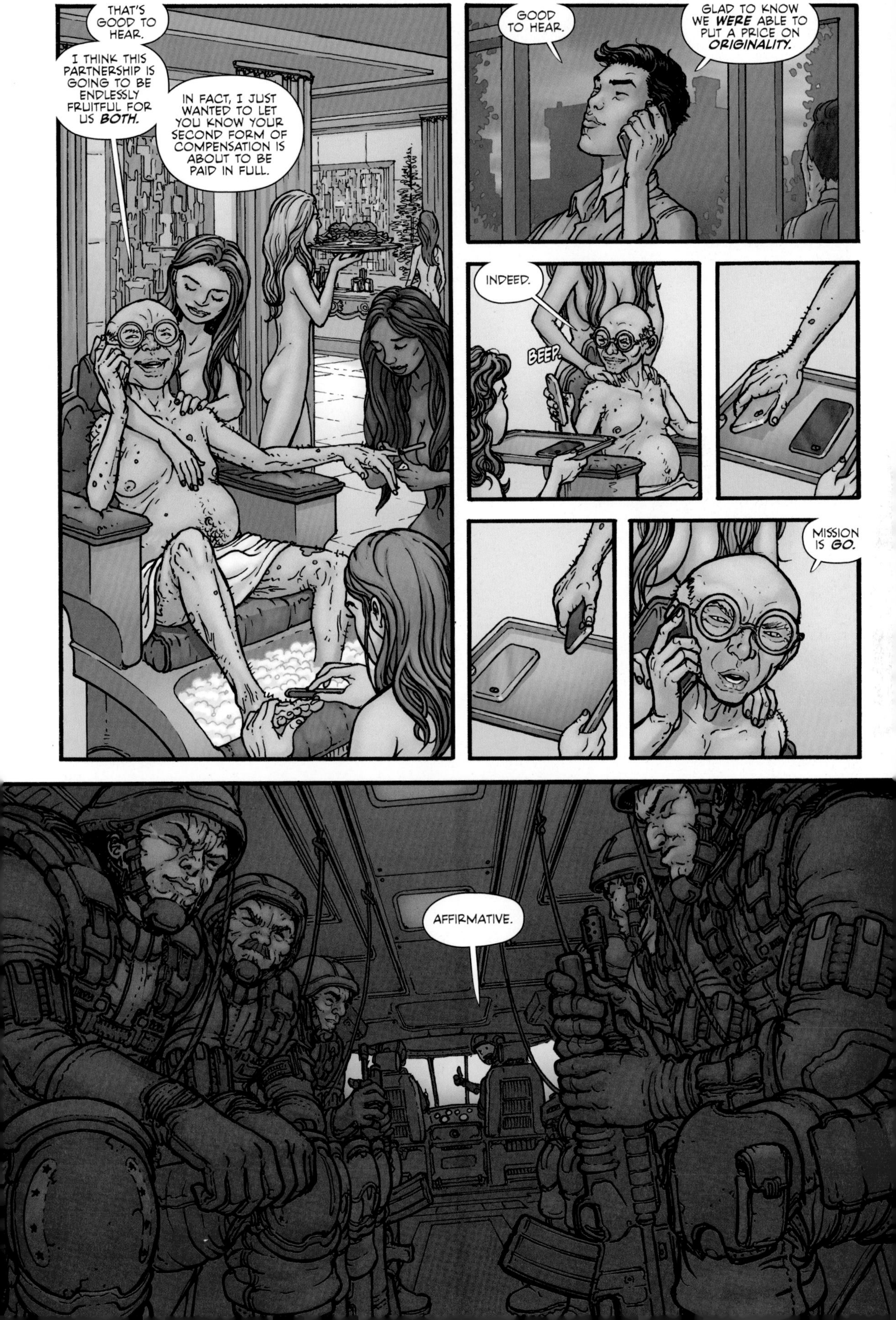
THAT'S GOOD TO HEAR.
I THINK THIS PARTNERSHIP IS GOING TO BE ENDLESSLY FRUITFUL FOR US BOTH.
IN FACT, I JUST WANTED TO LET YOU KNOW YOUR SECOND FORM OF COMPENSATION IS ABOUT TO BE PAID IN FULL.
GOOD TO HEAR.
GLAD TO KNOW WE WERE ABLE TO PUT A PRICE ON ORIGINALITY.
INDEED.
BEEP.
MISSION IS GO.
AFFIRMATIVE.

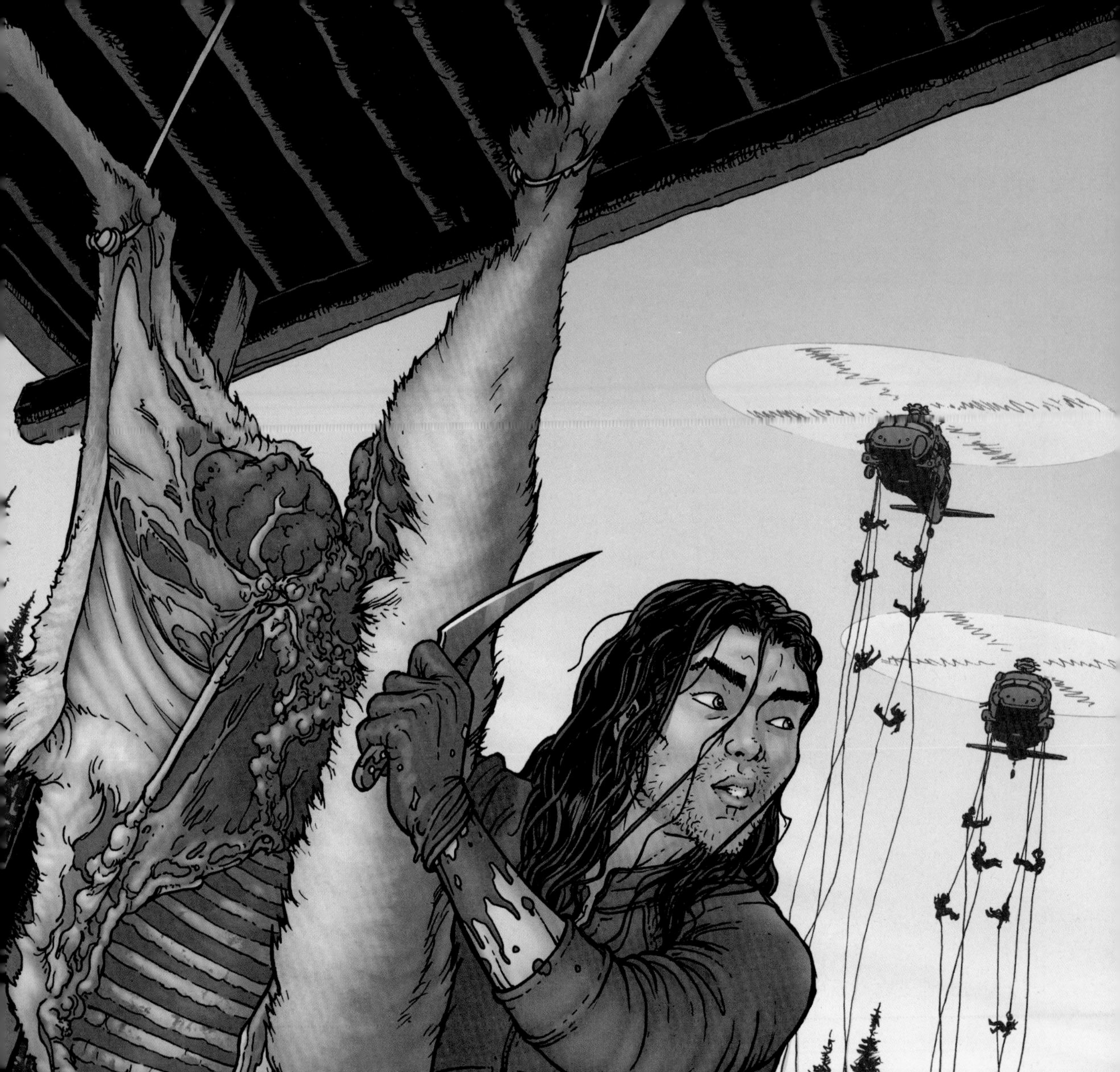

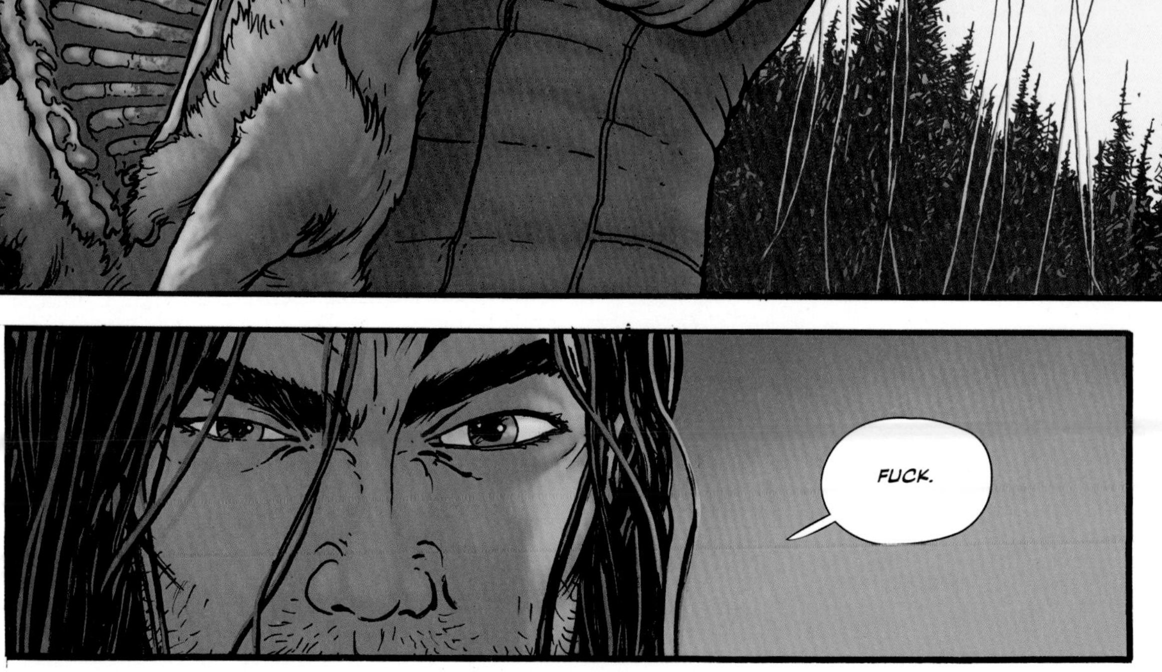
FUCK.

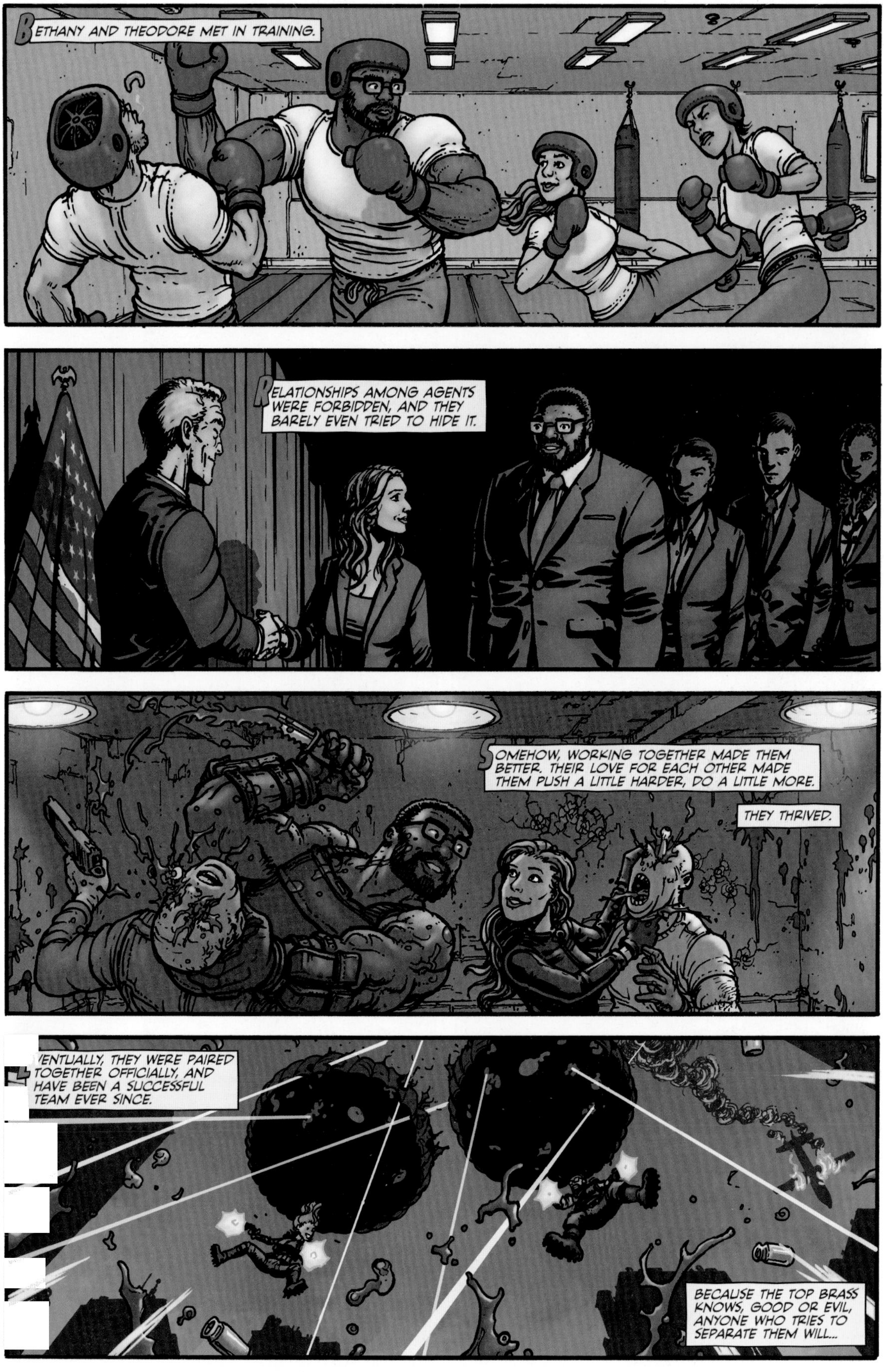
BETHANY AND THEODORE MET IN TRAINING.
RELATIONSHIPS AMONG AGENTS WERE FORBIDDEN, AND THEY BARELY EVEN TRIED TO HIDE IT.
SOMEHOW, WORKING TOGETHER MADE THEM BETTER. THEIR LOVE FOR EACH OTHER MADE THEM PUSH A LITTLE HARDER, DO A LITTLE MORE.
THEY THRIVED.
EVENTUALLY, THEY WERE PAIRED TOGETHER OFFICIALLY, AND HAVE BEEN A SUCCESSFUL TEAM EVER SINCE.
BECAUSE THE TOP BRASS KNOWS, GOOD OR EVIL, ANYONE WHO TRIES TO SEPARATE THEM WILL...

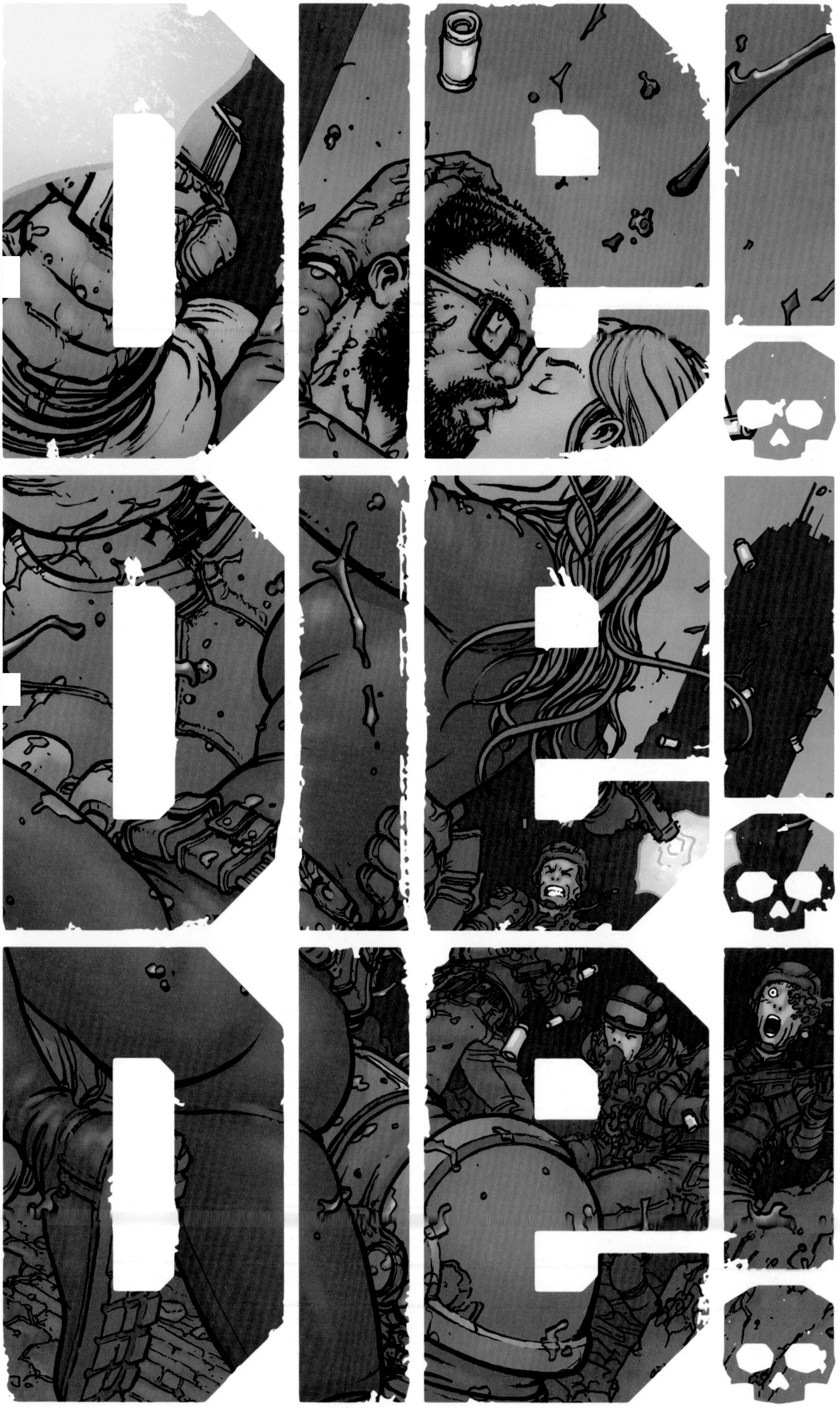
DIE!
DIE!
DIE!

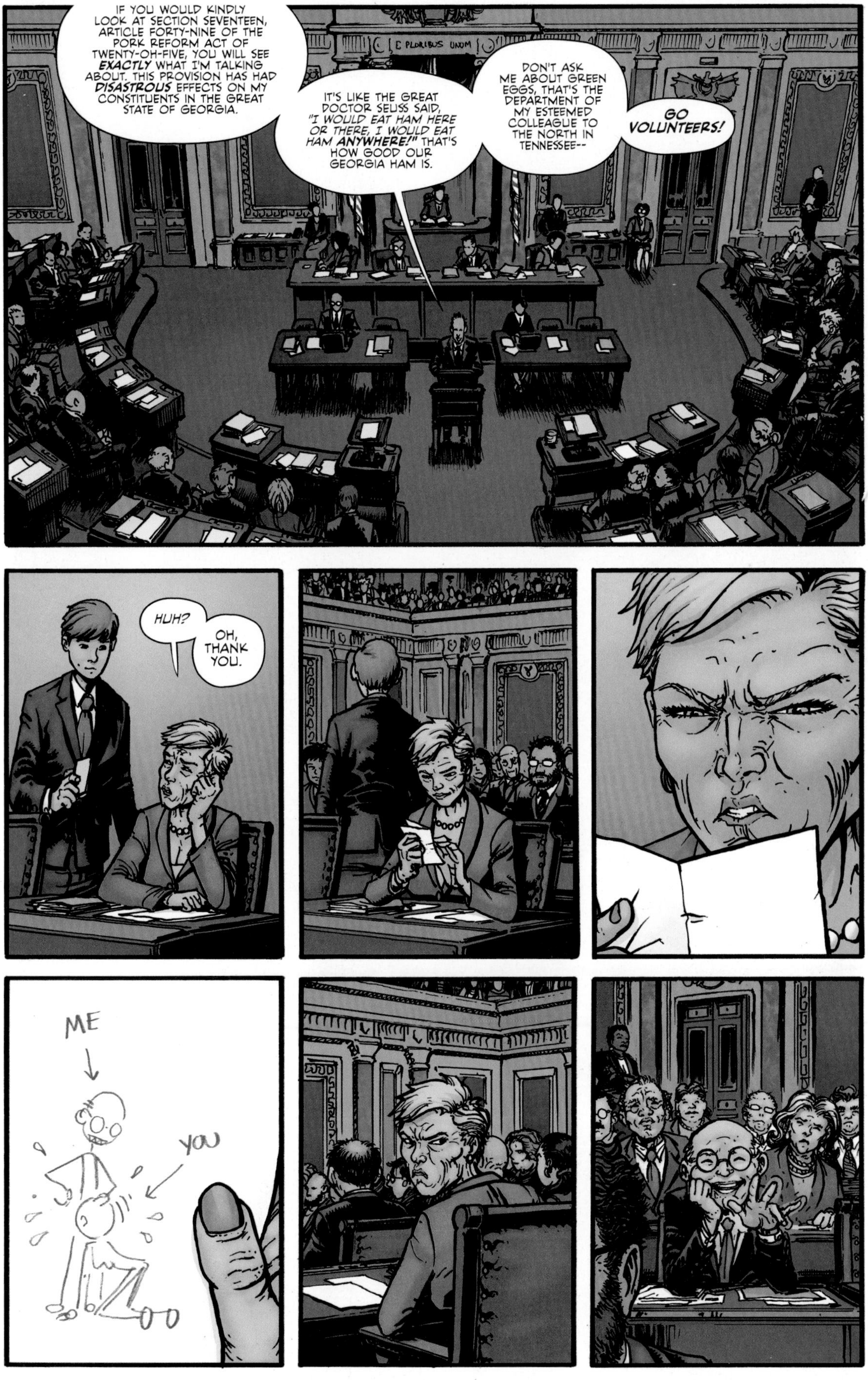
IF YOU WOULD KINDLY LOOK AT SECTION SEVENTEEN, ARTICLE FORTY-NINE OF THE PORK REFORM ACT OF TWENTY-OH-FIVE, YOU WILL SEE EXACTLY WHAT I'M TALKING ABOUT. THIS PROVISION HAS HAD DISASTROUS EFFECTS ON MY CONSTITUENTS IN THE GREAT STATE OF GEORGIA.
E PLURIBUS UNUM
IT'S LIKE THE GREAT DOCTOR SEUSS SAID, "I WOULD EAT HAM HERE OR THERE, I WOULD EAT HAM ANYWHERE!" THAT'S HOW GOOD OUR GEORGIA HAM IS.
DON'T ASK ME ABOUT GREEN EGGS, THAT'S THE DEPARTMENT OF MY ESTEEMED COLLEAGUE TO THE NORTH IN TENNESSEE--
GO VOLUNTEERS!
HUH?
OH, THANK YOU.
ME
YOU

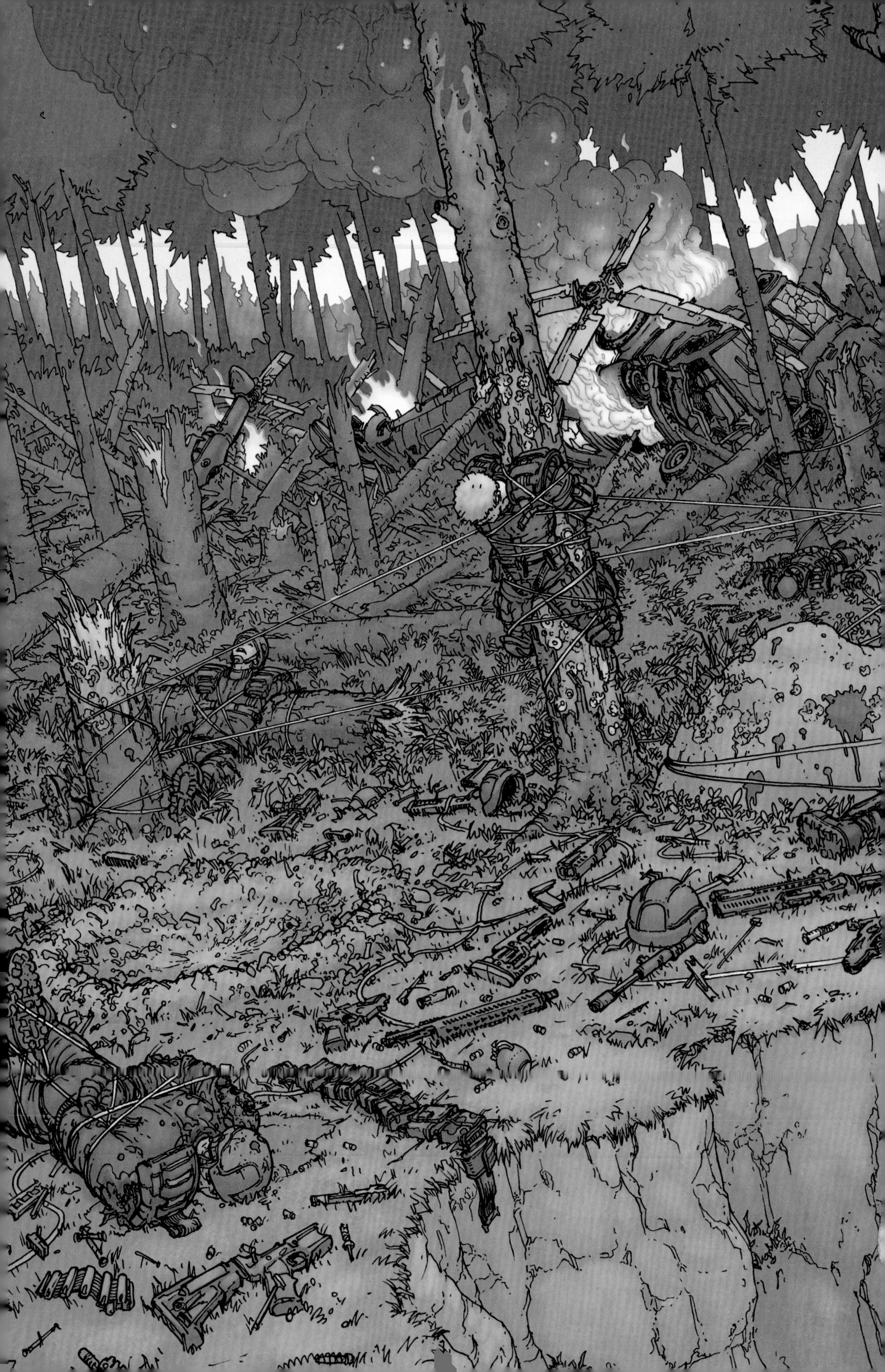

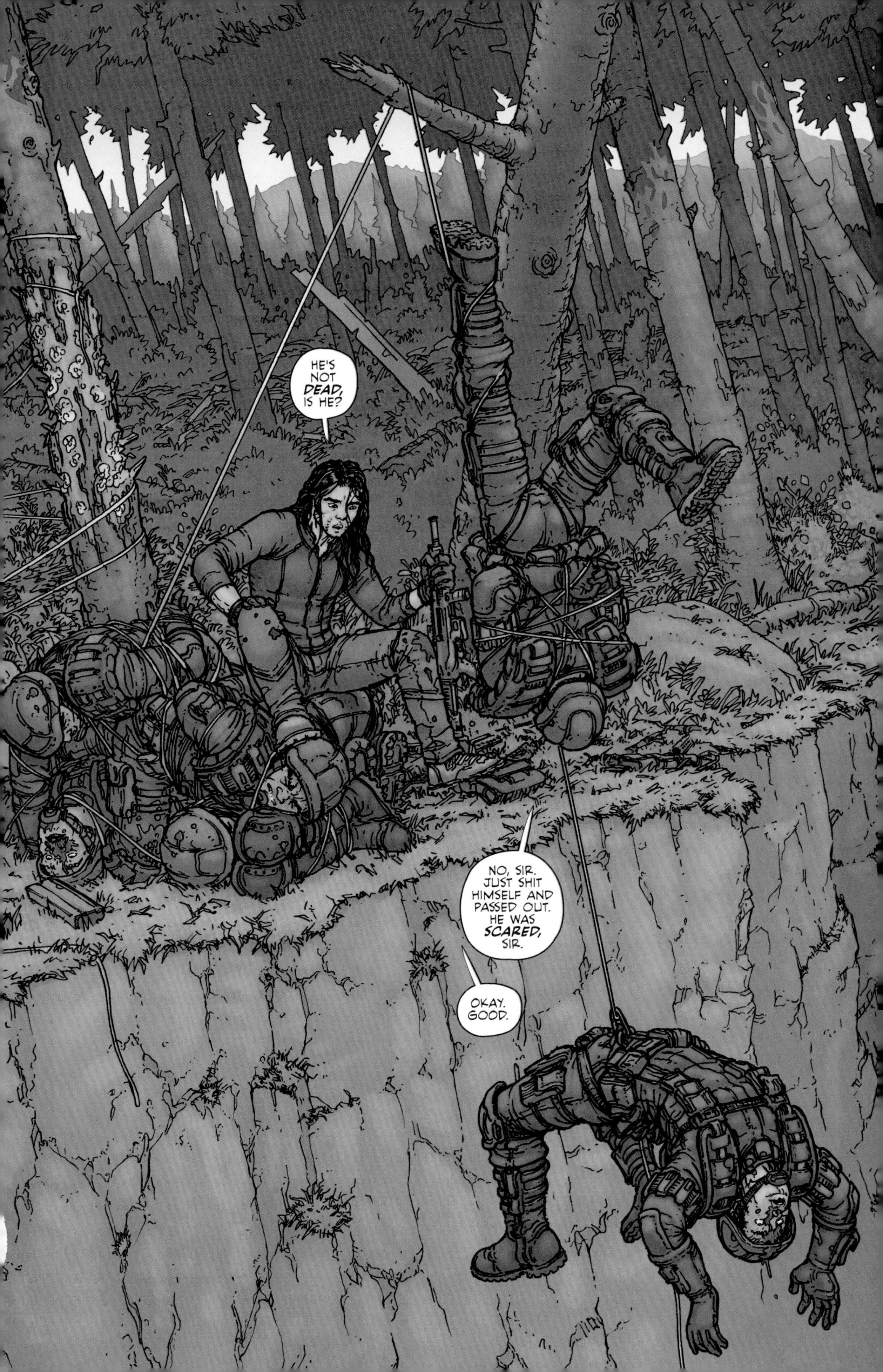
HE'S NOT DEAD, IS HE?
NO, SIR. JUST SHIT HIMSELF AND PASSED OUT. HE WAS SCARED, SIR.
OKAY. GOOD.

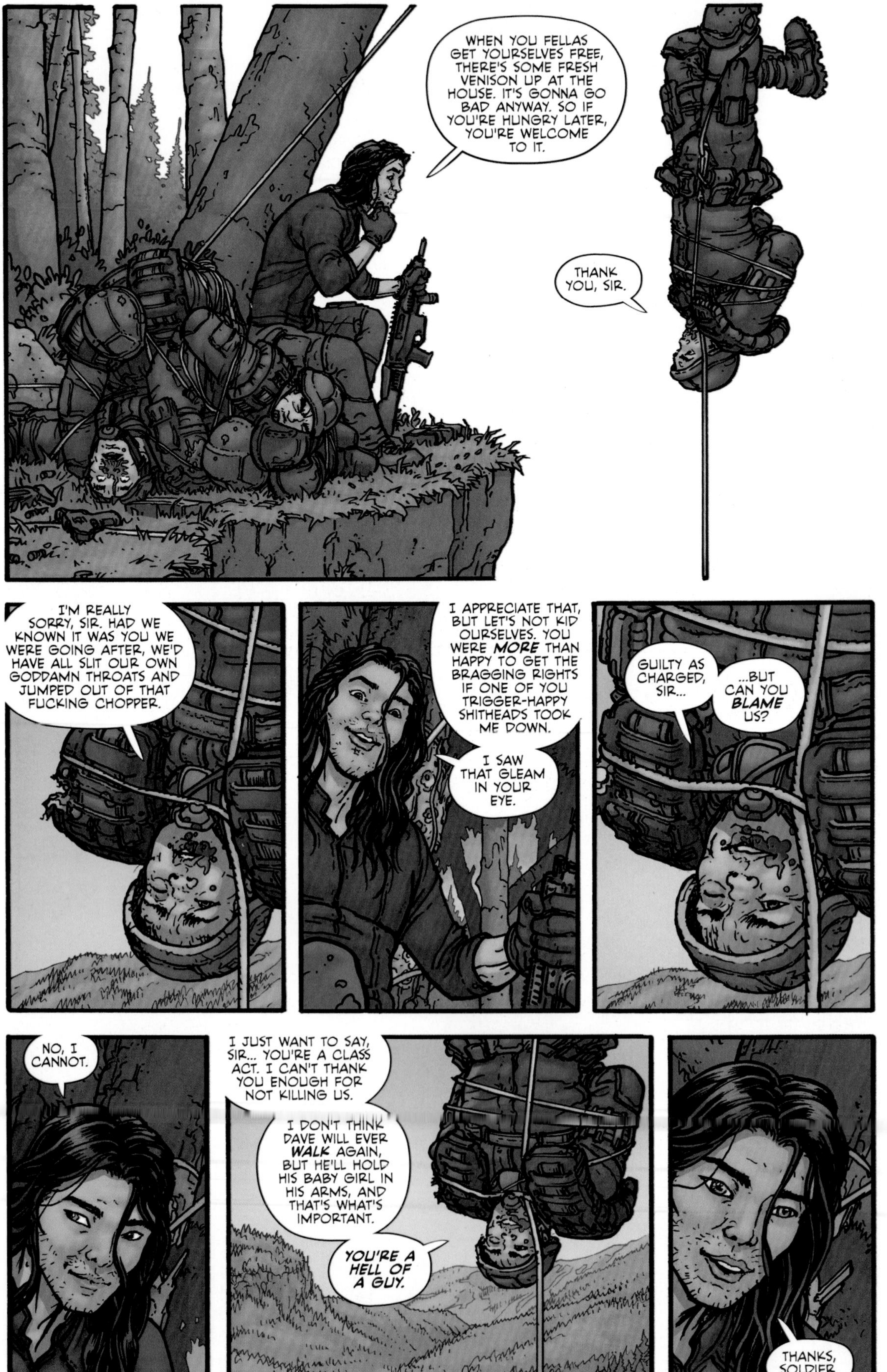
WHEN YOU FELLAS GET YOURSELVES FREE, THERE'S SOME FRESH VENISON UP AT THE HOUSE. IT'S GONNA GO BAD ANYWAY. SO IF YOU'RE HUNGRY LATER, YOU'RE WELCOME TO IT.
THANK YOU, SIR.
I'M REALLY SORRY, SIR. HAD WE KNOWN IT WAS YOU WE WERE GOING AFTER, WE'D HAVE ALL SLIT OUR OWN GODDAMN THROATS AND JUMPED OUT OF THAT FUCKING CHOPPER.
I APPRECIATE THAT, BUT LET'S NOT KID OURSELVES. YOU WERE MORE THAN HAPPY TO GET THE BRAGGING RIGHTS IF ONE OF YOU TRIGGER-HAPPY SHITHEADS TOOK ME DOWN.
I SAW THAT GLEAM IN YOUR EYE.
GUILTY AS CHARGED, SIR...
...BUT CAN YOU BLAME US?
NO, I CANNOT.
I JUST WANT TO SAY, SIR... YOU'RE A CLASS ACT. I CAN'T THANK YOU ENOUGH FOR NOT KILLING US.
I DON'T THINK DAVE WILL EVER WALK AGAIN, BUT HE'LL HOLD HIS BABY GIRL IN HIS ARMS, AND THAT'S WHAT'S IMPORTANT.
YOU'RE A HELL OF A GUY.
THANKS, SOLDIER.

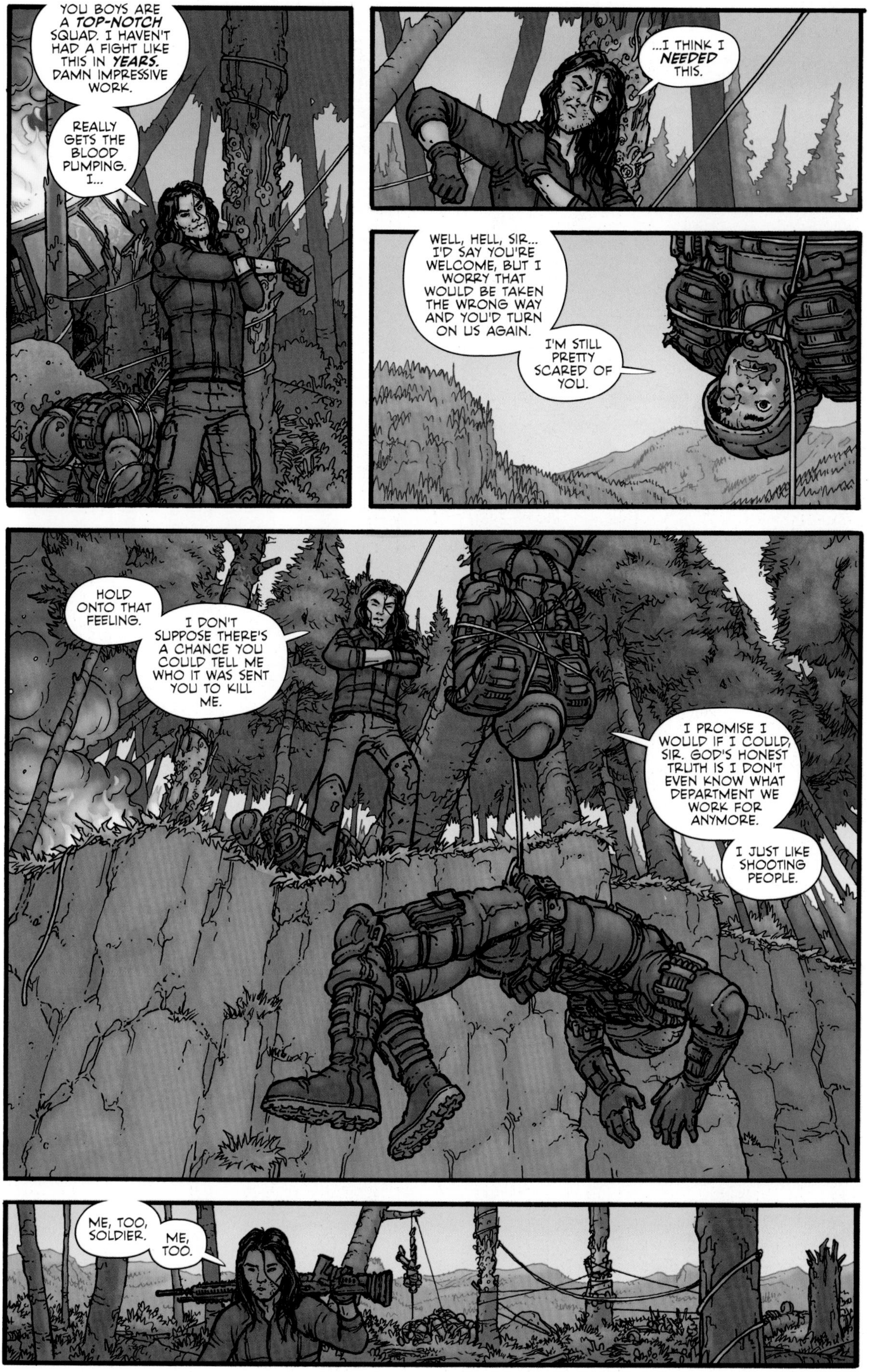
YOU BOYS ARE A TOP-NOTCH SQUAD. I HAVEN'T HAD A FIGHT LIKE THIS IN YEARS. DAMN IMPRESSIVE WORK.
REALLY GETS THE BLOOD PUMPING. I...
...I THINK I NEEDED THIS.
WELL, HELL, SIR... I'D SAY YOU'RE WELCOME, BUT I WORRY THAT WOULD BE TAKEN THE WRONG WAY AND YOU'D TURN ON US AGAIN.
I'M STILL PRETTY SCARED OF YOU.
HOLD ONTO THAT FEELING.
I DON'T SUPPOSE THERE'S A CHANCE YOU COULD TELL ME WHO IT WAS SENT YOU TO KILL ME.
I PROMISE I WOULD IF I COULD, SIR. GOD'S HONEST TRUTH IS I DON'T EVEN KNOW WHAT DEPARTMENT WE WORK FOR ANYMORE.
I JUST LIKE SHOOTING PEOPLE.
ME, TOO, SOLDIER.
ME, TOO.

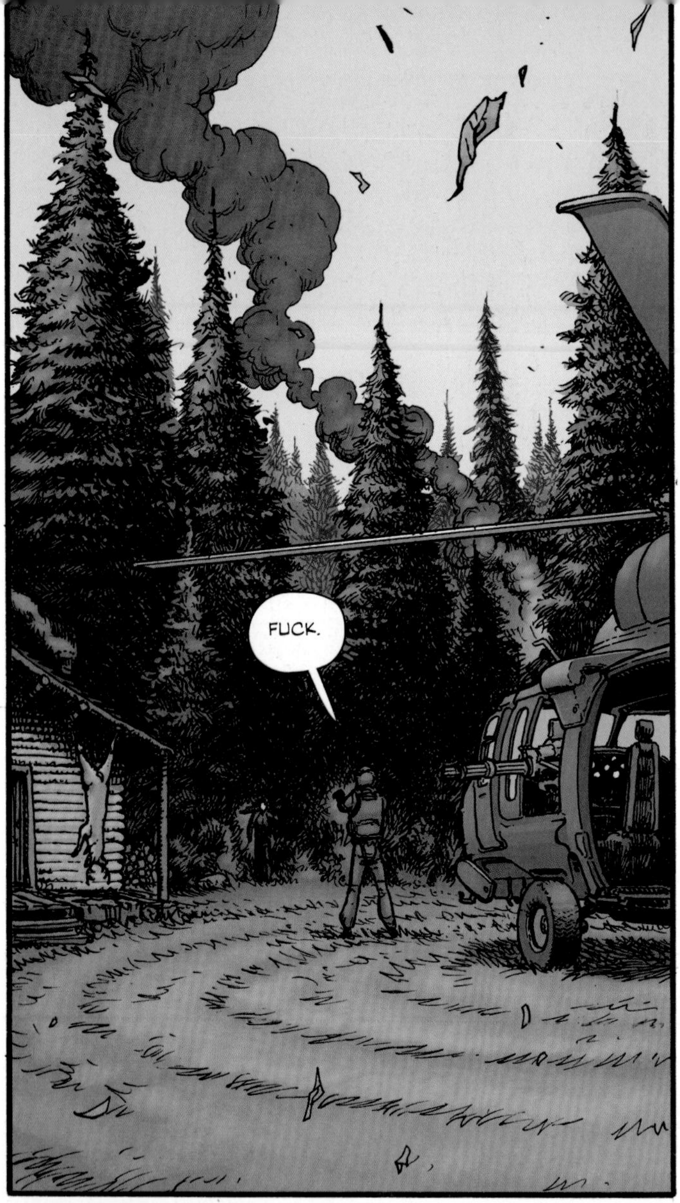
FUCK.

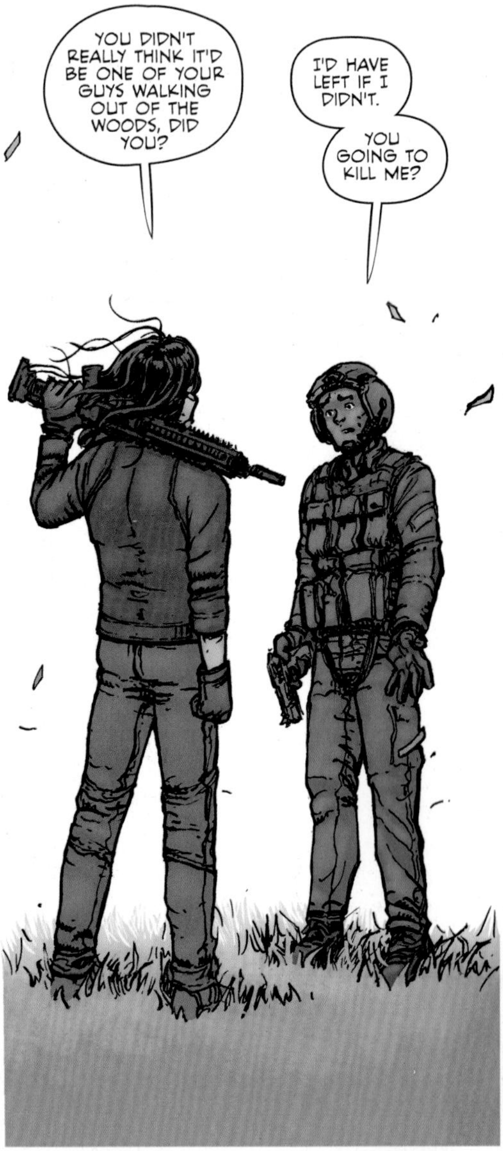
YOU DIDN'T REALLY THINK IT'D BE ONE OF YOUR GUYS WALKING OUT OF THE WOODS, DID YOU?
I'D HAVE LEFT IF I DIDN'T.
YOU GOING TO KILL ME?

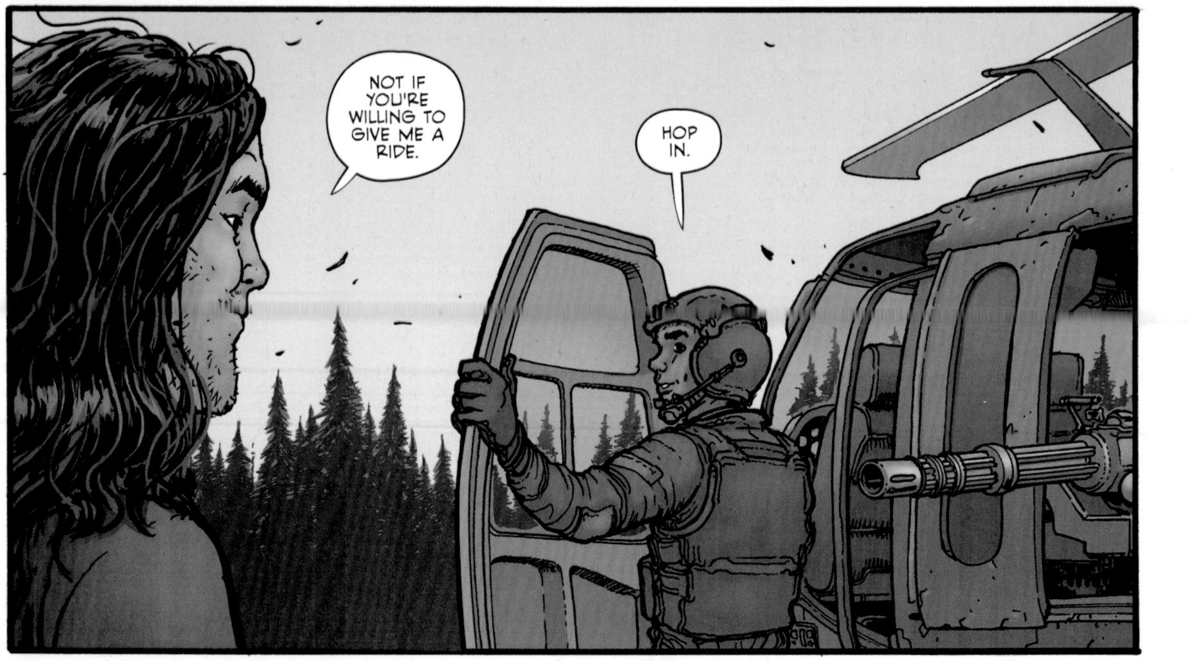
NOT IF YOU'RE WILLING TO GIVE ME A RIDE.
HOP IN.

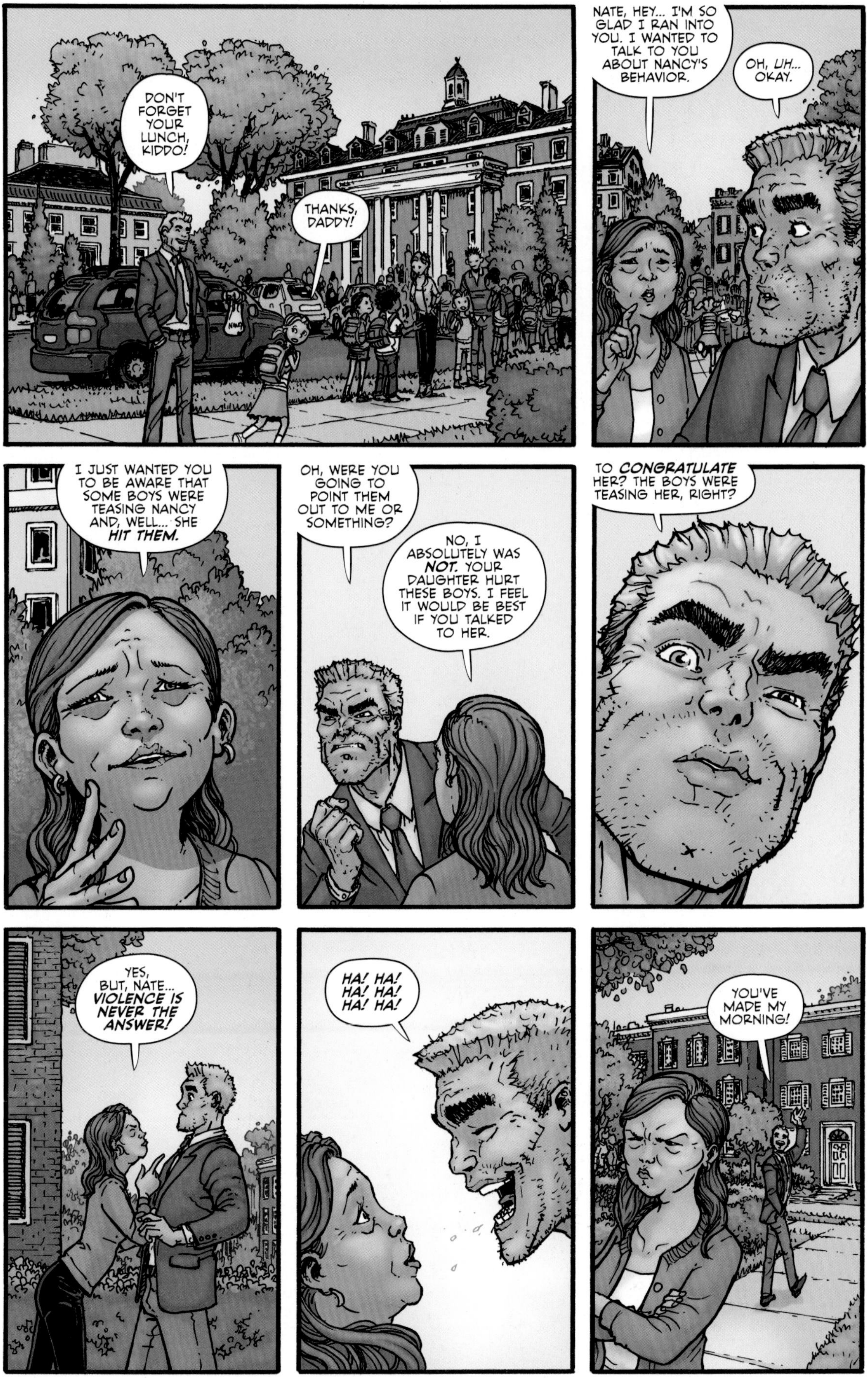

DON'T FORGET YOUR LUNCH, KIDDO!
THANKS, DADDY!
NATE, HEY... I'M SO GLAD I RAN INTO YOU. I WANTED TO TALK TO YOU ABOUT NANCY'S BEHAVIOR.
OH, UH... OKAY.
I JUST WANTED YOU TO BE AWARE THAT SOME BOYS WERE TEASING NANCY AND, WELL... SHE HIT THEM.
OH, WERE YOU GOING TO POINT THEM OUT TO ME OR SOMETHING?
NO, I ABSOLUTELY WAS NOT. YOUR DAUGHTER HURT THESE BOYS. I FEEL IT WOULD BE BEST IF YOU TALKED TO HER.
TO CONGRATULATE HER? THE BOYS WERE TEASING HER, RIGHT?
YES, BUT, NATE... VIOLENCE IS NEVER THE ANSWER!
HA! HA! HA! HA! HA! HA!
YOU'VE MADE MY MORNING!

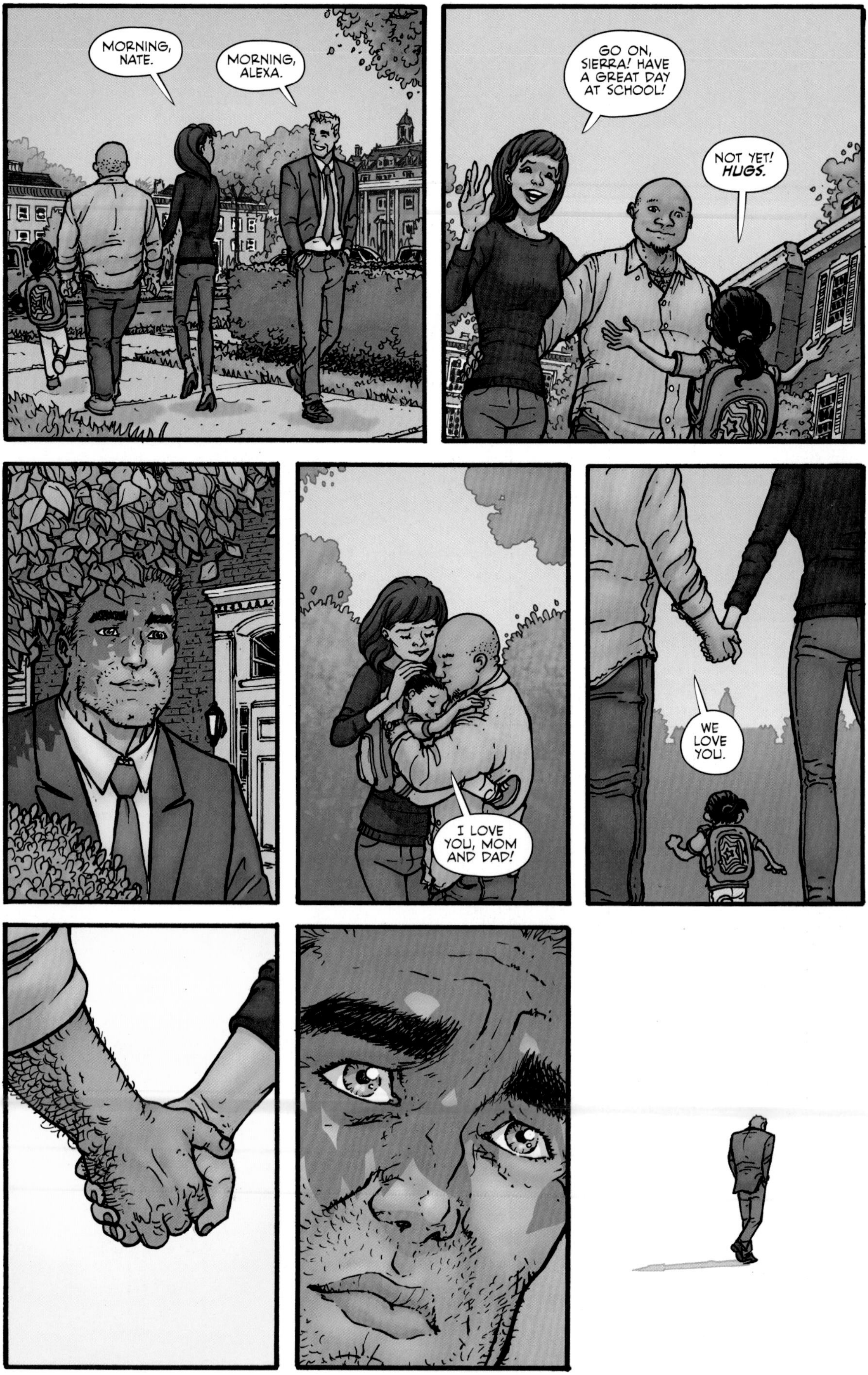
MORNING, NATE.
MORNING, ALEXA.
GO ON, SIERRA! HAVE A GREAT DAY AT SCHOOL!
NOT YET! HUGS.
I LOVE YOU, MOM AND DAD!
WE LOVE YOU.

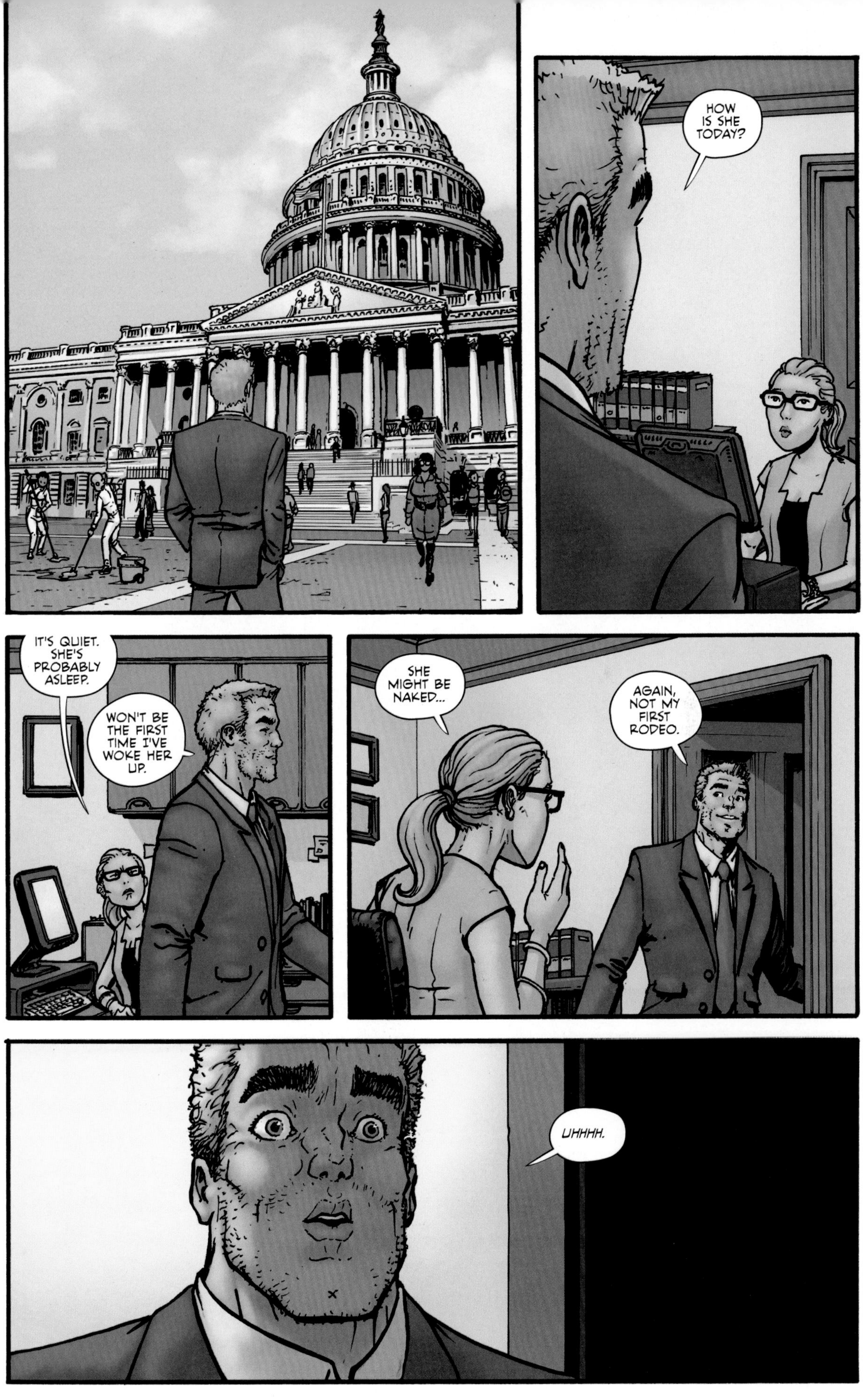
HOW IS SHE TODAY?
IT'S QUIET. SHE'S PROBABLY ASLEEP.
WON'T BE THE FIRST TIME I'VE WOKE HER UP.
SHE MIGHT BE NAKED...
AGAIN, NOT MY FIRST RODEO.
UHHHH.

PLEASE TELL JOHN THAT WE DIDN'T SEND A STRIKE TEAM TO KILL HIM, BEFORE HE BLOWS MY BRAINS OUT.

KEEP YOUR HANDS WHERE I CAN SEE THEM, NATE.

JOHN, WHAT MOTIVE COULD WE POSSIBLY HAVE? IF SOMEONE IS TRYING TO KILL YOU-- I'D HOPE YOU'D COME TO US FOR *HELP*.

WE CAN CALL PAUL AND GET HIM IN HERE. YOU TRUST PAUL, RIGHT?

...

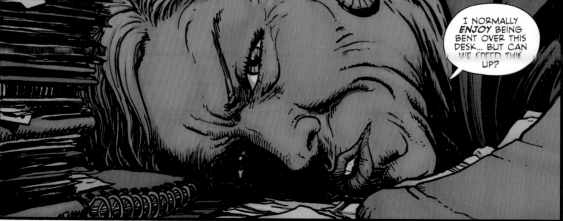

I NORMALLY *ENJOY* BEING BENT OVER THIS DESK... BUT CAN WE SPEED THIS UP?

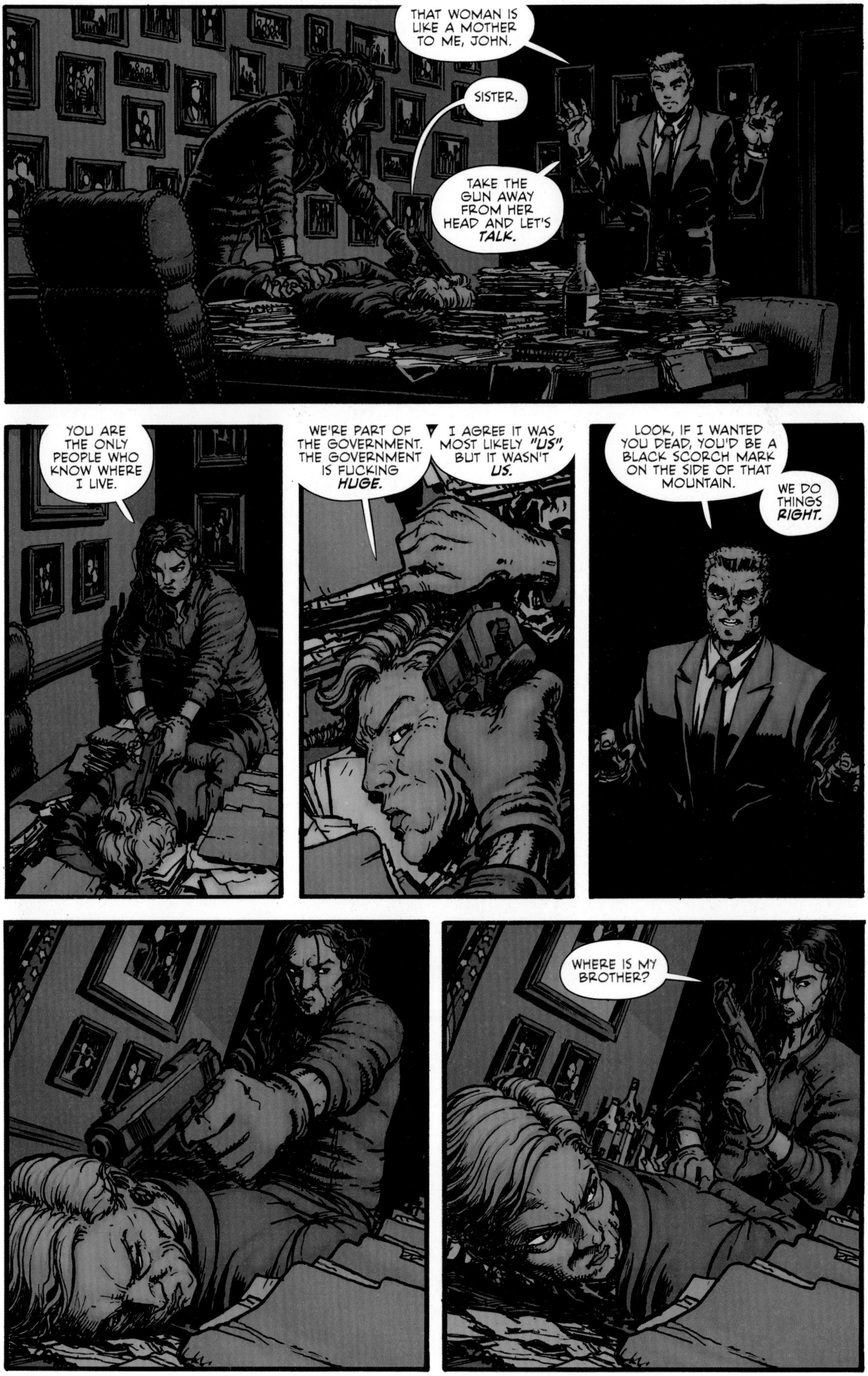
THAT WOMAN IS LIKE A MOTHER TO ME, JOHN.
SISTER.
TAKE THE GUN AWAY FROM HER HEAD AND LET'S TALK.
YOU ARE THE ONLY PEOPLE WHO KNOW WHERE I LIVE.
WE'RE PART OF THE GOVERNMENT. THE GOVERNMENT IS FUCKING HUGE.
I AGREE IT WAS MOST LIKELY "US", BUT IT WASN'T US.
LOOK, IF I WANTED YOU DEAD, YOU'D BE A BLACK SCORCH MARK ON THE SIDE OF THAT MOUNTAIN.
WE DO THINGS RIGHT.
WHERE IS MY BROTHER?

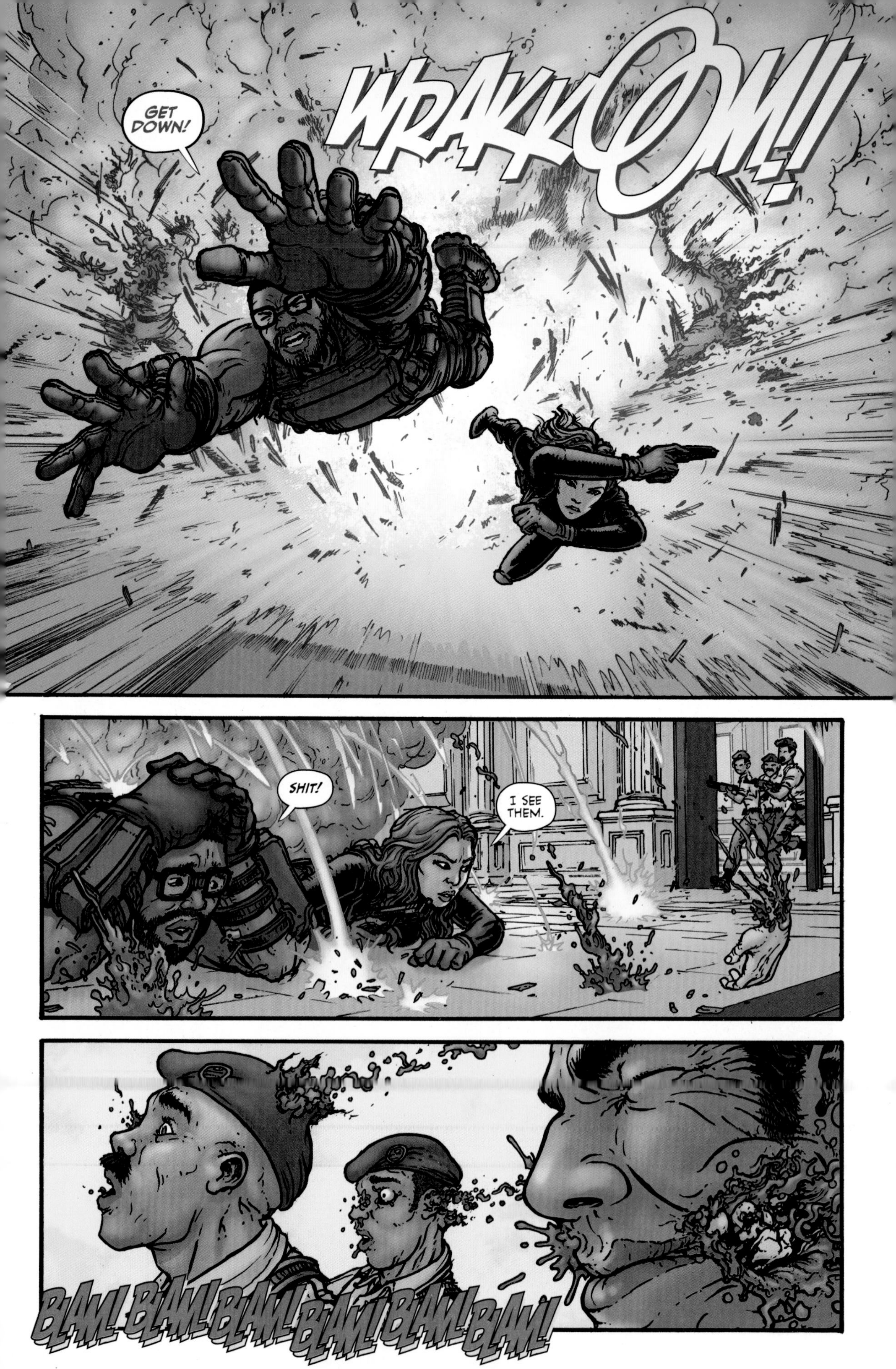
WRAKKOOM!!
GET DOWN!
SHIT!
I SEE THEM.
BLAM! BLAM! BLAM! BLAM! BLAM! BLAM!

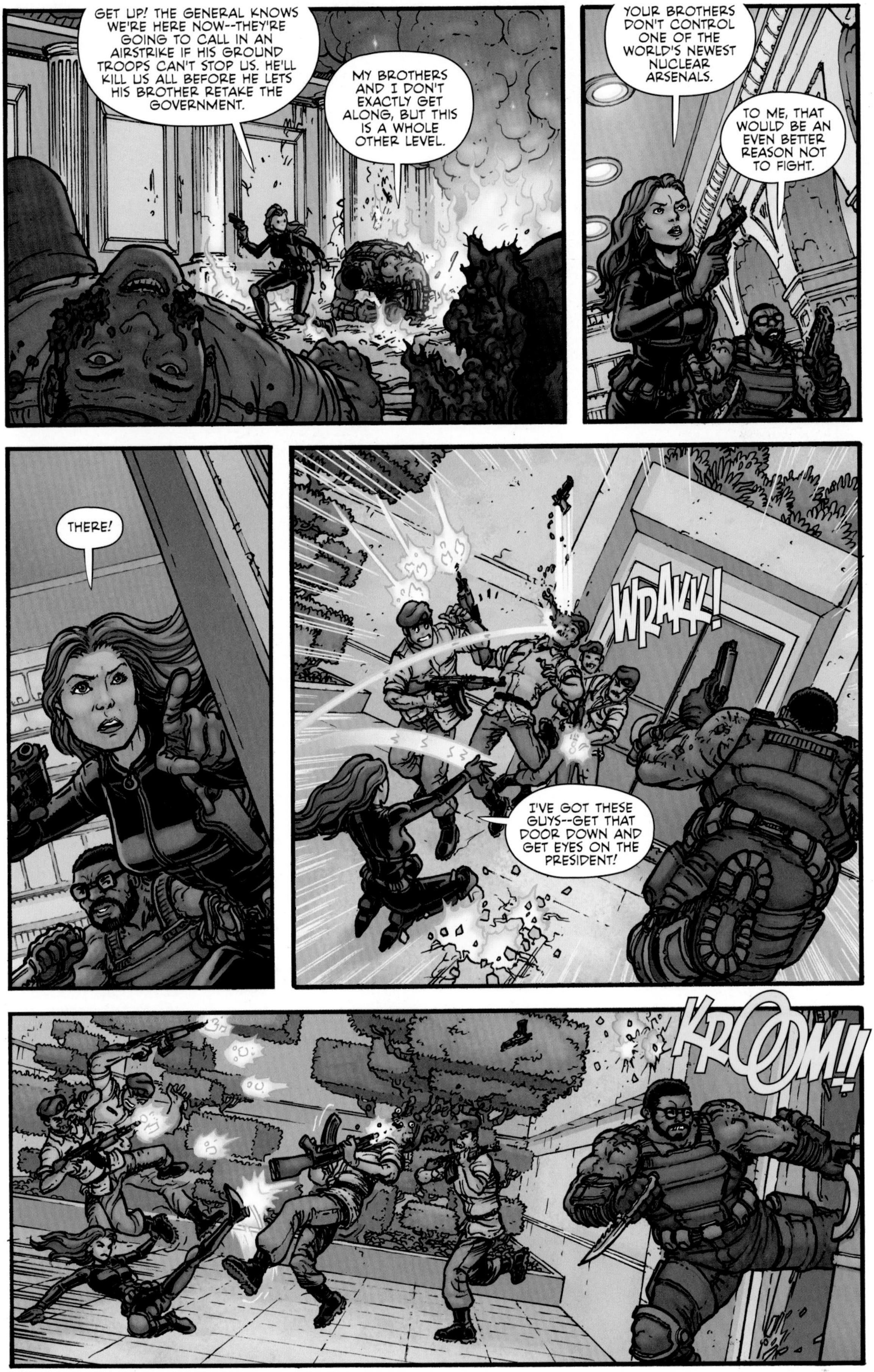
GET UP! THE GENERAL KNOWS WE'RE HERE NOW--THEY'RE GOING TO CALL IN AN AIRSTRIKE IF HIS GROUND TROOPS CAN'T STOP US. HE'LL KILL US ALL BEFORE HE LETS HIS BROTHER RETAKE THE GOVERNMENT.
MY BROTHERS AND I DON'T EXACTLY GET ALONG, BUT THIS IS A WHOLE OTHER LEVEL.
YOUR BROTHERS DON'T CONTROL ONE OF THE WORLD'S NEWEST NUCLEAR ARSENALS.
TO ME, THAT WOULD BE AN EVEN BETTER REASON NOT TO FIGHT.
THERE!
WRAKK!
I'VE GOT THESE GUYS--GET THAT DOOR DOWN AND GET EYES ON THE PRESIDENT!
KROOOM!!

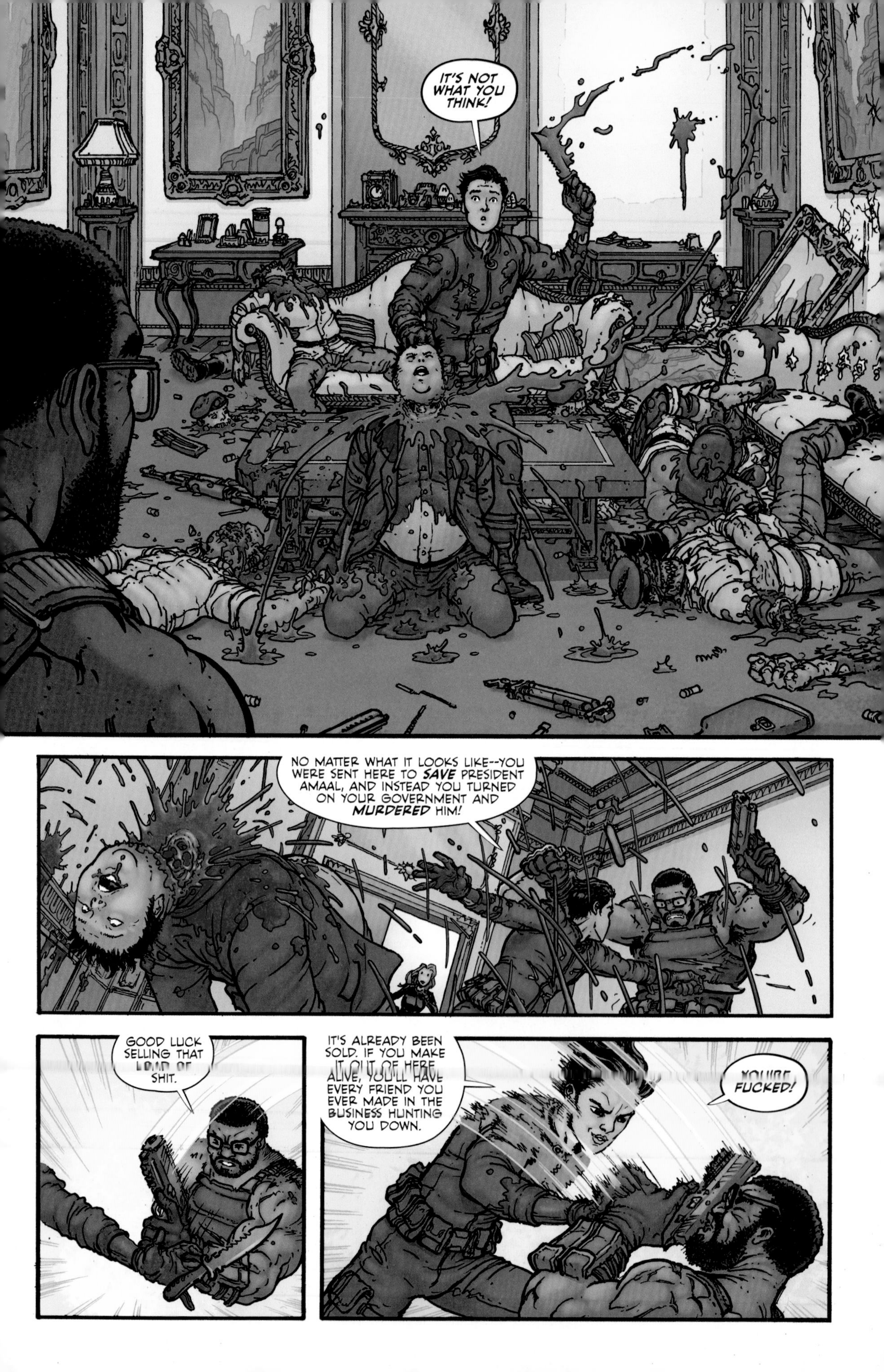
IT'S NOT WHAT YOU THINK!
NO MATTER WHAT IT LOOKS LIKE--YOU WERE SENT HERE TO SAVE PRESIDENT AMAAL, AND INSTEAD YOU TURNED ON YOUR GOVERNMENT AND MURDERED HIM!
GOOD LUCK SELLING THAT
SHIT.
IT'S ALREADY BEEN SOLD. IF YOU MAKE IT OUT OF HERE ALIVE, YOU'LL HAVE EVERY FRIEND YOU EVER MADE IN THE BUSINESS HUNTING YOU DOWN.
FUCKED!

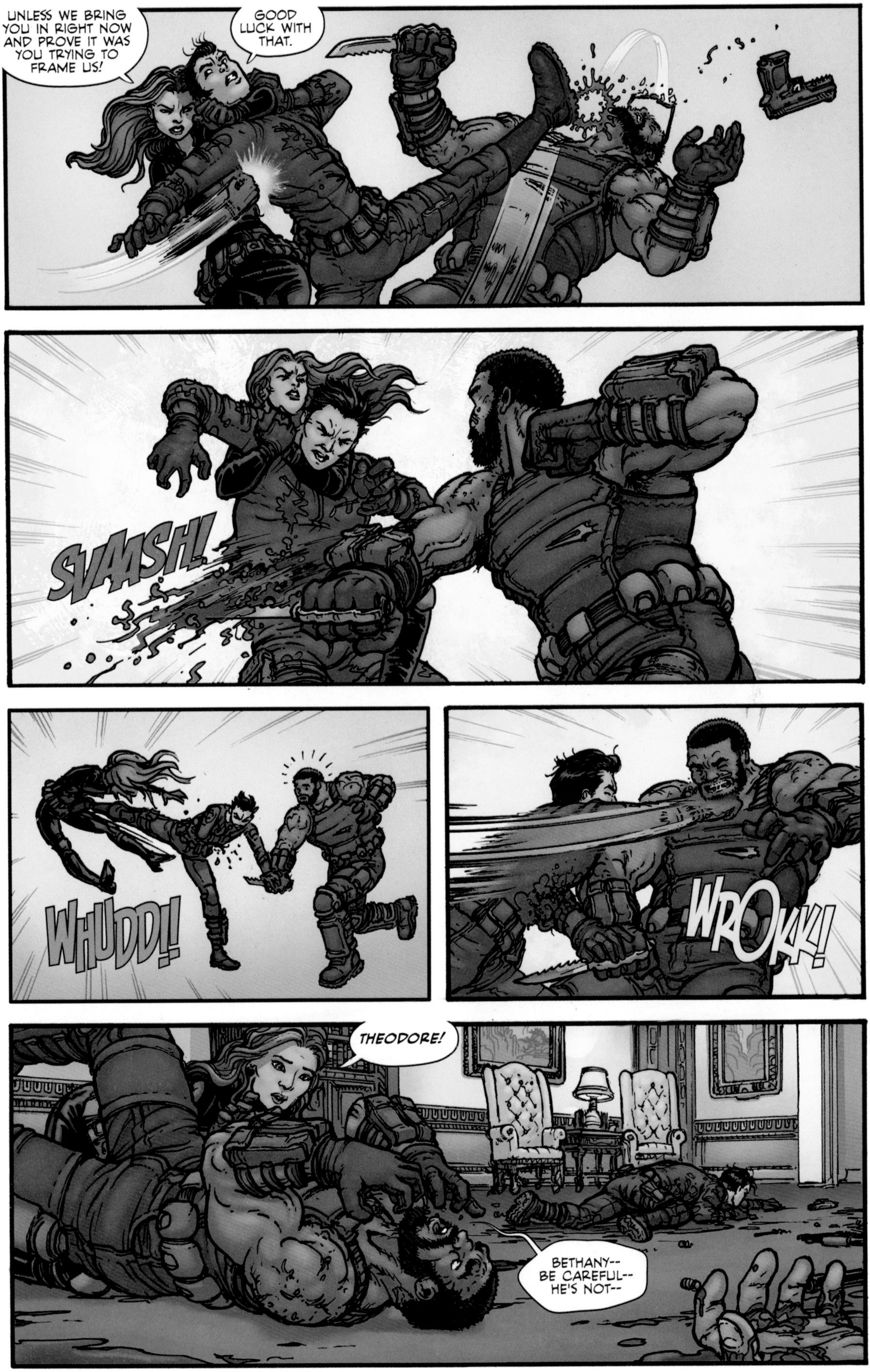
UNLESS WE BRING YOU IN RIGHT NOW AND PROVE IT WAS YOU TRYING TO FRAME US!
GOOD LUCK WITH THAT.
SVAASH!
WHUDD!!
WROKK!
THEODORE!
BETHANY-- BE CAREFUL-- HE'S NOT--

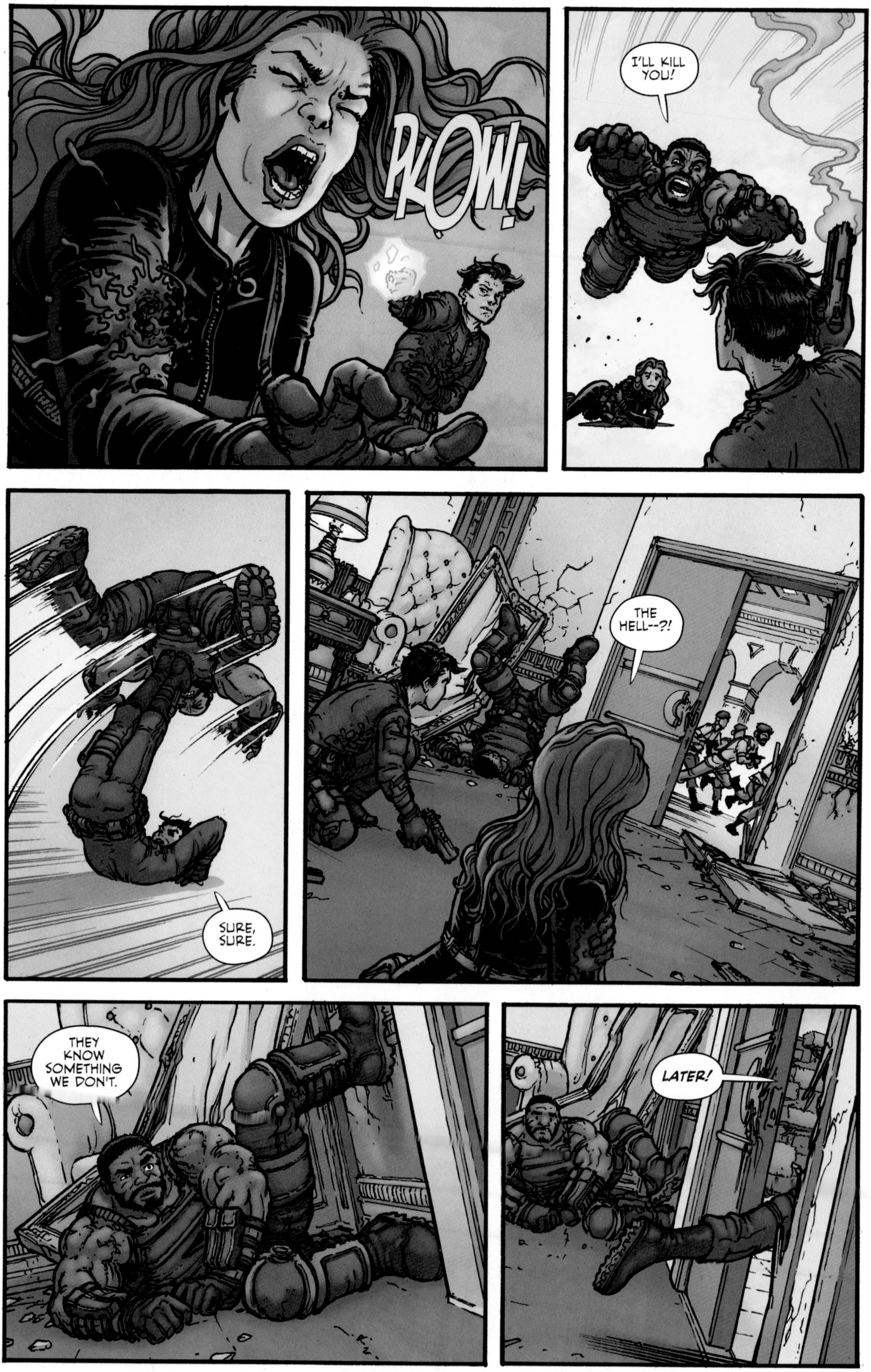
PKOW!
I'LL KILL YOU!
SURE, SURE.
THE HELL--?!
THEY KNOW SOMETHING WE DON'T.
LATER!

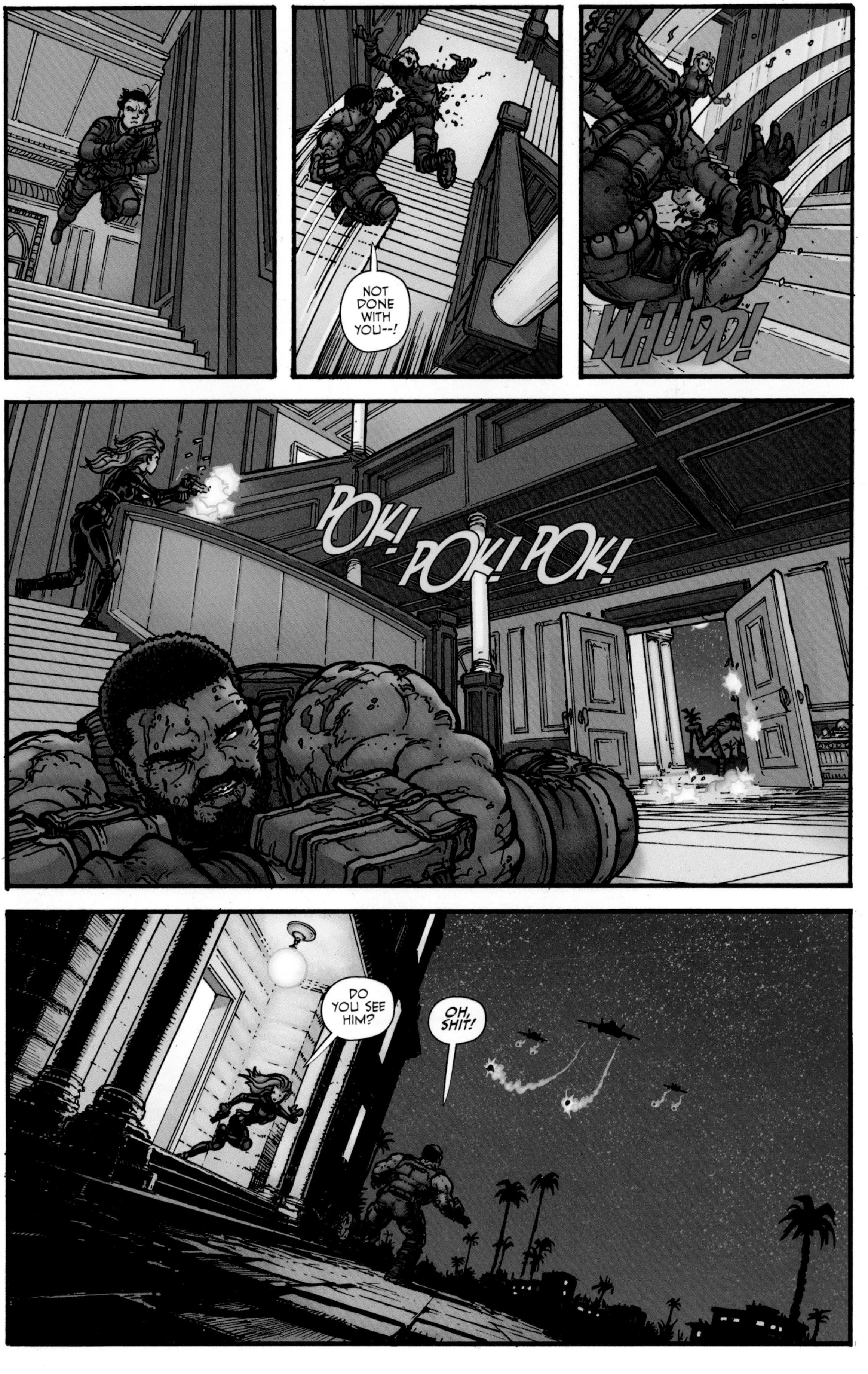
NOT DONE WITH YOU--!
WHUDD!
POK! POK! POK!
DO YOU SEE HIM?
OH, SHIT!

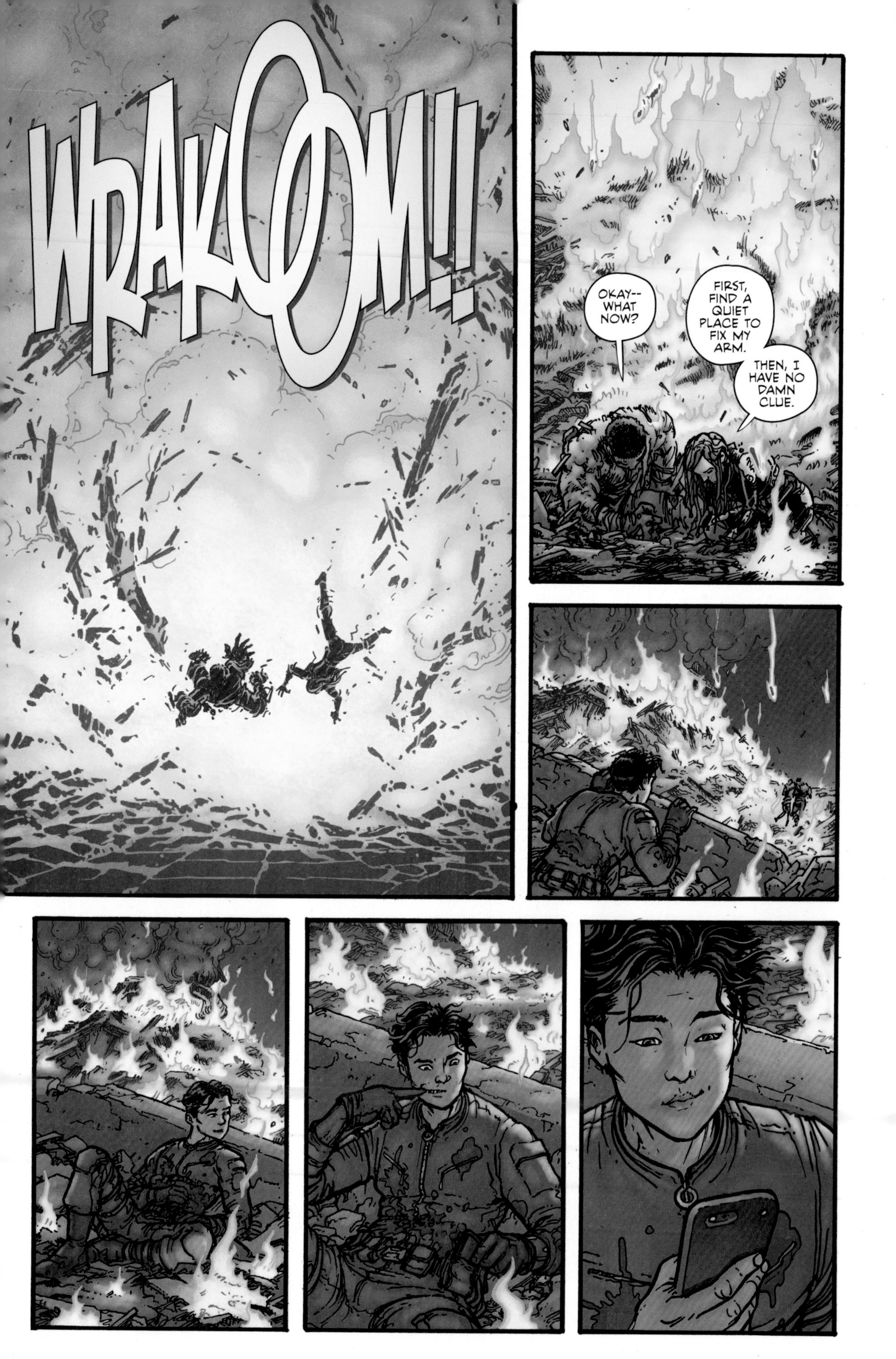
WRAKOOM!!
OKAY--WHAT NOW?
FIRST, FIND A QUIET PLACE TO FIX MY ARM.
THEN, I HAVE NO DAMN CLUE.

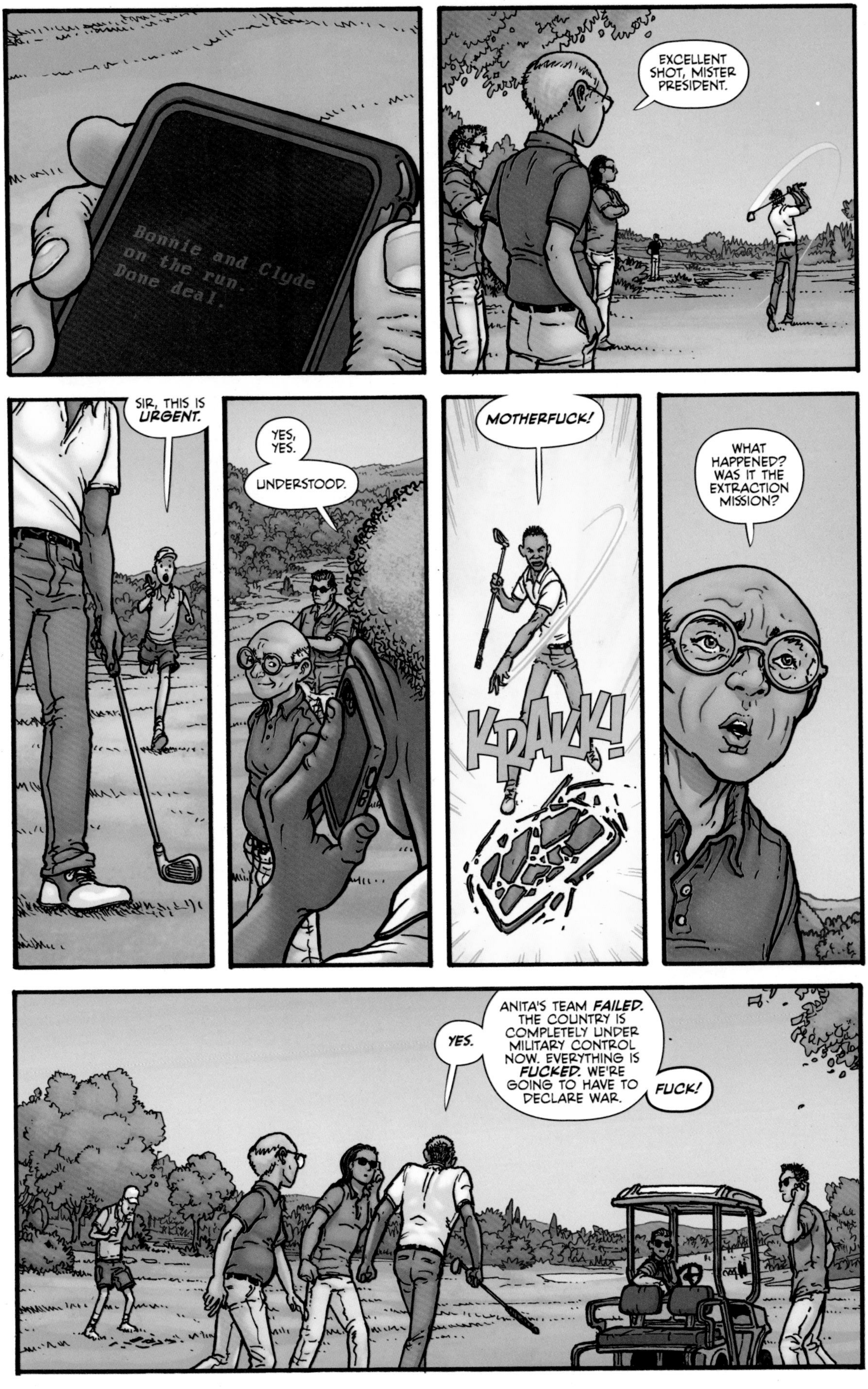
Bonnie and Clyde
on the run.
Done deal.
EXCELLENT SHOT, MISTER PRESIDENT.
SIR, THIS IS URGENT.
YES, YES.
UNDERSTOOD.
MOTHERFUCK!
KRAKK!
WHAT HAPPENED? WAS IT THE EXTRACTION MISSION?
YES.
ANITA'S TEAM FAILED. THE COUNTRY IS COMPLETELY UNDER MILITARY CONTROL NOW. EVERYTHING IS FUCKED. WE'RE GOING TO HAVE TO DECLARE WAR.
FUCK!

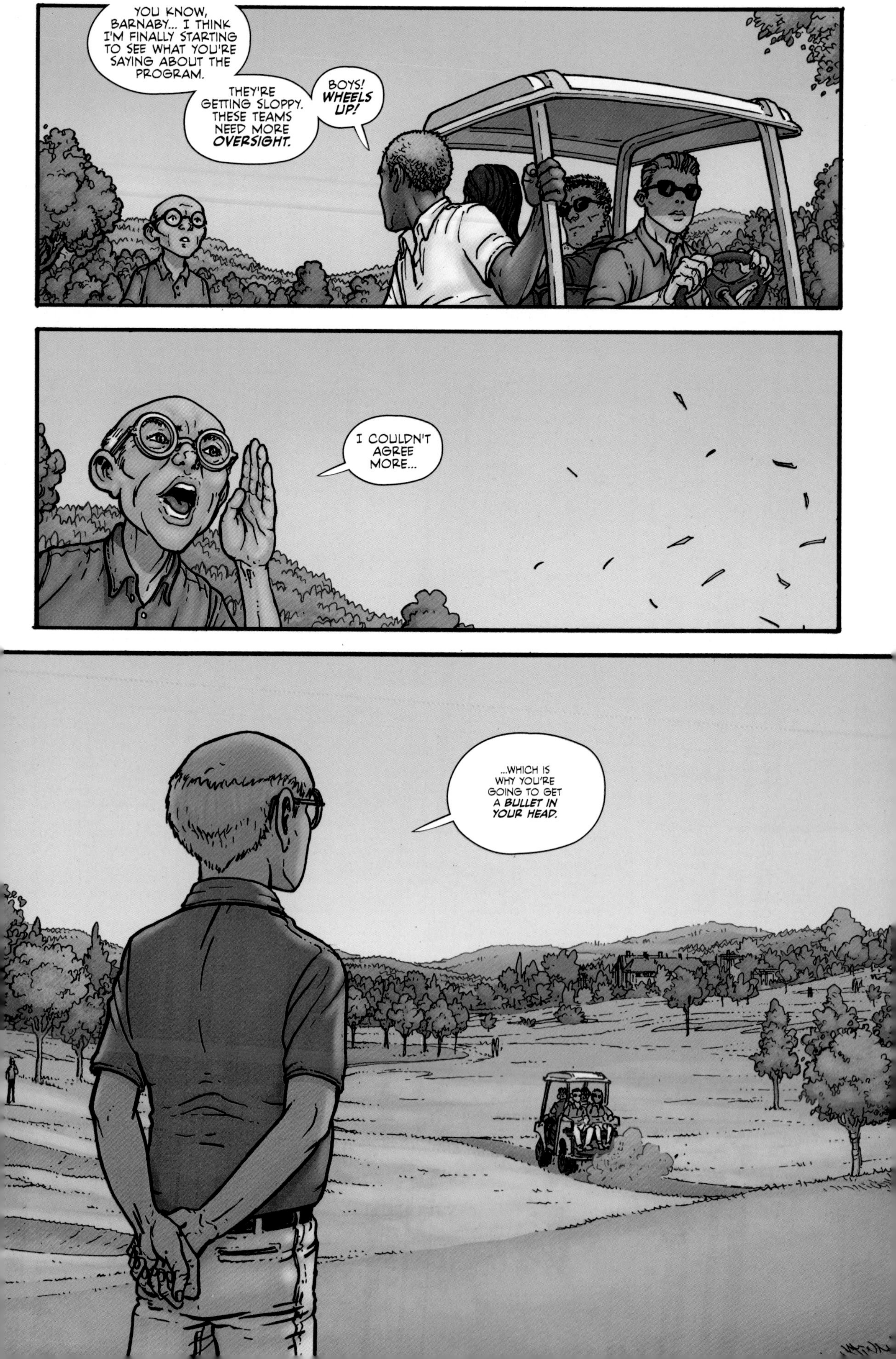
YOU KNOW, BARNABY... I THINK I'M FINALLY STARTING TO SEE WHAT YOU'RE SAYING ABOUT THE PROGRAM.
THEY'RE GETTING SLOPPY. THESE TEAMS NEED MORE OVERSIGHT.
BOYS! WHEELS UP!
I COULDN'T AGREE MORE...
...WHICH IS WHY YOU'RE GOING TO GET A BULLET IN YOUR HEAD.

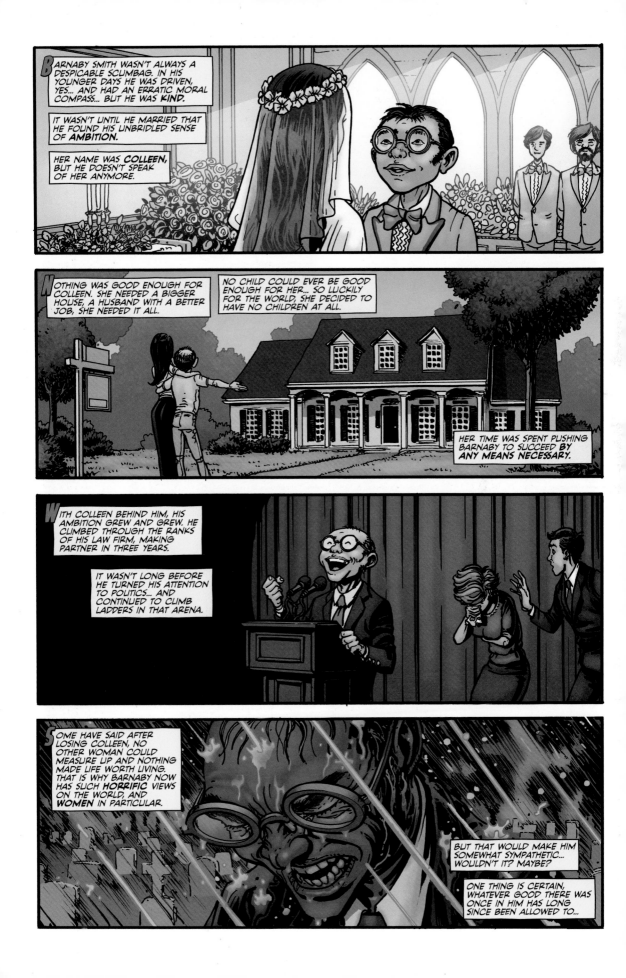

BARNABY SMITH WASN'T ALWAYS A DESPICABLE SCUMBAG. IN HIS YOUNGER DAYS HE WAS DRIVEN, YES... AND HAD AN ERRATIC MORAL COMPASS... BUT HE WAS **KIND.**

IT WASN'T UNTIL HE MARRIED THAT HE FOUND HIS UNBRIDLED SENSE OF **AMBITION.**

HER NAME WAS **COLLEEN,** BUT HE DOESN'T SPEAK OF HER ANYMORE.

NOTHING WAS GOOD ENOUGH FOR COLLEEN. SHE NEEDED A BIGGER HOUSE, A HUSBAND WITH A BETTER JOB, SHE NEEDED IT ALL.

NO CHILD COULD EVER BE GOOD ENOUGH FOR HER... SO LUCKILY FOR THE WORLD, SHE DECIDED TO HAVE NO CHILDREN AT ALL.

HER TIME WAS SPENT PUSHING BARNABY TO SUCCEED **BY ANY MEANS NECESSARY.**

WITH COLLEEN BEHIND HIM, HIS AMBITION GREW AND GREW. HE CLIMBED THROUGH THE RANKS OF HIS LAW FIRM, MAKING PARTNER IN THREE YEARS.

IT WASN'T LONG BEFORE HE TURNED HIS ATTENTION TO POLITICS... AND CONTINUED TO CLIMB LADDERS IN THAT ARENA.

SOME HAVE SAID AFTER LOSING COLLEEN, NO OTHER WOMAN COULD MEASURE UP AND NOTHING MADE LIFE WORTH LIVING. THAT IS WHY BARNABY NOW HAS SUCH **HORRIFIC** VIEWS ON THE WORLD, AND **WOMEN** IN PARTICULAR.

BUT THAT WOULD MAKE HIM SOMEWHAT SYMPATHETIC... WOULDN'T IT? MAYBE?

ONE THING IS CERTAIN, WHATEVER GOOD THERE WAS ONCE IN HIM HAS LONG SINCE BEEN ALLOWED TO...

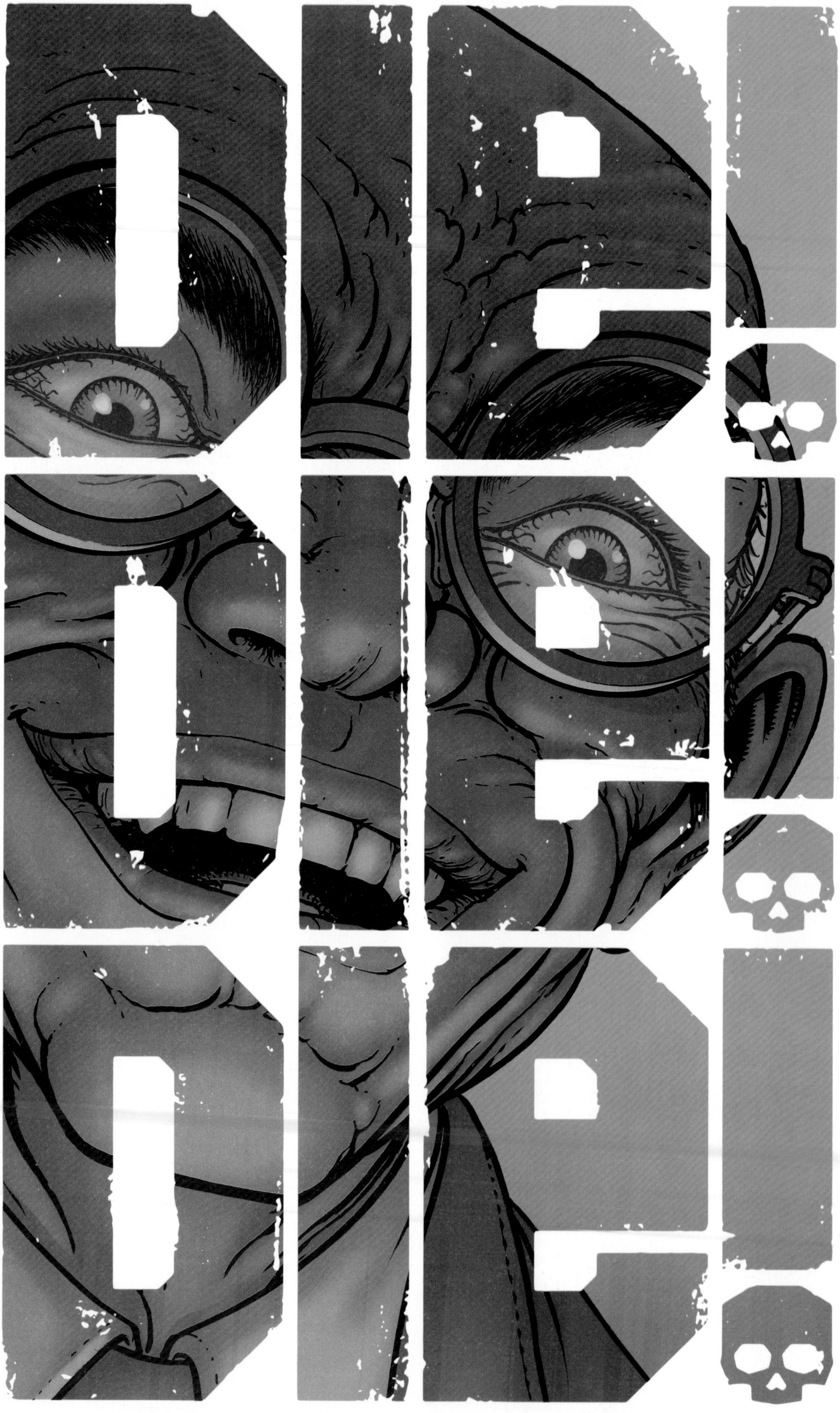
DIE!
DIE!
DIE!

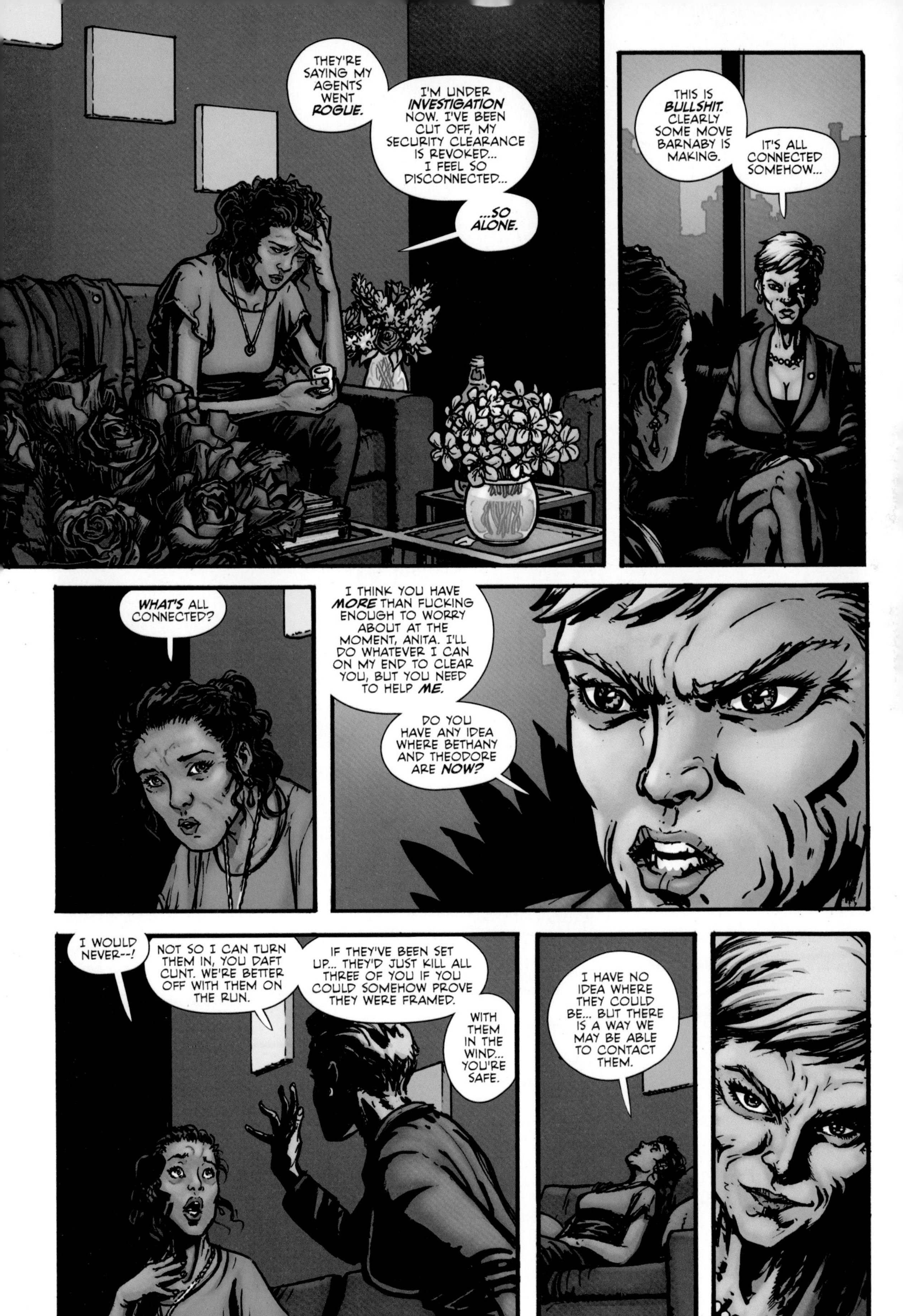
THEY'RE SAYING MY AGENTS WENT *ROGUE.*
I'M UNDER *INVESTIGATION* NOW. I'VE BEEN CUT OFF, MY SECURITY CLEARANCE IS REVOKED... I FEEL SO DISCONNECTED...
...SO *ALONE.*
THIS IS *BULLSHIT.* CLEARLY SOME MOVE BARNABY IS MAKING.
IT'S ALL CONNECTED SOMEHOW...
WHAT'S ALL CONNECTED?
I THINK YOU HAVE *MORE* THAN FUCKING ENOUGH TO WORRY ABOUT AT THE MOMENT, ANITA. I'LL DO WHATEVER I CAN ON MY END TO CLEAR YOU, BUT YOU NEED TO HELP *ME.*
DO YOU HAVE ANY IDEA WHERE BETHANY AND THEODORE ARE *NOW?*
I WOULD NEVER--!
NOT SO I CAN TURN THEM IN, YOU DAFT CUNT. WE'RE BETTER OFF WITH THEM ON THE RUN.
IF THEY'VE BEEN SET UP... THEY'D JUST KILL ALL THREE OF YOU IF YOU COULD SOMEHOW PROVE THEY WERE FRAMED.
WITH THEM IN THE WIND... YOU'RE SAFE.
I HAVE NO IDEA WHERE THEY COULD BE... BUT THERE IS A WAY WE MAY BE ABLE TO CONTACT THEM.

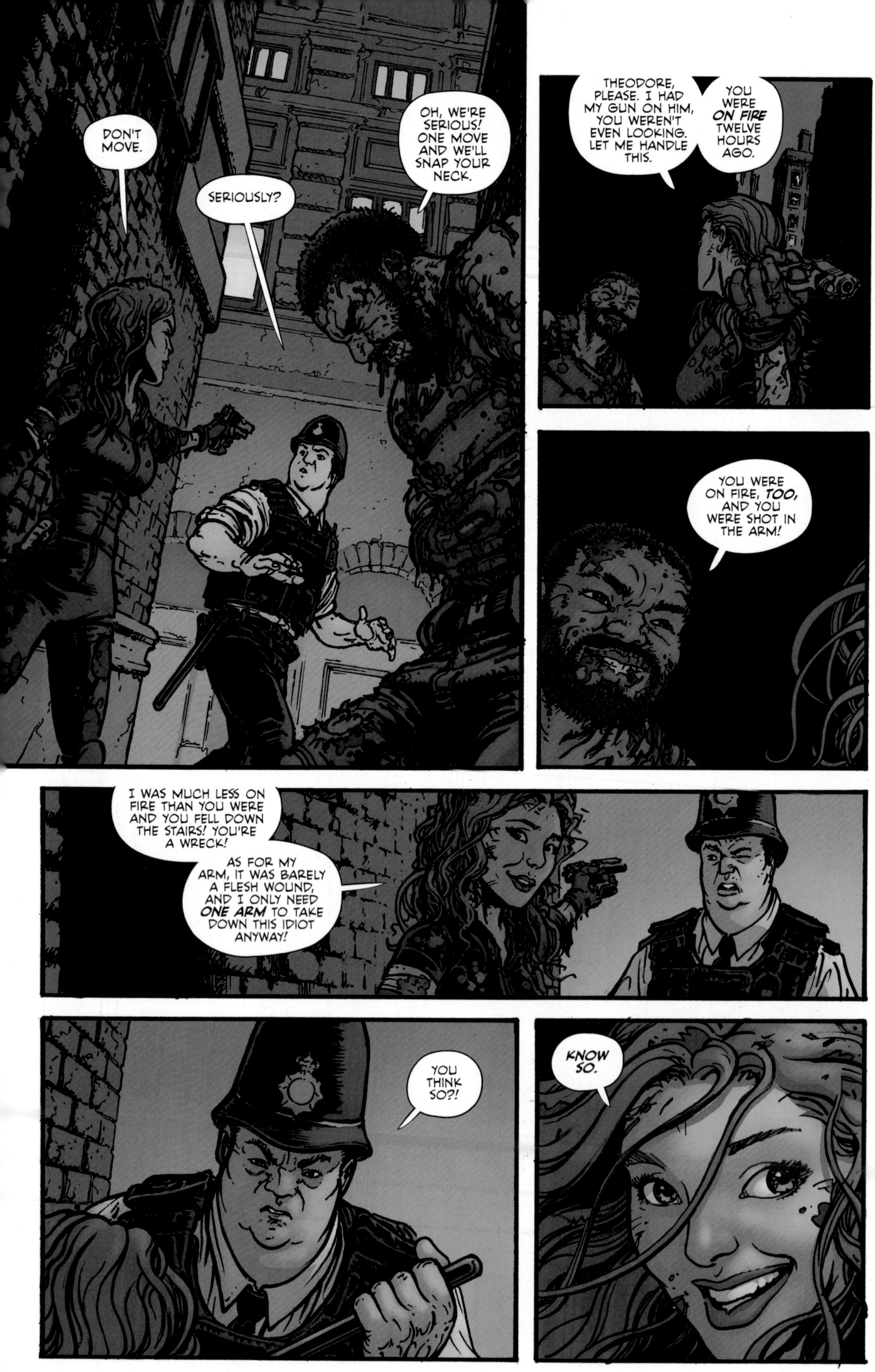
DON'T MOVE.
SERIOUSLY?
OH, WE'RE SERIOUS! ONE MOVE AND WE'LL SNAP YOUR NECK.
THEODORE, PLEASE. I HAD MY GUN ON HIM, YOU WEREN'T EVEN LOOKING. LET ME HANDLE THIS.
YOU WERE ON FIRE TWELVE HOURS AGO.
YOU WERE ON FIRE, TOO, AND YOU WERE SHOT IN THE ARM!
I WAS MUCH LESS ON FIRE THAN YOU WERE AND YOU FELL DOWN THE STAIRS! YOU'RE A WRECK!
AS FOR MY ARM, IT WAS BARELY A FLESH WOUND, AND I ONLY NEED ONE ARM TO TAKE DOWN THIS IDIOT ANYWAY!
YOU THINK SO?!
KNOW SO.

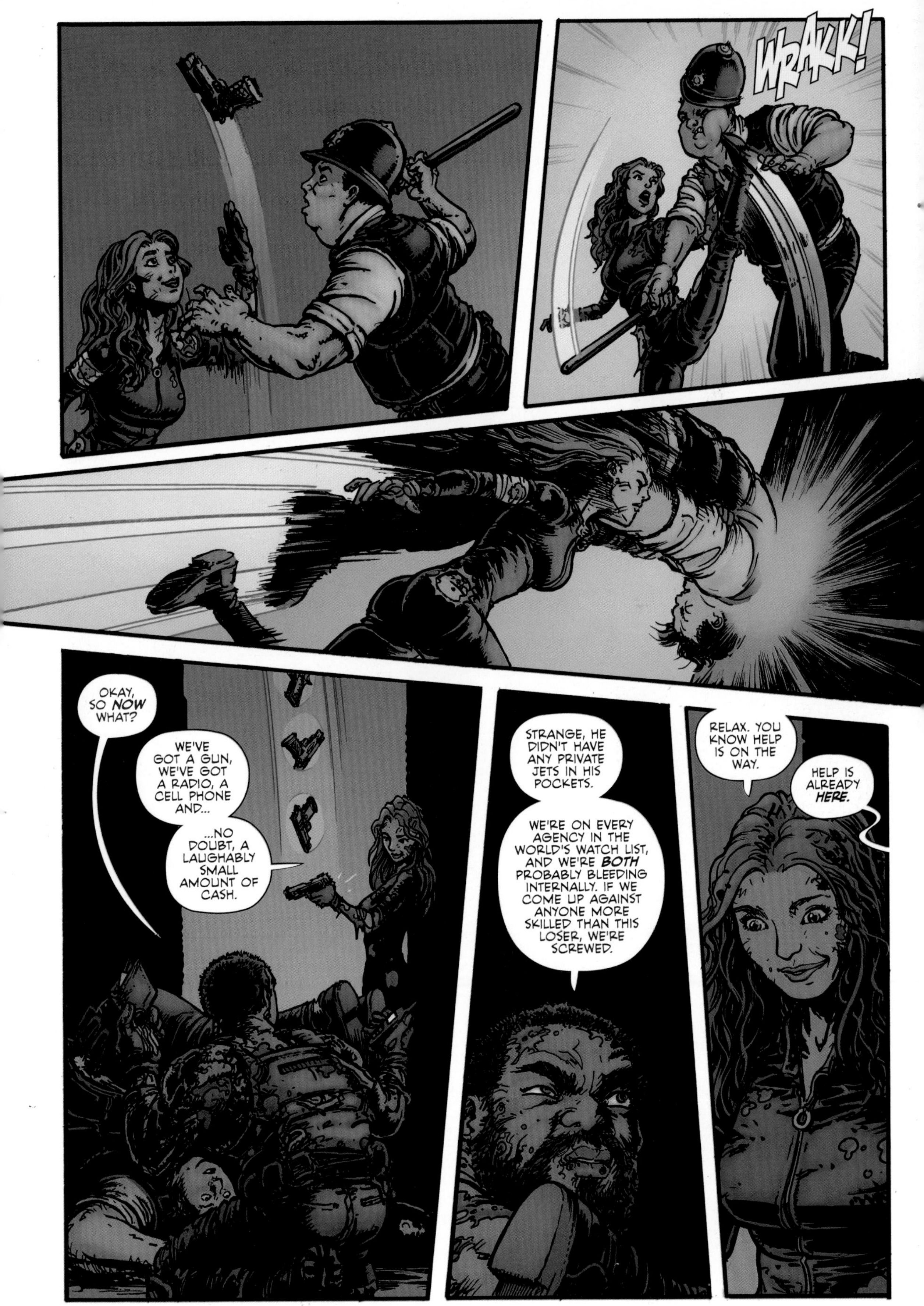

WRAKK!
OKAY, SO NOW WHAT?
WE'VE GOT A GUN, WE'VE GOT A RADIO, A CELL PHONE AND...
...NO DOUBT, A LAUGHABLY SMALL AMOUNT OF CASH.
STRANGE, HE DIDN'T HAVE ANY PRIVATE JETS IN HIS POCKETS.
WE'RE ON EVERY AGENCY IN THE WORLD'S WATCH LIST, AND WE'RE BOTH PROBABLY BLEEDING INTERNALLY. IF WE COME UP AGAINST ANYONE MORE SKILLED THAN THIS LOSER, WE'RE SCREWED.
RELAX. YOU KNOW HELP IS ON THE WAY.
HELP IS ALREADY HERE.

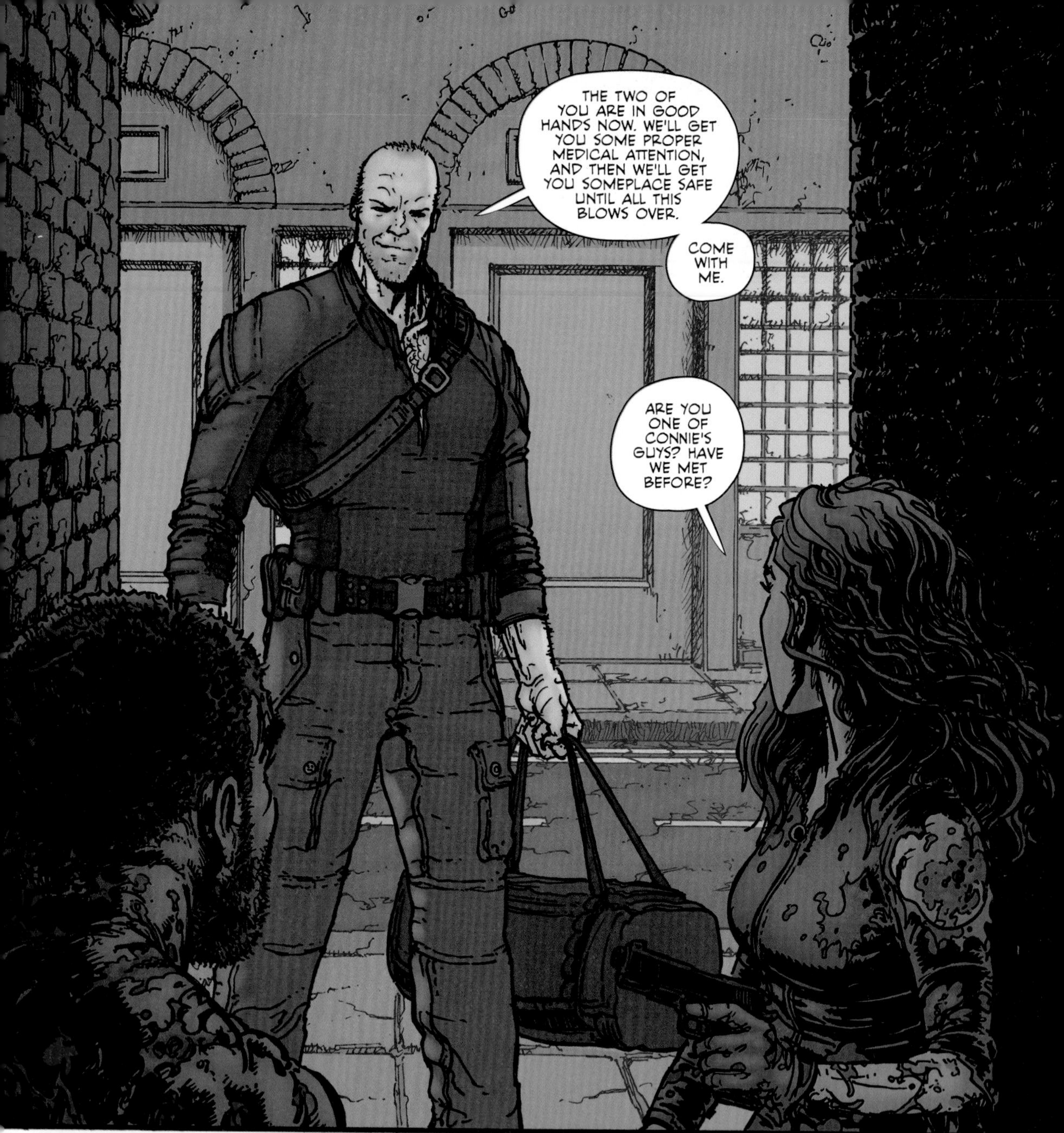
THE TWO OF YOU ARE IN GOOD HANDS NOW. WE'LL GET YOU SOME PROPER MEDICAL ATTENTION, AND THEN WE'LL GET YOU SOMEPLACE SAFE UNTIL ALL THIS BLOWS OVER.
COME WITH ME.
ARE YOU ONE OF CONNIE'S GUYS? HAVE WE MET BEFORE?

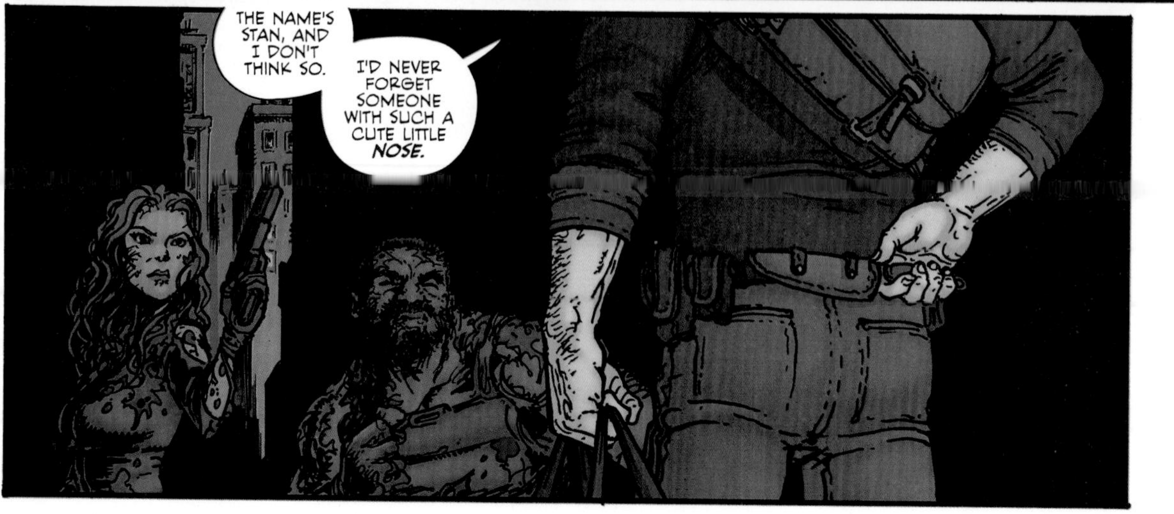
THE NAME'S STAN, AND I DON'T THINK SO.
I'D NEVER FORGET SOMEONE WITH SUCH A CUTE LITTLE ***NOSE.***

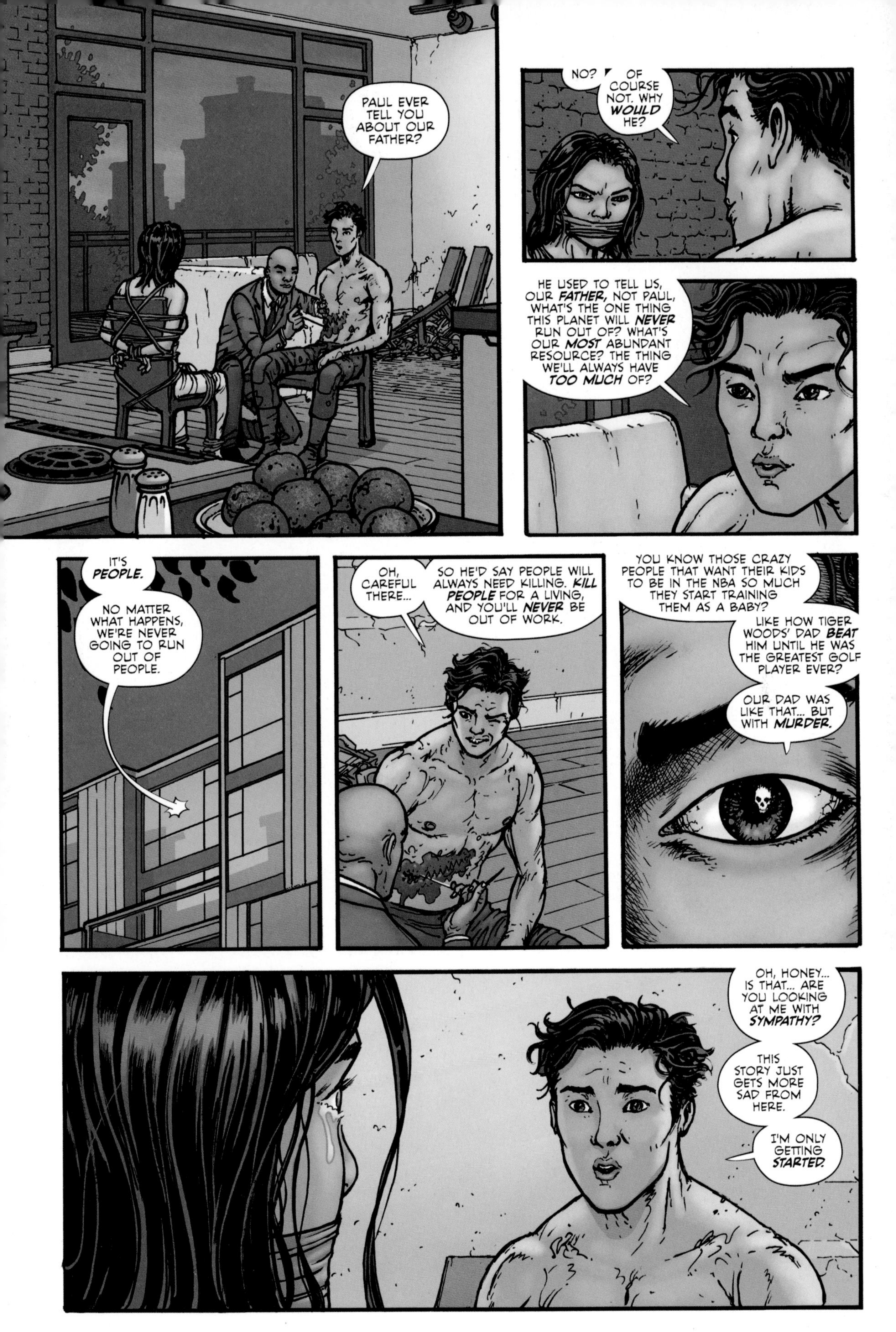
PAUL EVER TELL YOU ABOUT OUR FATHER?
NO?
OF COURSE NOT. WHY WOULD HE?
HE USED TO TELL US, OUR FATHER, NOT PAUL, WHAT'S THE ONE THING THIS PLANET WILL NEVER RUN OUT OF? WHAT'S OUR MOST ABUNDANT RESOURCE? THE THING WE'LL ALWAYS HAVE TOO MUCH OF?
IT'S PEOPLE.
NO MATTER WHAT HAPPENS, WE'RE NEVER GOING TO RUN OUT OF PEOPLE.
OH, CAREFUL THERE...
SO HE'D SAY PEOPLE WILL ALWAYS NEED KILLING. KILL PEOPLE FOR A LIVING, AND YOU'LL NEVER BE OUT OF WORK.
YOU KNOW THOSE CRAZY PEOPLE THAT WANT THEIR KIDS TO BE IN THE NBA SO MUCH THEY START TRAINING THEM AS A BABY?
LIKE HOW TIGER WOODS' DAD BEAT HIM UNTIL HE WAS THE GREATEST GOLF PLAYER EVER?
OUR DAD WAS LIKE THAT... BUT WITH MURDER.
OH, HONEY... IS THAT... ARE YOU LOOKING AT ME WITH SYMPATHY?
THIS STORY JUST GETS MORE SAD FROM HERE.
I'M ONLY GETTING STARTED.

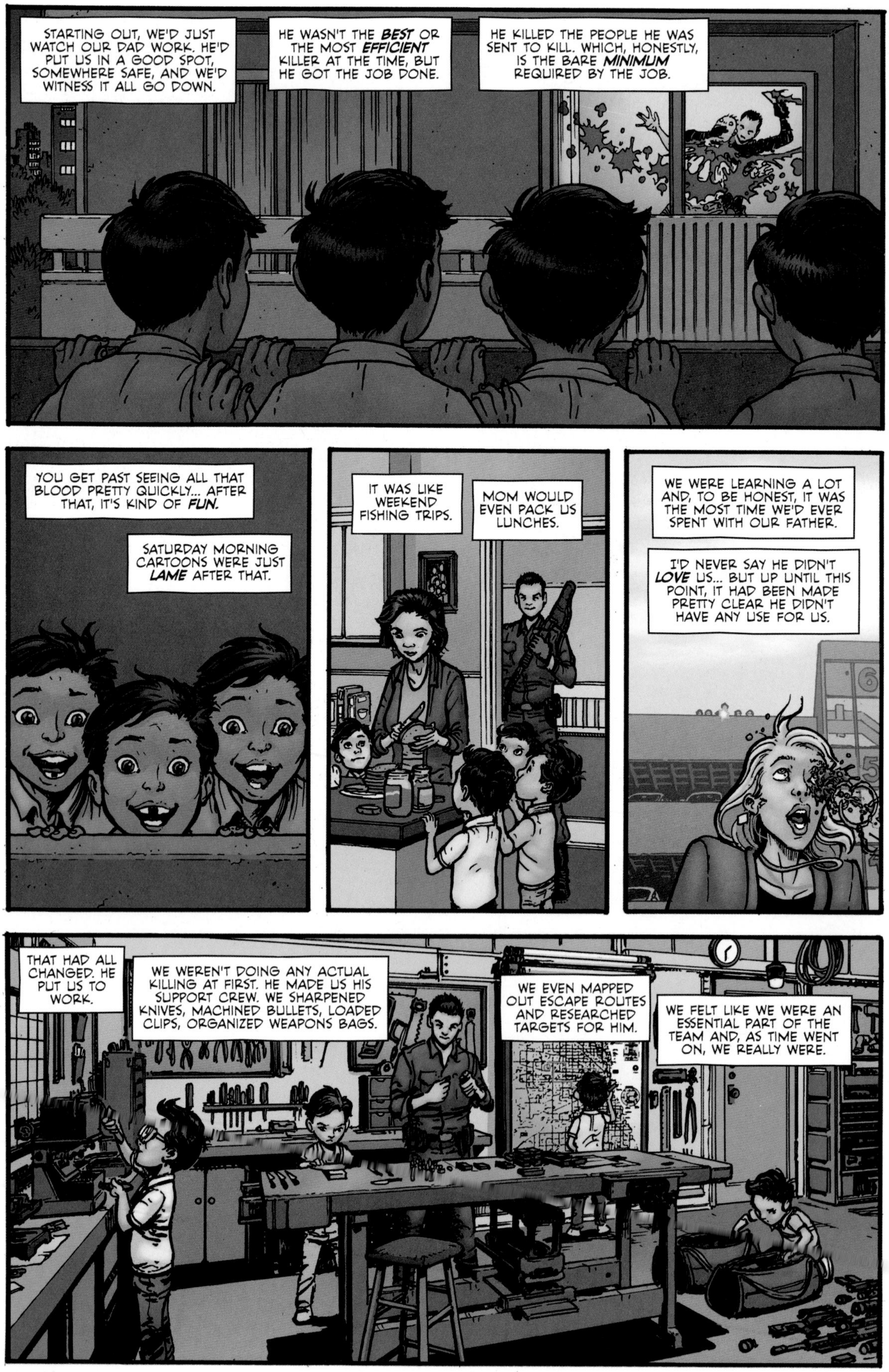
STARTING OUT, WE'D JUST WATCH OUR DAD WORK. HE'D PUT US IN A GOOD SPOT, SOMEWHERE SAFE, AND WE'D WITNESS IT ALL GO DOWN.
HE WASN'T THE BEST OR THE MOST EFFICIENT KILLER AT THE TIME, BUT HE GOT THE JOB DONE.
HE KILLED THE PEOPLE HE WAS SENT TO KILL. WHICH, HONESTLY, IS THE BARE MINIMUM REQUIRED BY THE JOB.
YOU GET PAST SEEING ALL THAT BLOOD PRETTY QUICKLY... AFTER THAT, IT'S KIND OF FUN.
SATURDAY MORNING CARTOONS WERE JUST LAME AFTER THAT.
IT WAS LIKE WEEKEND FISHING TRIPS.
MOM WOULD EVEN PACK US LUNCHES.
WE WERE LEARNING A LOT AND, TO BE HONEST, IT WAS THE MOST TIME WE'D EVER SPENT WITH OUR FATHER.
I'D NEVER SAY HE DIDN'T LOVE US... BUT UP UNTIL THIS POINT, IT HAD BEEN MADE PRETTY CLEAR HE DIDN'T HAVE ANY USE FOR US.
THAT HAD ALL CHANGED. HE PUT US TO WORK.
WE WEREN'T DOING ANY ACTUAL KILLING AT FIRST. HE MADE US HIS SUPPORT CREW. WE SHARPENED KNIVES, MACHINED BULLETS, LOADED CLIPS, ORGANIZED WEAPONS BAGS.
WE EVEN MAPPED OUT ESCAPE ROUTES AND RESEARCHED TARGETS FOR HIM.
WE FELT LIKE WE WERE AN ESSENTIAL PART OF THE TEAM AND, AS TIME WENT ON, WE REALLY WERE.

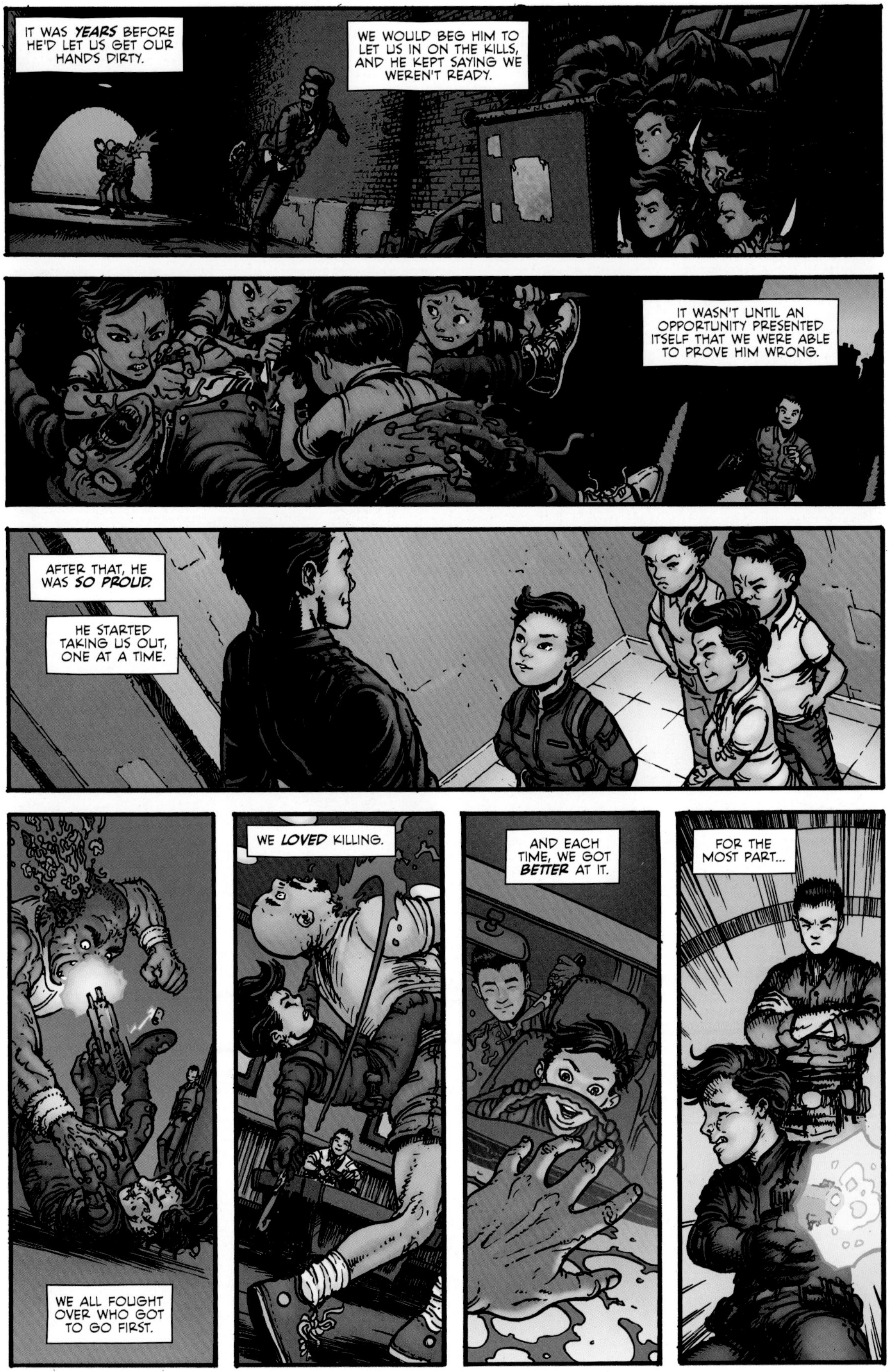
IT WAS YEARS BEFORE HE'D LET US GET OUR HANDS DIRTY.
WE WOULD BEG HIM TO LET US IN ON THE KILLS, AND HE KEPT SAYING WE WEREN'T READY.
IT WASN'T UNTIL AN OPPORTUNITY PRESENTED ITSELF THAT WE WERE ABLE TO PROVE HIM WRONG.
AFTER THAT, HE WAS SO PROUD.
HE STARTED TAKING US OUT, ONE AT A TIME.
WE ALL FOUGHT OVER WHO GOT TO GO FIRST.
WE LOVED KILLING.
AND EACH TIME, WE GOT BETTER AT IT.
FOR THE MOST PART...

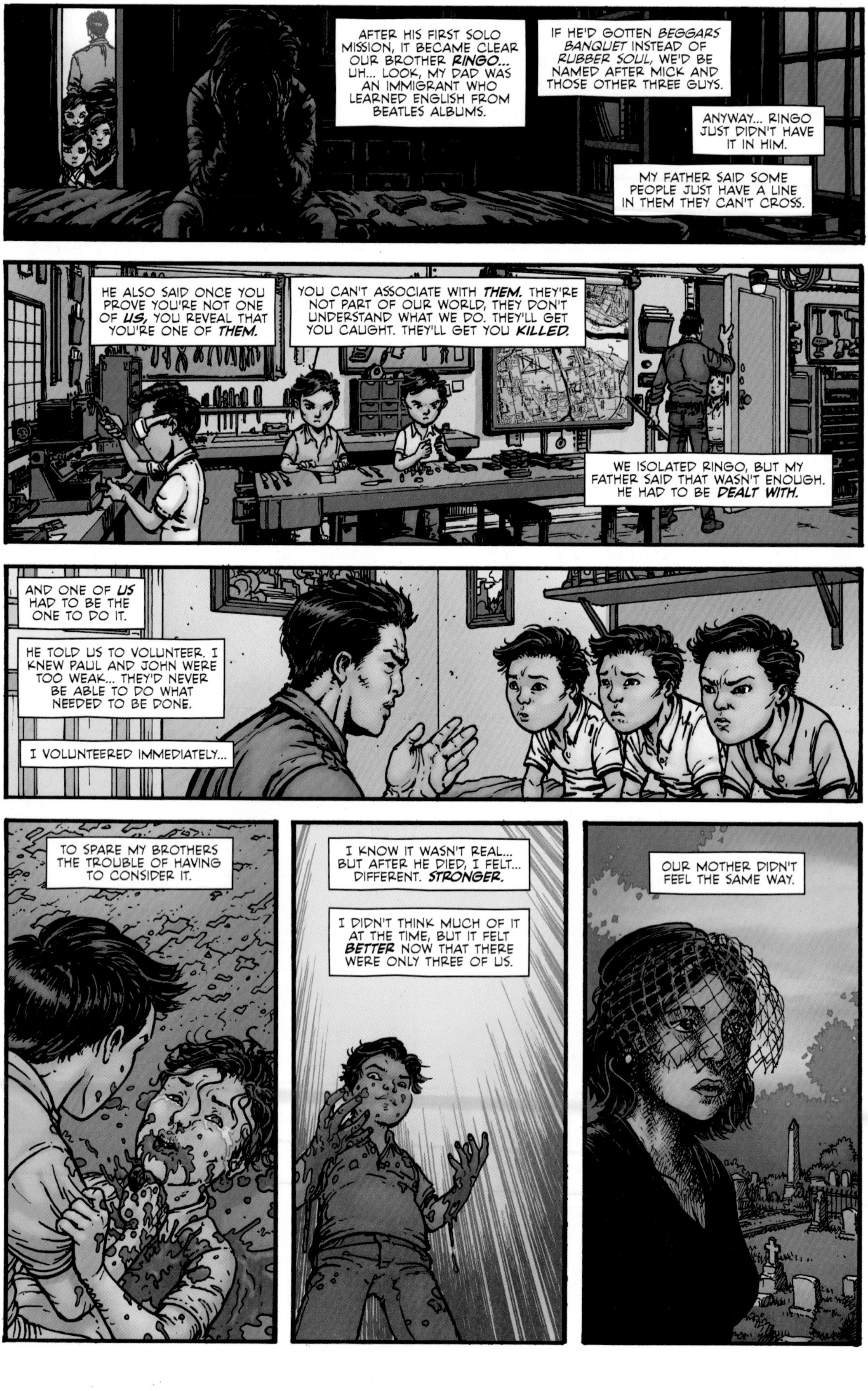
AFTER HIS FIRST SOLO MISSION, IT BECAME CLEAR OUR BROTHER RINGO... UH... LOOK, MY DAD WAS AN IMMIGRANT WHO LEARNED ENGLISH FROM BEATLES ALBUMS.
IF HE'D GOTTEN BEGGARS BANQUET INSTEAD OF RUBBER SOUL, WE'D BE NAMED AFTER MICK AND THOSE OTHER THREE GUYS.
ANYWAY... RINGO JUST DIDN'T HAVE IT IN HIM.
MY FATHER SAID SOME PEOPLE JUST HAVE A LINE IN THEM THEY CAN'T CROSS.
HE ALSO SAID ONCE YOU PROVE YOU'RE NOT ONE OF US, YOU REVEAL THAT YOU'RE ONE OF THEM.
YOU CAN'T ASSOCIATE WITH THEM. THEY'RE NOT PART OF OUR WORLD, THEY DON'T UNDERSTAND WHAT WE DO. THEY'LL GET YOU CAUGHT. THEY'LL GET YOU KILLED.
WE ISOLATED RINGO, BUT MY FATHER SAID THAT WASN'T ENOUGH. HE HAD TO BE DEALT WITH.
AND ONE OF US HAD TO BE THE ONE TO DO IT.
HE TOLD US TO VOLUNTEER. I KNEW PAUL AND JOHN WERE TOO WEAK... THEY'D NEVER BE ABLE TO DO WHAT NEEDED TO BE DONE.
I VOLUNTEERED IMMEDIATELY...
TO SPARE MY BROTHERS THE TROUBLE OF HAVING TO CONSIDER IT.
I KNOW IT WASN'T REAL... BUT AFTER HE DIED, I FELT... DIFFERENT. STRONGER.
I DIDN'T THINK MUCH OF IT AT THE TIME, BUT IT FELT BETTER NOW THAT THERE WERE ONLY THREE OF US.
OUR MOTHER DIDN'T FEEL THE SAME WAY.

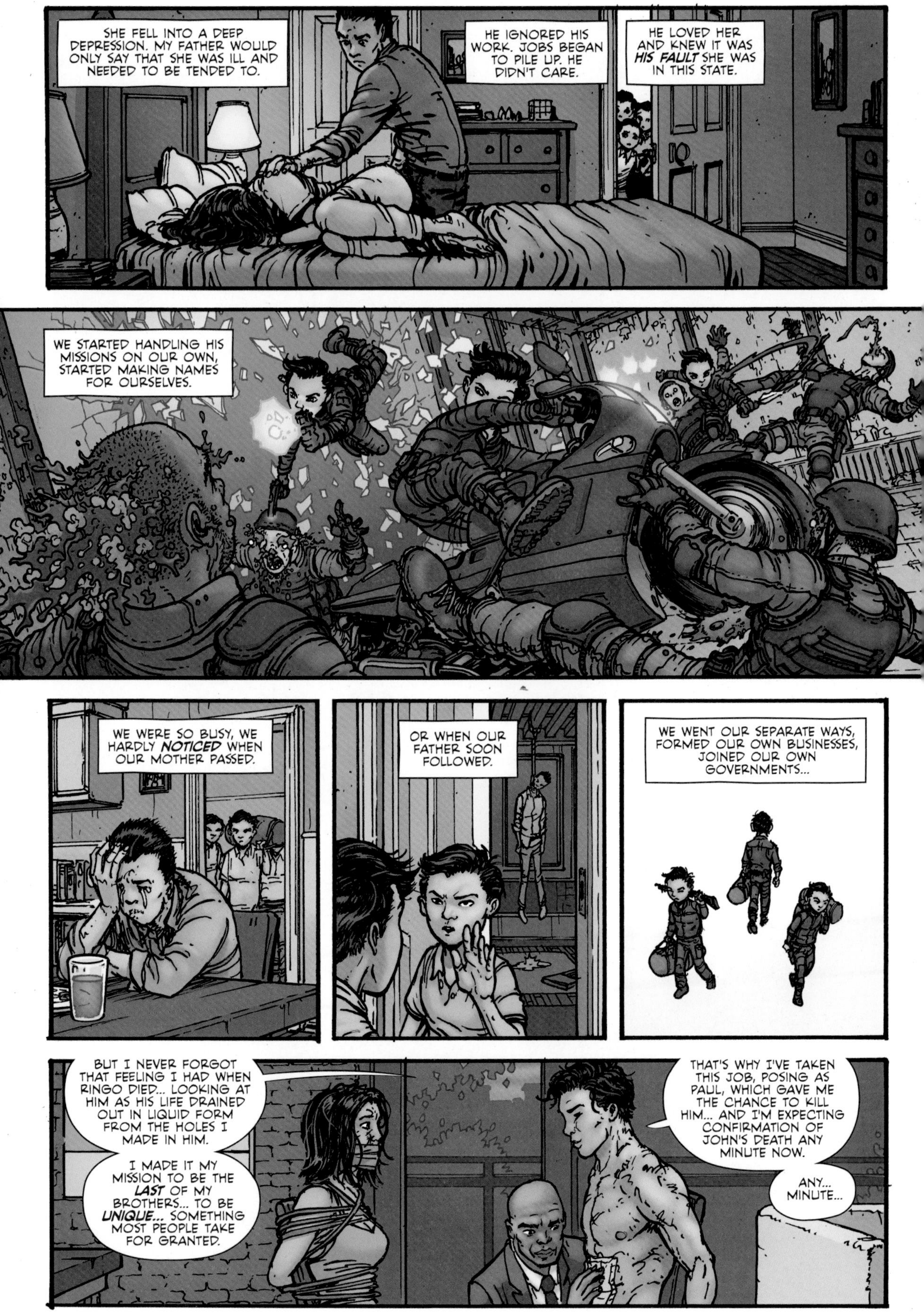
SHE FELL INTO A DEEP DEPRESSION. MY FATHER WOULD ONLY SAY THAT SHE WAS ILL AND NEEDED TO BE TENDED TO.
HE IGNORED HIS WORK. JOBS BEGAN TO PILE UP. HE DIDN'T CARE.
HE LOVED HER AND KNEW IT WAS ***HIS FAULT*** SHE WAS IN THIS STATE.
WE STARTED HANDLING HIS MISSIONS ON OUR OWN, STARTED MAKING NAMES FOR OURSELVES.
WE WERE SO BUSY, WE HARDLY ***NOTICED*** WHEN OUR MOTHER PASSED.
OR WHEN OUR FATHER SOON FOLLOWED.
WE WENT OUR SEPARATE WAYS, FORMED OUR OWN BUSINESSES, JOINED OUR OWN GOVERNMENTS...
BUT I NEVER FORGOT THAT FEELING I HAD WHEN RINGO DIED... LOOKING AT HIM AS HIS LIFE DRAINED OUT IN LIQUID FORM FROM THE HOLES I MADE IN HIM.
I MADE IT MY MISSION TO BE THE ***LAST*** OF MY BROTHERS... TO BE ***UNIQUE...*** SOMETHING MOST PEOPLE TAKE FOR GRANTED.
THAT'S WHY I'VE TAKEN THIS JOB, POSING AS PAUL, WHICH GAVE ME THE CHANCE TO KILL HIM... AND I'M EXPECTING CONFIRMATION OF JOHN'S DEATH ANY MINUTE NOW.
ANY... MINUTE...

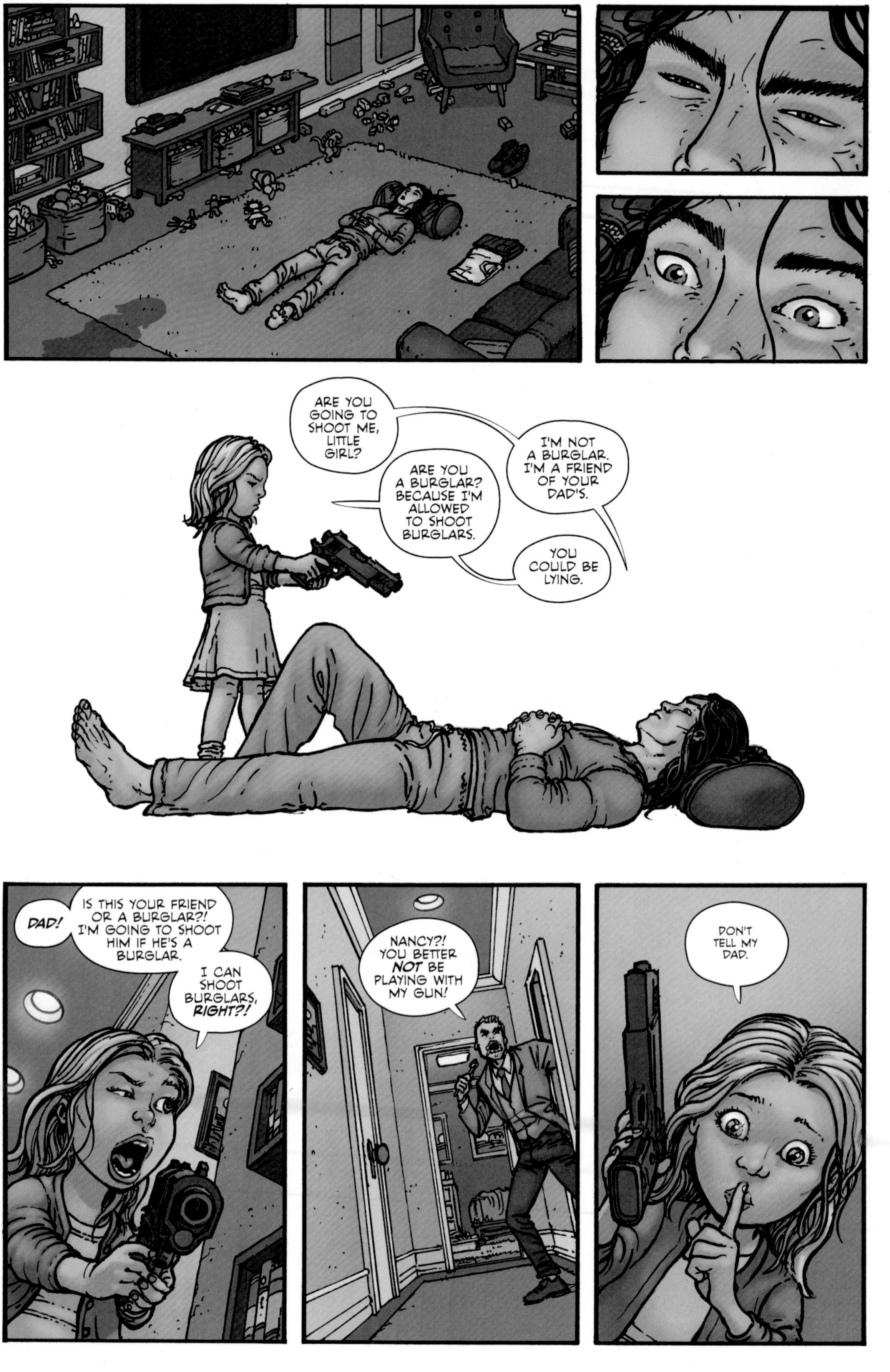
ARE YOU GOING TO SHOOT ME, LITTLE GIRL?
ARE YOU A BURGLAR? BECAUSE I'M ALLOWED TO SHOOT BURGLARS.
I'M NOT A BURGLAR. I'M A FRIEND OF YOUR DAD'S.
YOU COULD BE LYING.
DAD!
IS THIS YOUR FRIEND OR A BURGLAR?! I'M GOING TO SHOOT HIM IF HE'S A BURGLAR.
I CAN SHOOT BURGLARS, RIGHT?!
NANCY?! YOU BETTER NOT BE PLAYING WITH MY GUN!
DON'T TELL MY DAD.

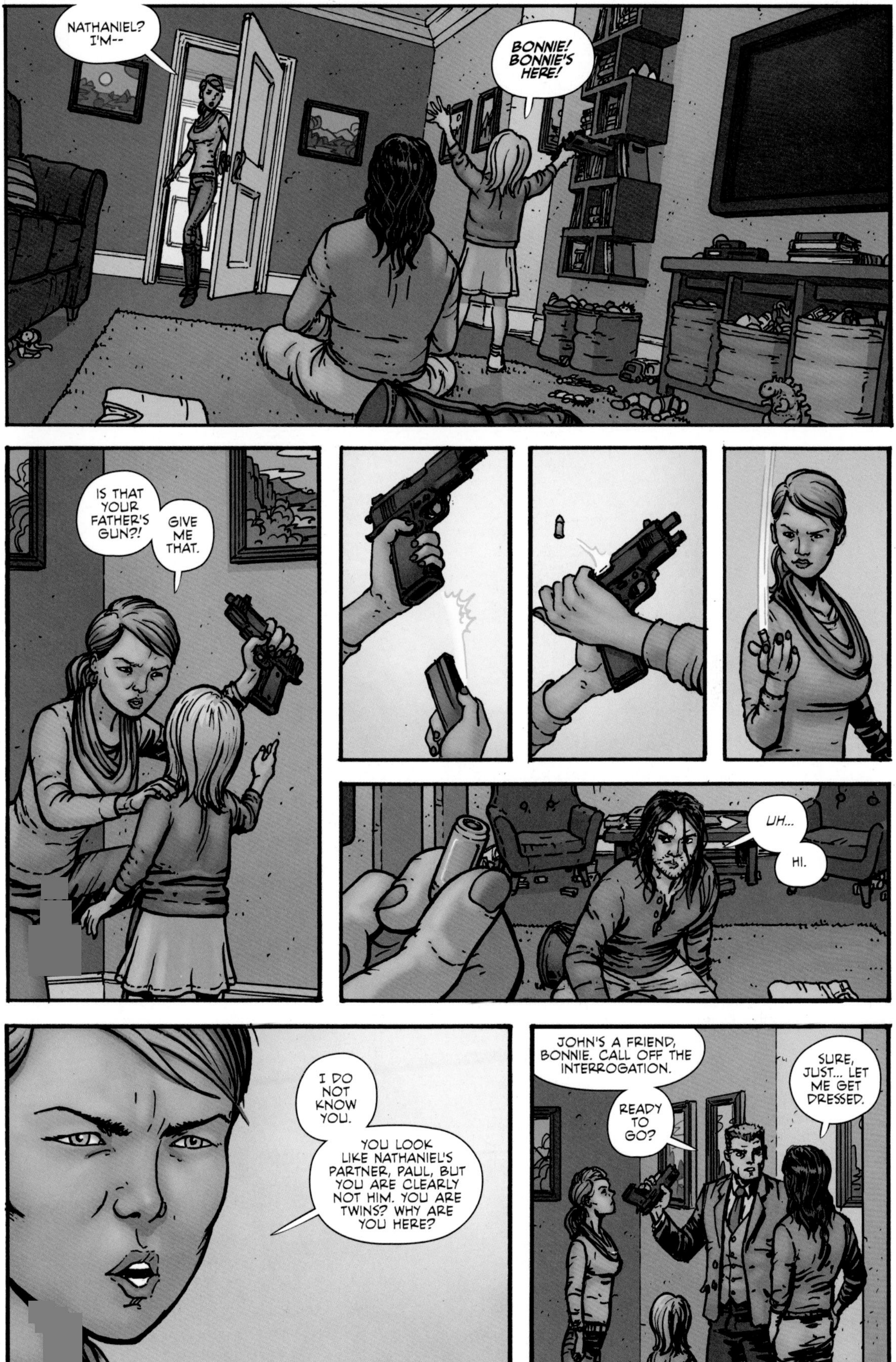
NATHANIEL? I'M--
BONNIE! BONNIE'S HERE!
IS THAT YOUR FATHER'S GUN?!
GIVE ME THAT.
UH...
HI.
I DO NOT KNOW YOU.
YOU LOOK LIKE NATHANIEL'S PARTNER, PAUL, BUT YOU ARE CLEARLY NOT HIM. YOU ARE TWINS? WHY ARE YOU HERE?
JOHN'S A FRIEND, BONNIE. CALL OFF THE INTERROGATION.
READY TO GO?
SURE, JUST... LET ME GET DRESSED.

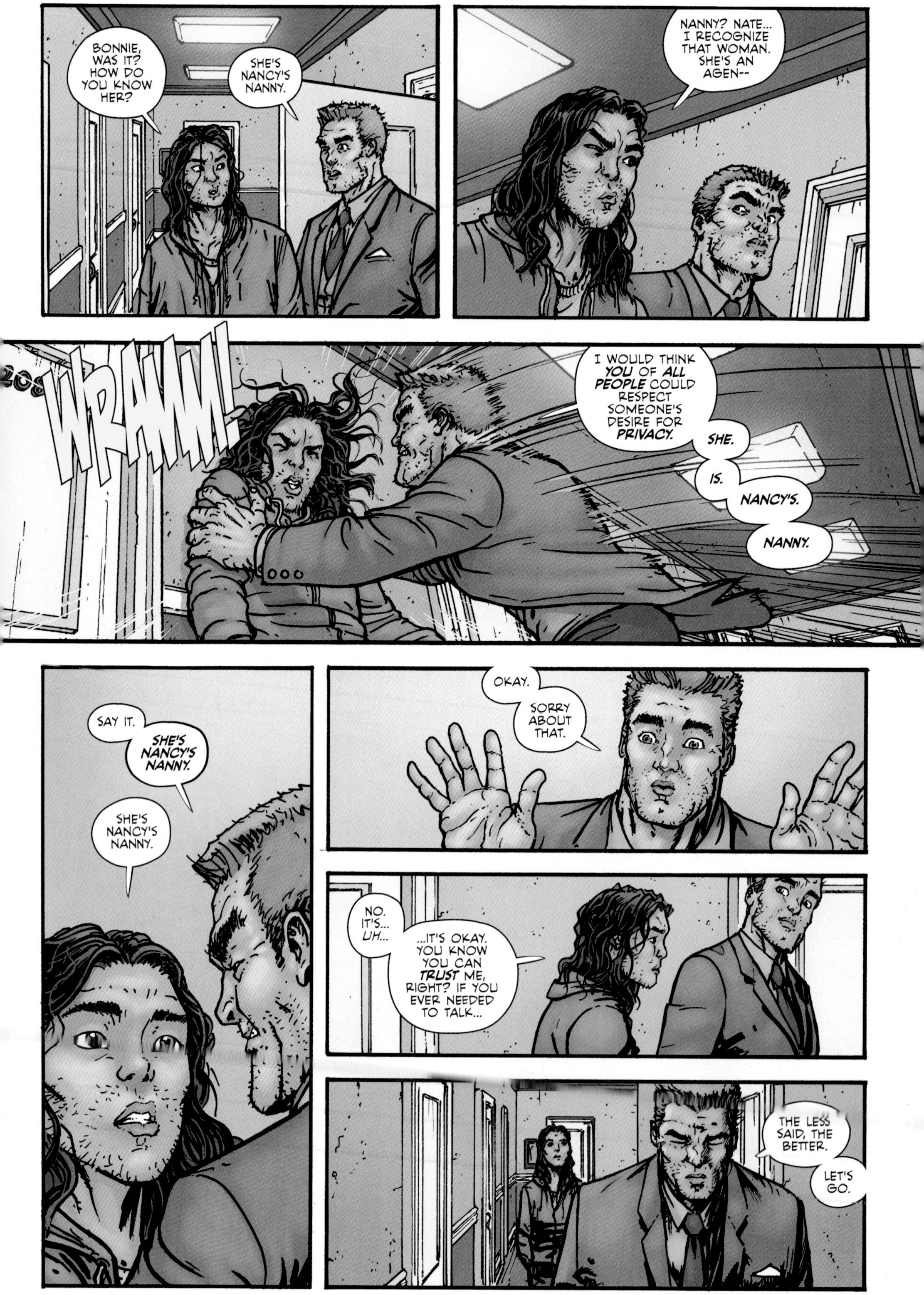
BONNIE, WAS IT? HOW DO YOU KNOW HER?
SHE'S NANCY'S NANNY.
NANNY? NATE... I RECOGNIZE THAT WOMAN. SHE'S AN AGEN--
WRAMM!
I WOULD THINK YOU OF ALL PEOPLE COULD RESPECT SOMEONE'S DESIRE FOR PRIVACY.
SHE.
IS.
NANCY'S.
NANNY.
SAY IT.
SHE'S NANCY'S NANNY.
SHE'S NANCY'S NANNY.
OKAY.
SORRY ABOUT THAT.
NO. IT'S... UH...
...IT'S OKAY. YOU KNOW YOU CAN TRUST ME, RIGHT? IF YOU EVER NEEDED TO TALK...
THE LESS SAID, THE BETTER.
LET'S GO.

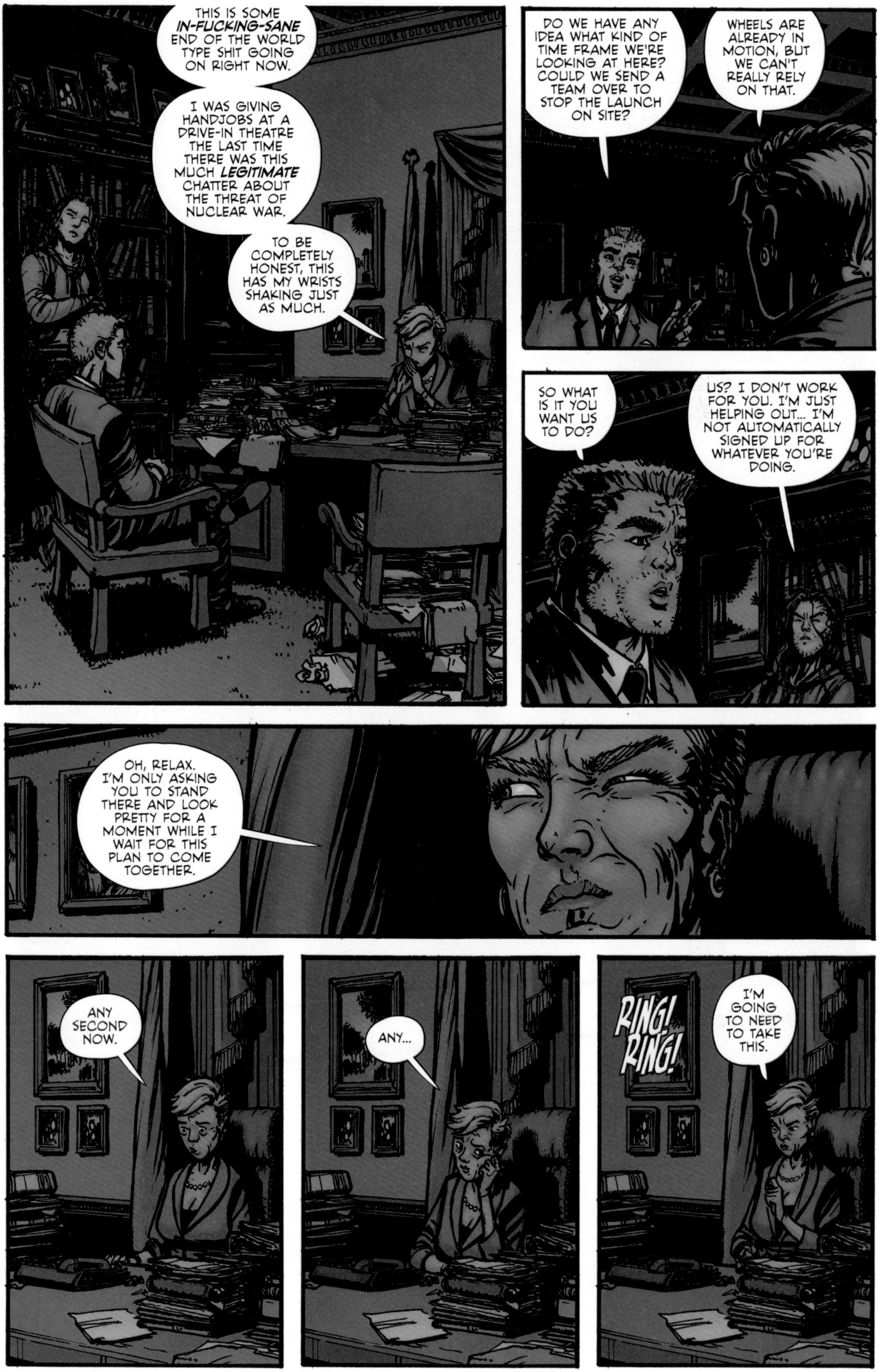
THIS IS SOME IN-FUCKING-SANE END OF THE WORLD TYPE SHIT GOING ON RIGHT NOW.
I WAS GIVING HANDJOBS AT A DRIVE-IN THEATRE THE LAST TIME THERE WAS THIS MUCH LEGITIMATE CHATTER ABOUT THE THREAT OF NUCLEAR WAR.
TO BE COMPLETELY HONEST, THIS HAS MY WRISTS SHAKING JUST AS MUCH.
DO WE HAVE ANY IDEA WHAT KIND OF TIME FRAME WE'RE LOOKING AT HERE? COULD WE SEND A TEAM OVER TO STOP THE LAUNCH ON SITE?
WHEELS ARE ALREADY IN MOTION, BUT WE CAN'T REALLY RELY ON THAT.
SO WHAT IS IT YOU WANT US TO DO?
US? I DON'T WORK FOR YOU. I'M JUST HELPING OUT... I'M NOT AUTOMATICALLY SIGNED UP FOR WHATEVER YOU'RE DOING.
OH, RELAX. I'M ONLY ASKING YOU TO STAND THERE AND LOOK PRETTY FOR A MOMENT WHILE I WAIT FOR THIS PLAN TO COME TOGETHER.
ANY SECOND NOW.
ANY...
RING! RING!
I'M GOING TO NEED TO TAKE THIS.

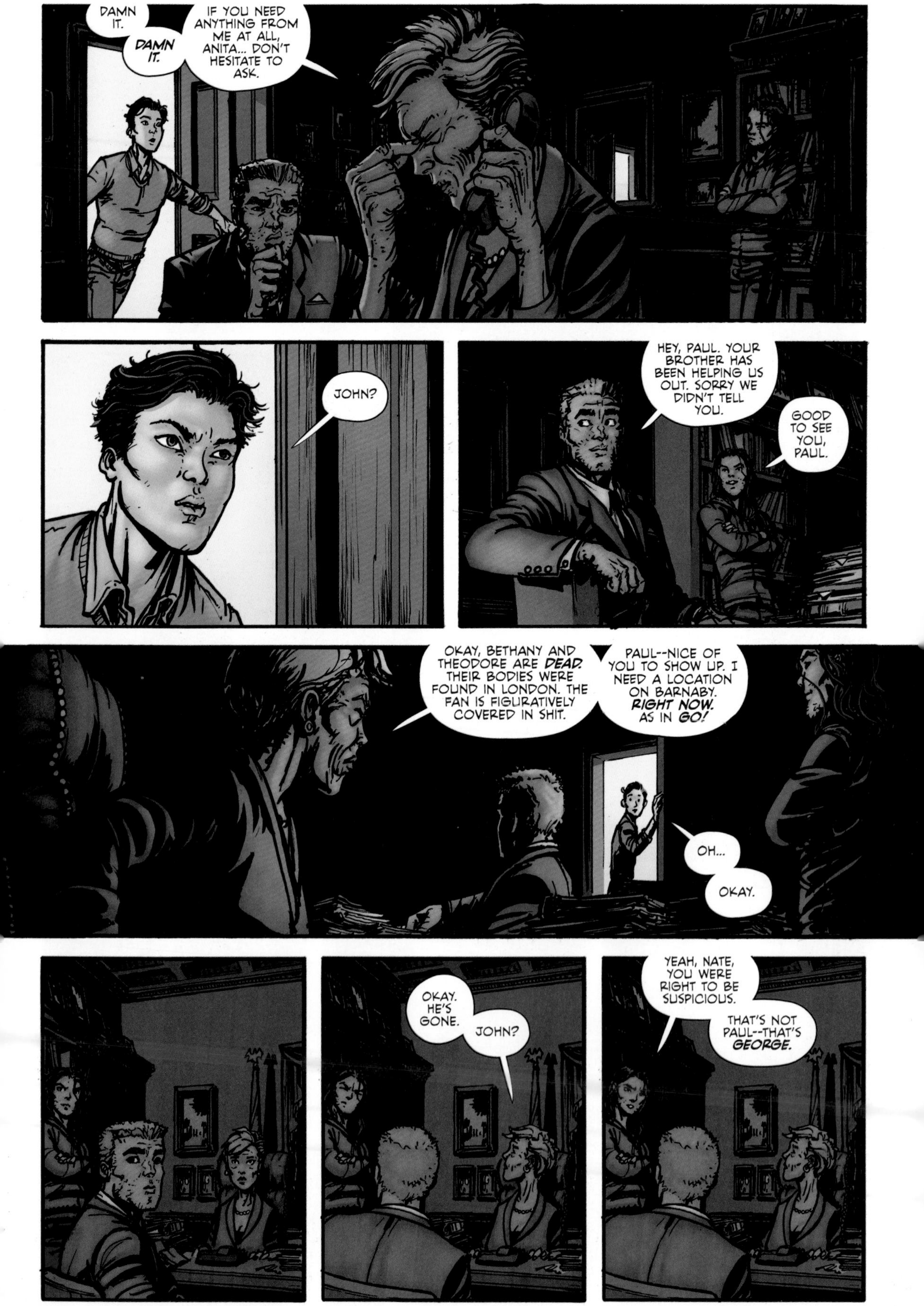
DAMN IT.
DAMN IT.
IF YOU NEED ANYTHING FROM ME AT ALL, ANITA... DON'T HESITATE TO ASK.
JOHN?
HEY, PAUL. YOUR BROTHER HAS BEEN HELPING US OUT. SORRY WE DIDN'T TELL YOU.
GOOD TO SEE YOU, PAUL.
OKAY, BETHANY AND THEODORE ARE DEAD. THEIR BODIES WERE FOUND IN LONDON. THE FAN IS FIGURATIVELY COVERED IN SHIT.
PAUL--NICE OF YOU TO SHOW UP. I NEED A LOCATION ON BARNABY. RIGHT NOW. AS IN GO!
OH...
OKAY.
OKAY. HE'S GONE.
JOHN?
YEAH, NATE, YOU WERE RIGHT TO BE SUSPICIOUS.
THAT'S NOT PAUL--THAT'S GEORGE.

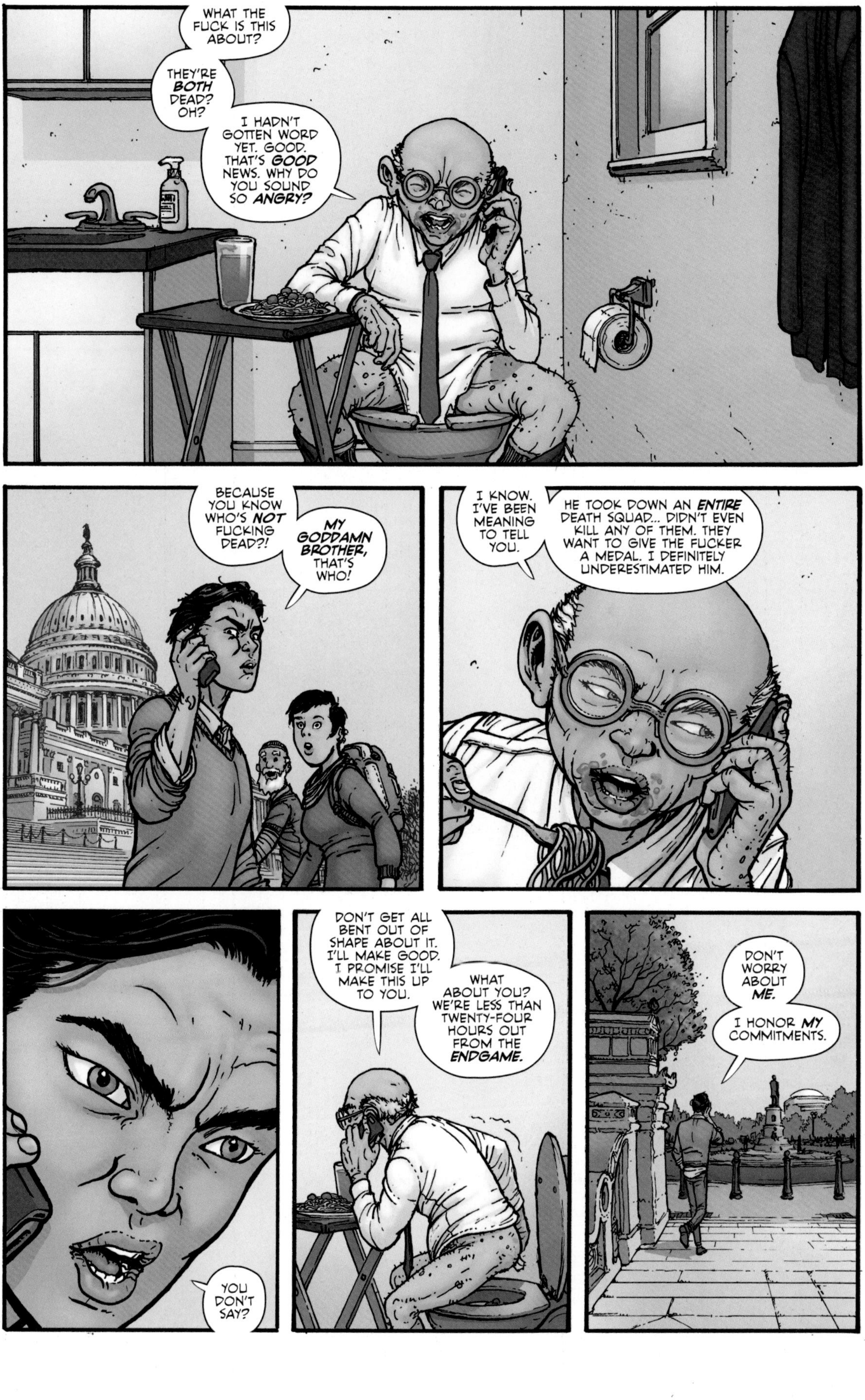
WHAT THE FUCK IS THIS ABOUT?
THEY'RE BOTH DEAD? OH?
I HADN'T GOTTEN WORD YET. GOOD. THAT'S GOOD NEWS. WHY DO YOU SOUND SO ANGRY?
BECAUSE YOU KNOW WHO'S NOT FUCKING DEAD?!
MY GODDAMN BROTHER, THAT'S WHO!
I KNOW. I'VE BEEN MEANING TO TELL YOU.
HE TOOK DOWN AN ENTIRE DEATH SQUAD... DIDN'T EVEN KILL ANY OF THEM. THEY WANT TO GIVE THE FUCKER A MEDAL. I DEFINITELY UNDERESTIMATED HIM.
YOU DON'T SAY?
DON'T GET ALL BENT OUT OF SHAPE ABOUT IT. I'LL MAKE GOOD. I PROMISE I'LL MAKE THIS UP TO YOU.
WHAT ABOUT YOU? WE'RE LESS THAN TWENTY-FOUR HOURS OUT FROM THE ENDGAME.
DON'T WORRY ABOUT ME.
I HONOR MY COMMITMENTS.

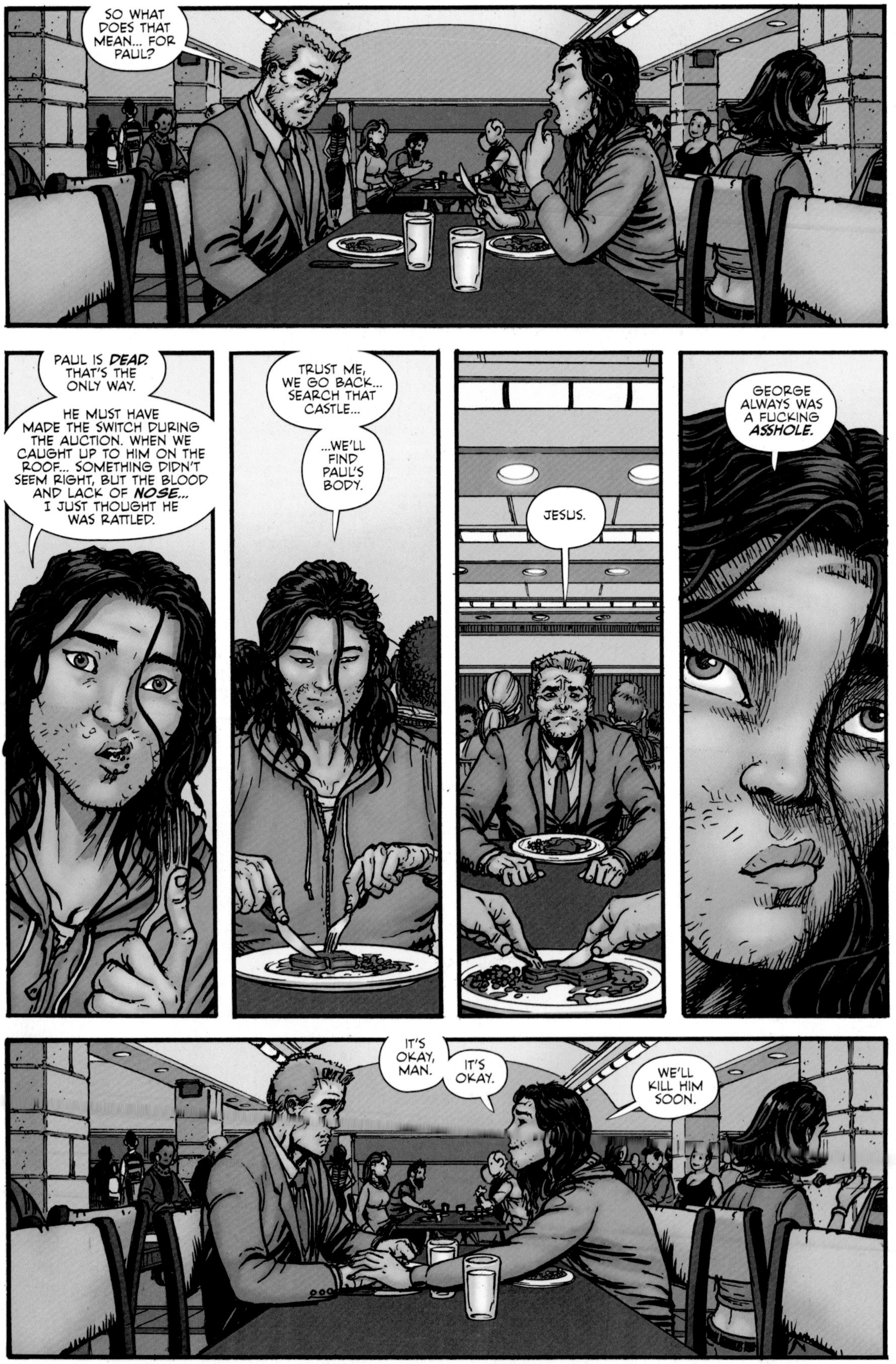
SO WHAT DOES THAT MEAN... FOR PAUL?
PAUL IS DEAD. THAT'S THE ONLY WAY.
HE MUST HAVE MADE THE SWITCH DURING THE AUCTION. WHEN WE CAUGHT UP TO HIM ON THE ROOF... SOMETHING DIDN'T SEEM RIGHT, BUT THE BLOOD AND LACK OF NOSE... I JUST THOUGHT HE WAS RATTLED.
TRUST ME, WE GO BACK... SEARCH THAT CASTLE...
...WE'LL FIND PAUL'S BODY.
JESUS.
GEORGE ALWAYS WAS A FUCKING ASSHOLE.
IT'S OKAY, MAN.
IT'S OKAY.
WE'LL KILL HIM SOON.

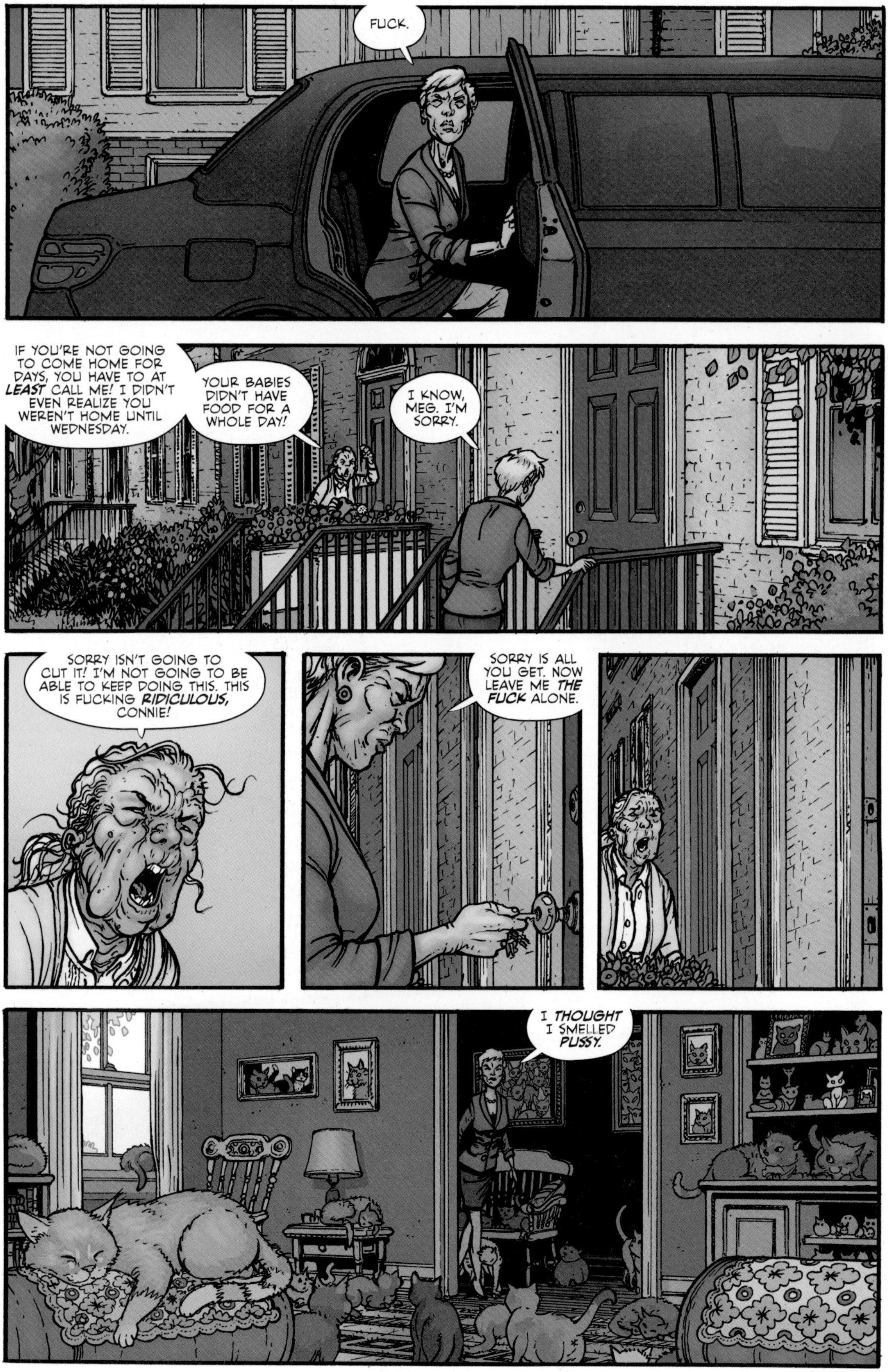
FUCK.
IF YOU'RE NOT GOING TO COME HOME FOR DAYS, YOU HAVE TO AT LEAST CALL ME! I DIDN'T EVEN REALIZE YOU WEREN'T HOME UNTIL WEDNESDAY.
YOUR BABIES DIDN'T HAVE FOOD FOR A WHOLE DAY!
I KNOW, MEG. I'M SORRY.
SORRY ISN'T GOING TO CUT IT! I'M NOT GOING TO BE ABLE TO KEEP DOING THIS. THIS IS FUCKING RIDICULOUS, CONNIE!
SORRY IS ALL YOU GET. NOW LEAVE ME THE FUCK ALONE.
I THOUGHT I SMELLED PUSSY.

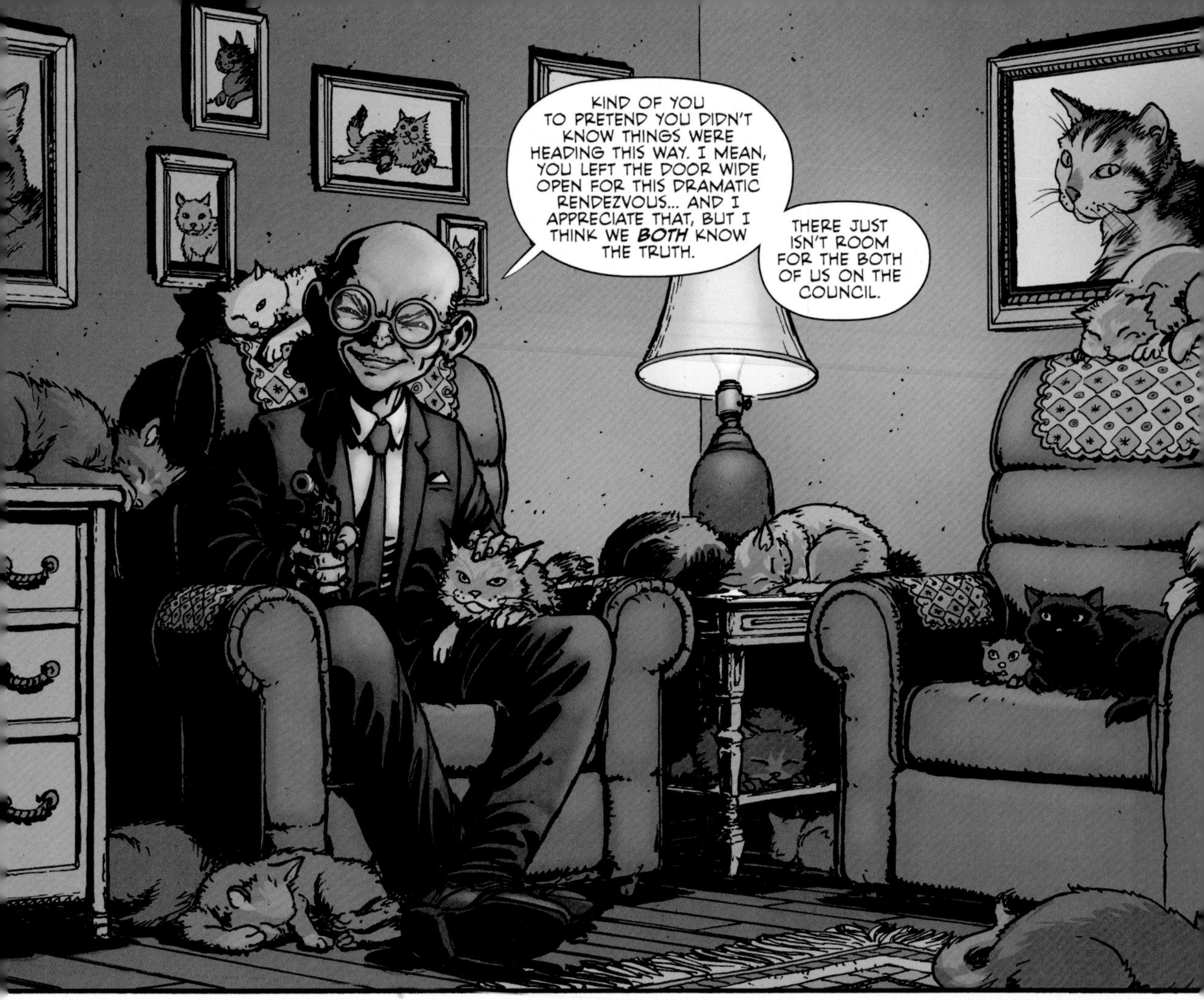
KIND OF YOU TO PRETEND YOU DIDN'T KNOW THINGS WERE HEADING THIS WAY. I MEAN, YOU LEFT THE DOOR WIDE OPEN FOR THIS DRAMATIC RENDEZVOUS... AND I APPRECIATE THAT, BUT I THINK WE BOTH KNOW THE TRUTH.
THERE JUST ISN'T ROOM FOR THE BOTH OF US ON THE COUNCIL.

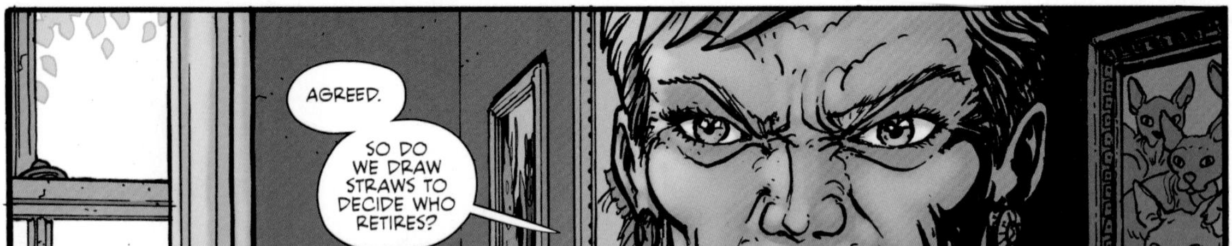
AGREED.
SO DO WE DRAW STRAWS TO DECIDE WHO RETIRES?

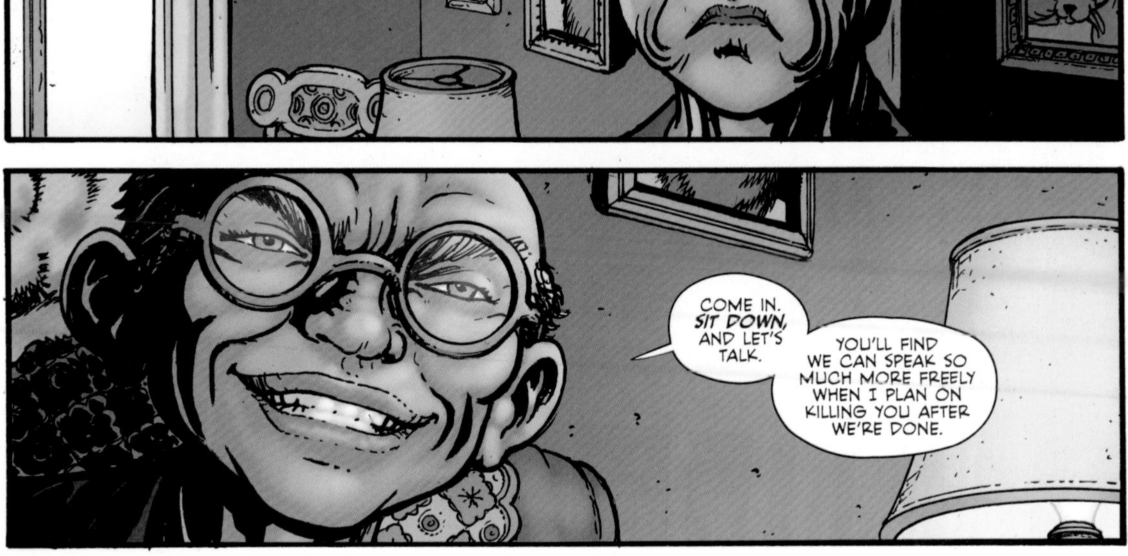
COME IN. SIT DOWN, AND LET'S TALK.
YOU'LL FIND WE CAN SPEAK SO MUCH MORE FREELY WHEN I PLAN ON KILLING YOU AFTER WE'RE DONE.

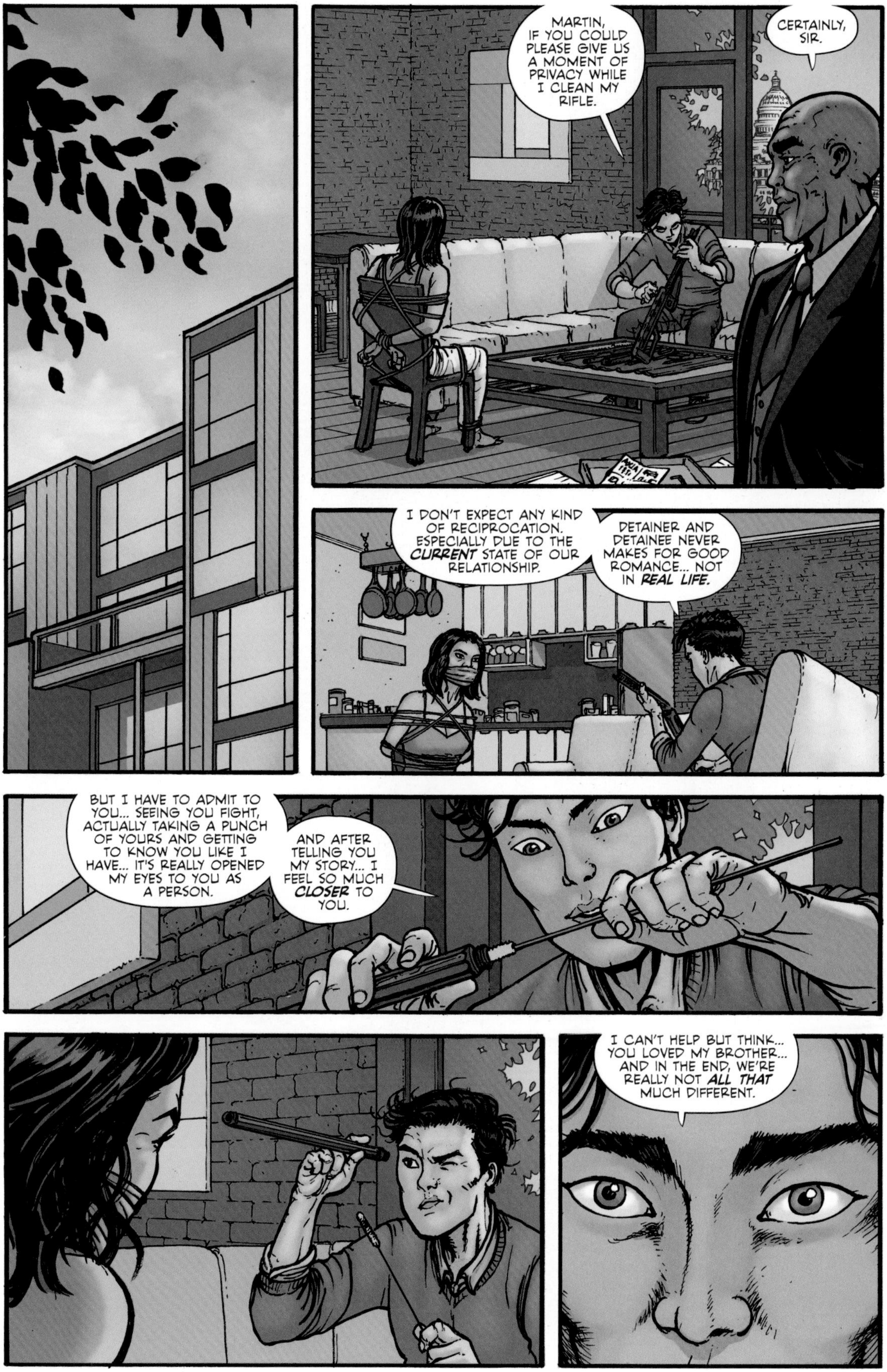
MARTIN, IF YOU COULD PLEASE GIVE US A MOMENT OF PRIVACY WHILE I CLEAN MY RIFLE.
CERTAINLY, SIR.
I DON'T EXPECT ANY KIND OF RECIPROCATION. ESPECIALLY DUE TO THE CURRENT STATE OF OUR RELATIONSHIP.
DETAINER AND DETAINEE NEVER MAKES FOR GOOD ROMANCE... NOT IN REAL LIFE.
BUT I HAVE TO ADMIT TO YOU... SEEING YOU FIGHT, ACTUALLY TAKING A PUNCH OF YOURS AND GETTING TO KNOW YOU LIKE I HAVE... IT'S REALLY OPENED MY EYES TO YOU AS A PERSON.
AND AFTER TELLING YOU MY STORY... I FEEL SO MUCH CLOSER TO YOU.
I CAN'T HELP BUT THINK... YOU LOVED MY BROTHER... AND IN THE END, WE'RE REALLY NOT ALL THAT MUCH DIFFERENT.

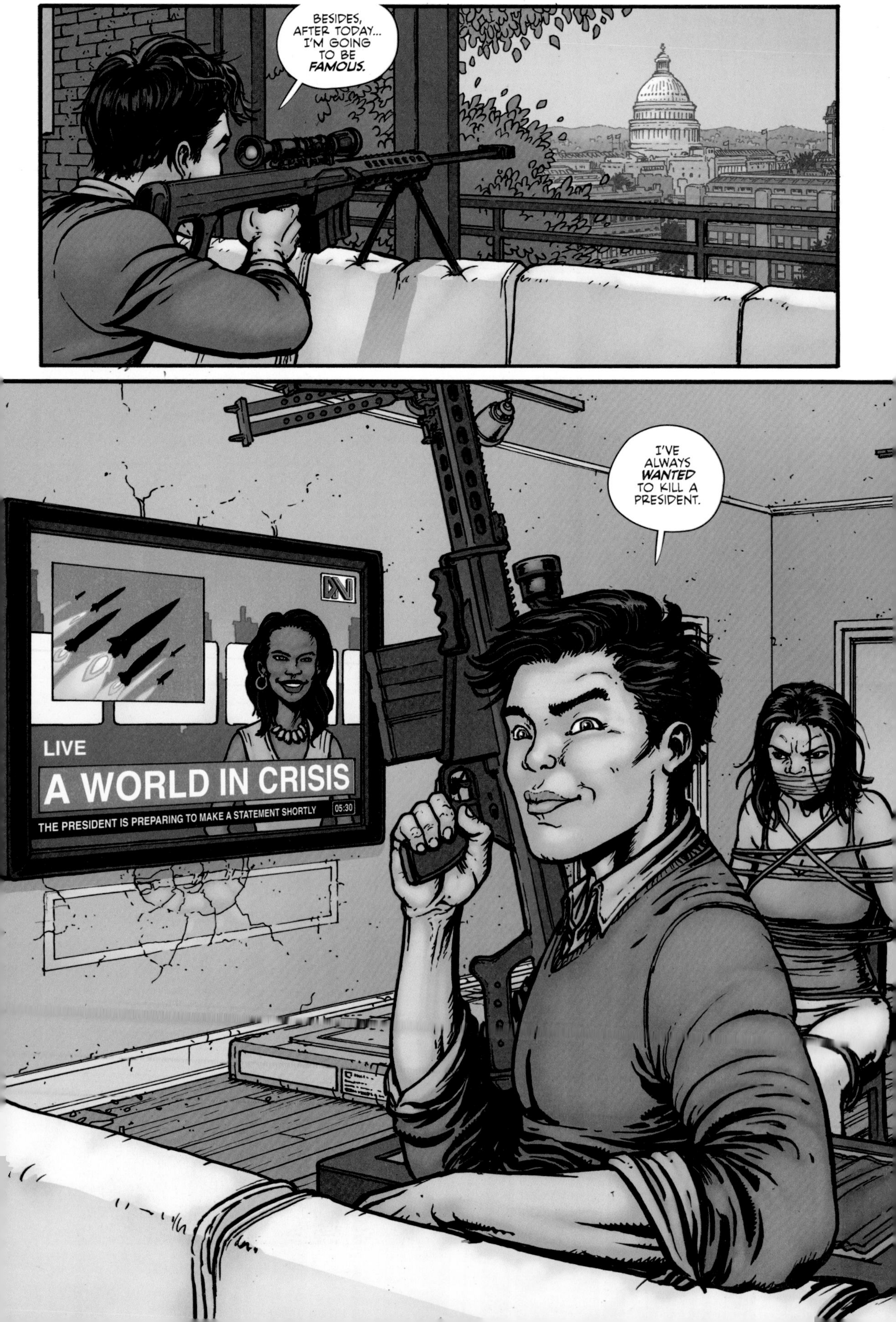
BESIDES, AFTER TODAY... I'M GOING TO BE FAMOUS.
I'VE ALWAYS WANTED TO KILL A PRESIDENT.
LIVE
A WORLD IN CRISIS
THE PRESIDENT IS PREPARING TO MAKE A STATEMENT SHORTLY
05:30

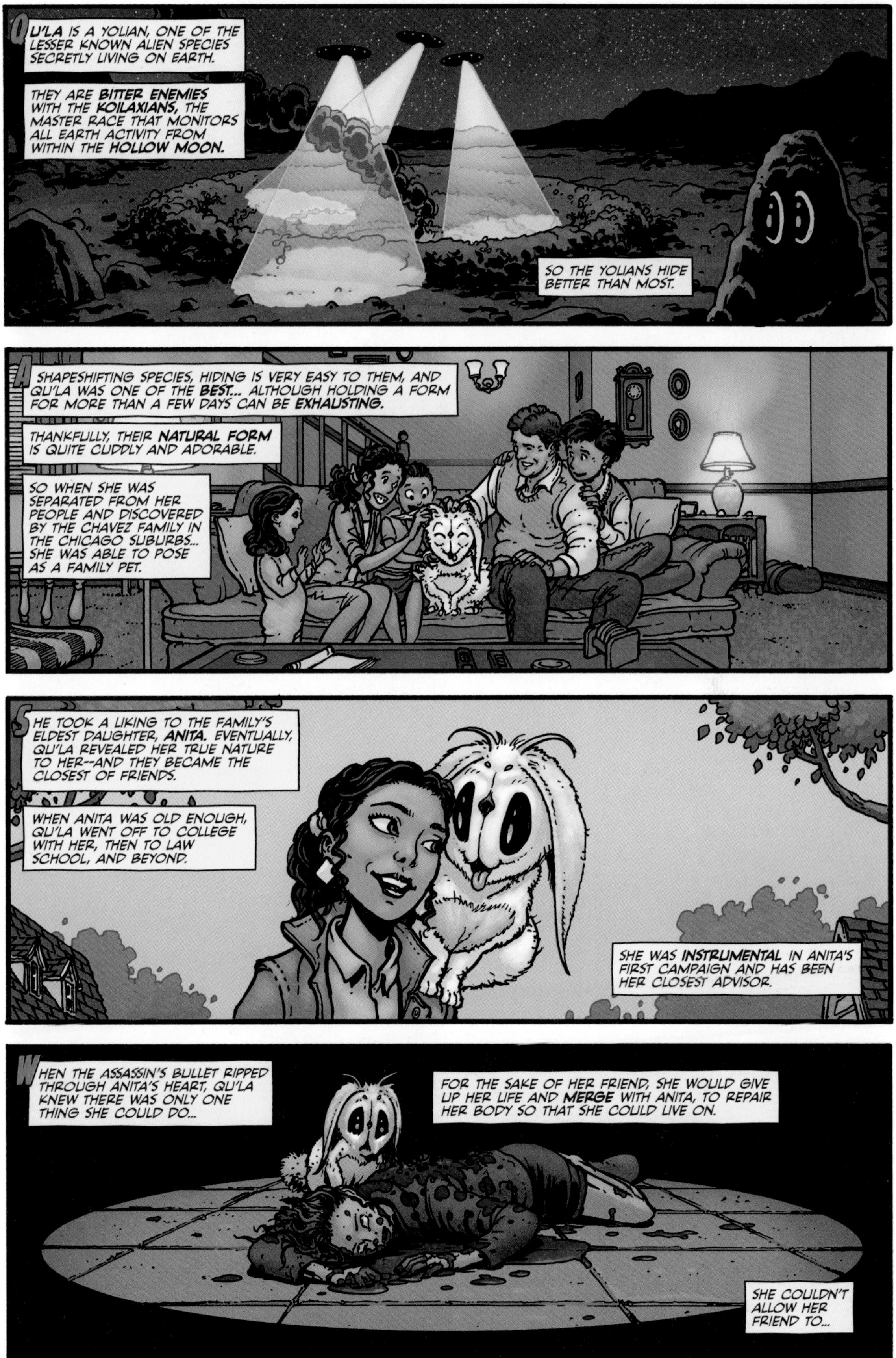
QU'LA IS A YOLIAN, ONE OF THE LESSER KNOWN ALIEN SPECIES SECRETLY LIVING ON EARTH.
THEY ARE BITTER ENEMIES WITH THE KOILAXIANS, THE MASTER RACE THAT MONITORS ALL EARTH ACTIVITY FROM WITHIN THE HOLLOW MOON.
SO THE YOLIANS HIDE BETTER THAN MOST.
A SHAPESHIFTING SPECIES, HIDING IS VERY EASY TO THEM, AND QU'LA WAS ONE OF THE BEST... ALTHOUGH HOLDING A FORM FOR MORE THAN A FEW DAYS CAN BE EXHAUSTING.
THANKFULLY, THEIR NATURAL FORM IS QUITE CUDDLY AND ADORABLE.
SO WHEN SHE WAS SEPARATED FROM HER PEOPLE AND DISCOVERED BY THE CHAVEZ FAMILY IN THE CHICAGO SUBURBS... SHE WAS ABLE TO POSE AS A FAMILY PET.
SHE TOOK A LIKING TO THE FAMILY'S ELDEST DAUGHTER, ANITA. EVENTUALLY, QU'LA REVEALED HER TRUE NATURE TO HER--AND THEY BECAME THE CLOSEST OF FRIENDS.
WHEN ANITA WAS OLD ENOUGH, QU'LA WENT OFF TO COLLEGE WITH HER, THEN TO LAW SCHOOL, AND BEYOND.
SHE WAS INSTRUMENTAL IN ANITA'S FIRST CAMPAIGN AND HAS BEEN HER CLOSEST ADVISOR.
WHEN THE ASSASSIN'S BULLET RIPPED THROUGH ANITA'S HEART, QU'LA KNEW THERE WAS ONLY ONE THING SHE COULD DO...
FOR THE SAKE OF HER FRIEND, SHE WOULD GIVE UP HER LIFE AND MERGE WITH ANITA, TO REPAIR HER BODY SO THAT SHE COULD LIVE ON.
SHE COULDN'T ALLOW HER FRIEND TO...

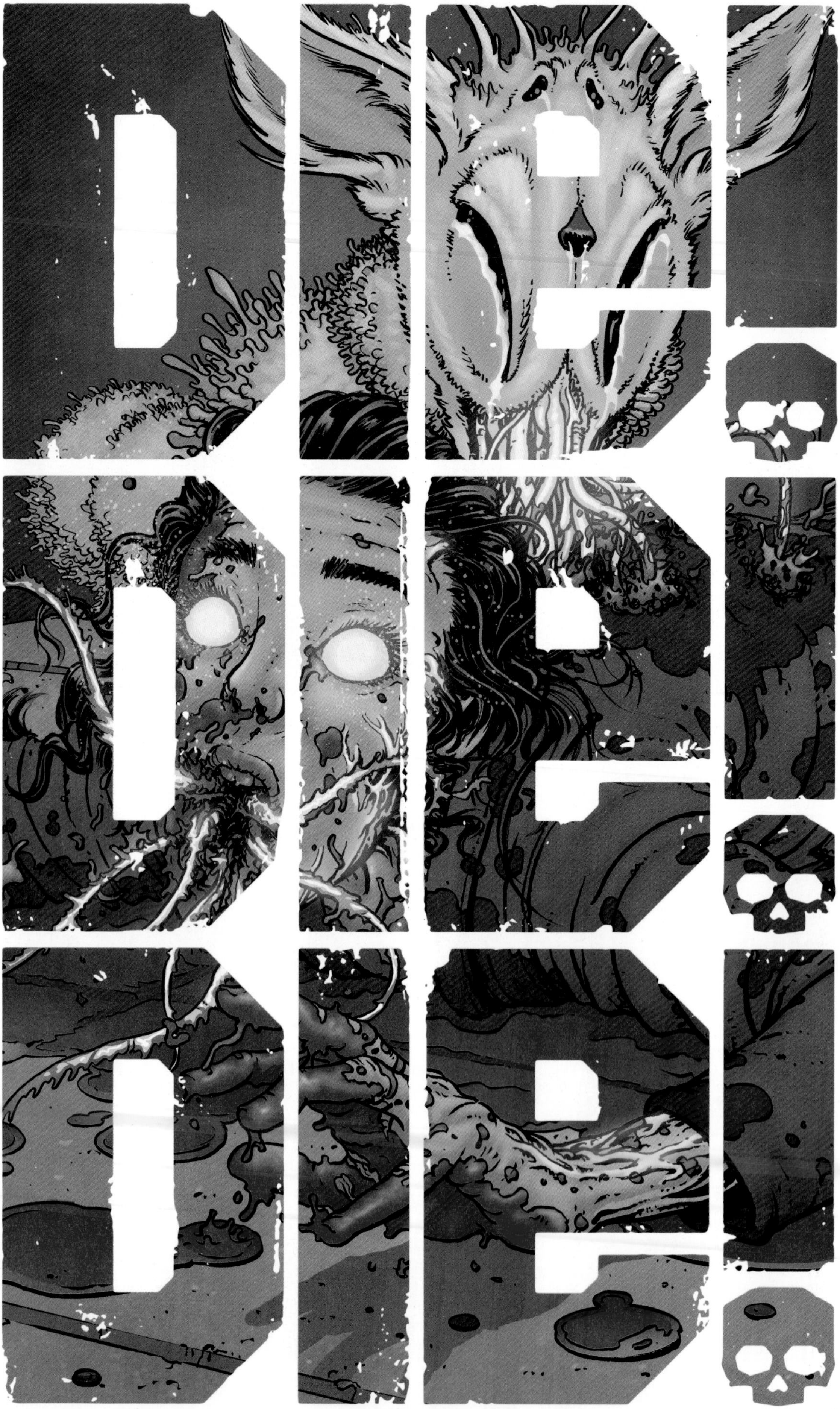
DIE!
DIE!
DIE!

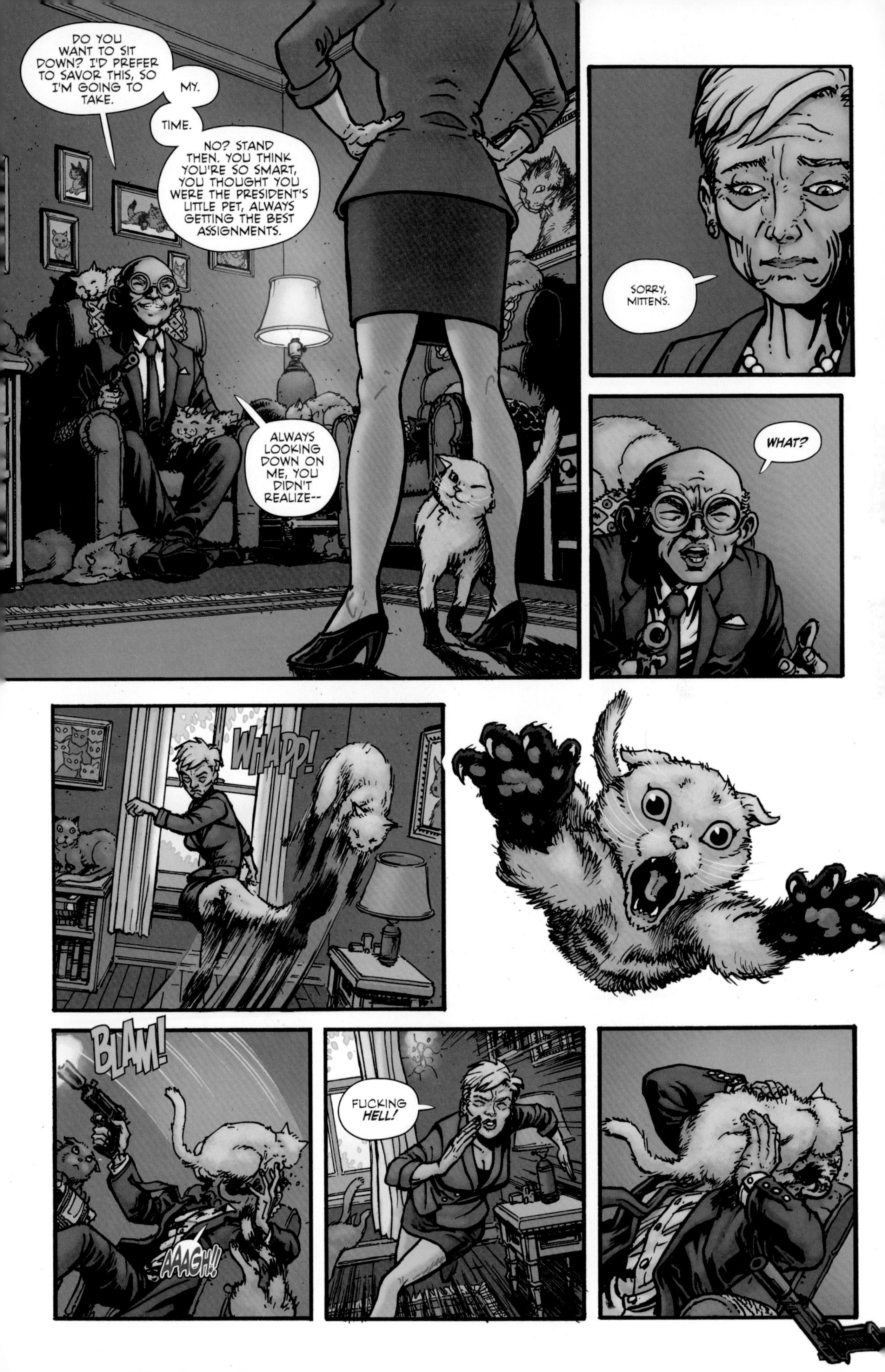
DO YOU WANT TO SIT DOWN? I'D PREFER TO SAVOR THIS, SO I'M GOING TO TAKE.
MY.
TIME.
NO? STAND THEN. YOU THINK YOU'RE SO SMART, YOU THOUGHT YOU WERE THE PRESIDENT'S LITTLE PET, ALWAYS GETTING THE BEST ASSIGNMENTS.
ALWAYS LOOKING DOWN ON ME, YOU DIDN'T REALIZE--
SORRY, MITTENS.
WHAT?
WHAPP!
BLAM!
AAAGH!!
FUCKING HELL!

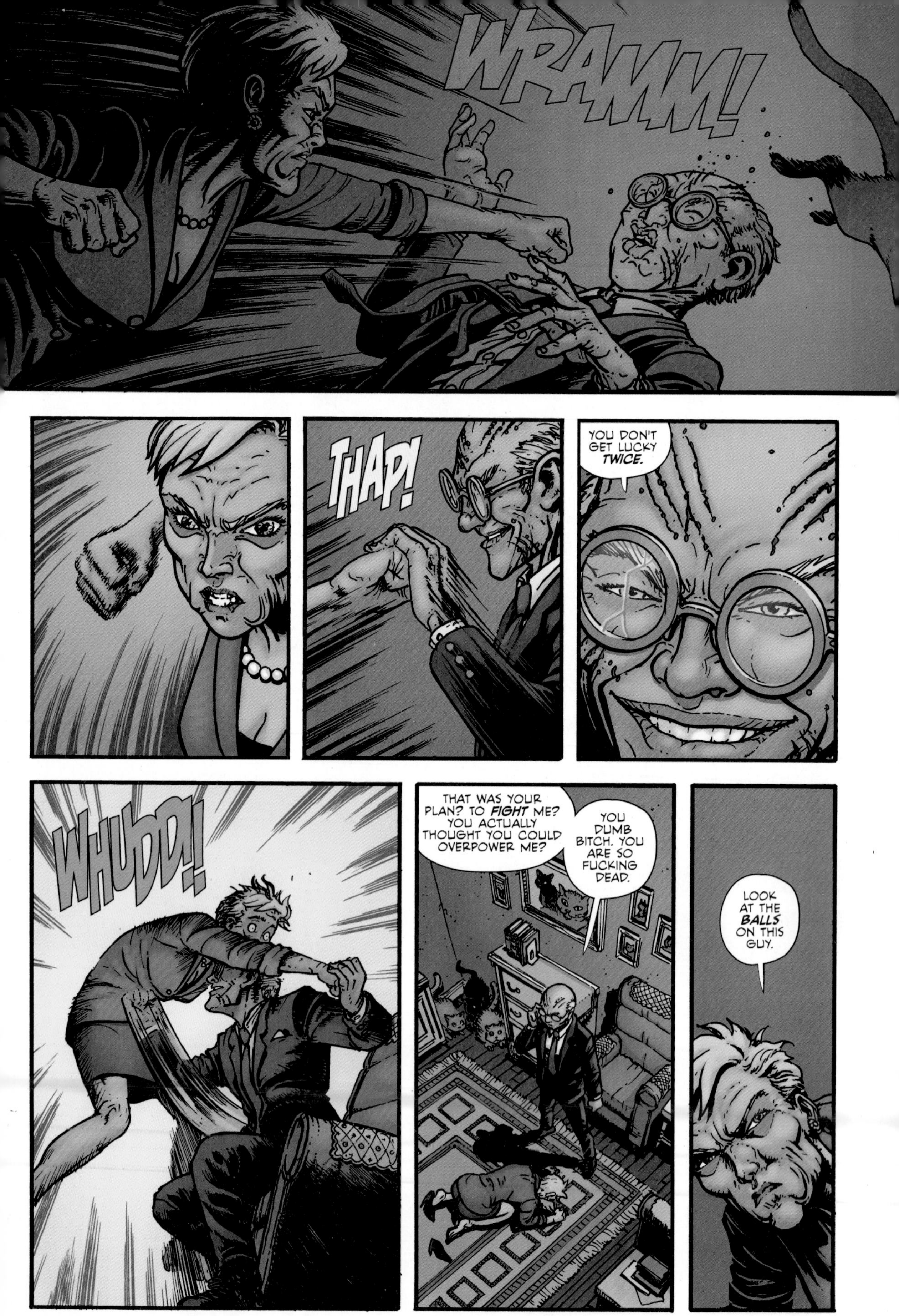
WRAMM!
THAP!
YOU DON'T GET LUCKY TWICE.
WHUDD!!
THAT WAS YOUR PLAN? TO FIGHT ME? YOU ACTUALLY THOUGHT YOU COULD OVERPOWER ME?
YOU DUMB BITCH. YOU ARE SO FUCKING DEAD.
LOOK AT THE BALLS ON THIS GUY.

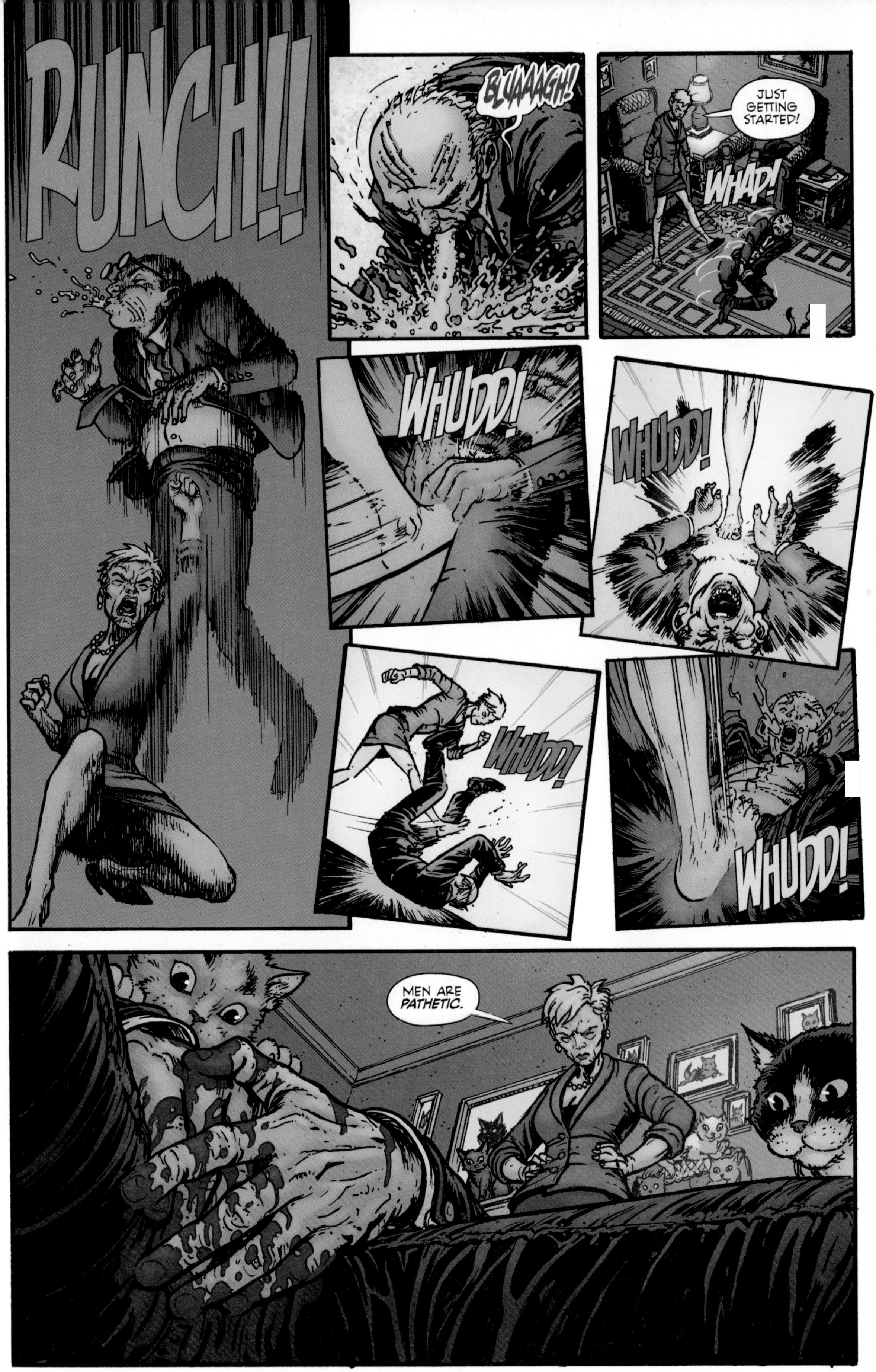
PUNCH!!!
BLUAAAGH!
JUST GETTING STARTED!
WHAP!
WHUDD!
WHUDD!
WHUDD!
WHUDD!
MEN ARE PATHETIC.

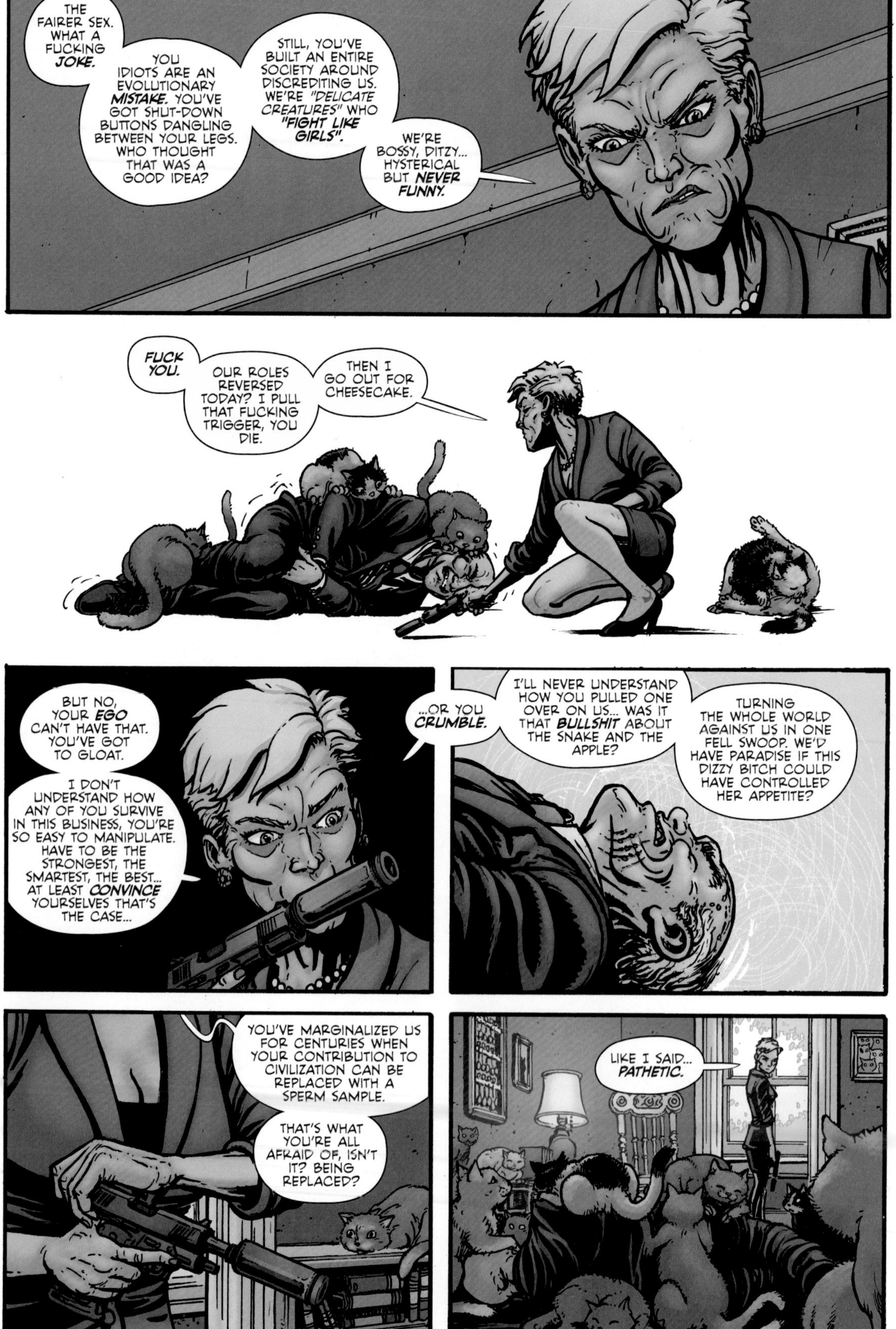
THE FAIRER SEX. WHAT A FUCKING JOKE.
YOU IDIOTS ARE AN EVOLUTIONARY MISTAKE. YOU'VE GOT SHUT-DOWN BUTTONS DANGLING BETWEEN YOUR LEGS. WHO THOUGHT THAT WAS A GOOD IDEA?
STILL, YOU'VE BUILT AN ENTIRE SOCIETY AROUND DISCREDITING US. WE'RE "DELICATE CREATURES" WHO "FIGHT LIKE GIRLS".
WE'RE BOSSY, DITZY... HYSTERICAL BUT NEVER FUNNY.
FUCK YOU.
OUR ROLES REVERSED TODAY? I PULL THAT FUCKING TRIGGER, YOU DIE.
THEN I GO OUT FOR CHEESECAKE.
BUT NO, YOUR EGO CAN'T HAVE THAT. YOU'VE GOT TO GLOAT.
I DON'T UNDERSTAND HOW ANY OF YOU SURVIVE IN THIS BUSINESS, YOU'RE SO EASY TO MANIPULATE. HAVE TO BE THE STRONGEST, THE SMARTEST, THE BEST... AT LEAST CONVINCE YOURSELVES THAT'S THE CASE...
...OR YOU CRUMBLE.
I'LL NEVER UNDERSTAND HOW YOU PULLED ONE OVER ON US... WAS IT THAT BULLSHIT ABOUT THE SNAKE AND THE APPLE?
TURNING THE WHOLE WORLD AGAINST US IN ONE FELL SWOOP. WE'D HAVE PARADISE IF THIS DIZZY BITCH COULD HAVE CONTROLLED HER APPETITE?
YOU'VE MARGINALIZED US FOR CENTURIES WHEN YOUR CONTRIBUTION TO CIVILIZATION CAN BE REPLACED WITH A SPERM SAMPLE.
THAT'S WHAT YOU'RE ALL AFRAID OF, ISN'T IT? BEING REPLACED?
LIKE I SAID... PATHETIC.

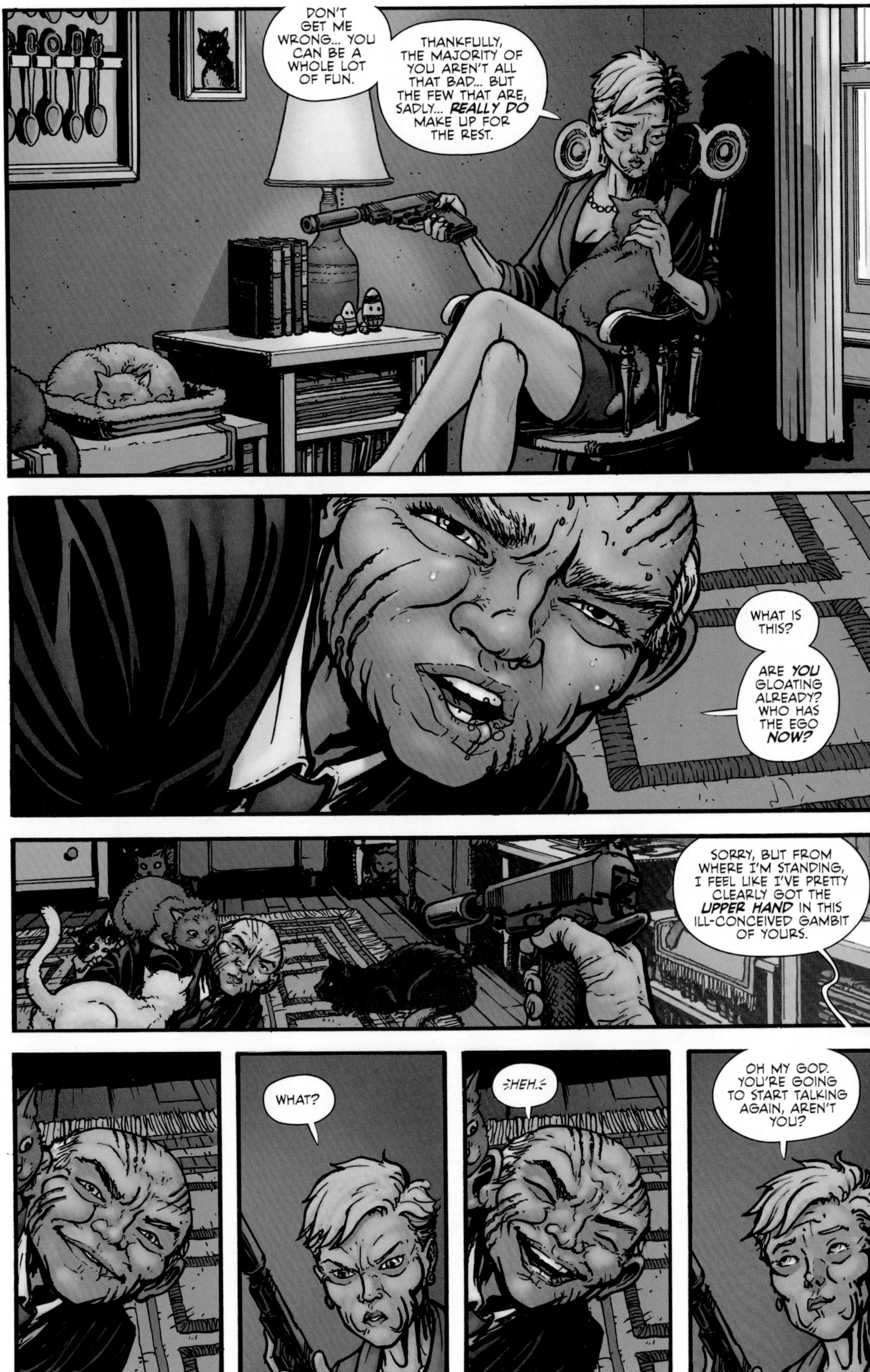
DON'T GET ME WRONG... YOU CAN BE A WHOLE LOT OF FUN.
THANKFULLY, THE MAJORITY OF YOU AREN'T ALL THAT BAD... BUT THE FEW THAT ARE, SADLY... REALLY DO MAKE UP FOR THE REST.
WHAT IS THIS?
ARE YOU GLOATING ALREADY? WHO HAS THE EGO NOW?
SORRY, BUT FROM WHERE I'M STANDING, I FEEL LIKE I'VE PRETTY CLEARLY GOT THE UPPER HAND IN THIS ILL-CONCEIVED GAMBIT OF YOURS.
WHAT?
HEH.
OH MY GOD. YOU'RE GOING TO START TALKING AGAIN, AREN'T YOU?

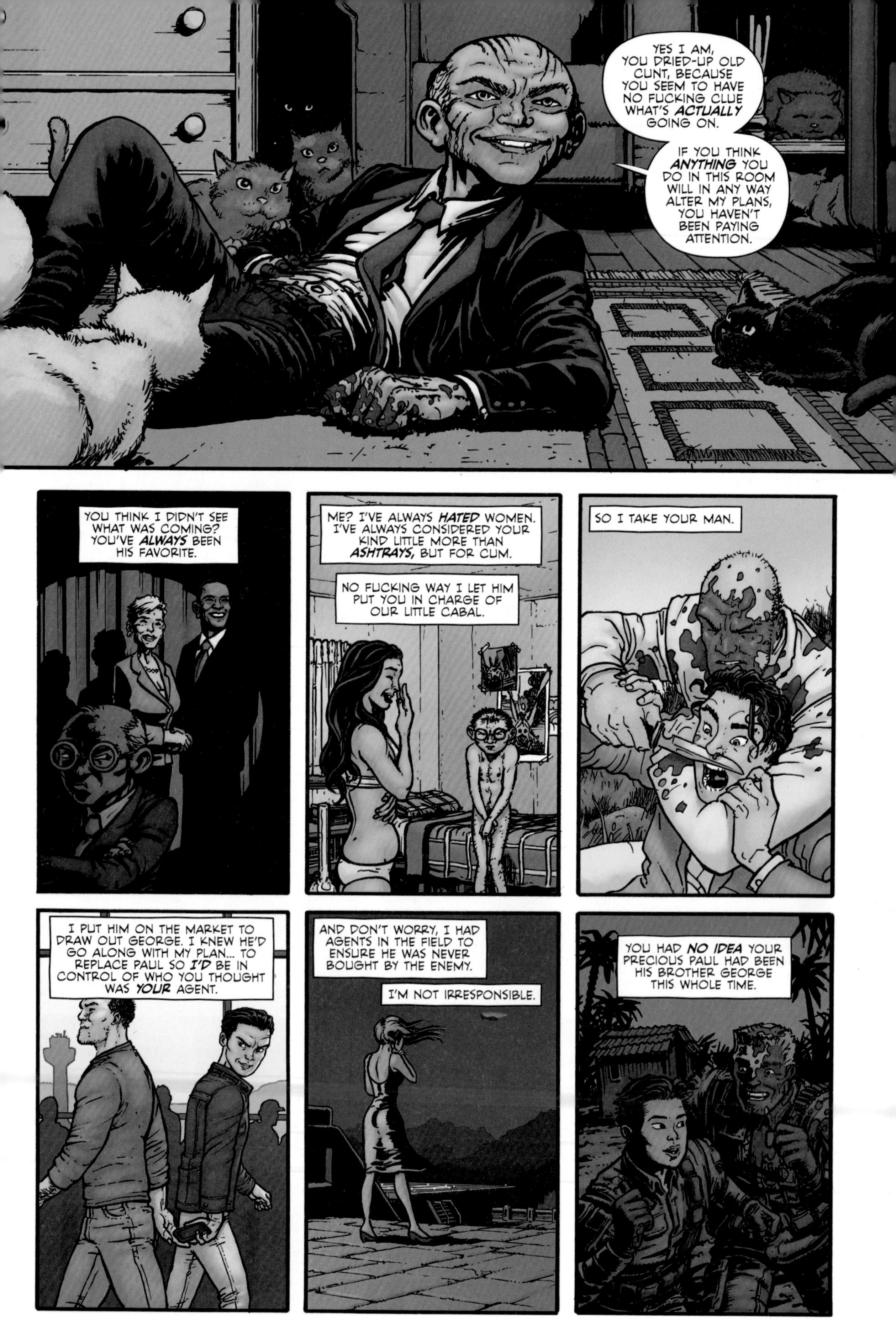
YES I AM, YOU DRIED-UP OLD CUNT, BECAUSE YOU SEEM TO HAVE NO FUCKING CLUE WHAT'S ACTUALLY GOING ON.
IF YOU THINK ANYTHING YOU DO IN THIS ROOM WILL IN ANY WAY ALTER MY PLANS, YOU HAVEN'T BEEN PAYING ATTENTION.
YOU THINK I DIDN'T SEE WHAT WAS COMING? YOU'VE ALWAYS BEEN HIS FAVORITE.
ME? I'VE ALWAYS HATED WOMEN. I'VE ALWAYS CONSIDERED YOUR KIND LITTLE MORE THAN ASHTRAYS, BUT FOR CUM.
NO FUCKING WAY I LET HIM PUT YOU IN CHARGE OF OUR LITTLE CABAL.
SO I TAKE YOUR MAN.
I PUT HIM ON THE MARKET TO DRAW OUT GEORGE. I KNEW HE'D GO ALONG WITH MY PLAN... TO REPLACE PAUL SO I'D BE IN CONTROL OF WHO YOU THOUGHT WAS YOUR AGENT.
AND DON'T WORRY, I HAD AGENTS IN THE FIELD TO ENSURE HE WAS NEVER BOUGHT BY THE ENEMY.
I'M NOT IRRESPONSIBLE.
YOU HAD NO IDEA YOUR PRECIOUS PAUL HAD BEEN HIS BROTHER GEORGE THIS WHOLE TIME.

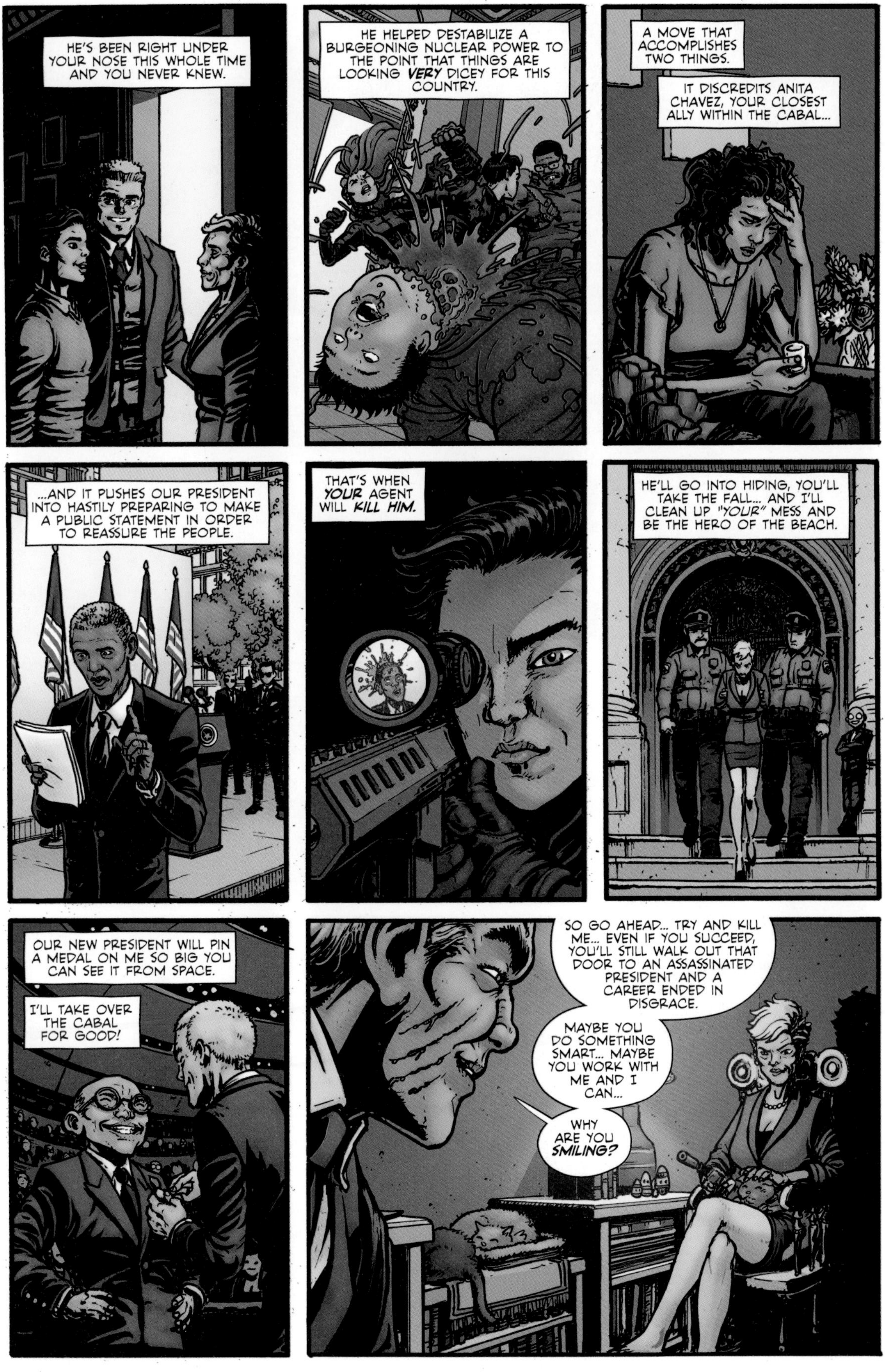
HE'S BEEN RIGHT UNDER YOUR NOSE THIS WHOLE TIME AND YOU NEVER KNEW.
HE HELPED DESTABILIZE A BURGEONING NUCLEAR POWER TO THE POINT THAT THINGS ARE LOOKING **VERY** DICEY FOR THIS COUNTRY.
A MOVE THAT ACCOMPLISHES TWO THINGS.
IT DISCREDITS ANITA CHAVEZ, YOUR CLOSEST ALLY WITHIN THE CABAL...
...AND IT PUSHES OUR PRESIDENT INTO HASTILY PREPARING TO MAKE A PUBLIC STATEMENT IN ORDER TO REASSURE THE PEOPLE.
THAT'S WHEN ***YOUR*** AGENT WILL ***KILL HIM.***
HE'LL GO INTO HIDING, YOU'LL TAKE THE FALL... AND I'LL CLEAN UP *"YOUR"* MESS AND BE THE HERO OF THE BEACH.
OUR NEW PRESIDENT WILL PIN A MEDAL ON ME SO BIG YOU CAN SEE IT FROM SPACE.
I'LL TAKE OVER THE CABAL FOR GOOD!
SO GO AHEAD... TRY AND KILL ME... EVEN IF YOU SUCCEED, YOU'LL STILL WALK OUT THAT DOOR TO AN ASSASSINATED PRESIDENT AND A CAREER ENDED IN DISGRACE.
MAYBE YOU DO SOMETHING SMART... MAYBE YOU WORK WITH ME AND I CAN...
WHY ARE YOU ***SMILING?***

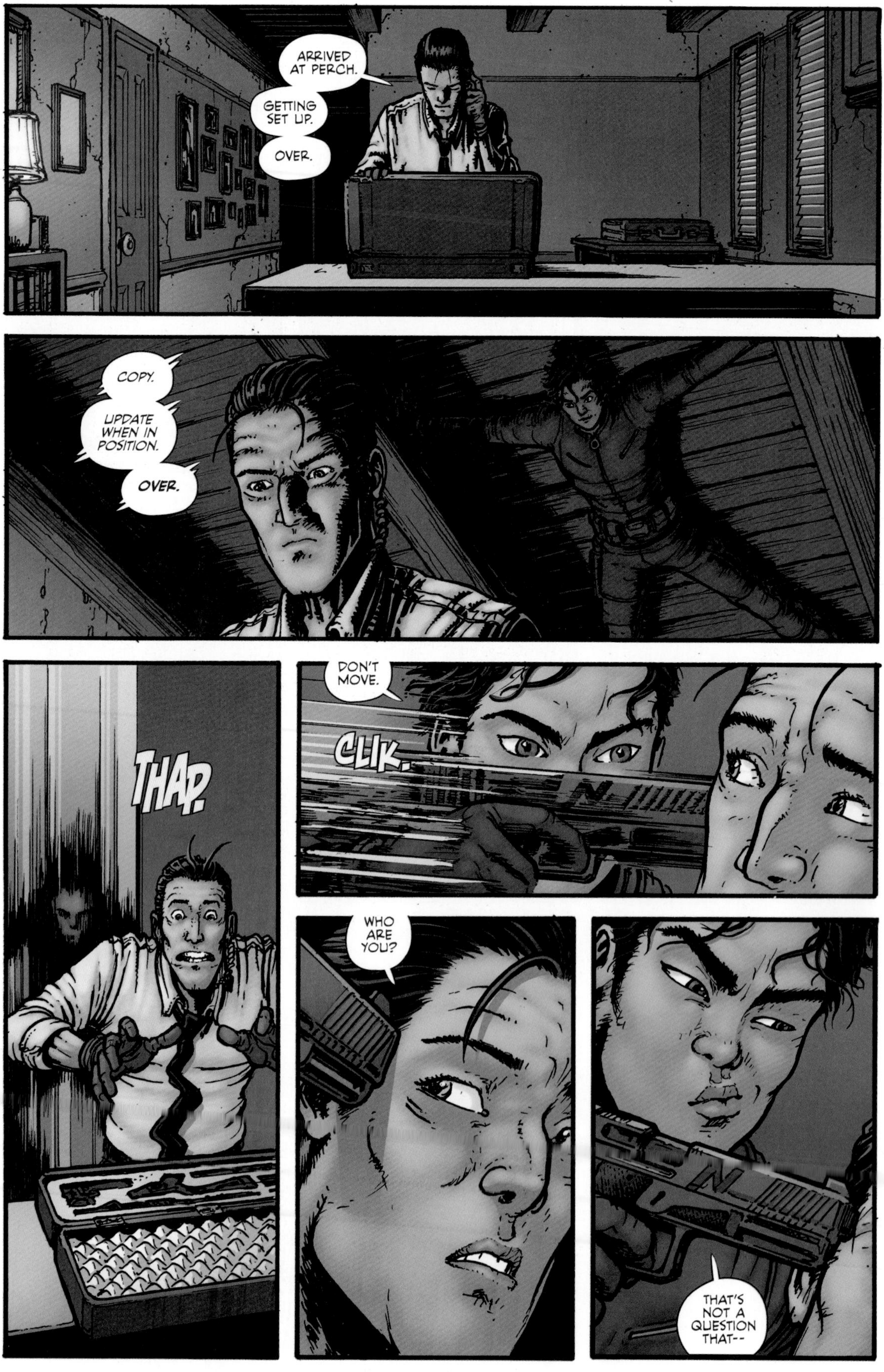
ARRIVED AT PERCH.
GETTING SET UP.
OVER.
COPY.
UPDATE WHEN IN POSITION.
OVER.
THAP.
DON'T MOVE.
CLIK.
WHO ARE YOU?
THAT'S NOT A QUESTION THAT--

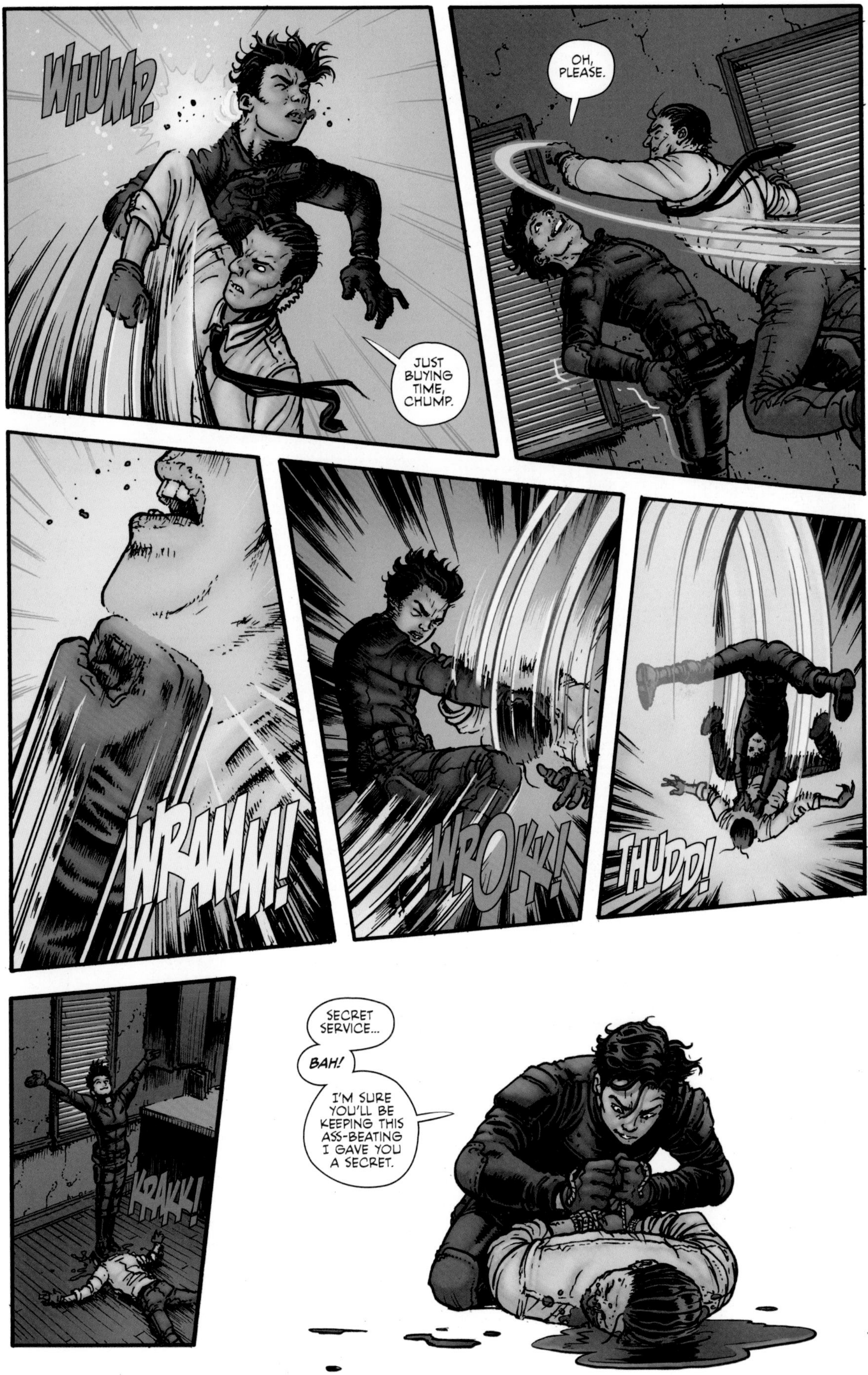
WHUMP.
JUST BUYING TIME, CHUMP.
OH, PLEASE.
WRAMM!
WROKK!
THUDD!
KRAKK!
SECRET SERVICE...
BAH!
I'M SURE YOU'LL BE KEEPING THIS ASS-BEATING I GAVE YOU A SECRET.

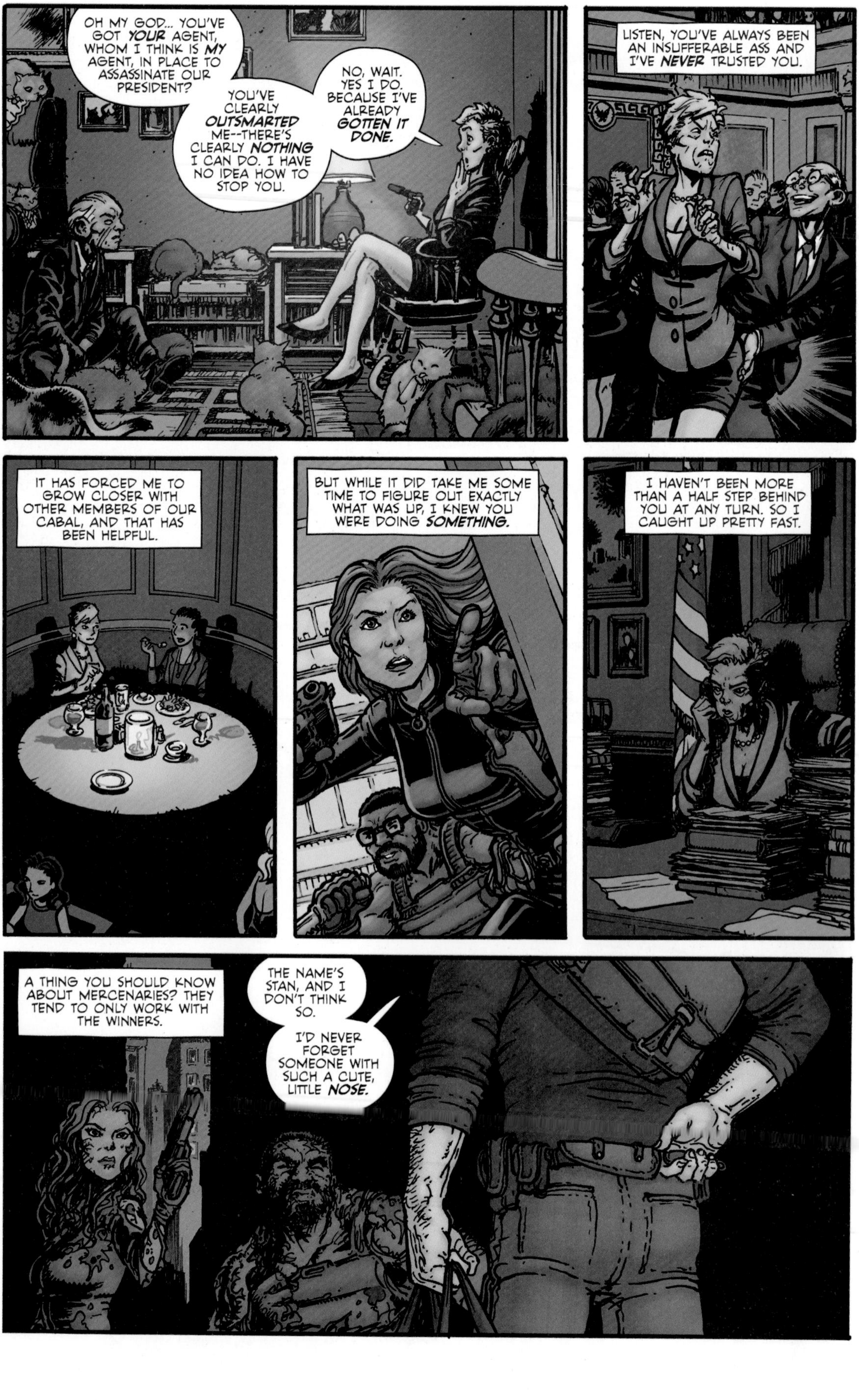
OH MY GOD... YOU'VE GOT YOUR AGENT, WHOM I THINK IS MY AGENT, IN PLACE TO ASSASSINATE OUR PRESIDENT?
YOU'VE CLEARLY OUTSMARTED ME--THERE'S CLEARLY NOTHING I CAN DO. I HAVE NO IDEA HOW TO STOP YOU.
NO, WAIT. YES I DO. BECAUSE I'VE ALREADY GOTTEN IT DONE.
LISTEN, YOU'VE ALWAYS BEEN AN INSUFFERABLE ASS AND I'VE NEVER TRUSTED YOU.
IT HAS FORCED ME TO GROW CLOSER WITH OTHER MEMBERS OF OUR CABAL, AND THAT HAS BEEN HELPFUL.
BUT WHILE IT DID TAKE ME SOME TIME TO FIGURE OUT EXACTLY WHAT WAS UP, I KNEW YOU WERE DOING SOMETHING.
I HAVEN'T BEEN MORE THAN A HALF STEP BEHIND YOU AT ANY TURN. SO I CAUGHT UP PRETTY FAST.
A THING YOU SHOULD KNOW ABOUT MERCENARIES? THEY TEND TO ONLY WORK WITH THE WINNERS.
THE NAME'S STAN, AND I DON'T THINK SO.
I'D NEVER FORGET SOMEONE WITH SUCH A CUTE, LITTLE NOSE.

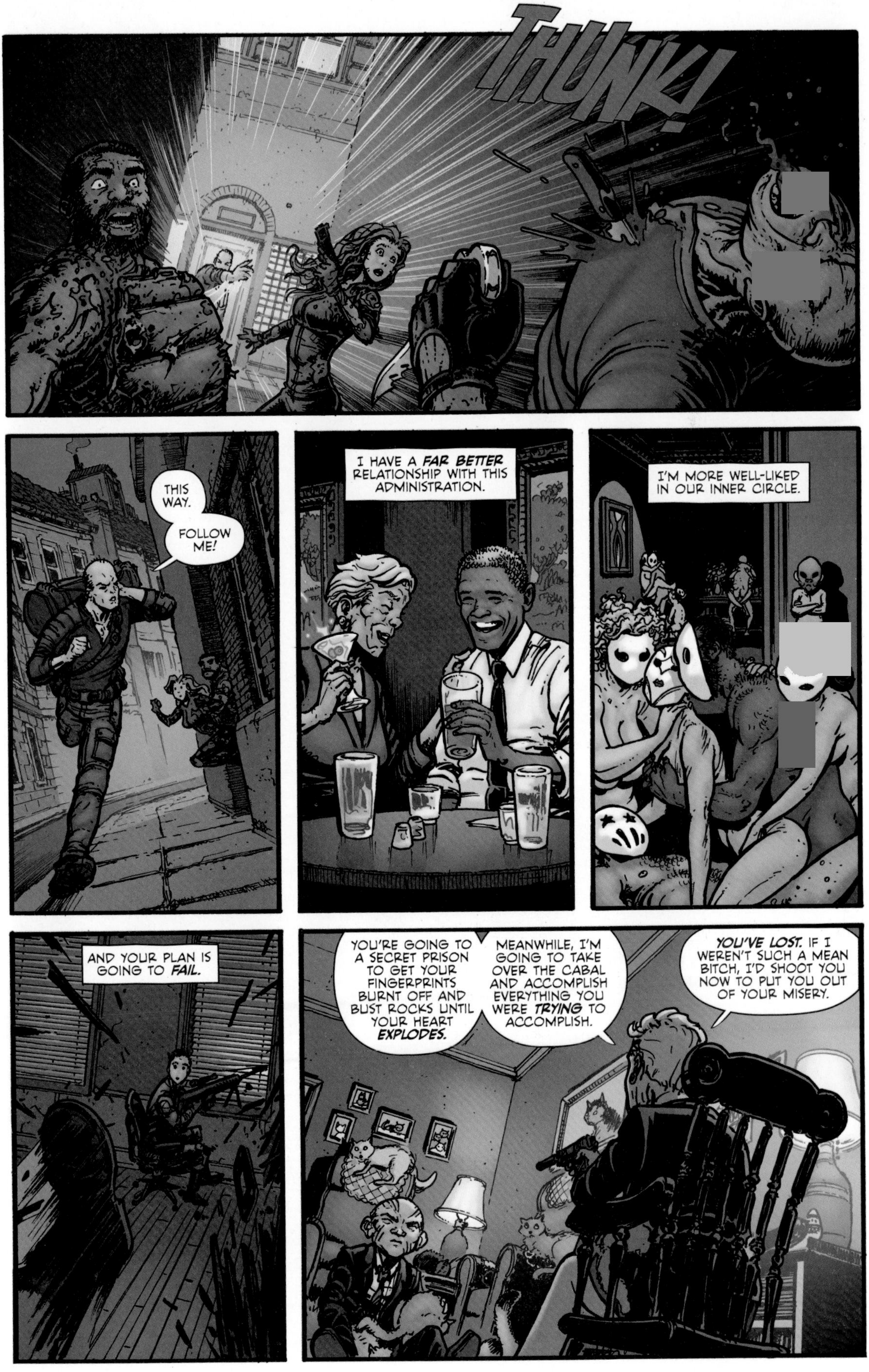
THUNK!
THIS WAY.
FOLLOW ME!
I HAVE A FAR BETTER RELATIONSHIP WITH THIS ADMINISTRATION.
I'M MORE WELL-LIKED IN OUR INNER CIRCLE.
AND YOUR PLAN IS GOING TO FAIL.
YOU'RE GOING TO A SECRET PRISON TO GET YOUR FINGERPRINTS BURNT OFF AND BUST ROCKS UNTIL YOUR HEART EXPLODES.
MEANWHILE, I'M GOING TO TAKE OVER THE CABAL AND ACCOMPLISH EVERYTHING TRYING TO ACCOMPLISH.
YOU'VE LOST. IF I WEREN'T SUCH A MEAN BITCH, I'D SHOOT YOU NOW TO PUT YOU OUT OF YOUR MISERY.

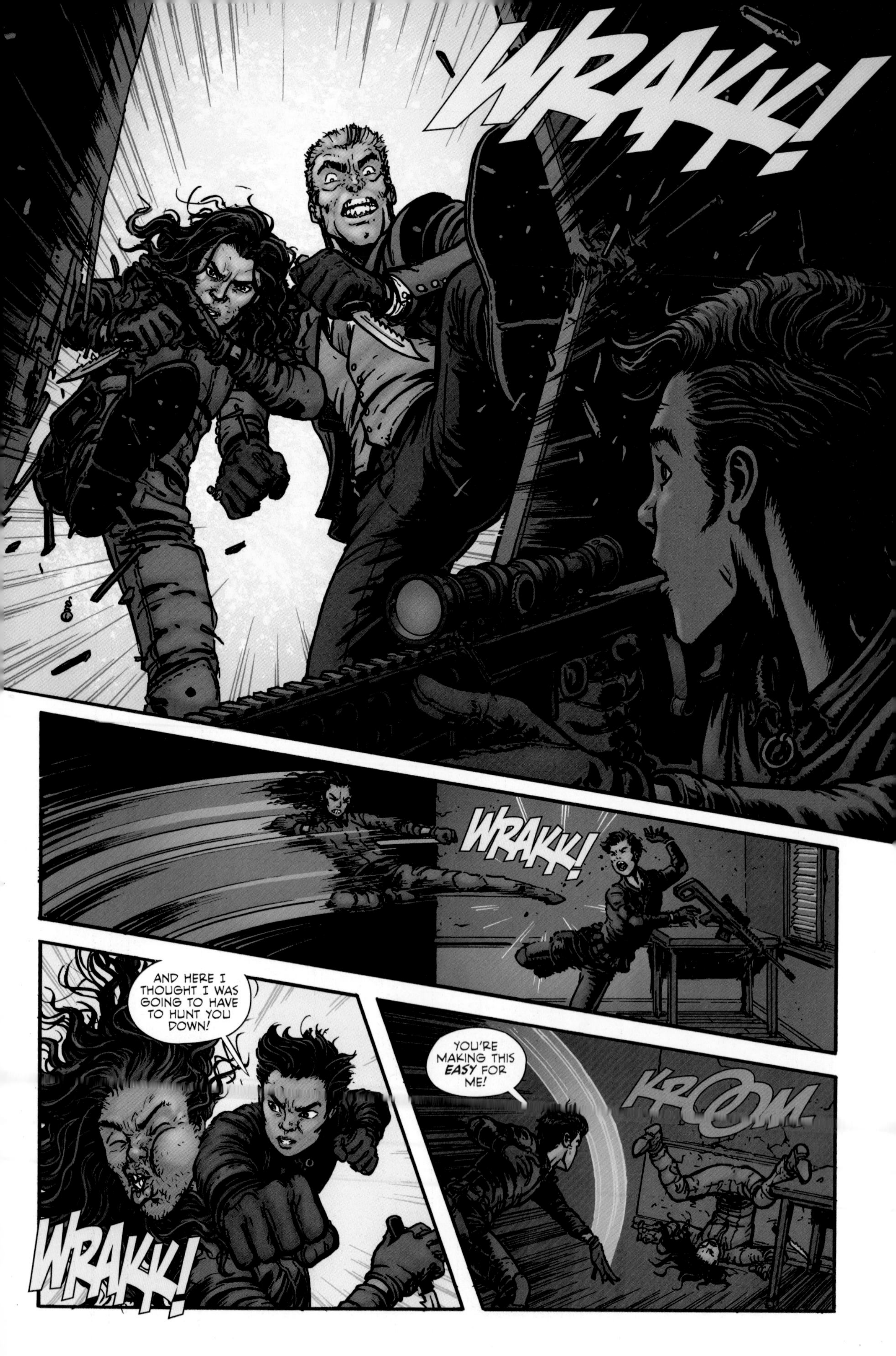
WRAKK!
WRAKK!
AND HERE I THOUGHT I WAS GOING TO HAVE TO HUNT YOU DOWN!
WRAKK!
YOU'RE MAKING THIS EASY FOR ME!
KROOM

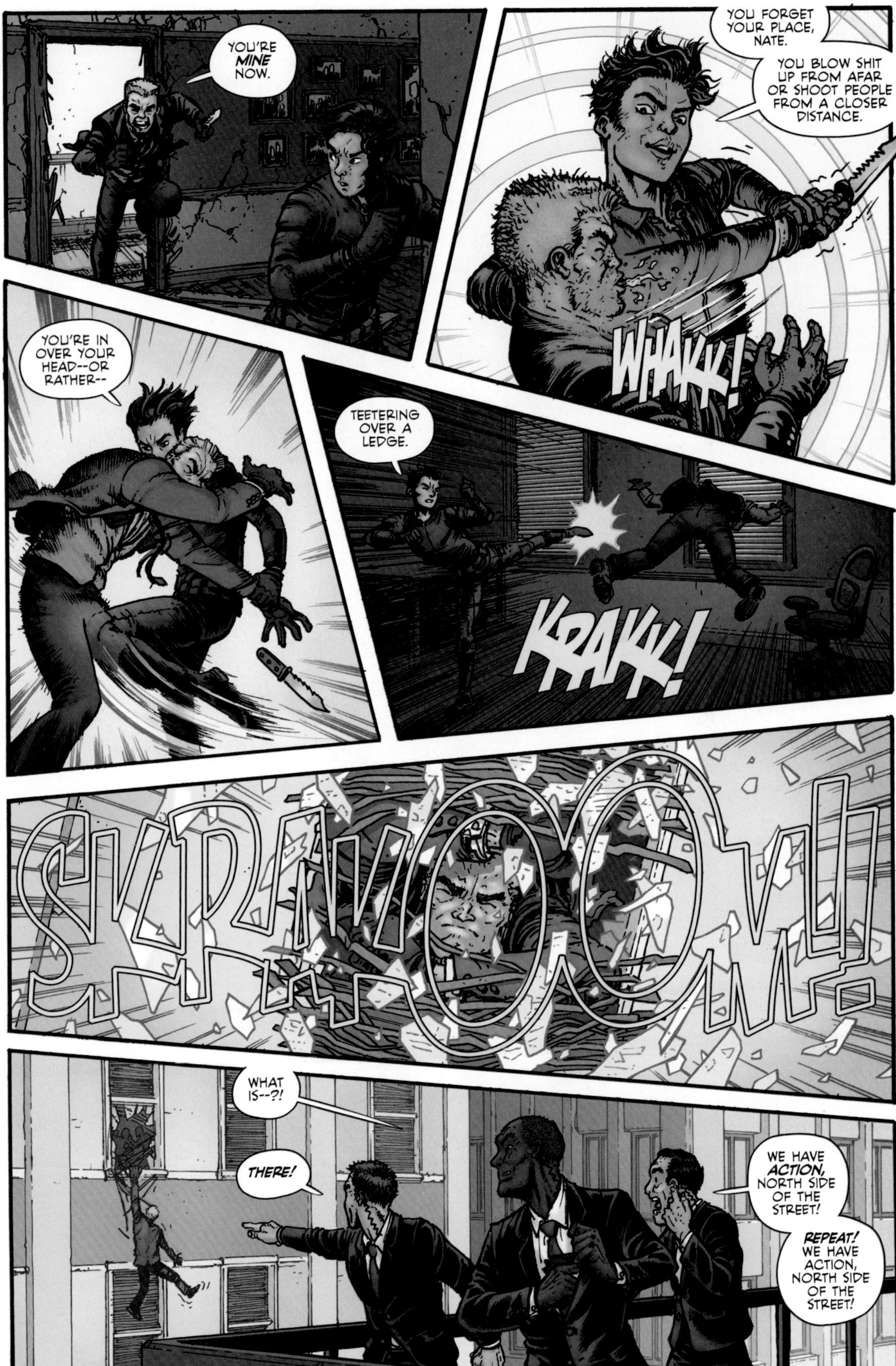
YOU'RE *MINE* NOW.
YOU FORGET YOUR PLACE, NATE.
YOU BLOW SHIT UP FROM AFAR OR SHOOT PEOPLE FROM A CLOSER DISTANCE.
WHAKK!
YOU'RE IN OVER YOUR HEAD--OR RATHER--
TEETERING OVER A LEDGE.
KRAKK!
SKRAWOOOM!
WHAT IS--?!
THERE!
WE HAVE *ACTION,* NORTH SIDE OF THE STREET!
REPEAT! WE HAVE ACTION, NORTH SIDE OF THE STREET!

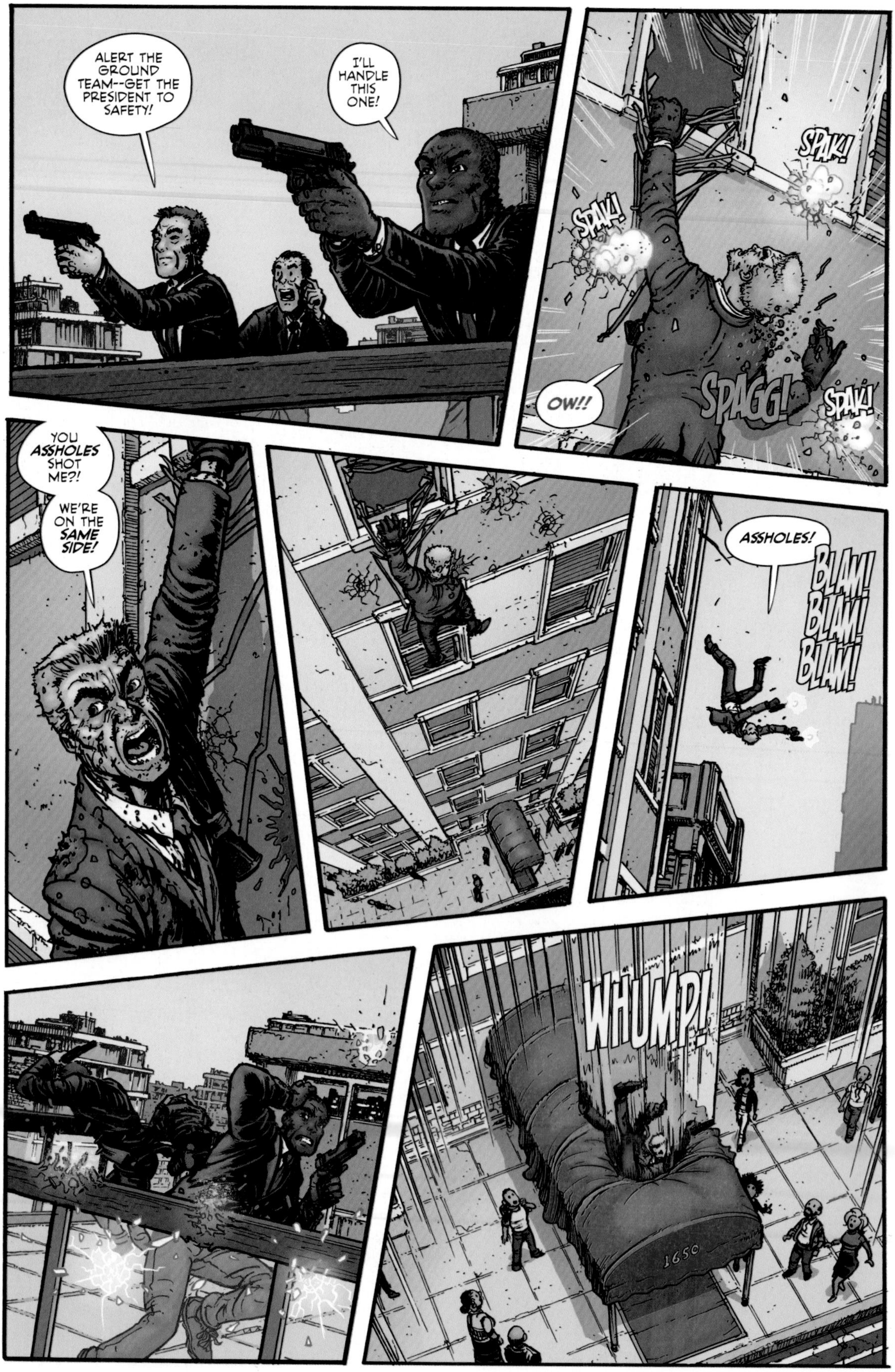

ALERT THE GROUND TEAM--GET THE PRESIDENT TO SAFETY!
I'LL HANDLE THIS ONE!
SPAK!
SPAK!
OW!!
SPAGG!
SPAK!
YOU *ASSHOLES* SHOT ME?!
WE'RE ON THE *SAME SIDE!*
ASSHOLES!
BLAM! BLAM! BLAM!
WHUMP!
1650

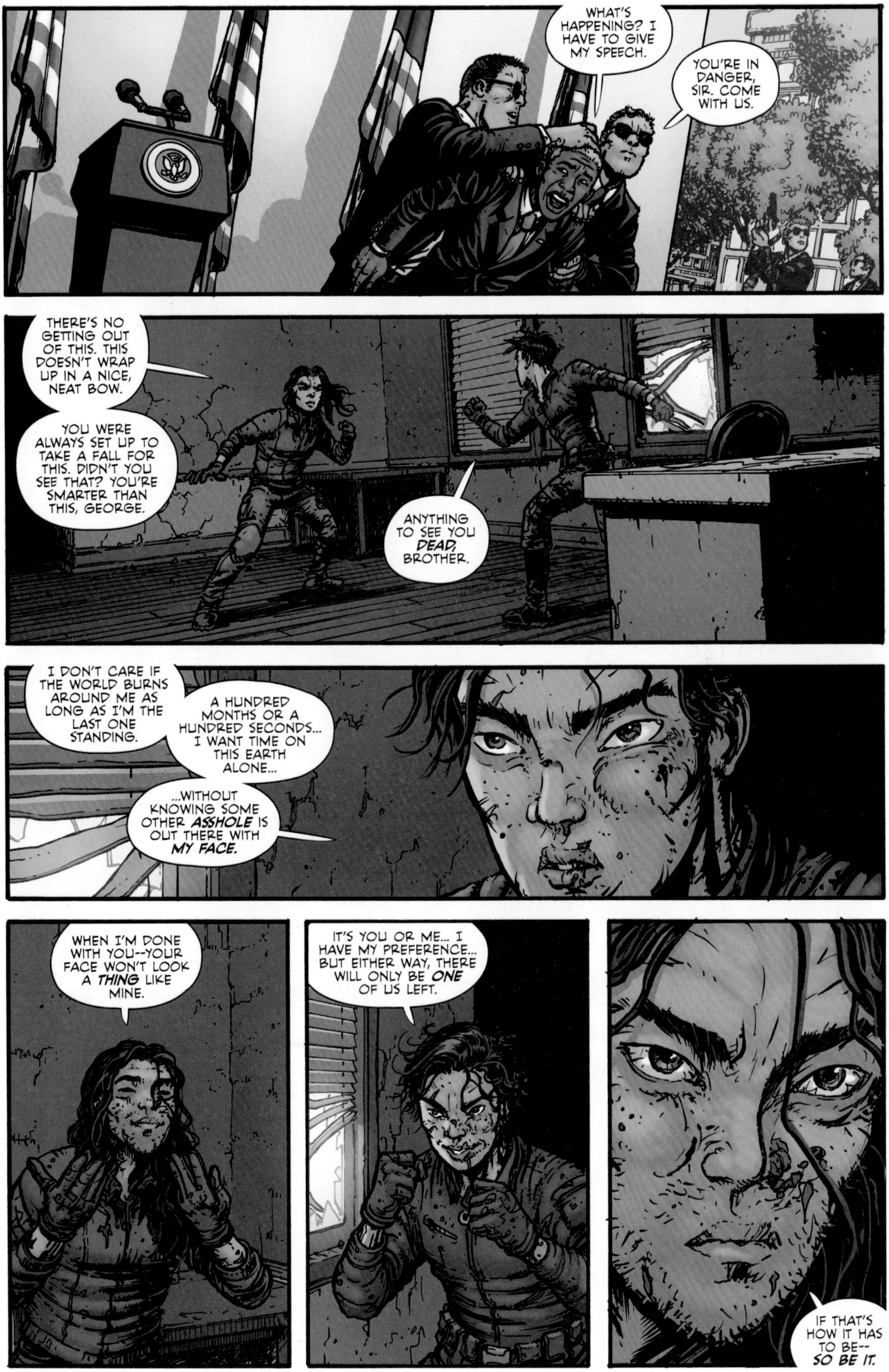

WHAT'S HAPPENING? I HAVE TO GIVE MY SPEECH.
YOU'RE IN DANGER, SIR. COME WITH US.
THERE'S NO GETTING OUT OF THIS. THIS DOESN'T WRAP UP IN A NICE, NEAT BOW.
YOU WERE ALWAYS SET UP TO TAKE A FALL FOR THIS. DIDN'T YOU SEE THAT? YOU'RE SMARTER THAN THIS, GEORGE.
ANYTHING TO SEE YOU *DEAD,* BROTHER.
I DON'T CARE IF THE WORLD BURNS AROUND ME AS LONG AS I'M THE LAST ONE STANDING.
A HUNDRED MONTHS OR A HUNDRED SECONDS... I WANT TIME ON THIS EARTH ALONE...
...WITHOUT KNOWING SOME OTHER ***ASSHOLE*** IS OUT THERE WITH ***MY FACE.***
WHEN I'M DONE WITH YOU--YOUR FACE WON'T LOOK A *THING* LIKE MINE.
IT'S YOU OR ME... I HAVE MY PREFERENCE... BUT EITHER WAY, THERE WILL ONLY BE *ONE* OF US LEFT.
IF THAT'S HOW IT HAS TO BE-- ***SO BE IT.***

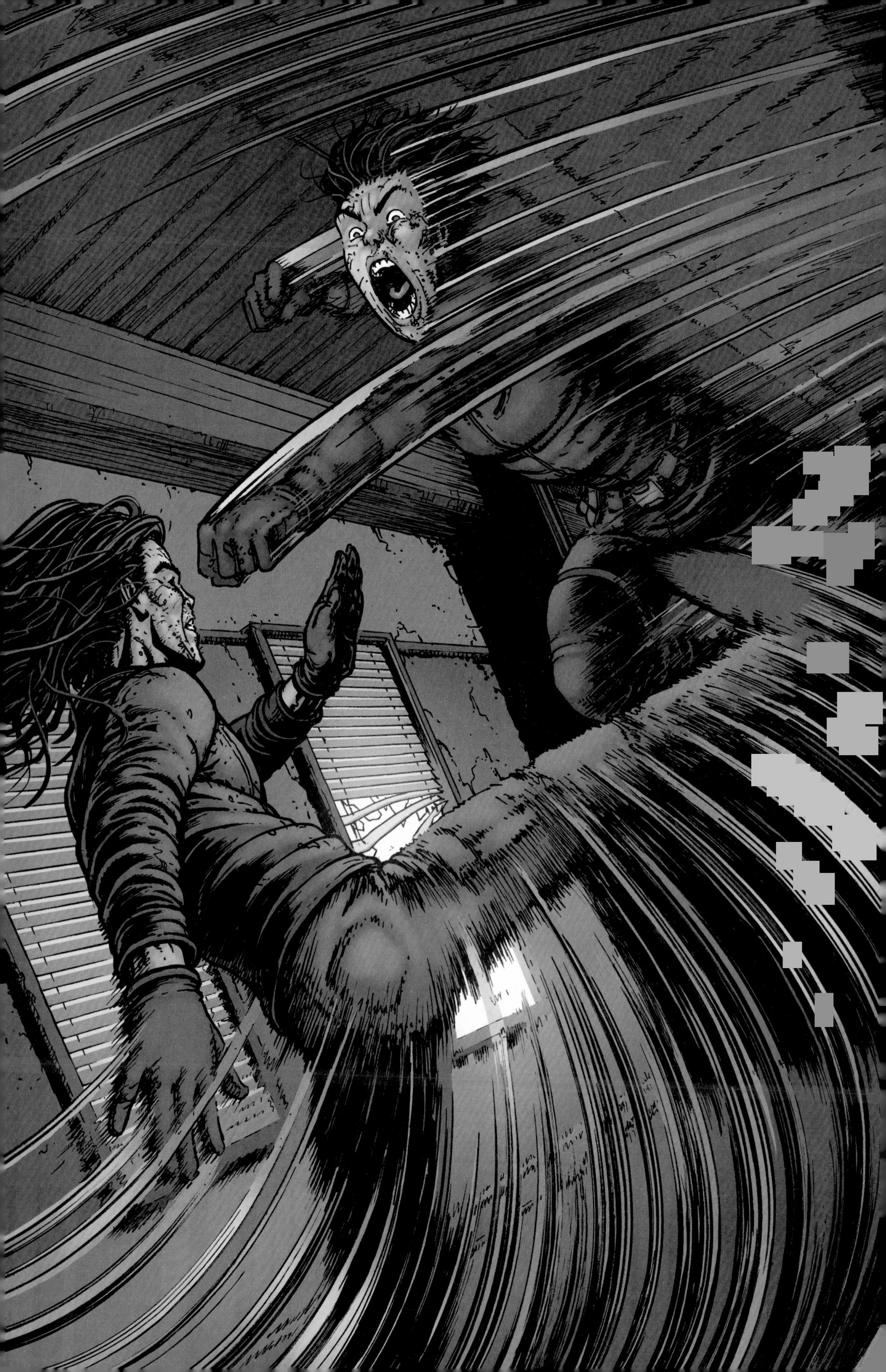

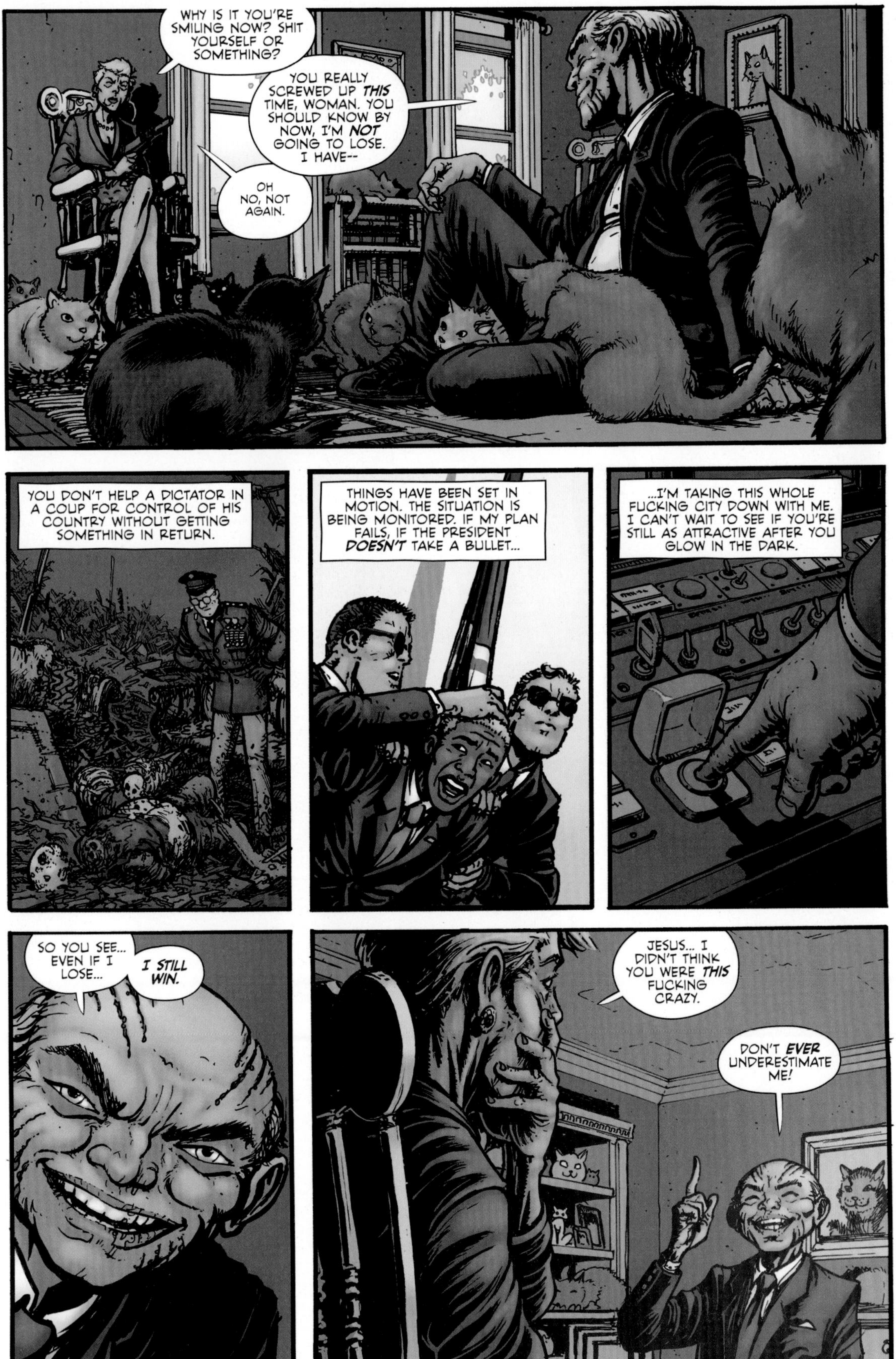
WHY IS IT YOU'RE SMILING NOW? SHIT YOURSELF OR SOMETHING?
YOU REALLY SCREWED UP **THIS** TIME, WOMAN. YOU SHOULD KNOW BY NOW, I'M **NOT** GOING TO LOSE. I HAVE--
OH NO, NOT AGAIN.
YOU DON'T HELP A DICTATOR IN A COUP FOR CONTROL OF HIS COUNTRY WITHOUT GETTING SOMETHING IN RETURN.
THINGS HAVE BEEN SET IN MOTION. THE SITUATION IS BEING MONITORED. IF MY PLAN FAILS, IF THE PRESIDENT **DOESN'T** TAKE A BULLET...
...I'M TAKING THIS WHOLE FUCKING CITY DOWN WITH ME. I CAN'T WAIT TO SEE IF YOU'RE STILL AS ATTRACTIVE AFTER YOU GLOW IN THE DARK.
SO YOU SEE... EVEN IF I LOSE...
I STILL WIN.
JESUS... I DIDN'T THINK YOU WERE **THIS** FUCKING CRAZY.
DON'T **EVER** UNDERESTIMATE ME!

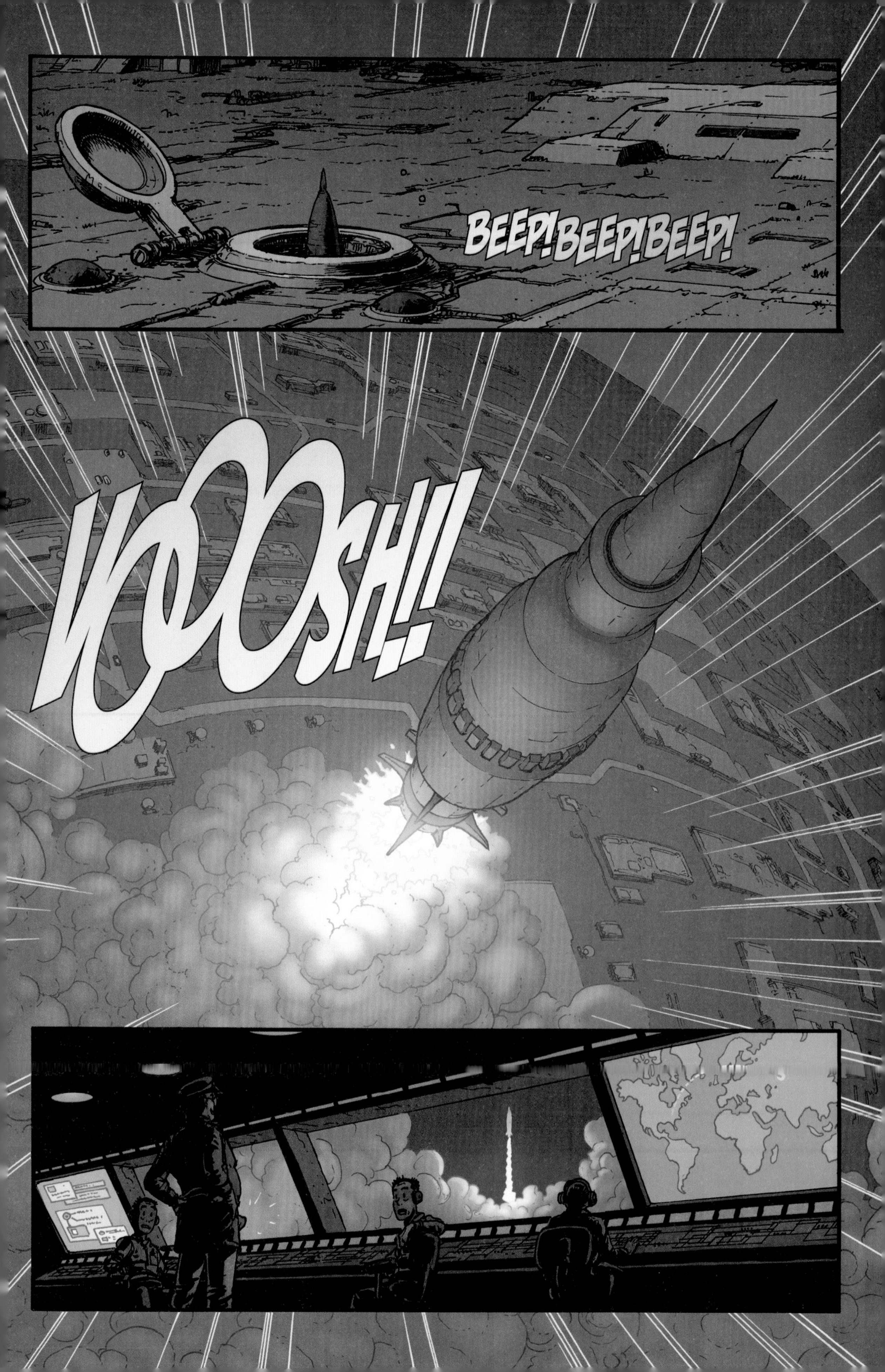
BEEP! BEEP! BEEP!
WOOSH!!

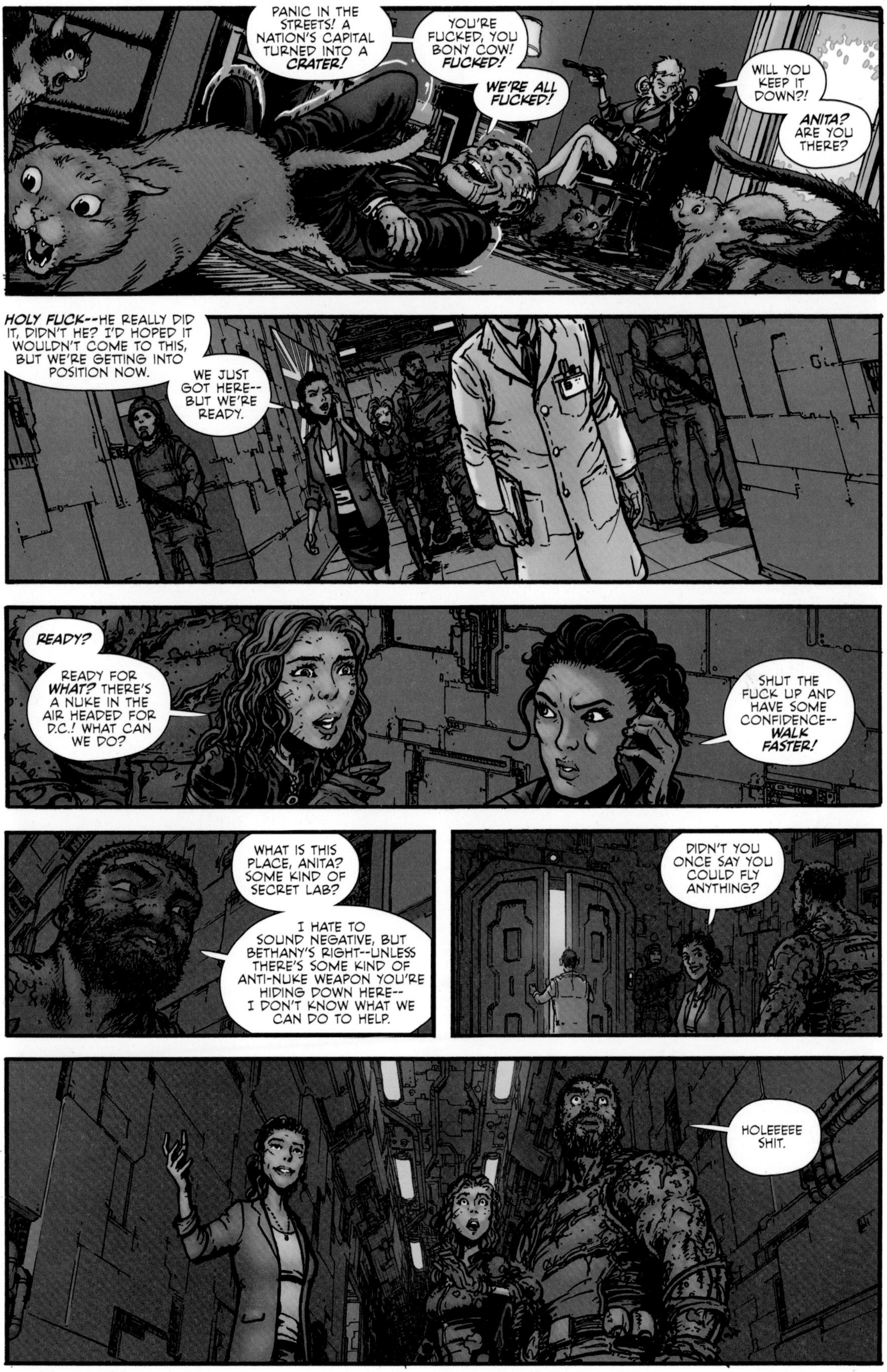
PANIC IN THE STREETS! A NATION'S CAPITAL TURNED INTO A ***CRATER!***
YOU'RE FUCKED, YOU BONY COW! ***FUCKED!***
WE'RE ALL FUCKED!
WILL YOU KEEP IT DOWN?!
ANITA? ARE YOU THERE?
HOLY FUCK-- HE REALLY DID IT, DIDN'T HE? I'D HOPED IT WOULDN'T COME TO THIS, BUT WE'RE GETTING INTO POSITION NOW.
WE JUST GOT HERE-- BUT WE'RE READY.
READY?
READY FOR ***WHAT?*** THERE'S A NUKE IN THE AIR HEADED FOR D.C.! WHAT CAN WE DO?
SHUT THE FUCK UP AND HAVE SOME CONFIDENCE-- ***WALK FASTER!***
WHAT IS THIS PLACE, ANITA? SOME KIND OF SECRET LAB?
I HATE TO SOUND NEGATIVE, BUT BETHANY'S RIGHT--UNLESS THERE'S SOME KIND OF ANTI-NUKE WEAPON YOU'RE HIDING DOWN HERE-- I DON'T KNOW WHAT WE CAN DO TO HELP.
DIDN'T YOU ONCE SAY YOU COULD FLY ANYTHING?
HOLEEEEE SHIT.

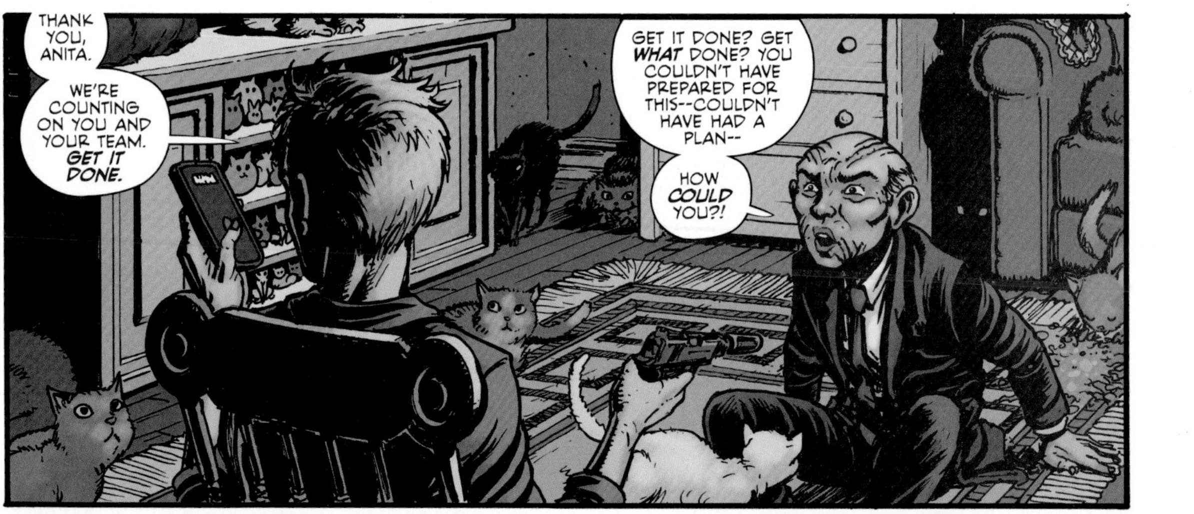
THANK YOU, ANITA.
WE'RE COUNTING ON YOU AND YOUR TEAM. GET IT DONE.
GET IT DONE? GET WHAT DONE? YOU COULDN'T HAVE PREPARED FOR THIS--COULDN'T HAVE HAD A PLAN--
HOW COULD YOU?!

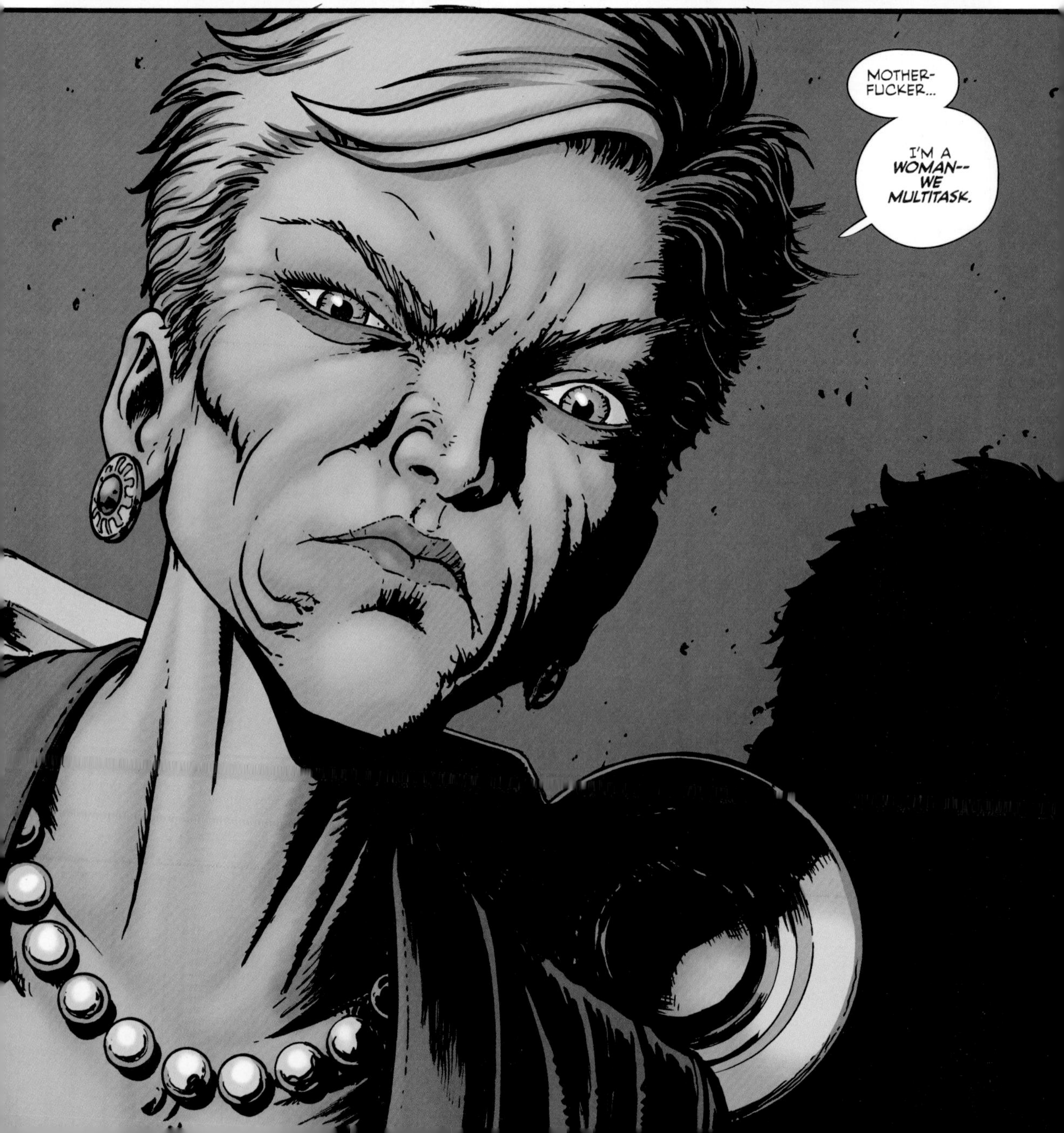
MOTHER-FUCKER...
I'M A WOMAN--WE MULTITASK.

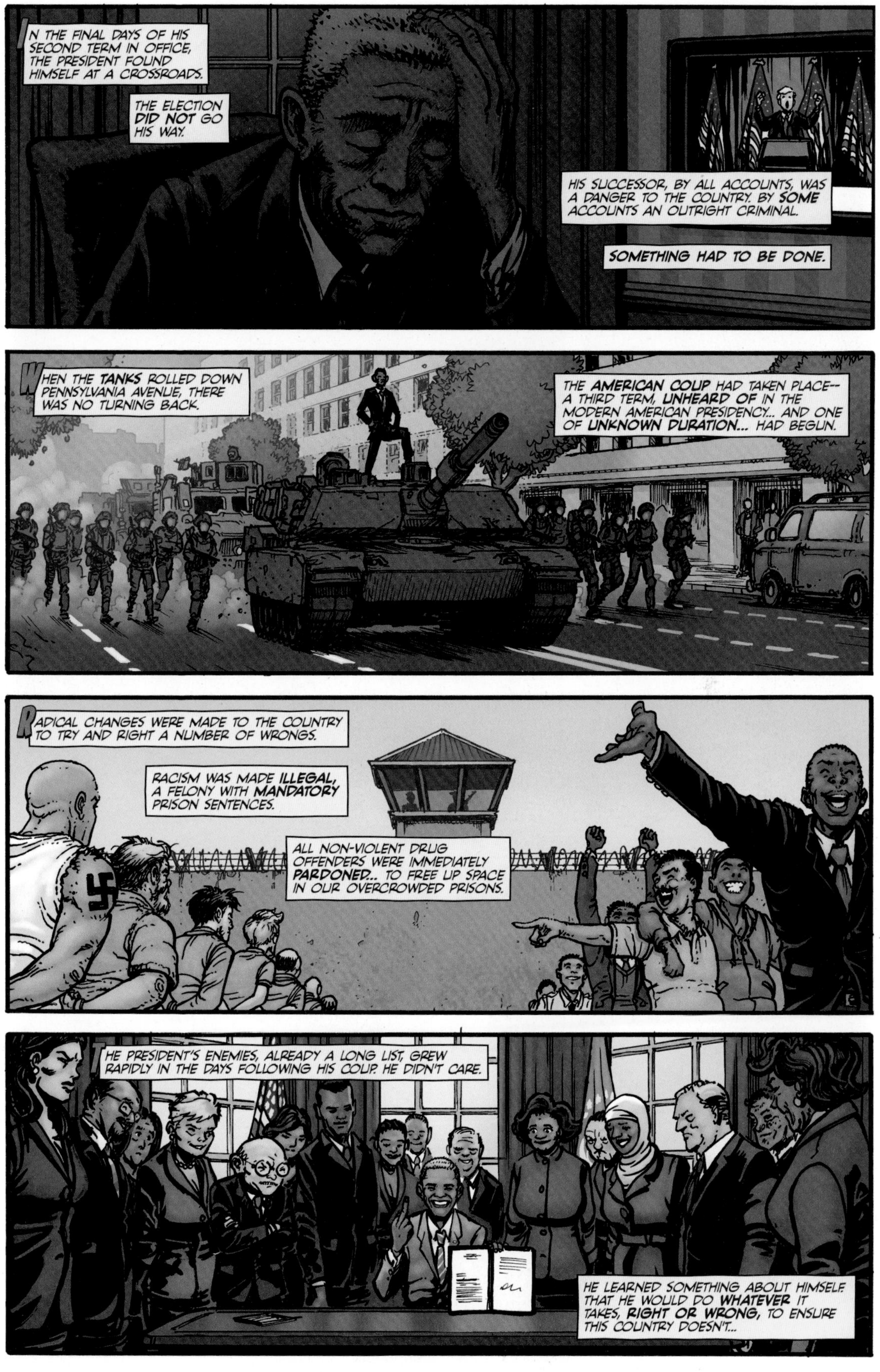
IN THE FINAL DAYS OF HIS SECOND TERM IN OFFICE, THE PRESIDENT FOUND HIMSELF AT A CROSSROADS.
THE ELECTION **DID NOT** GO HIS WAY.
HIS SUCCESSOR, BY ALL ACCOUNTS, WAS A DANGER TO THE COUNTRY. BY **SOME** ACCOUNTS AN OUTRIGHT CRIMINAL.
SOMETHING HAD TO BE DONE.
WHEN THE **TANKS** ROLLED DOWN PENNSYLVANIA AVENUE, THERE WAS NO TURNING BACK.
THE **AMERICAN COUP** HAD TAKEN PLACE-- A THIRD TERM, **UNHEARD OF** IN THE MODERN AMERICAN PRESIDENCY... AND ONE OF **UNKNOWN DURATION...** HAD BEGUN.
RADICAL CHANGES WERE MADE TO THE COUNTRY TO TRY AND RIGHT A NUMBER OF WRONGS.
RACISM WAS MADE **ILLEGAL,** A FELONY WITH **MANDATORY** PRISON SENTENCES.
ALL NON-VIOLENT DRUG OFFENDERS WERE IMMEDIATELY **PARDONED...** TO FREE UP SPACE IN OUR OVERCROWDED PRISONS.
THE PRESIDENT'S ENEMIES, ALREADY A LONG LIST, GREW RAPIDLY IN THE DAYS FOLLOWING HIS COUP. HE DIDN'T CARE.
HE LEARNED SOMETHING ABOUT HIMSELF. THAT HE WOULD DO **WHATEVER** IT TAKES, **RIGHT OR WRONG,** TO ENSURE THIS COUNTRY DOESN'T...

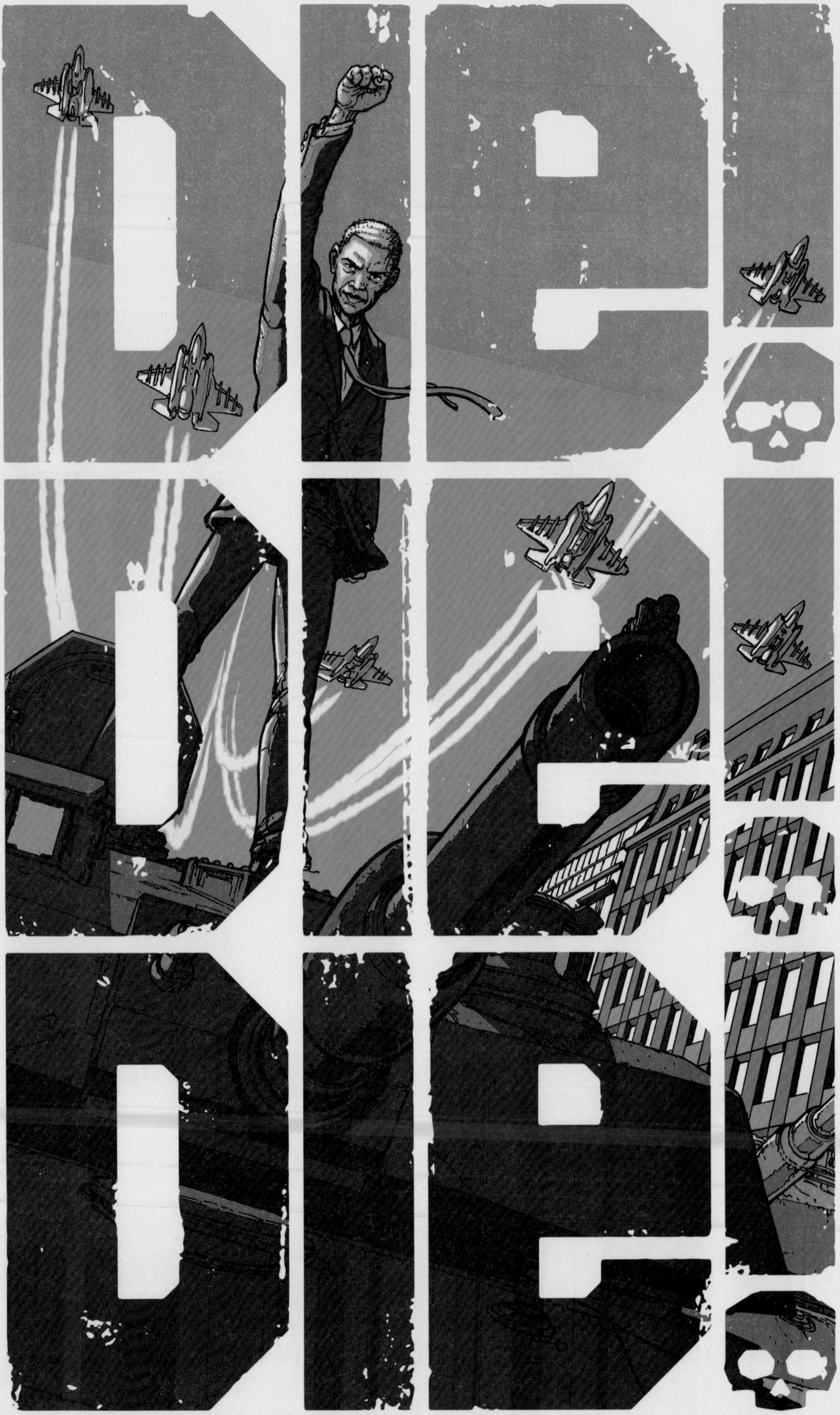
DIE!
DIE!
DIE!

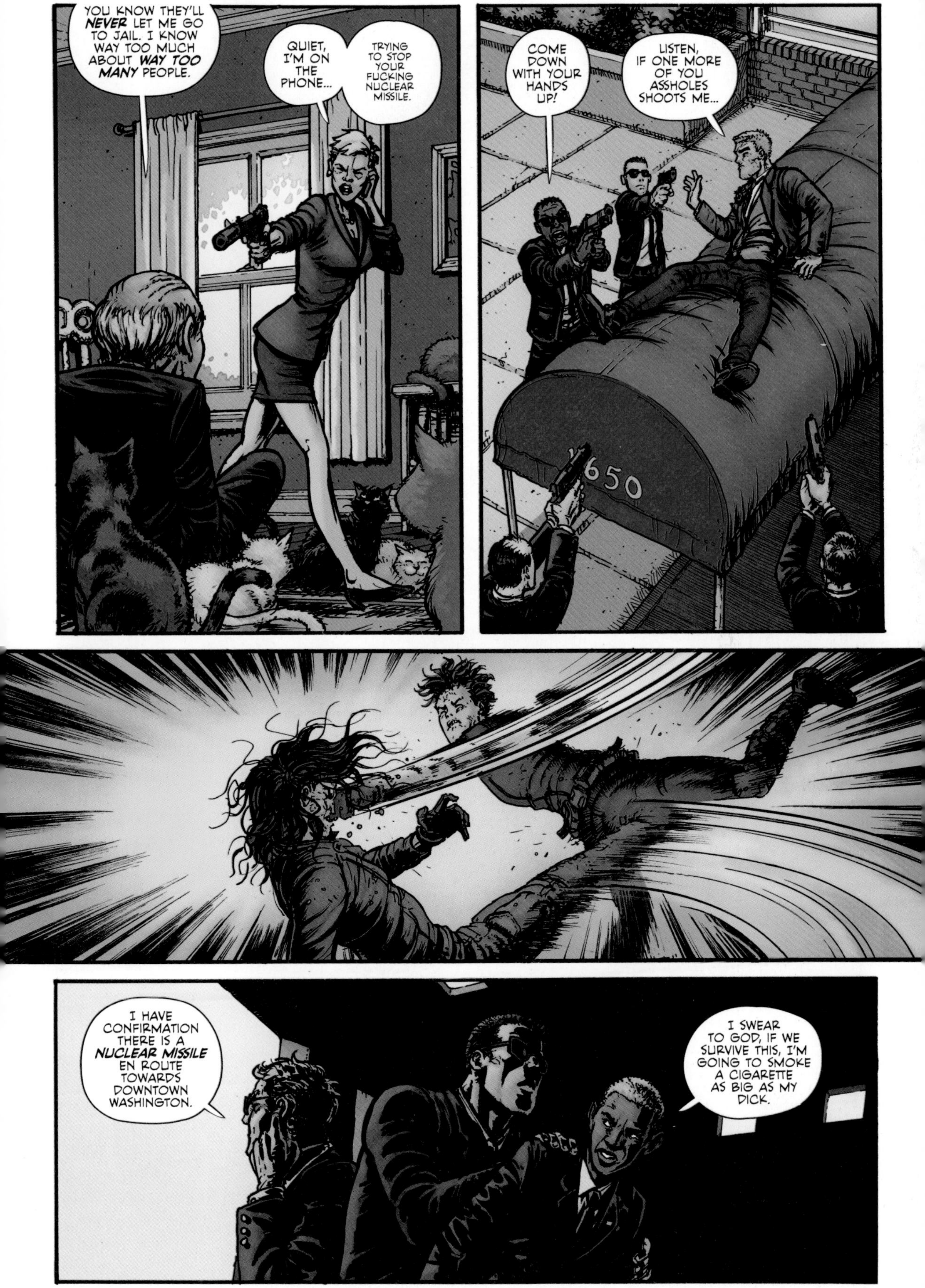
YOU KNOW THEY'LL NEVER LET ME GO TO JAIL. I KNOW WAY TOO MUCH ABOUT WAY TOO MANY PEOPLE.
QUIET, I'M ON THE PHONE...
TRYING TO STOP YOUR FUCKING NUCLEAR MISSILE.
COME DOWN WITH YOUR HANDS UP!
LISTEN, IF ONE MORE OF YOU ASSHOLES SHOOTS ME...
I HAVE CONFIRMATION THERE IS A NUCLEAR MISSILE EN ROUTE TOWARDS DOWNTOWN WASHINGTON.
I SWEAR TO GOD, IF WE SURVIVE THIS, I'M GOING TO SMOKE A CIGARETTE AS BIG AS MY DICK.

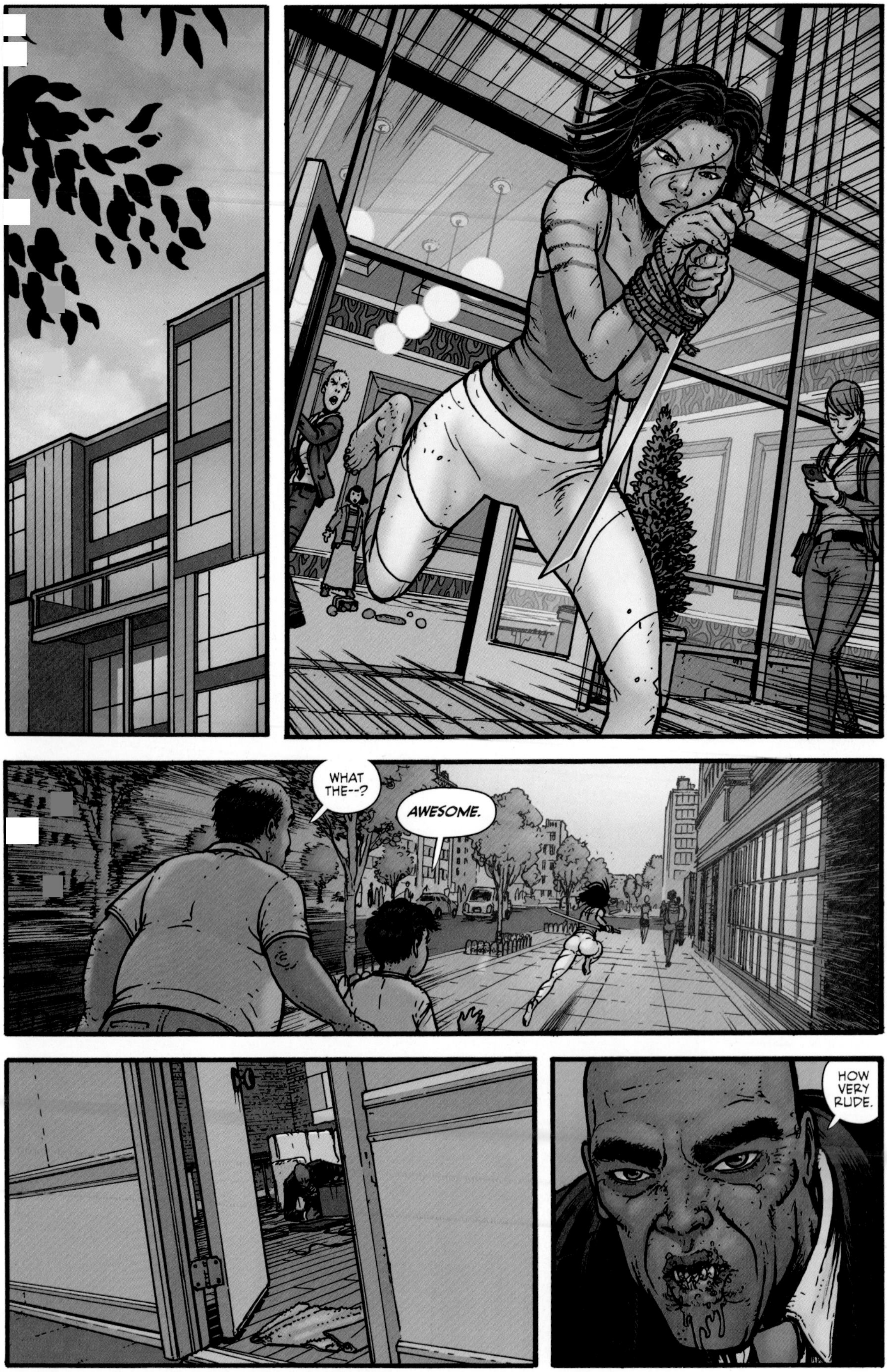
WHAT THE--?
AWESOME.
HOW VERY RUDE.

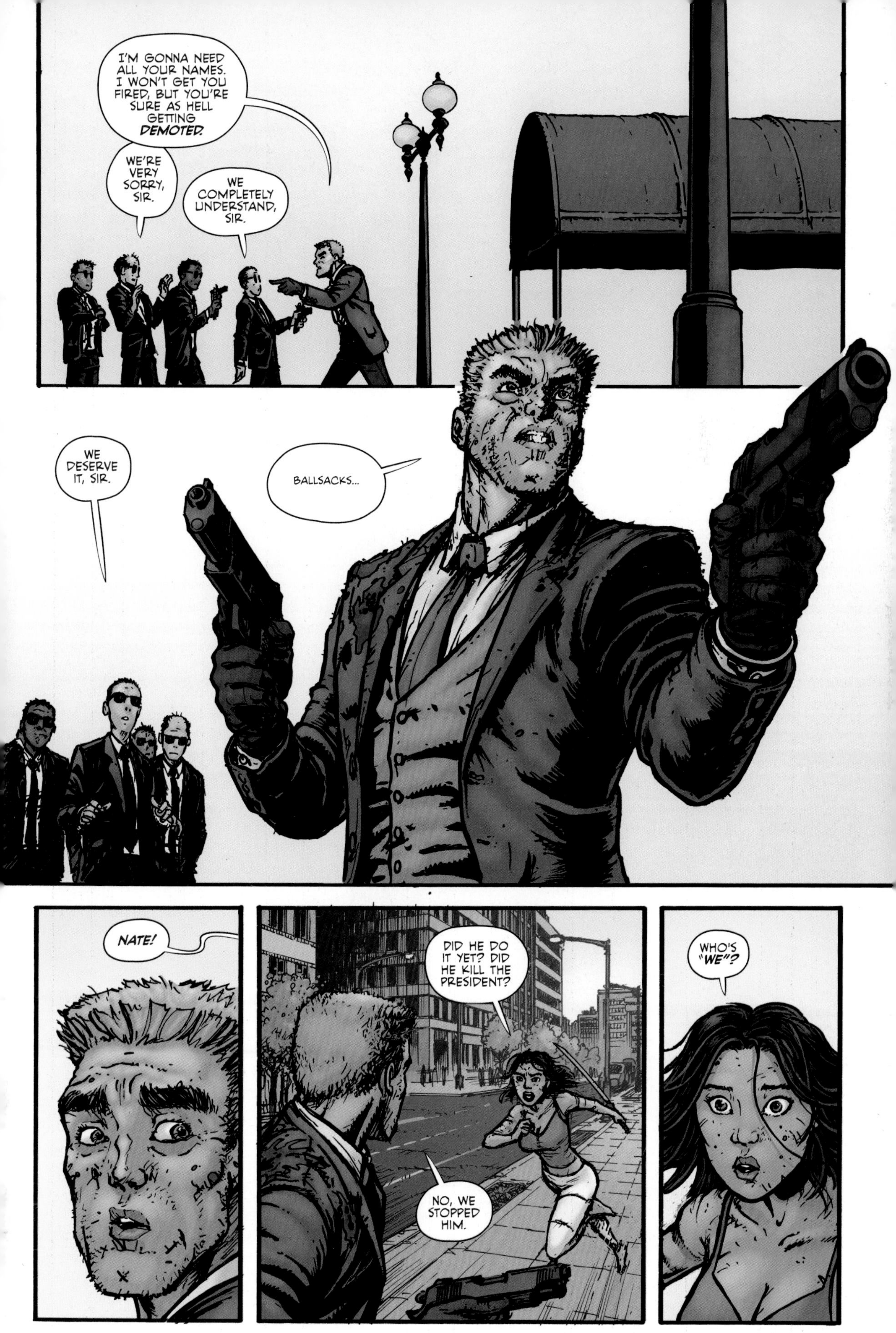
I'M GONNA NEED ALL YOUR NAMES. I WON'T GET YOU FIRED, BUT YOU'RE SURE AS HELL GETTING ***DEMOTED.***
WE'RE VERY SORRY, SIR.
WE COMPLETELY UNDERSTAND, SIR.
WE DESERVE IT, SIR.
BALLSACKS...
NATE!
DID HE DO IT YET? DID HE KILL THE PRESIDENT?
NO, WE STOPPED HIM.
WHO'S "***WE***"?

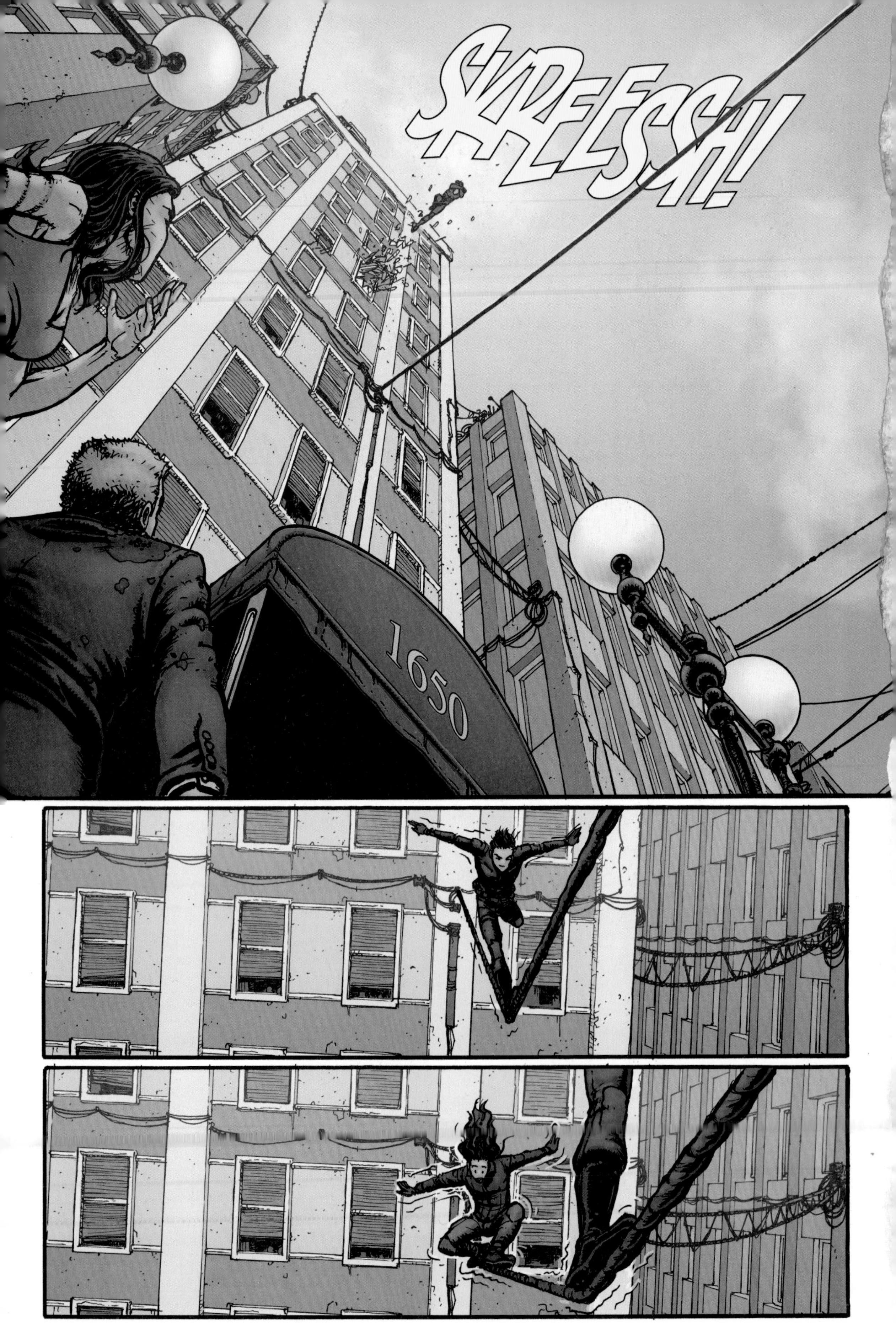
SKREESSH!
1650

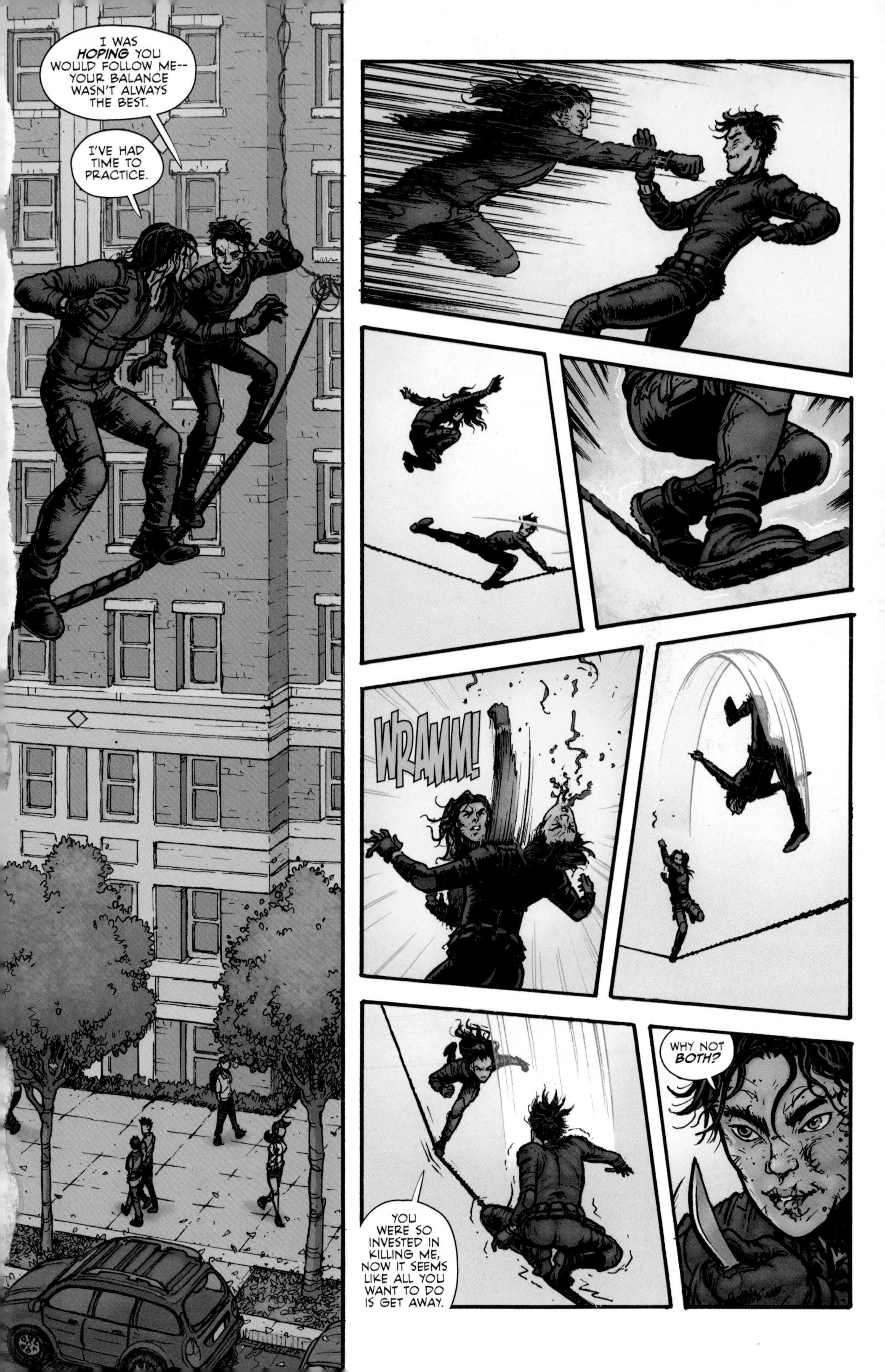
I WAS *HOPING* YOU WOULD FOLLOW ME-- YOUR BALANCE WASN'T ALWAYS THE BEST.
I'VE HAD TIME TO PRACTICE.
WRAMM!
YOU WERE SO INVESTED IN KILLING ME, NOW IT SEEMS LIKE ALL YOU WANT TO DO IS GET AWAY.
WHY NOT *BOTH?*

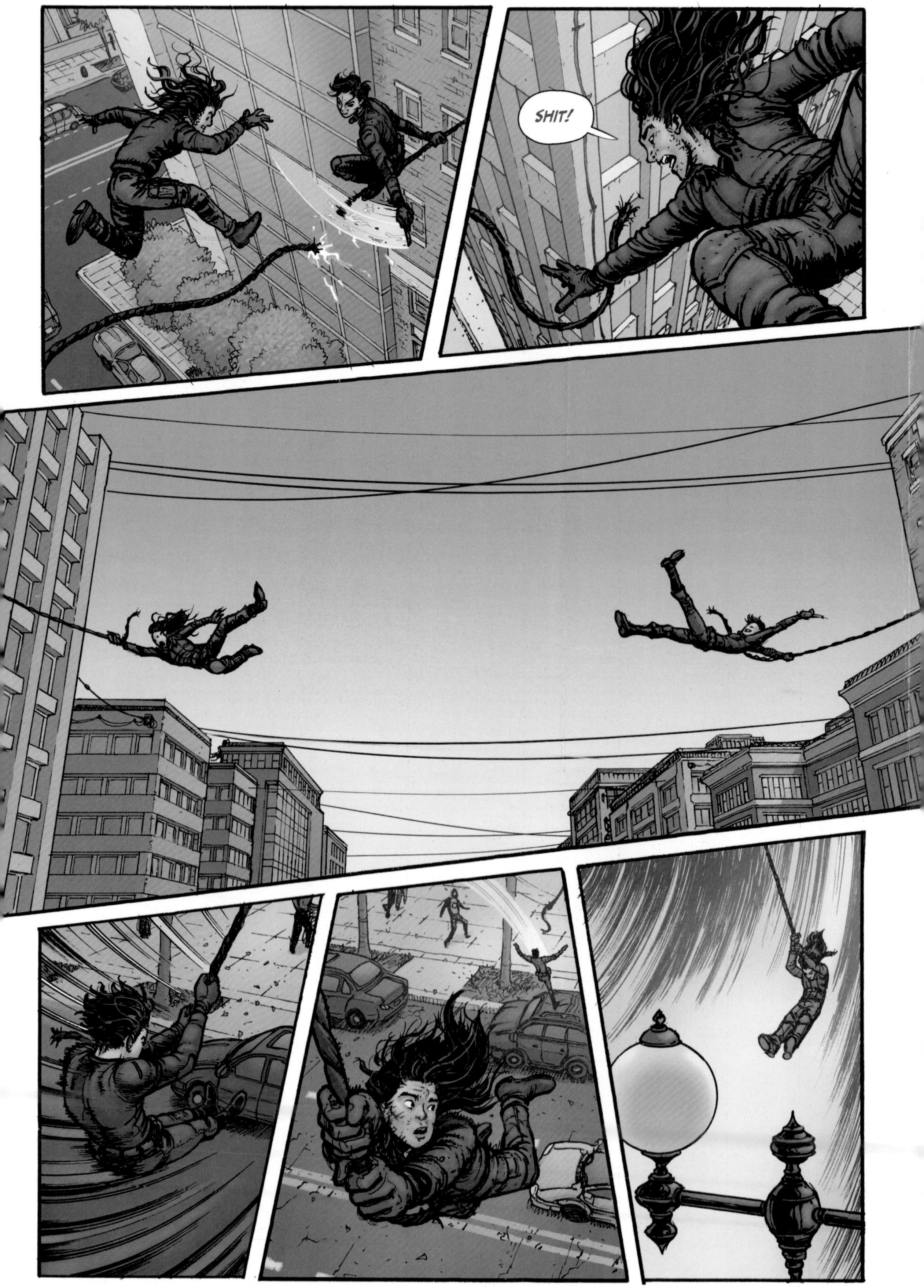
SHIT!

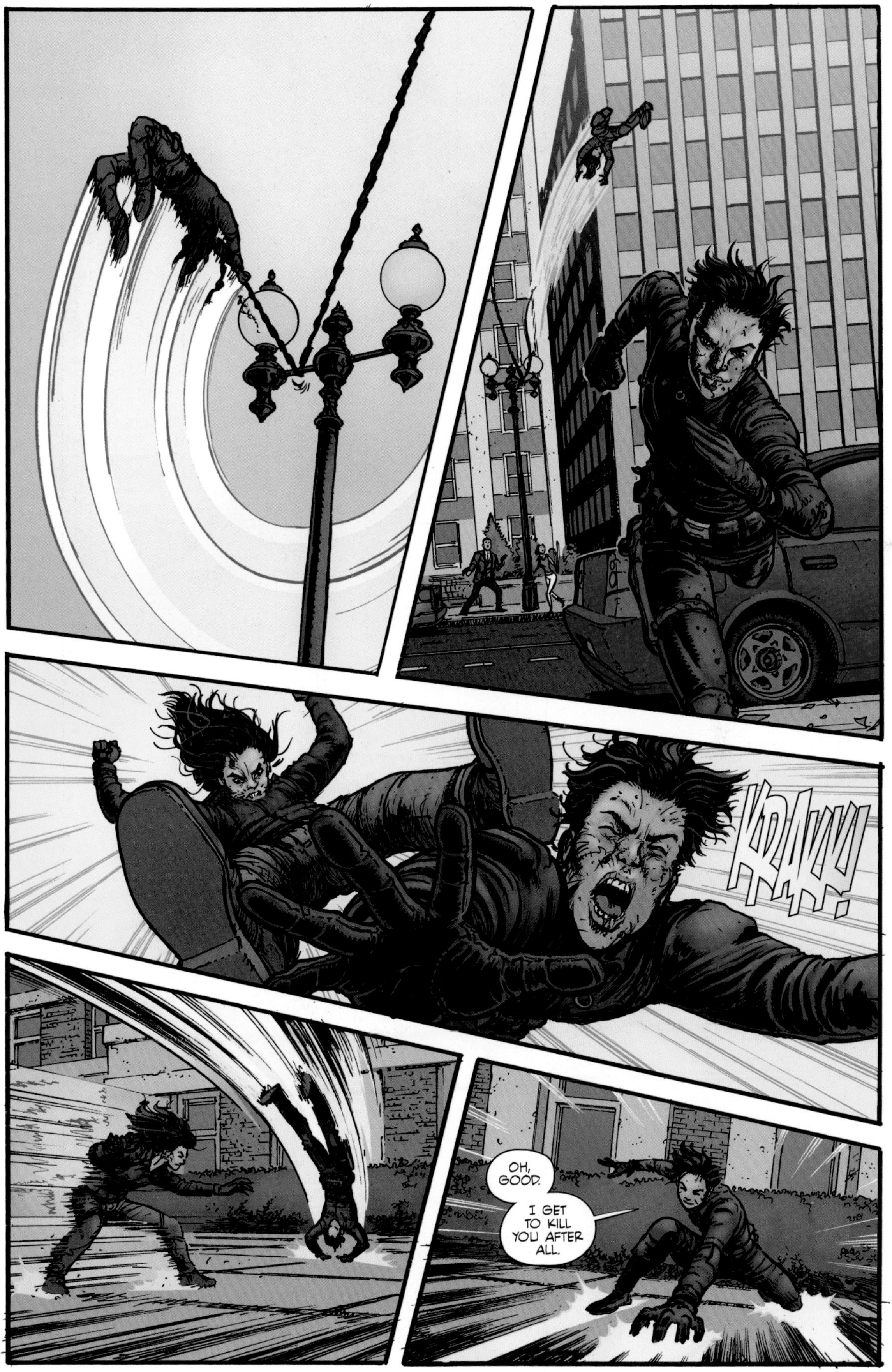
KRAKK!
OH, GOOD.
I GET TO KILL YOU AFTER ALL.

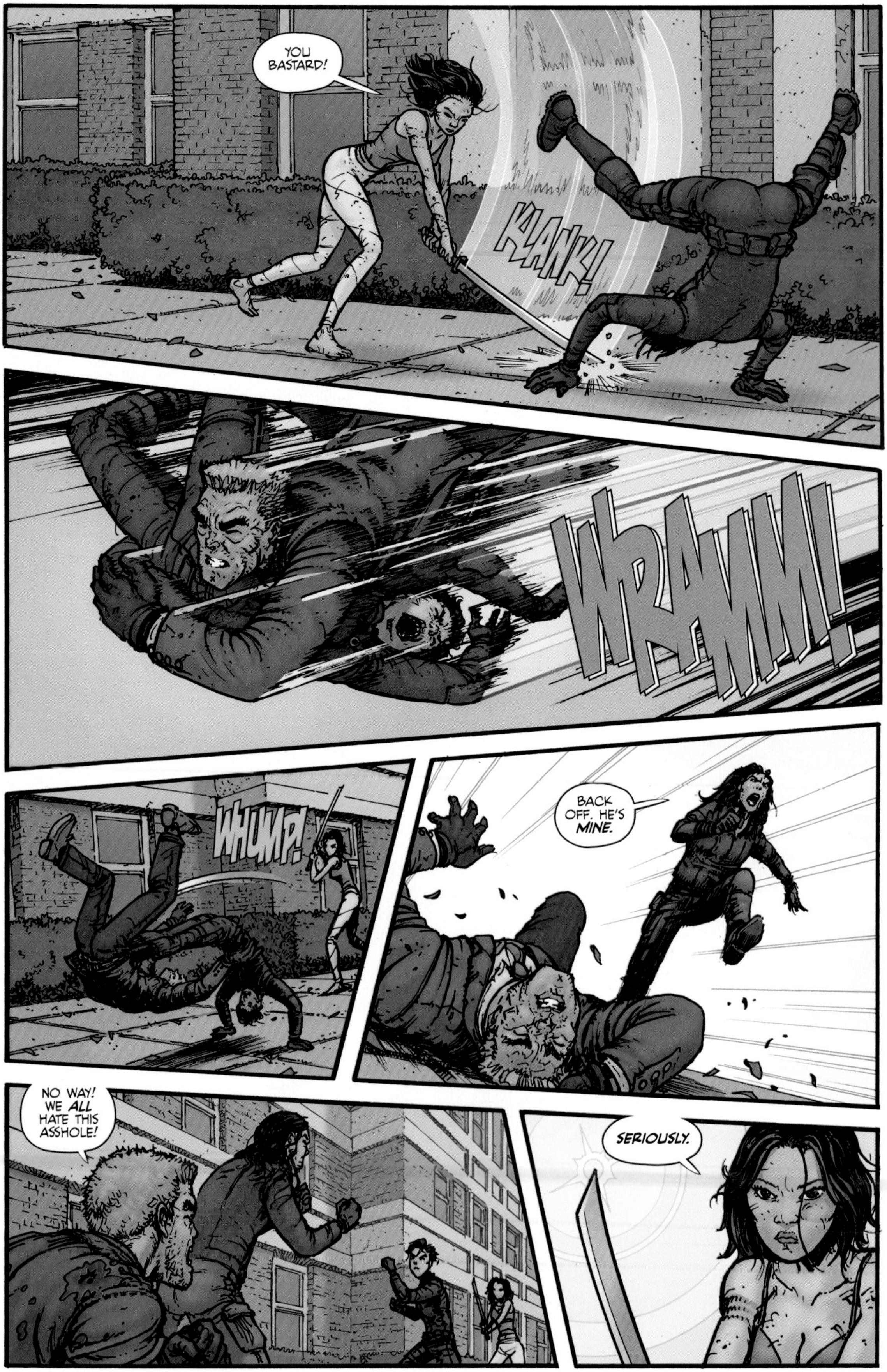
YOU BASTARD!
KLANK!
WRAMM!
WHUMP!
BACK OFF. HE'S MINE.
NO WAY! WE ALL HATE THIS ASSHOLE!
SERIOUSLY.

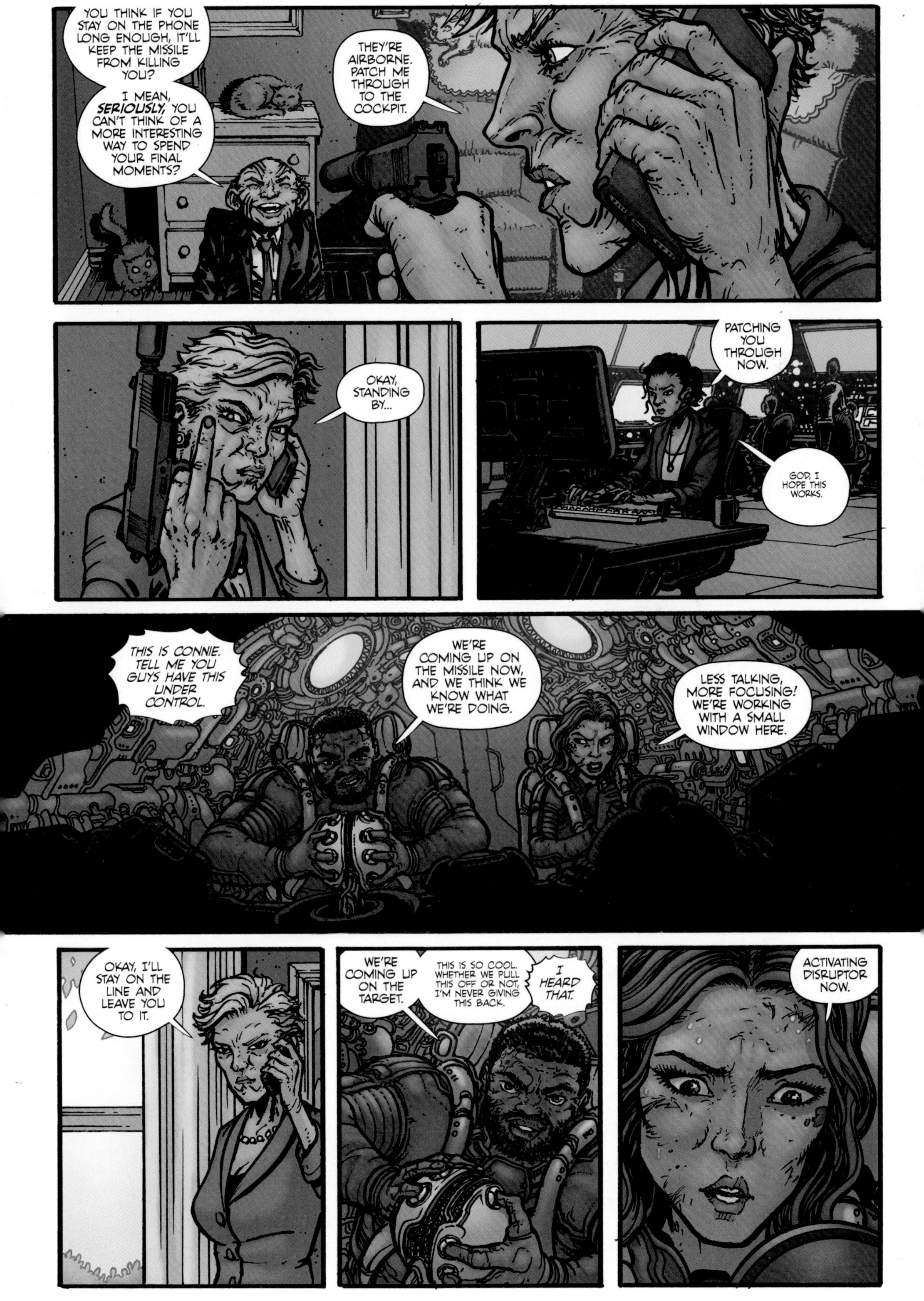
YOU THINK IF YOU STAY ON THE PHONE LONG ENOUGH, IT'LL KEEP THE MISSILE FROM KILLING YOU?
I MEAN, SERIOUSLY, YOU CAN'T THINK OF A MORE INTERESTING WAY TO SPEND YOUR FINAL MOMENTS?
THEY'RE AIRBORNE. PATCH ME THROUGH TO THE COCKPIT.
OKAY, STANDING BY...
PATCHING YOU THROUGH NOW.
GOD, I HOPE THIS WORKS.
THIS IS CONNIE. TELL ME YOU GUYS HAVE THIS UNDER CONTROL.
WE'RE COMING UP ON THE MISSILE NOW, AND WE THINK WE KNOW WHAT WE'RE DOING.
LESS TALKING, MORE FOCUSING! WE'RE WORKING WITH A SMALL WINDOW HERE.
OKAY, I'LL STAY ON THE LINE AND LEAVE YOU TO IT.
WE'RE COMING UP ON THE TARGET.
THIS IS SO COOL. WHETHER WE PULL THIS OFF OR NOT, I'M NEVER GIVING THIS BACK.
I HEARD THAT.
ACTIVATING DISRUPTOR NOW.

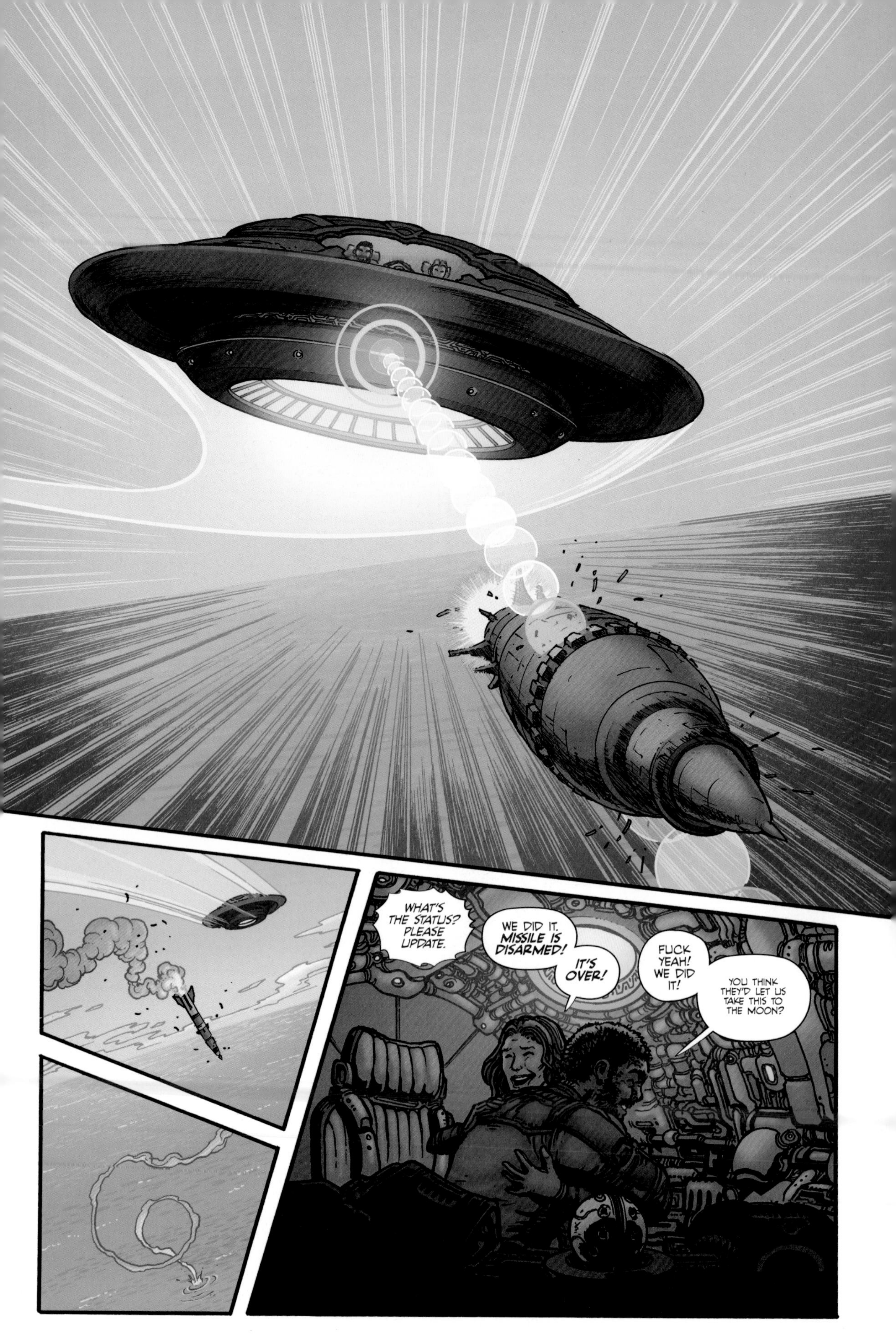
WHAT'S THE STATUS? PLEASE UPDATE.
WE DID IT. MISSILE IS DISARMED!
IT'S OVER!
FUCK YEAH! WE DID IT!
YOU THINK THEY'D LET US TAKE THIS TO THE MOON?

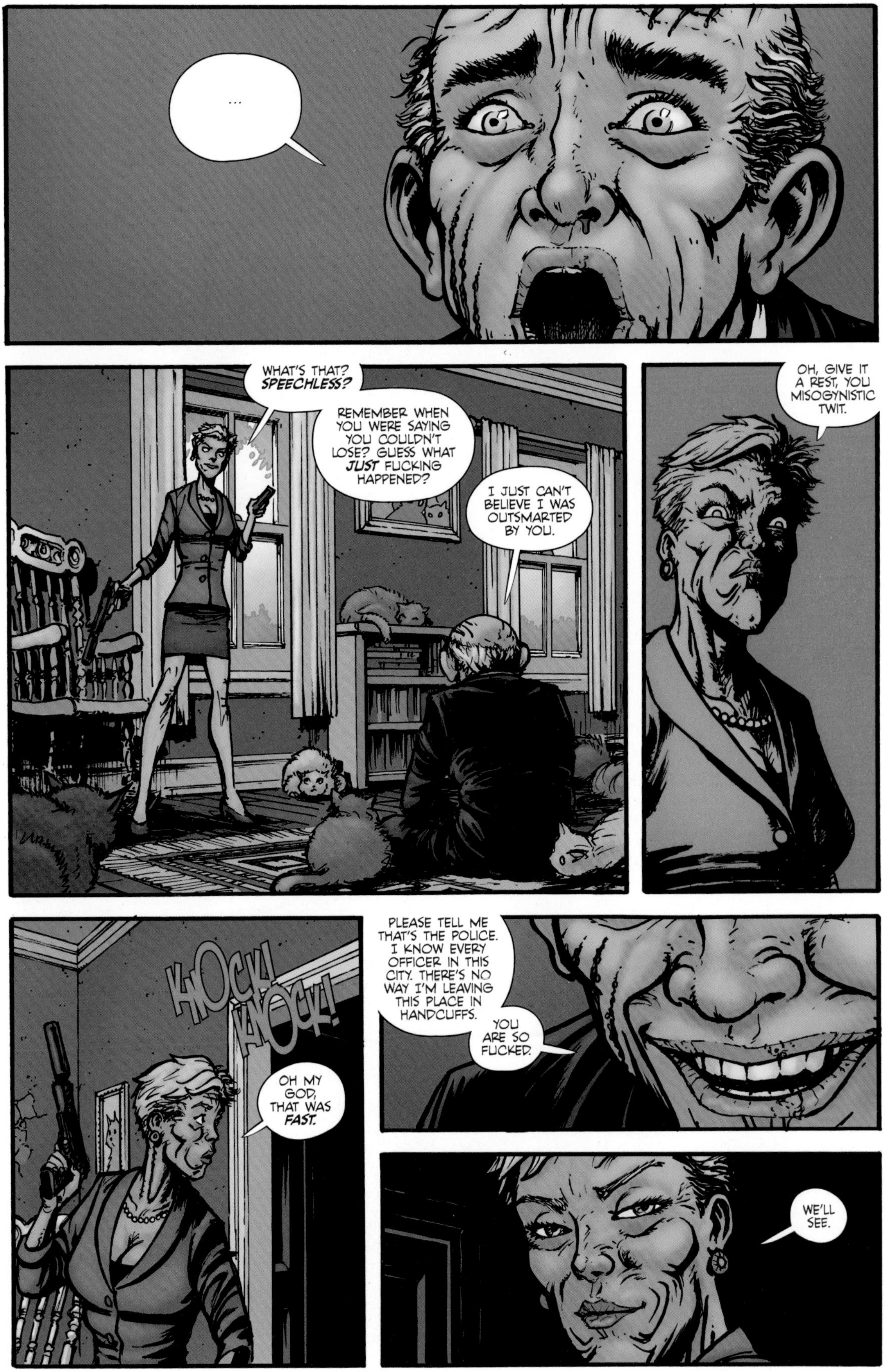
...
WHAT'S THAT? SPEECHLESS?
REMEMBER WHEN YOU WERE SAYING YOU COULDN'T LOSE? GUESS WHAT JUST FUCKING HAPPENED?
I JUST CAN'T BELIEVE I WAS OUTSMARTED BY YOU.
OH, GIVE IT A REST, YOU MISOGYNISTIC TWIT.
KNOCK! KNOCK!
OH MY GOD, THAT WAS FAST.
PLEASE TELL ME THAT'S THE POLICE. I KNOW EVERY OFFICER IN THIS CITY. THERE'S NO WAY I'M LEAVING THIS PLACE IN HANDCUFFS.
YOU ARE SO FUCKED.
WE'LL SEE.

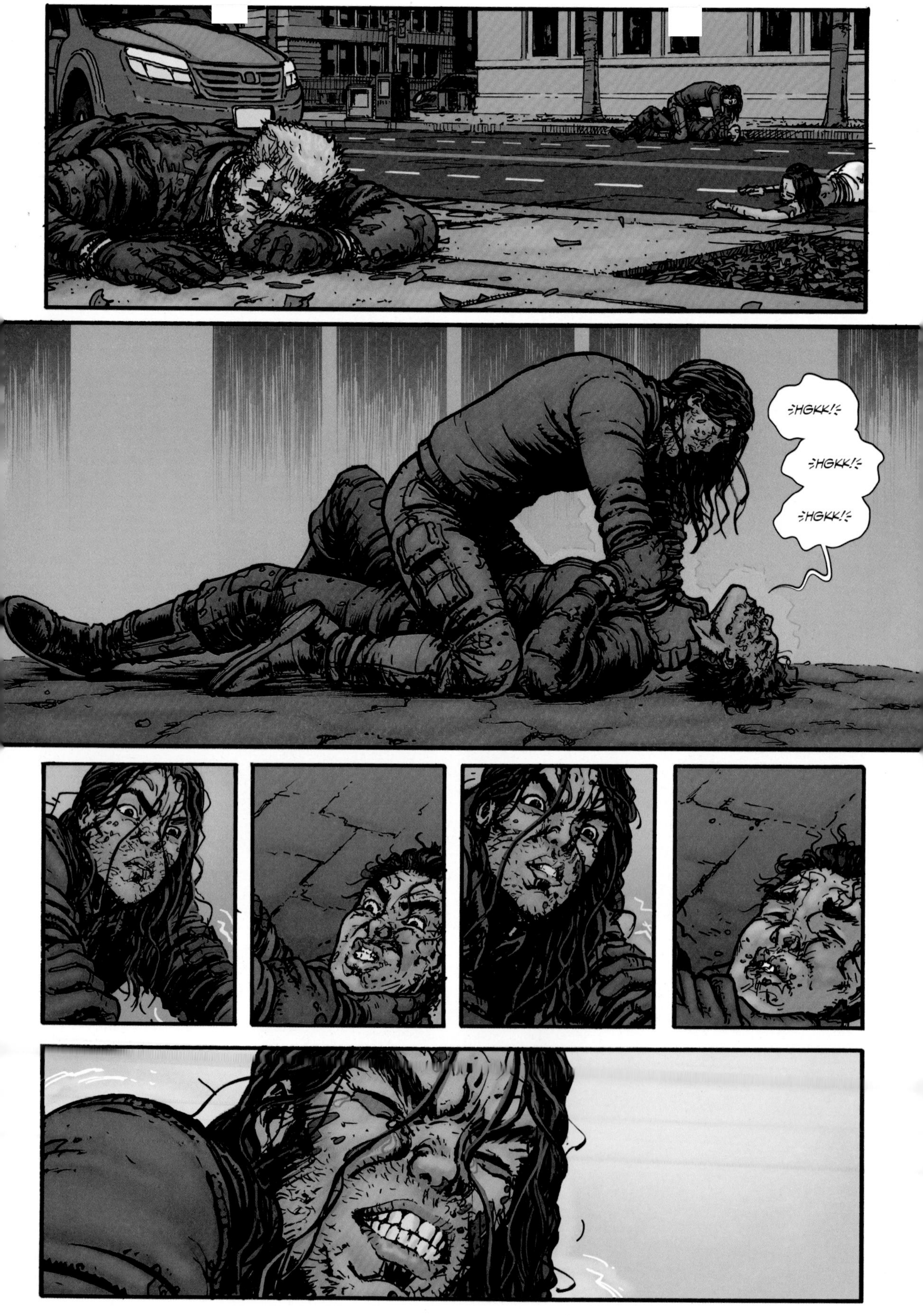
HGKK!
HGKK!
HGKK!

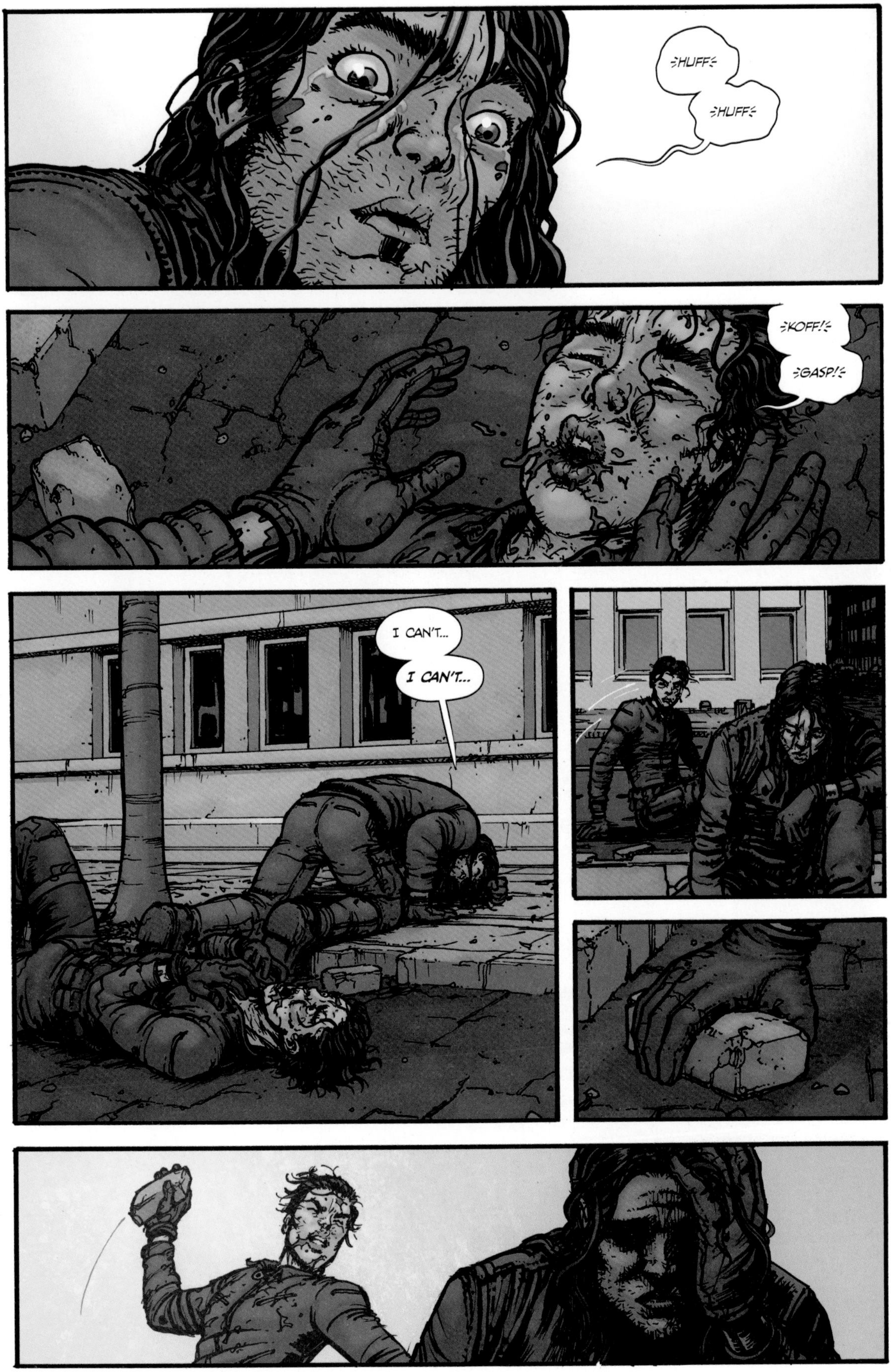
HUFF
HUFF
KOFF!
GASP!
I CAN'T...
I CAN'T...

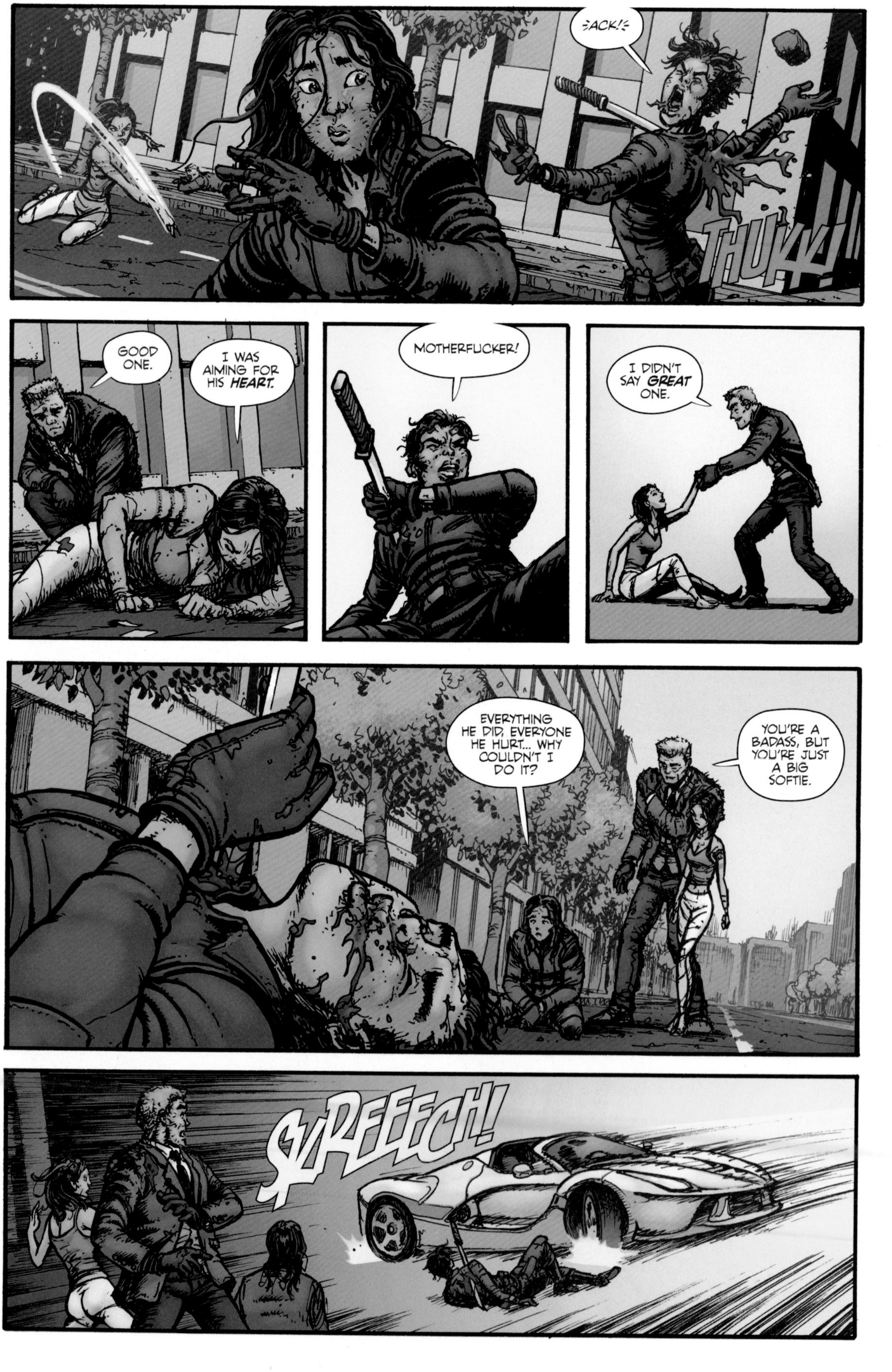
ACK!
THUKK!
GOOD ONE.
I WAS AIMING FOR HIS HEART.
MOTHERFUCKER!
I DIDN'T SAY GREAT ONE.
EVERYTHING HE DID, EVERYONE HE HURT... WHY COULDN'T I DO IT?
YOU'RE A BADASS, BUT YOU'RE JUST A BIG SOFTIE.
SKREEECH!

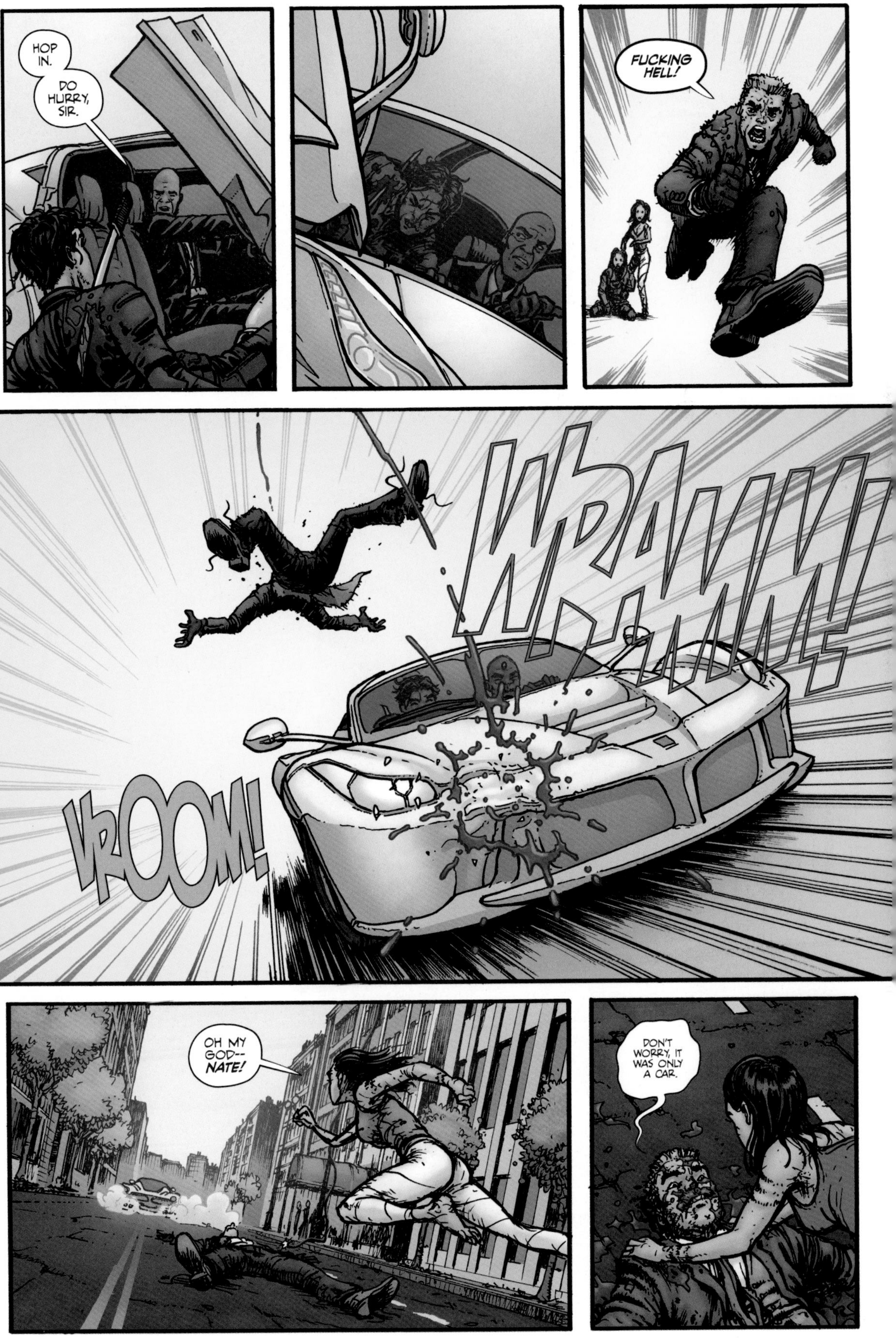
HOP IN.
DO HURRY, SIR.
FUCKING HELL!
WRAMM!
VROOM!
OH MY GOD-- NATE!
DON'T WORRY, IT WAS ONLY A CAR.

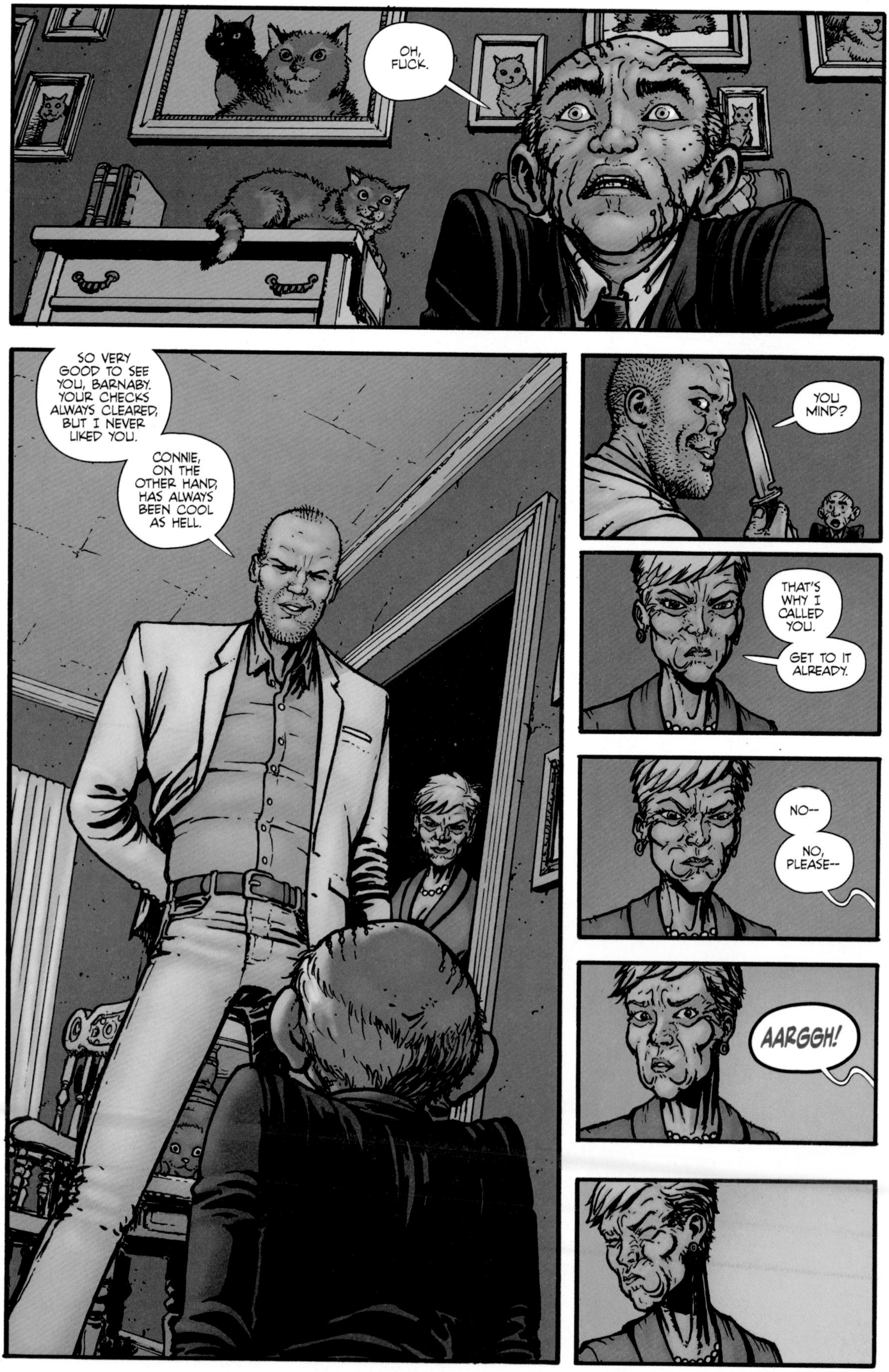
OH, FUCK.
SO VERY GOOD TO SEE YOU, BARNABY. YOUR CHECKS ALWAYS CLEARED, BUT I NEVER LIKED YOU.
CONNIE, ON THE OTHER HAND, HAS ALWAYS BEEN COOL AS HELL.
YOU MIND?
THAT'S WHY I CALLED YOU.
GET TO IT ALREADY.
NO--
NO, PLEASE--
AARGGH!

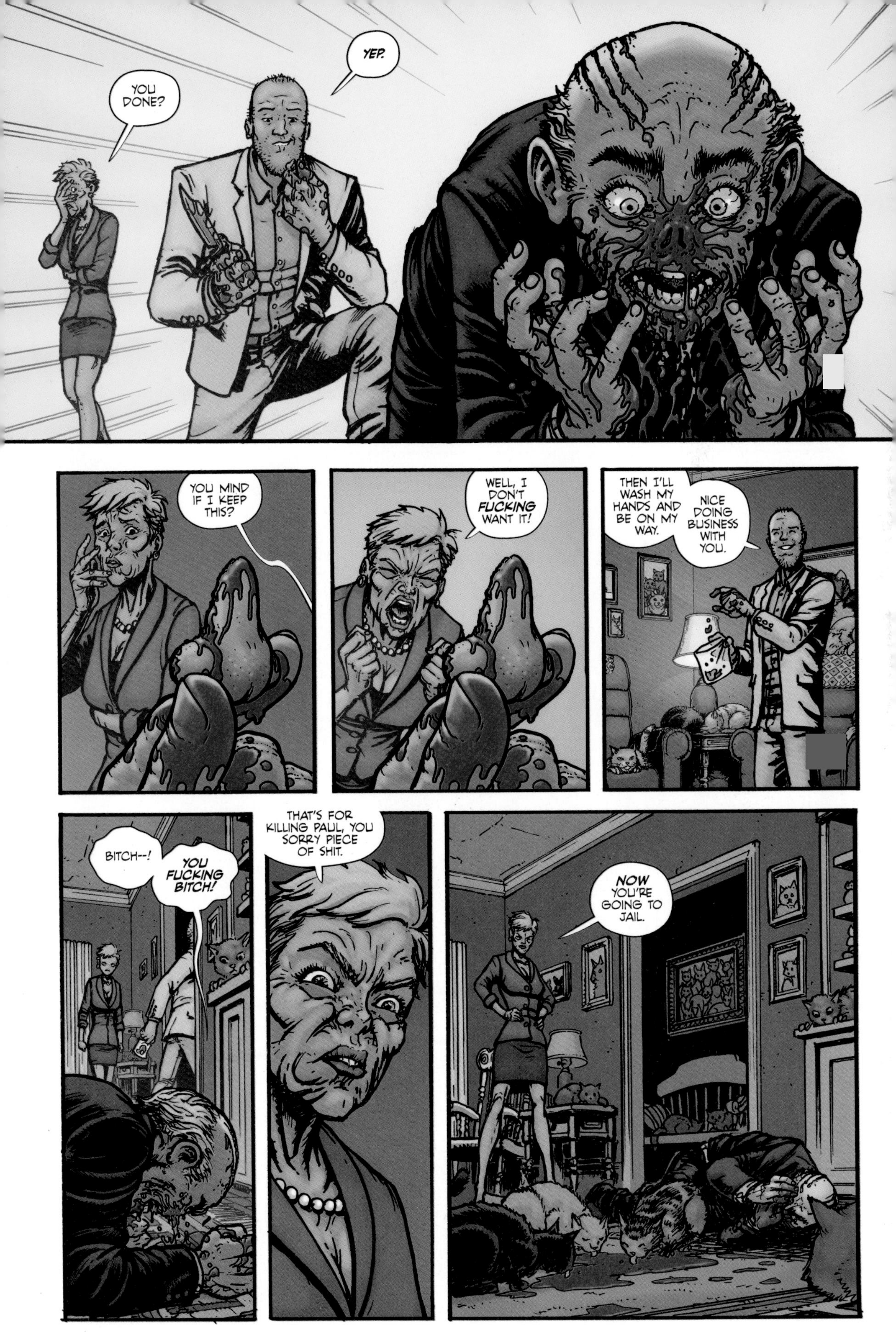
YOU DONE?
YEP.
YOU MIND IF I KEEP THIS?
WELL, I DON'T FUCKING WANT IT!
THEN I'LL WASH MY HANDS AND BE ON MY WAY.
NICE DOING BUSINESS WITH YOU.
BITCH--!
YOU FUCKING BITCH!
THAT'S FOR KILLING PAUL, YOU SORRY PIECE OF SHIT.
NOW YOU'RE GOING TO JAIL.

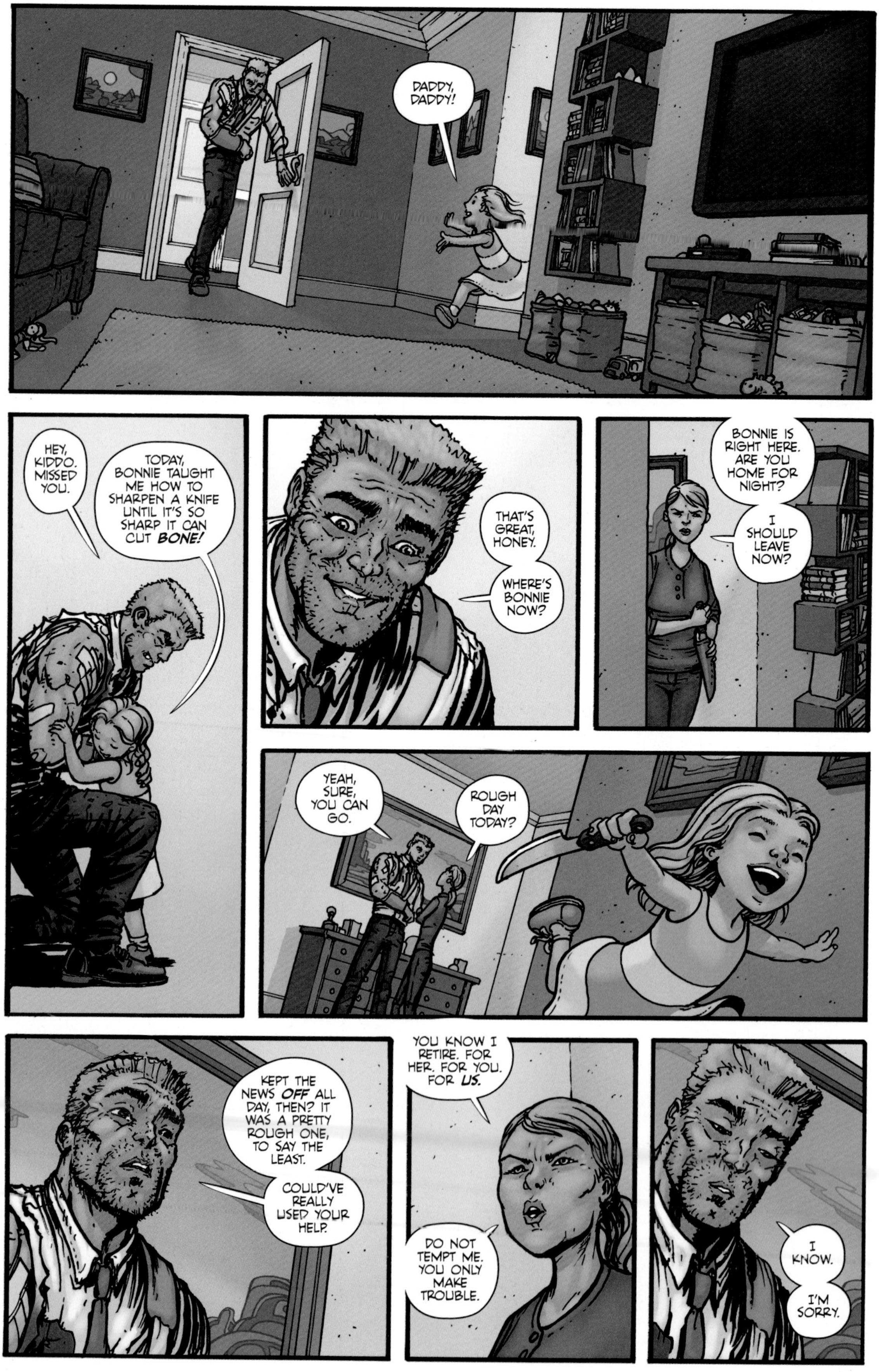
DADDY, DADDY!
HEY, KIDDO. MISSED YOU.
TODAY, BONNIE TAUGHT ME HOW TO SHARPEN A KNIFE UNTIL IT'S SO SHARP IT CAN CUT BONE!
THAT'S GREAT, HONEY.
WHERE'S BONNIE NOW?
BONNIE IS RIGHT HERE. ARE YOU HOME FOR NIGHT?
I SHOULD LEAVE NOW?
YEAH, SURE, YOU CAN GO.
ROUGH DAY TODAY?
KEPT THE NEWS OFF ALL DAY, THEN? IT WAS A PRETTY ROUGH ONE, TO SAY THE LEAST.
COULD'VE REALLY USED YOUR HELP.
YOU KNOW I RETIRE. FOR HER. FOR YOU. FOR US.
DO NOT TEMPT ME. YOU ONLY MAKE TROUBLE.
I KNOW.
I'M SORRY.

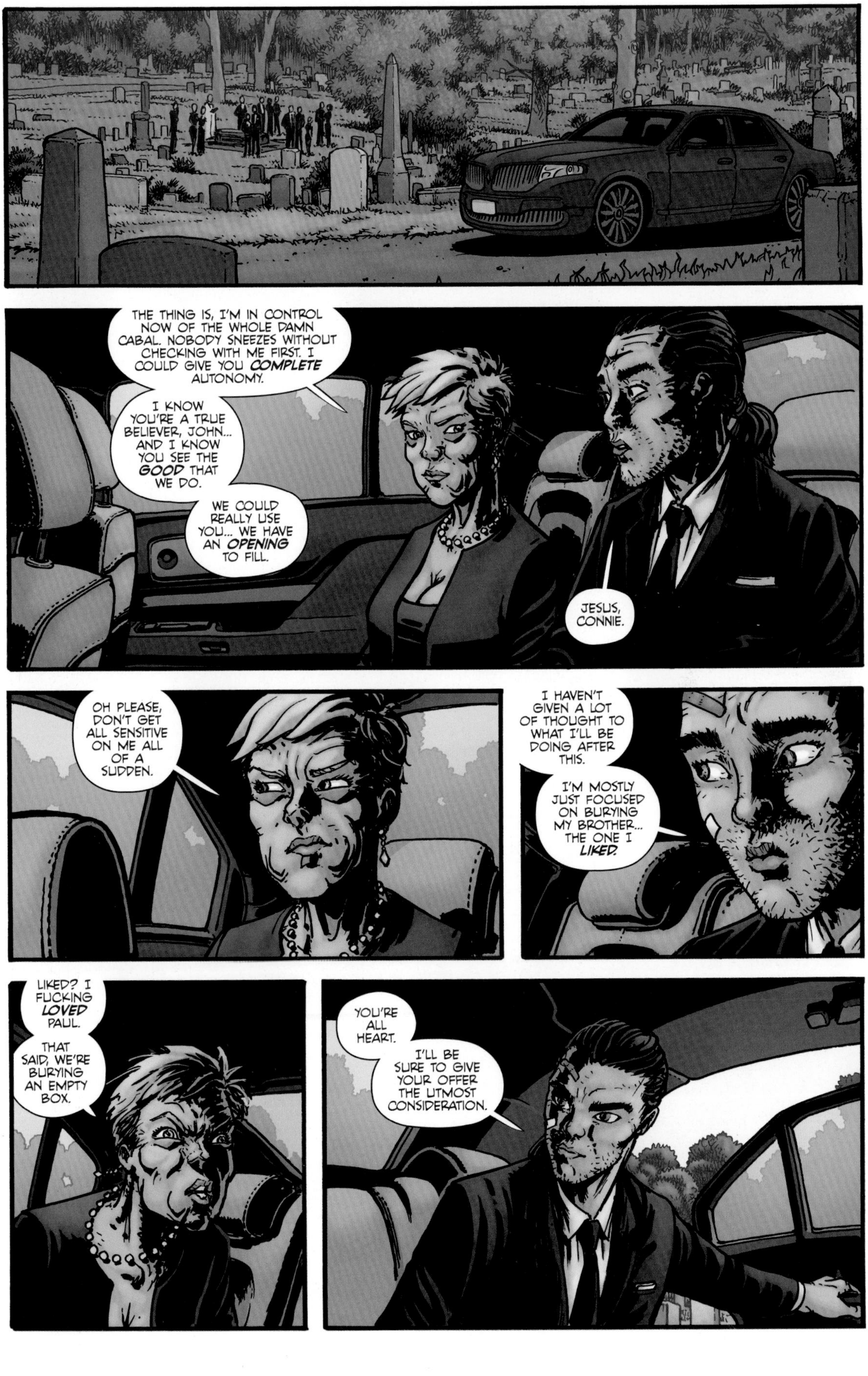
THE THING IS, I'M IN CONTROL NOW OF THE WHOLE DAMN CABAL. NOBODY SNEEZES WITHOUT CHECKING WITH ME FIRST. I COULD GIVE YOU COMPLETE AUTONOMY.
I KNOW YOU'RE A TRUE BELIEVER, JOHN... AND I KNOW YOU SEE THE GOOD THAT WE DO.
WE COULD REALLY USE YOU... WE HAVE AN OPENING TO FILL.
JESUS, CONNIE.
OH PLEASE, DON'T GET ALL SENSITIVE ON ME ALL OF A SUDDEN.
I HAVEN'T GIVEN A LOT OF THOUGHT TO WHAT I'LL BE DOING AFTER THIS.
I'M MOSTLY JUST FOCUSED ON BURYING MY BROTHER... THE ONE I LIKED.
LIKED? I FUCKING LOVED PAUL.
THAT SAID, WE'RE BURYING AN EMPTY BOX.
YOU'RE ALL HEART.
I'LL BE SURE TO GIVE YOUR OFFER THE UTMOST CONSIDERATION.

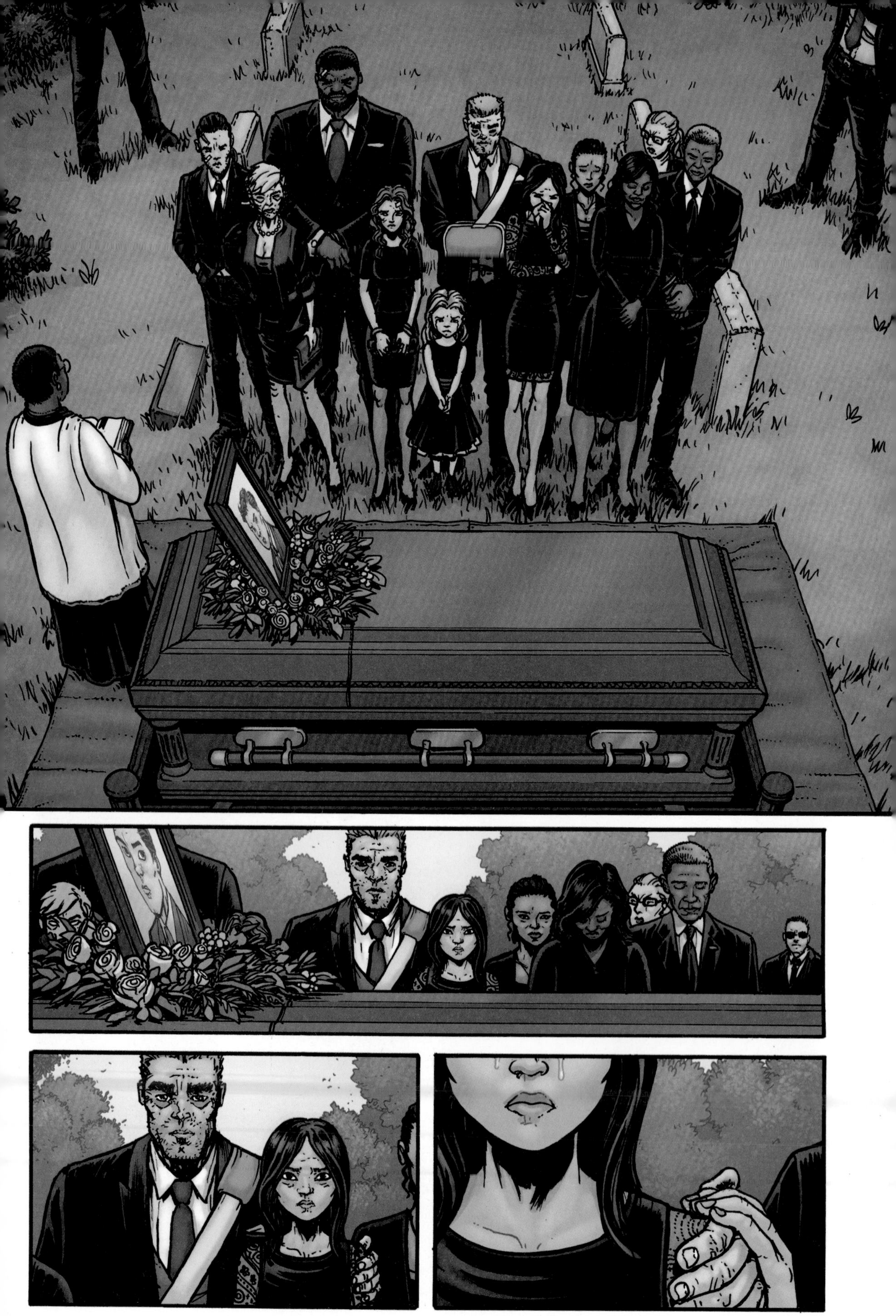

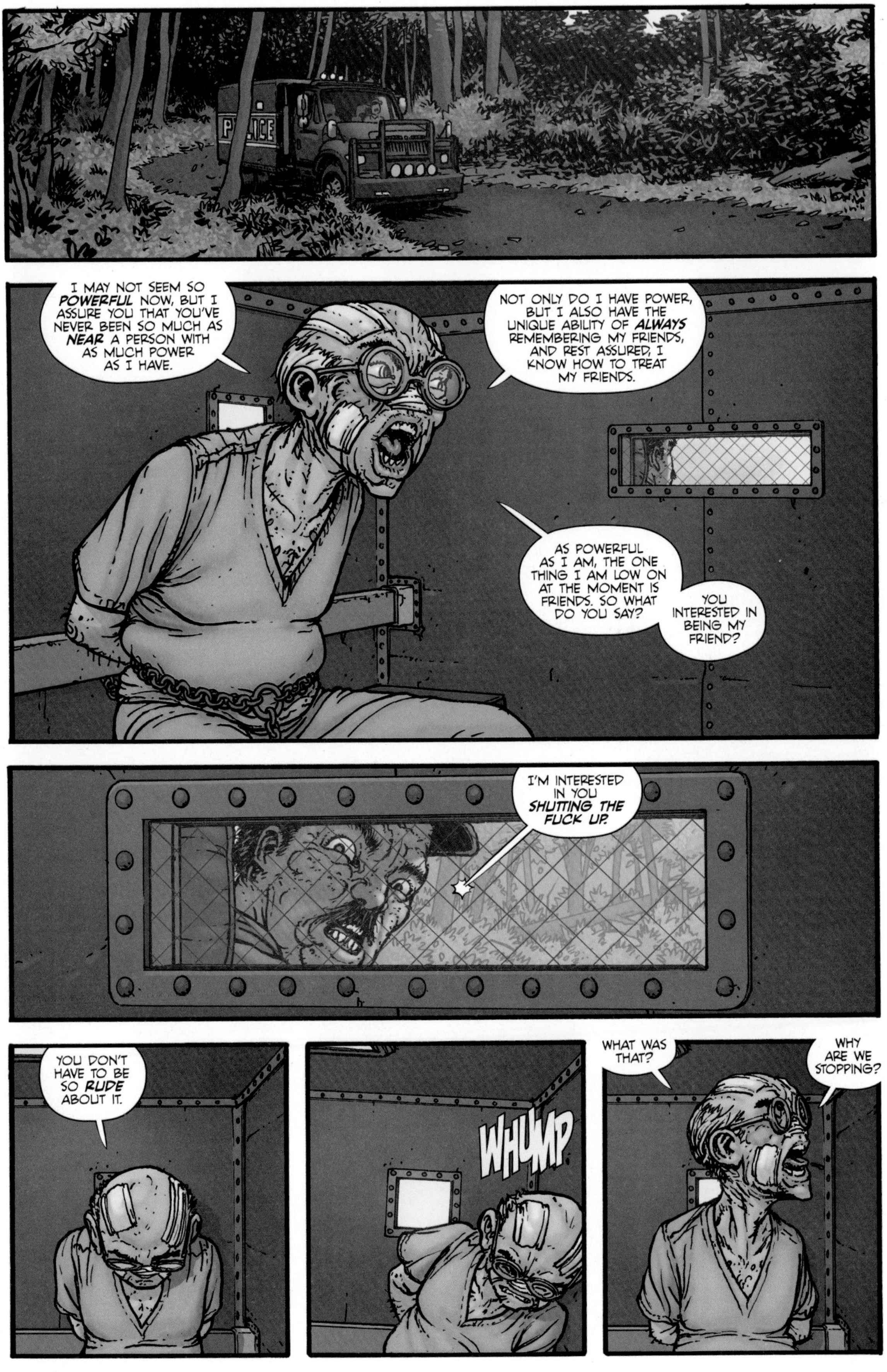
I MAY NOT SEEM SO POWERFUL NOW, BUT I ASSURE YOU THAT YOU'VE NEVER BEEN SO MUCH AS NEAR A PERSON WITH AS MUCH POWER AS I HAVE.
NOT ONLY DO I HAVE POWER, BUT I ALSO HAVE THE UNIQUE ABILITY OF ALWAYS REMEMBERING MY FRIENDS, AND REST ASSURED, I KNOW HOW TO TREAT MY FRIENDS.
AS POWERFUL AS I AM, THE ONE THING I AM LOW ON AT THE MOMENT IS FRIENDS. SO WHAT DO YOU SAY?
YOU INTERESTED IN BEING MY FRIEND?
I'M INTERESTED IN YOU SHUTTING THE FUCK UP.
YOU DON'T HAVE TO BE SO RUDE ABOUT IT.
WHUMP
WHAT WAS THAT?
WHY ARE WE STOPPING?

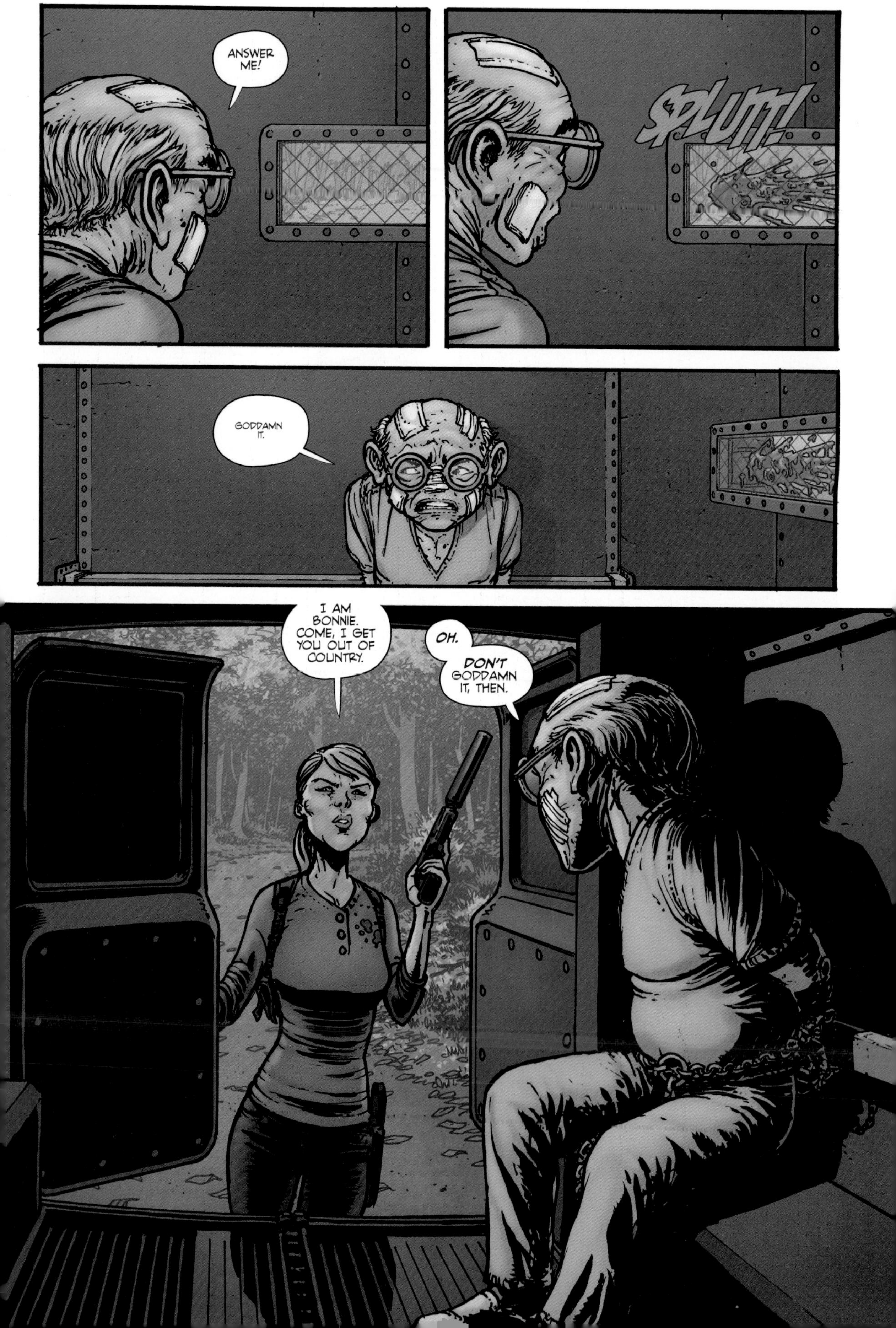
ANSWER ME!
SPLUTT!
GODDAMN IT.
I AM BONNIE. COME, I GET YOU OUT OF COUNTRY.
OH.
DON'T GODDAMN IT, THEN.

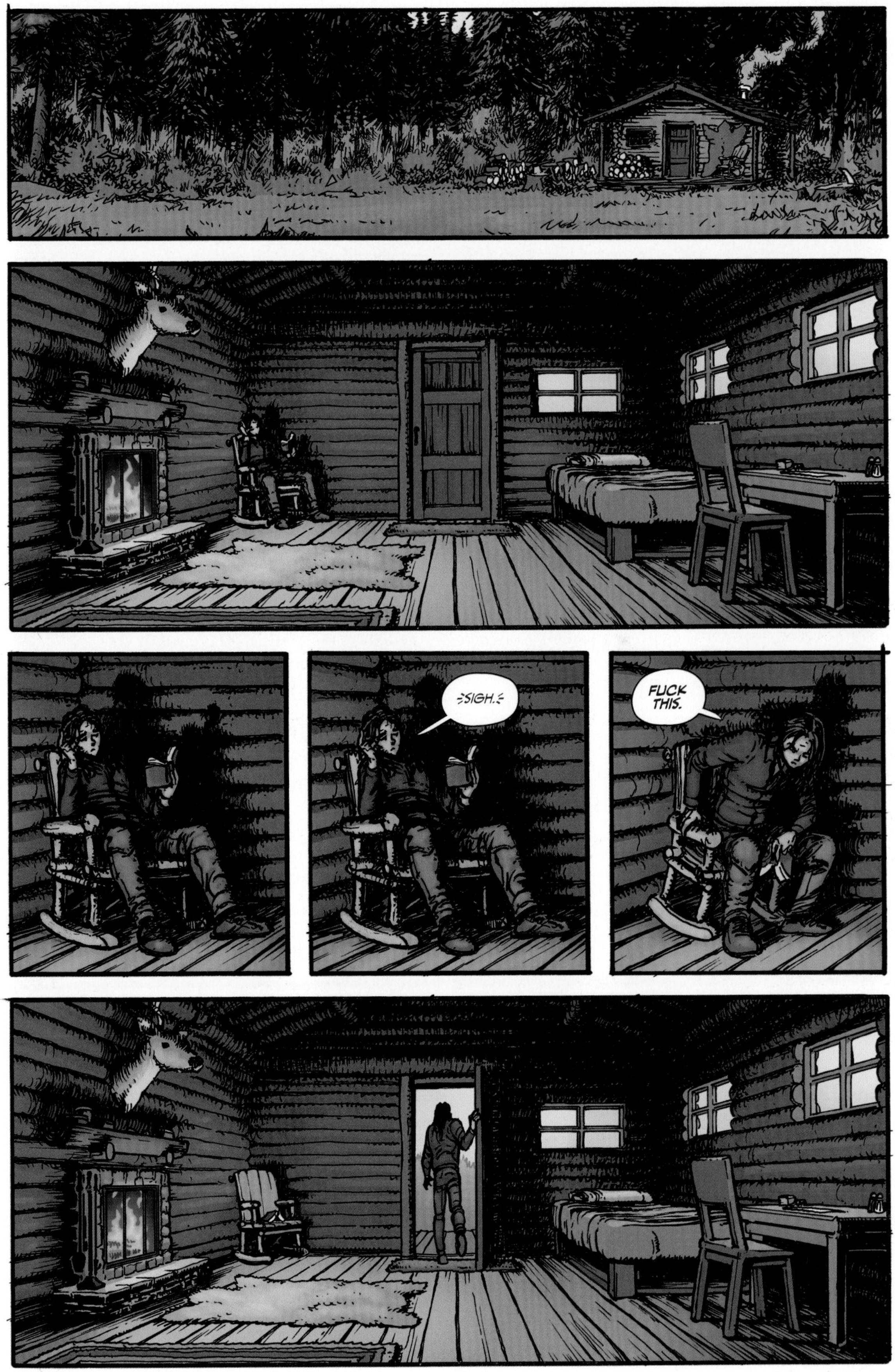
SIGH.
FUCK THIS.

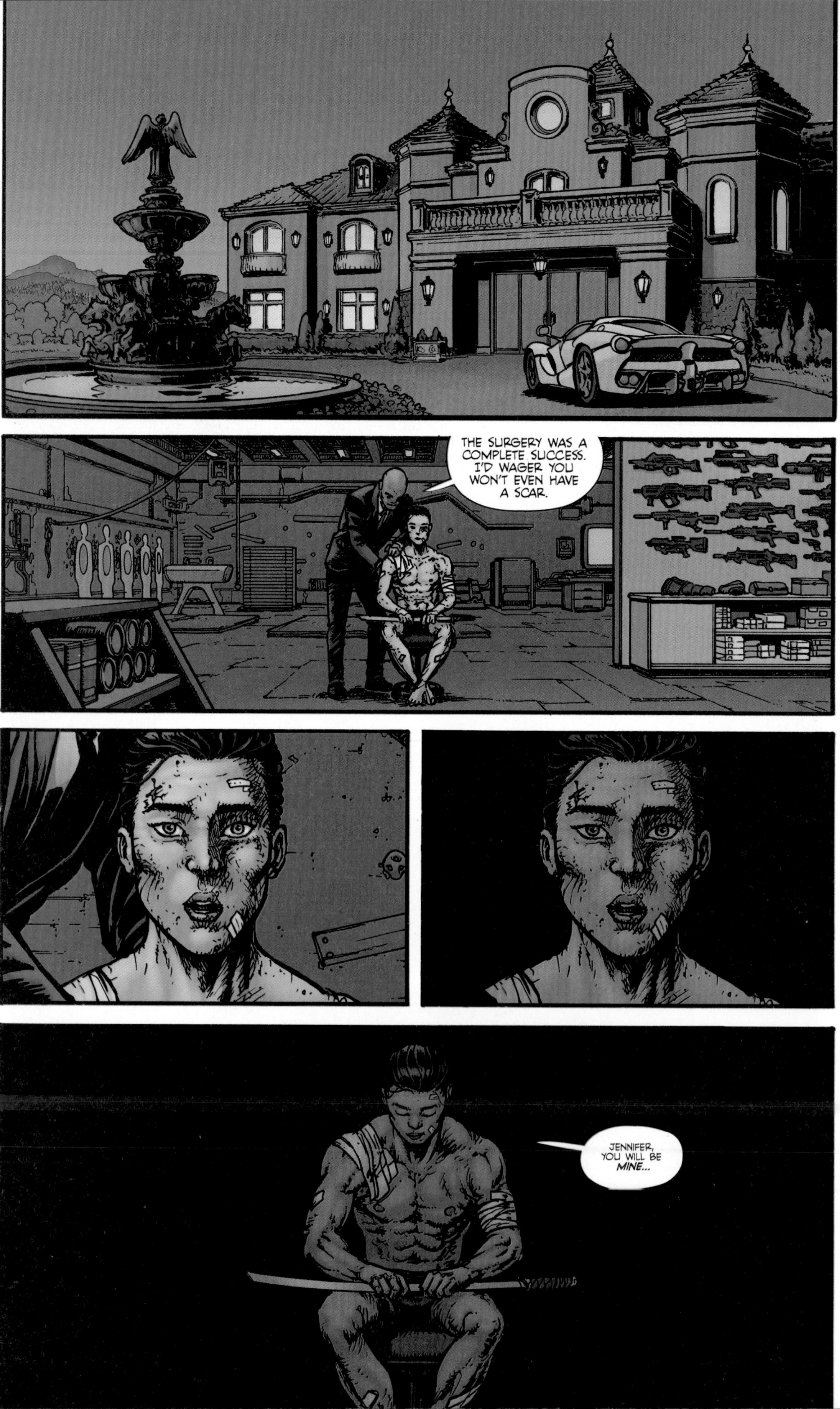
THE SURGERY WAS A COMPLETE SUCCESS. I'D WAGER YOU WON'T EVEN HAVE A SCAR.
JENNIFER, YOU WILL BE *MINE...*

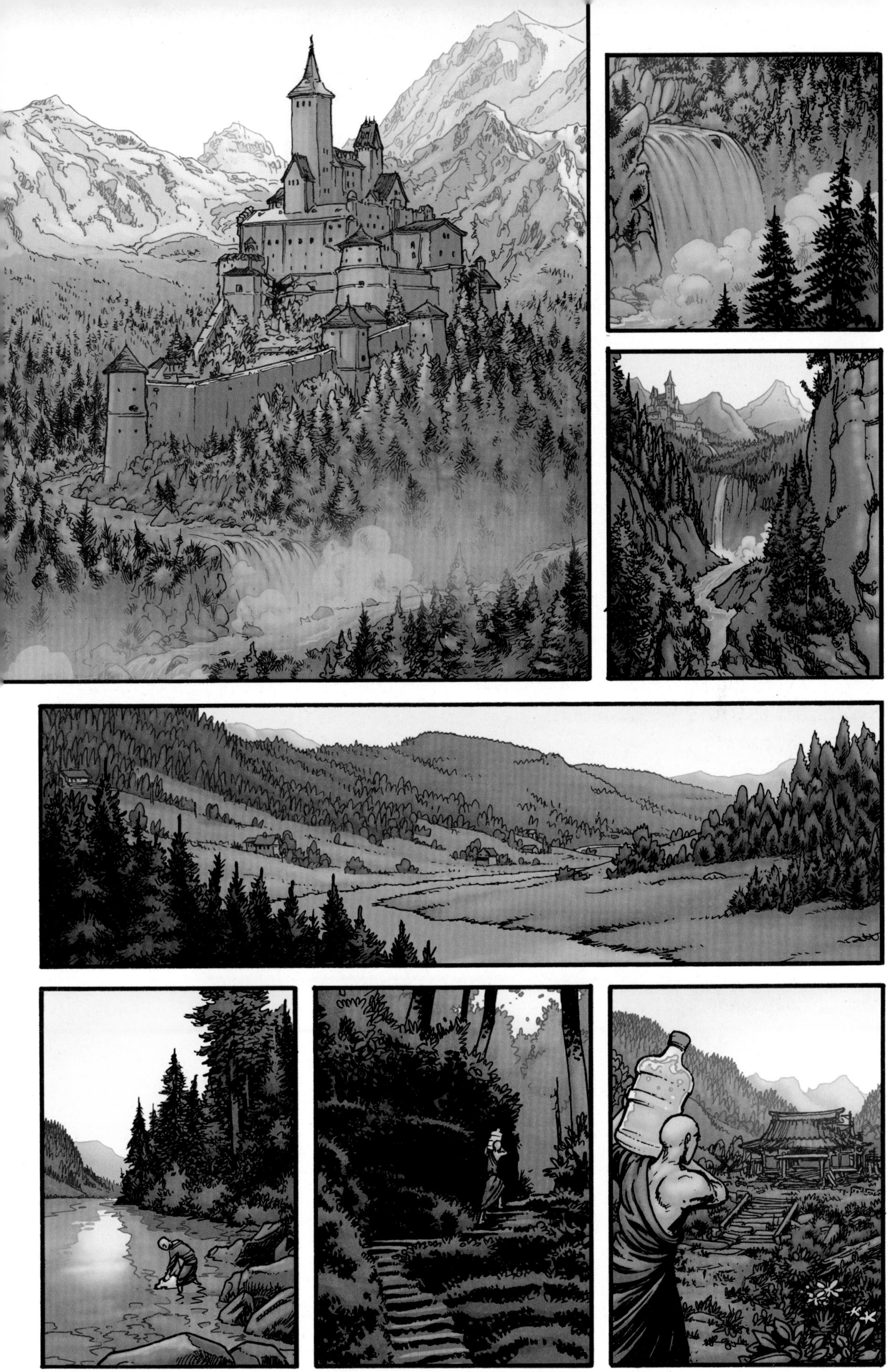

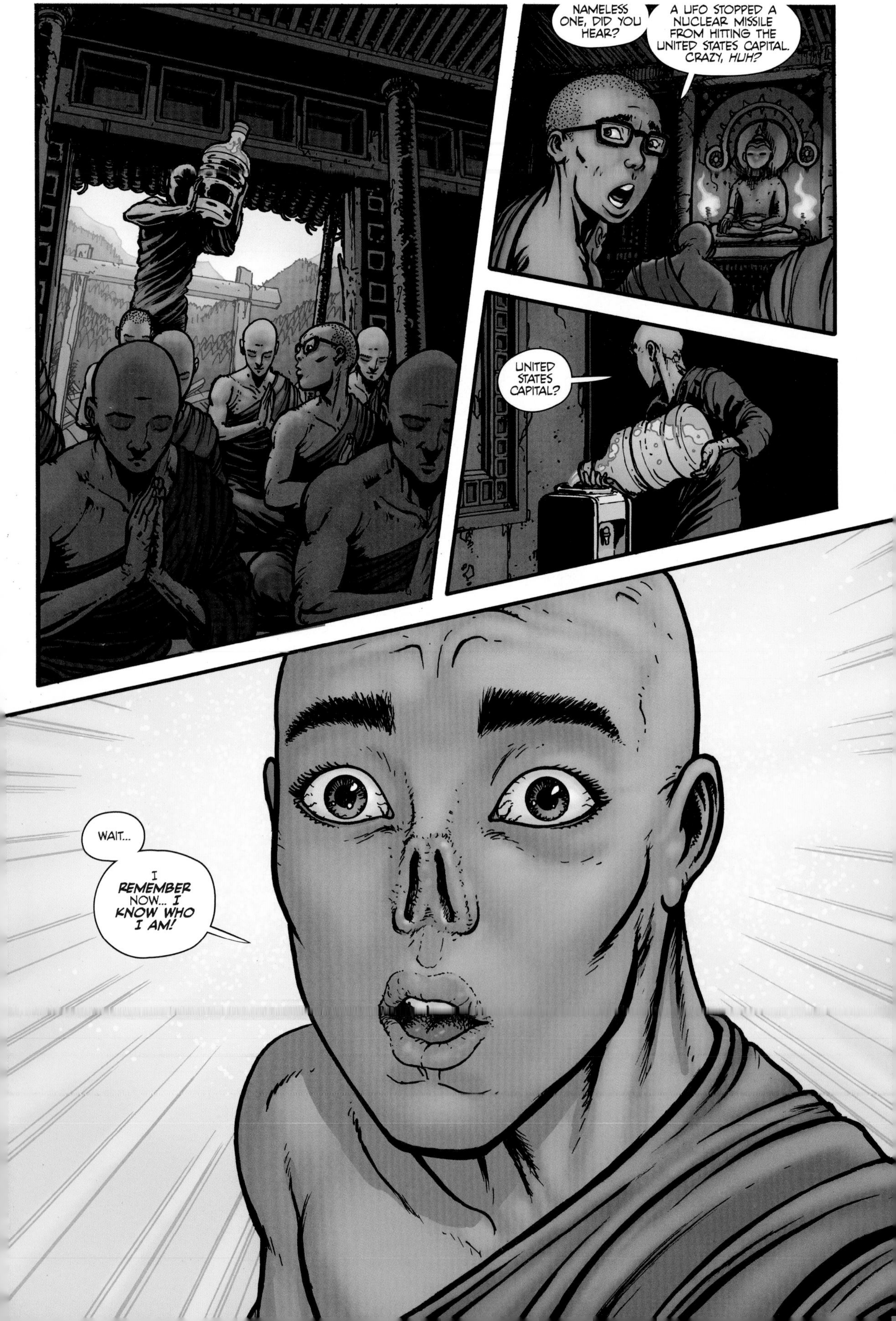
NAMELESS ONE, DID YOU HEAR?
A UFO STOPPED A NUCLEAR MISSILE FROM HITTING THE UNITED STATES CAPITAL. CRAZY, HUH?
UNITED STATES CAPITAL?
WAIT...
I REMEMBER NOW... I KNOW WHO I AM!

TO BE
CONTINUED

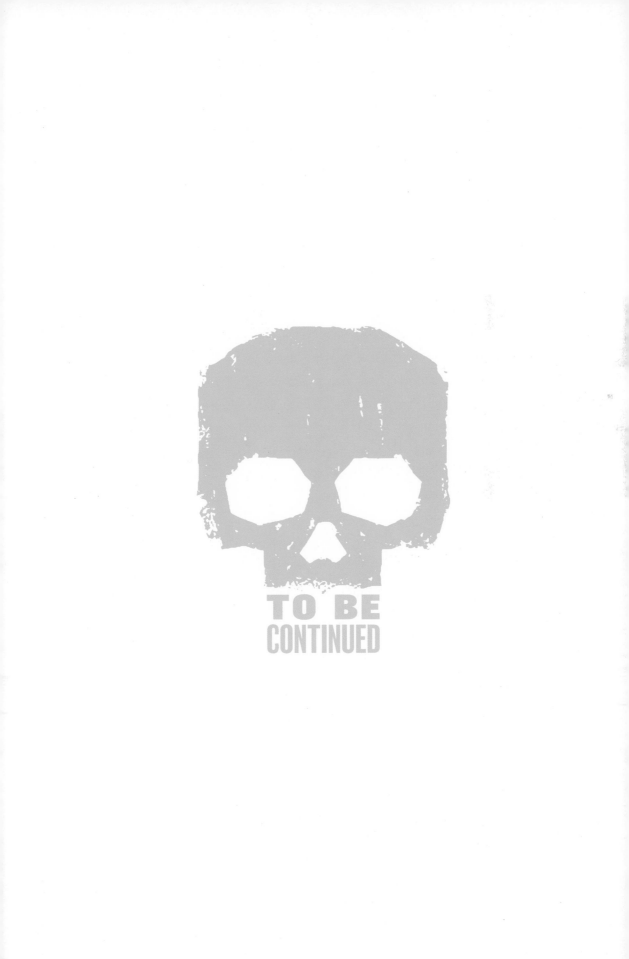

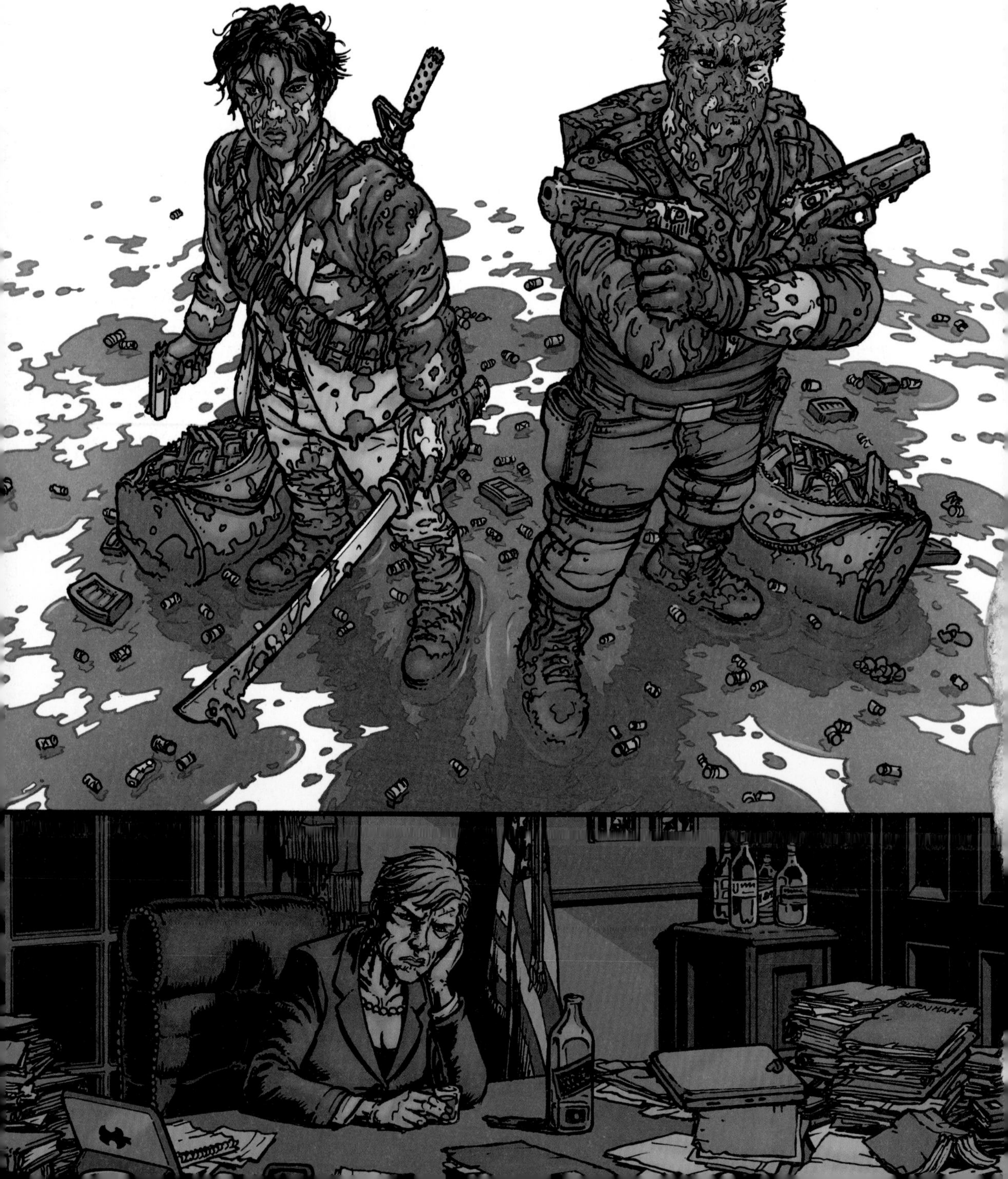

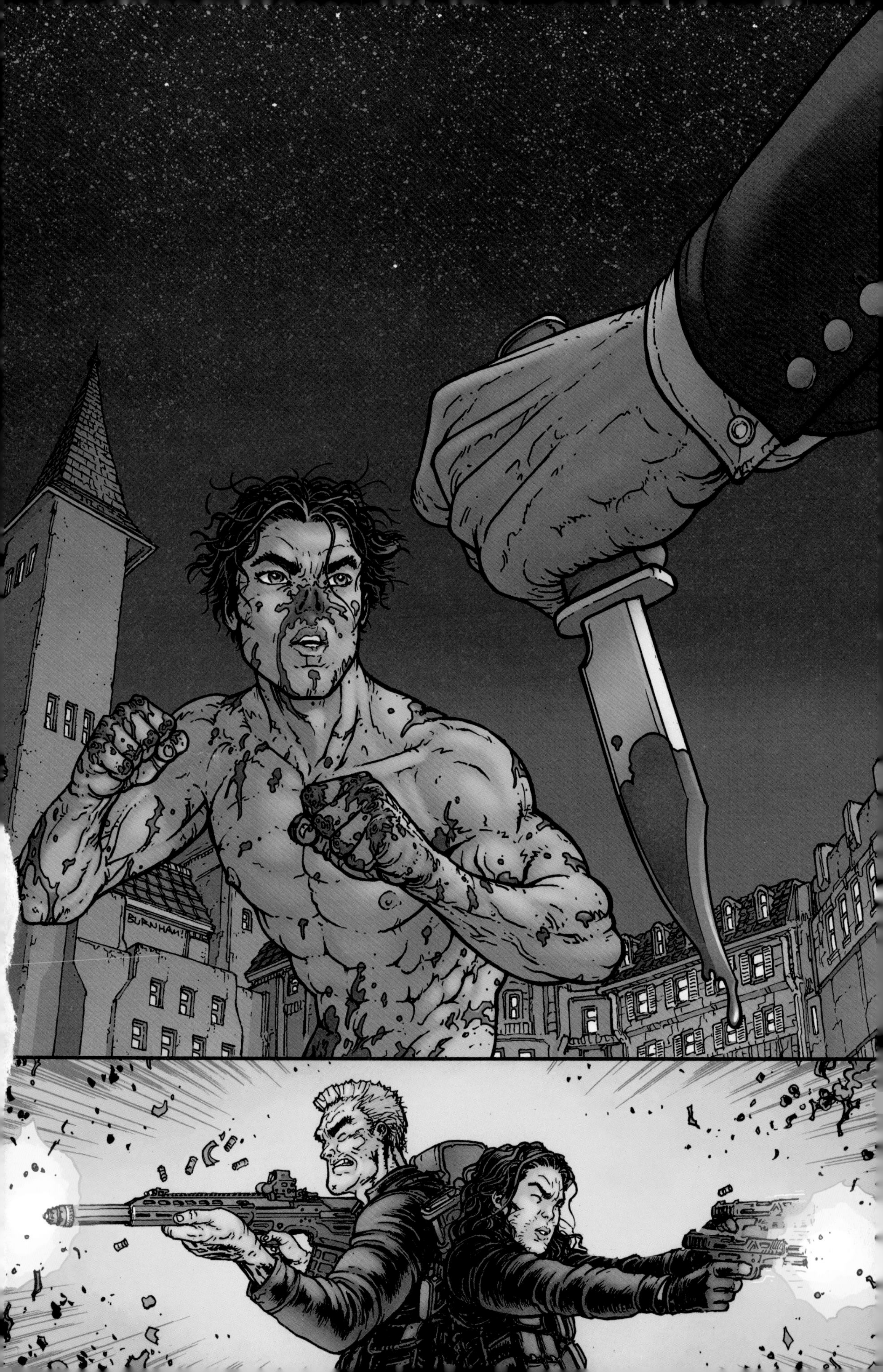
BURNHAM!

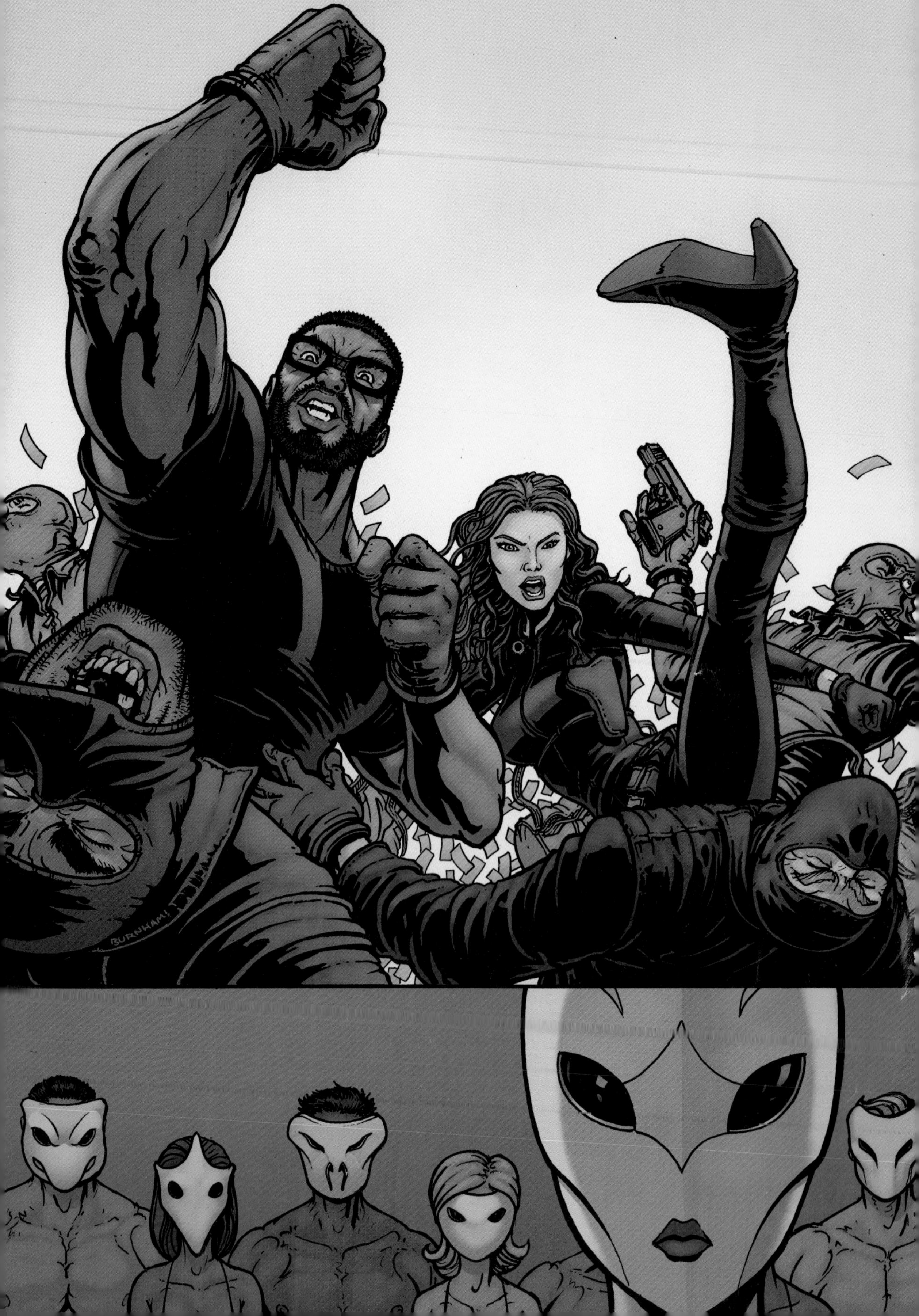
BURNHAM!

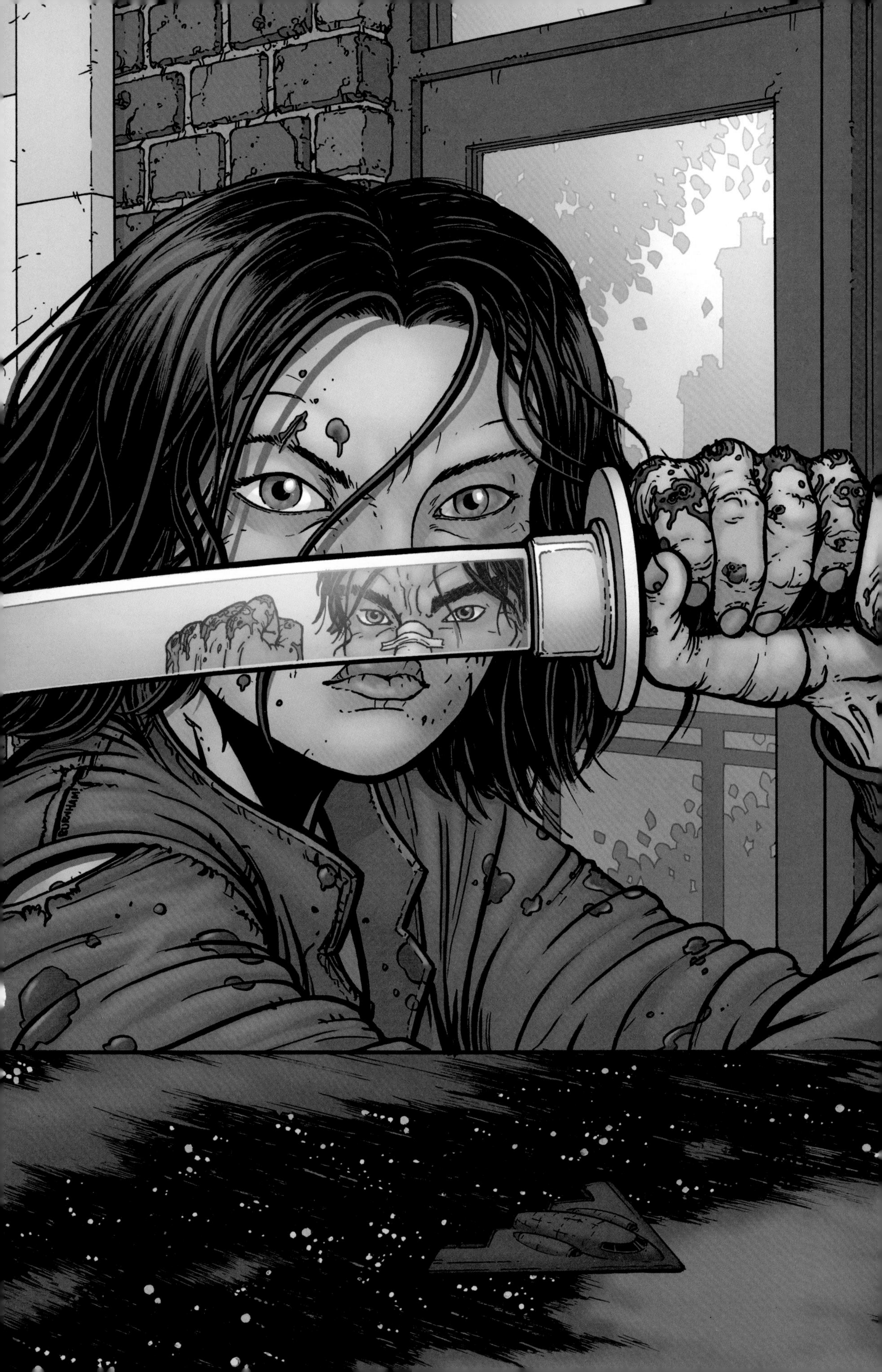

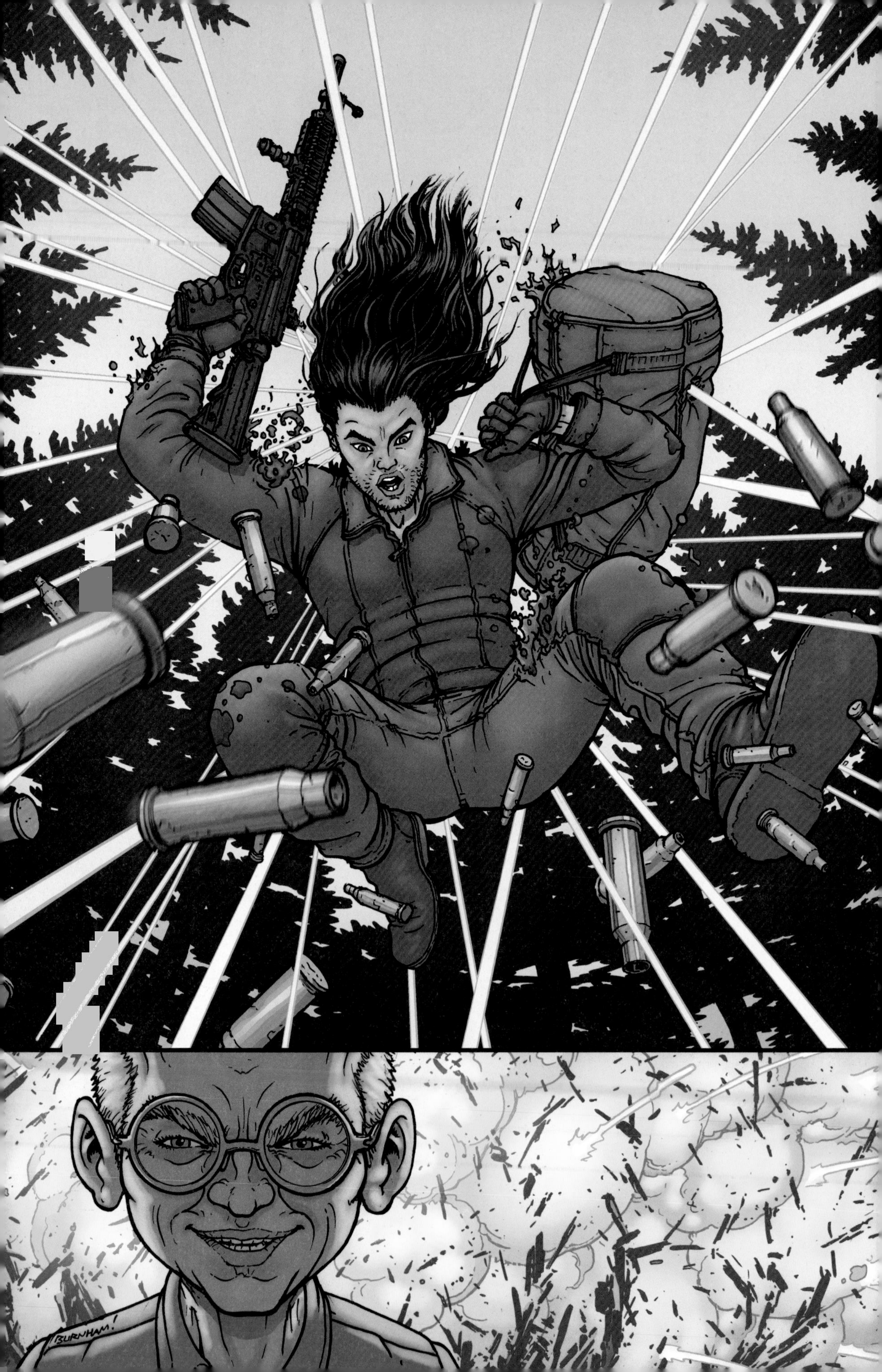
BURNHAM!

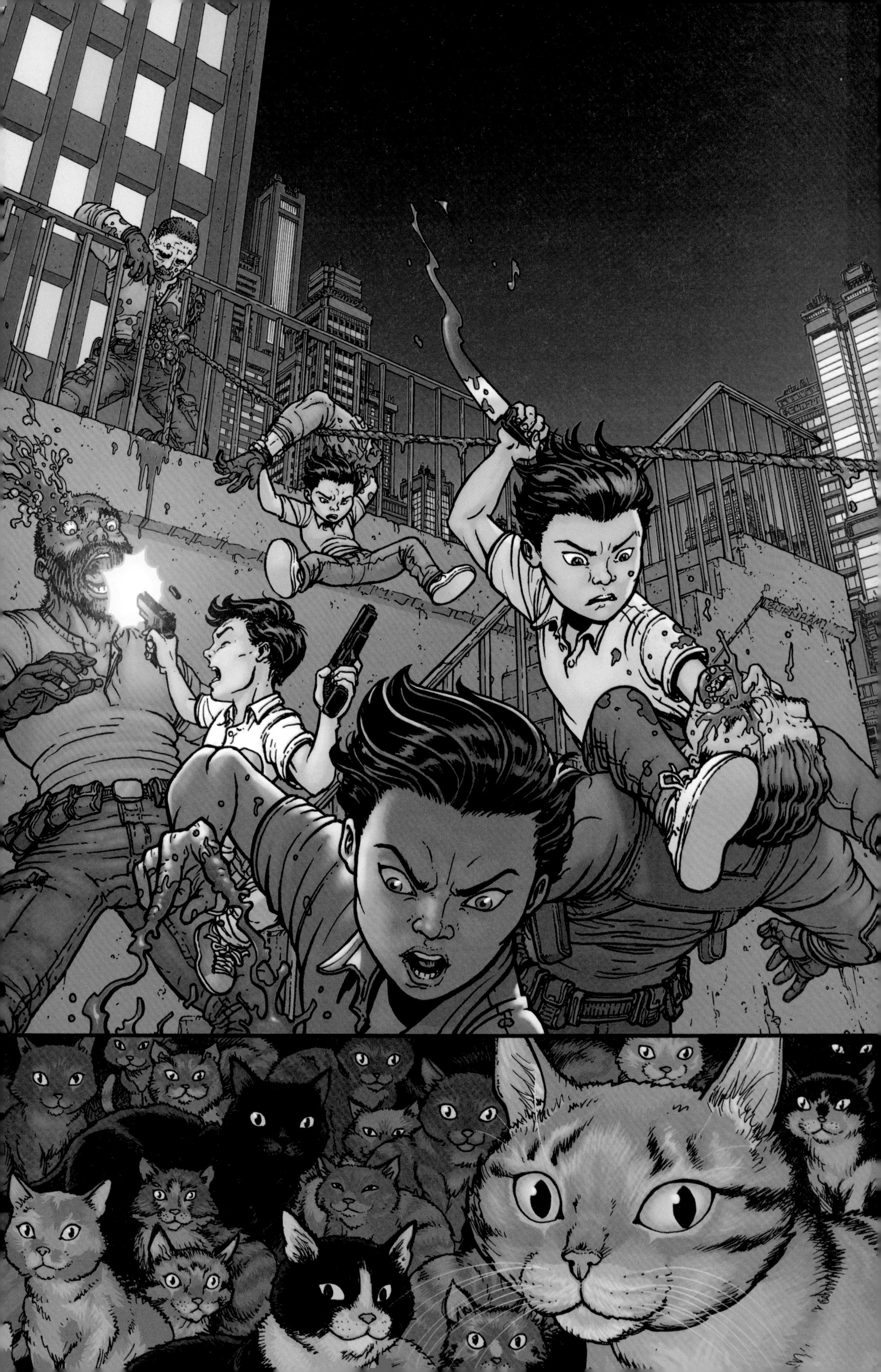
BURNHAM

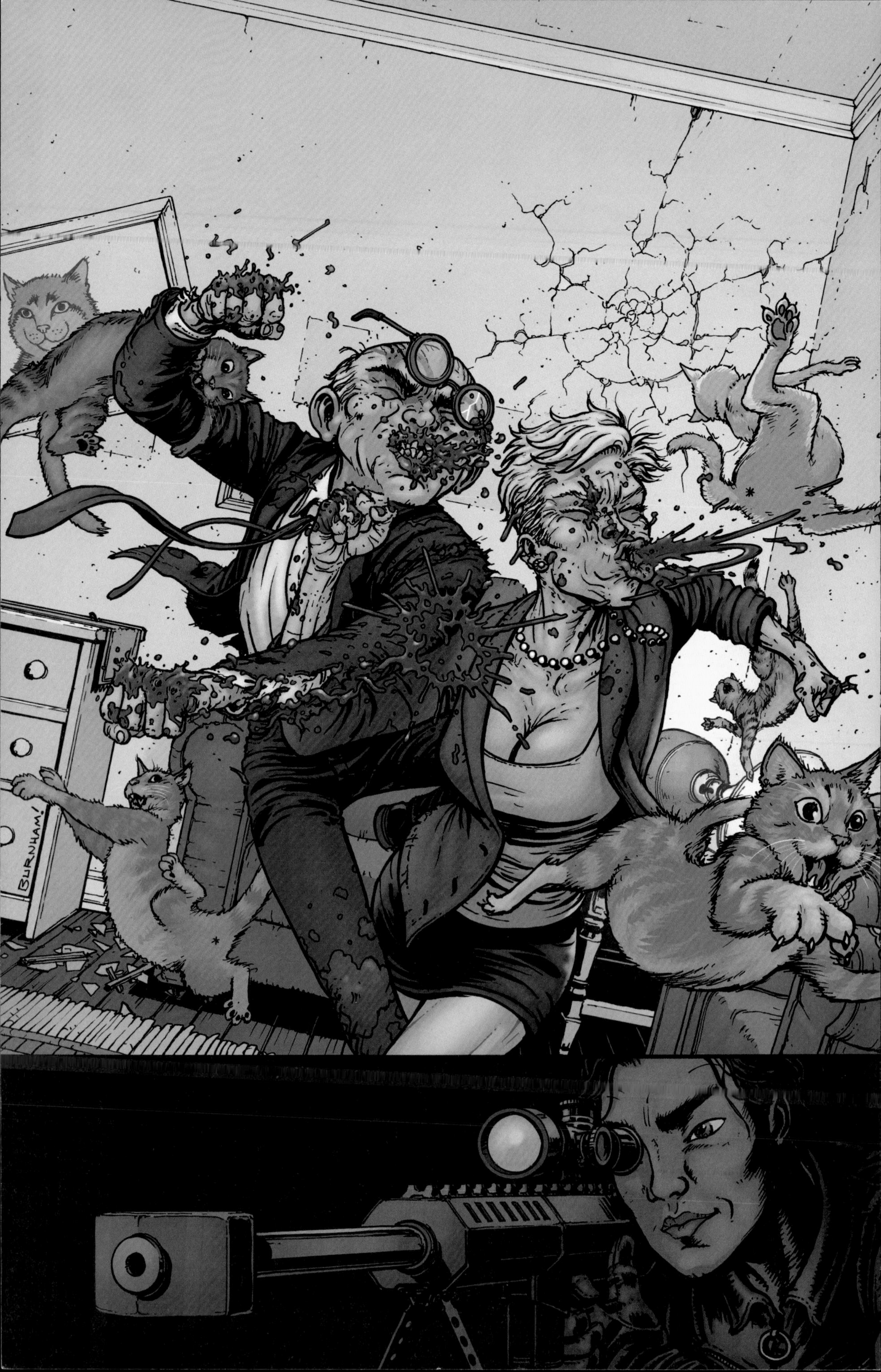
BURNHAM!

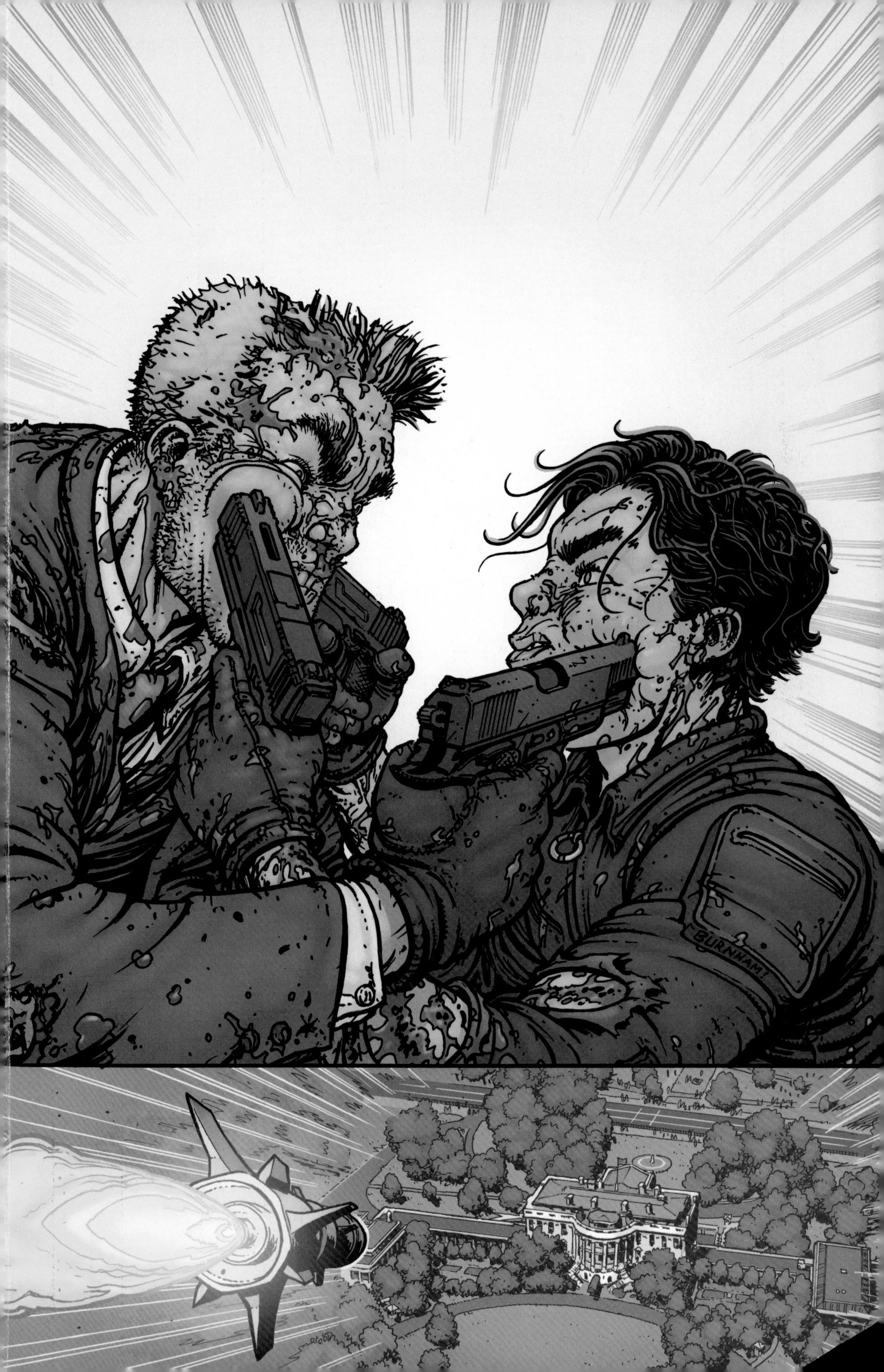
BURNHAM!

FOR MORE TALES FROM ROBERT KIRKMAN AND SKYBOUND